SO HERE'S
OUR LEO

SO HERE'S OUR LEO

D. G. COMPTON

WILDSIDE PRESS

CHAPTER 1

So here's our Leo. That's Leo Bresson, I know him well. Leo Anthony Bresson: the only child of a French-born music hall illusionist, Maurice Moon (né Breton) and a British Spiritualist medium, Madam Sara. When this story starts, way back in September 1983, Leo was forty-three years old and his father was no longer around. Maurice had died some thirty-odd years before, drunk and unmourned at the wheel of a friend's souped-up Ford Zephyr. Madam Sara, however, was still alive and—although aphasic as a result of two recent minor strokes—still determinedly kicking.

This had surprised nobody who knew her, either in her public life as a medium or in her hardly less copious private doings. Until her current afflictions, Madam Sara Bresson had been a woman of rare presence and determination. Not an easy individual—too full of her *Gift* and her *Mission*, too oversized, and too certain—but in any population there will always be quite a few people who welcome immoderacy and are comforted by certainty. Down the many years of her professional career, those who experienced the full Madam Sara very frequently came back for more.

She's been gone for quite a while now, of course, but she played an important part in Leo's dramas and he still misses her. And fears her. Indeed, that's mostly why he's talked me at last into putting together, with his help, this odd sort of third person memoir-cum-true-life-crime story. He's hoping, though he'd never admit it, to lay her ghost.

Leo Bresson… An inoffensive name, you'd think, but he's always disliked it. He'd probably have disliked whatever name fate had burdened him with. He's a life-long stammerer, you see, and stammerers tend to feel that way. Words in general are troublesome but names are particularly so. They can't be avoided. They aren't negotiable. When a man with a stammer is asked for his name and gets stuck, it's not something he can dodge or find other words for. He simply has to battle on. Names are a trial for all concerned.

Also, a stammered name instantly and clearly signals who/why/what its owner is.

Not that the intrusions of Leo's stammer will feature largely in this book. Certainly no attempt will be made to reproduce them on the page—a boring enterprise for all concerned and in any case of little use. No printed array of dashes or repeated consonants can give more than the feeblest idea of the sufferer's actual endeavours. But it needs a mention here because Leo's struggle to speak has always been a part of how he functions. It told him very early in his life that he was boring, embarrassing and often, with its facial contortions, downright ugly, and although by the 1980s, after thirty-odd years of piecemeal adjustments, his impediment was no longer a serious practical burden, it still significantly shaped—and even today continues to shape—his capacity both to give and to receive.

So anyway, here's our Leo, our story, stammer and all. It's an early evening in September, 1983, we're in Cirencester—your standard quaint old British Cotswold market town, narrow cobbled streets, worn golden stonework, muddy Land Rovers—and he's standing shoeless in the living room of his ex-lover Declan Finsey, exed by him just a few minutes ago.

Now his ex is leaning, heavily silent, on the balcony rail outside the room's French windows. Declan's flat is on the fifth floor of a sixties block situated on the outskirts of the town and offers, in daylight, very pleasant views of woods and plump, sheep-dotted hillsides. Not now, though. Night is falling, shading out all but the nearest rooftops and chimneys.

It's been a long hard day for Leo and frankly he's not at his best. Usually he might be said to have, at the very least, a certain boyish charm about him, but not this evening. This evening he's crumpled, grubby, hot under the arms, wild of eye, stammer going great guns. He's a mess.

Leo's in his socks, by the way, because his suede Hush Puppies have been left by the front door in deference to the flat's immaculate wall-to-wall white carpeting. Declan has style: his arm chairs and sofa are in Danish black leather and his coffee table, on which Leo dumped his scuffed old briefcase when he arrived, is Danish also, with a polished black slate top. He smokes Stuyvesants too, just in case anyone notices.

It's a great pity that Leo has to be introduced to the reader on this particular evening, when he's so stressed-out and charmless, so much not his best, but that can't be helped. No other opening would begin our story at such a perfect moment, one that presented anything like such a promising narrative hook. For this is the evening, Tuesday evening, 26th September 1983, when Leo's life, never all that fancy, changes (melo?)dramatically for the worse, and this story will concern that change, and how he deals with it.

On most evenings in his working week Leo would by now be back at home in nearby Cheltenham Spa, in the honey pine kitchen of his mother's Victorian gem, 81 Tivoli Street, whipping up something for their dinner. Today, though, is the last Tuesday in the month, and that's the day when, as his mother's secretary, Leo has to drive round a number of Cotswold towns and villages, *showing the flag* (her phrase) to her loyal team of *truthsayers* (her word for mediums), the men and women who run her local *guid-*

ance meetings (Madam Sara again, her term for séances), which are weekly events sponsored by her *Spiritualist Church of Truth* (a dubious title that she would claim to be honest and self-explanatory).

Predictably enough, truthsayers are a demanding lot and even on good days they tend to run Leo ragged. Today, though, was never going to be a good day for him. Today, as well as his mother's truthsayers, this present encounter with Declan has also loomed over him. The encounter that now finds him standing in his socks in his ex-lover's fifth floor Cirencester flat.

Declan, discreetly gay (a usage not common back in those days, of course) like Leo himself but less complicatedly, is one of Madam Sara's truthsayers and Leo's just faced up to formally ending their homosexual relationship. It's been lapsing recently anyway, certainly on his side, and he's made the break as gently as he could—he's rehearsed it a hundred times in his head—but it still hasn't been one of his better-scripted efforts. Now he's fussing unnecessarily with the zip-tag of his open anorak as he peers out through the living room French windows to where Declan, still not speaking, leans on the balcony's tubular metal handrail. Leo's looking anxiously for any clue as to what his ex-lover will do next.

Leo isn't bold. He may appear to be—tallish, six foot two with decent build, acceptable features, disciplined red-brown hair and beard, deep-set bright brown eyes, attentive manner—but the appearance is deceptive. The fact is, if Leo has a single defining characteristic, a single quality most helpful in getting to know him, it's a negative, it's what he isn't. He isn't bold. He lacks voltage. Intensity. He has other attributes, he plays quite a passable Charlie Kunz piano, but the clincher is, he isn't bold.

He can be brave, when absolutely necessary (*vide* his facing Declan with the truth this evening), but he's never bold. Never the casual, brassy gregariousness of bold.

It isn't a quality he once possessed and then somehow had it beaten out of him: he was born that way. There are babies who arrive with big feet; others come bad-tempered. Leo came not bold. And his early circumstances didn't help him to grow out of it. They probably made it worse.

Brief explanatory rewind, back to the London Metropolitan Borough of Paddington on the nineteenth of August 1940, the day of Leo's birth, and the first of those unhelpful early circumstances: his mother. To me, recently, shortly before her death and with unusual honesty, Madam Sara has been willing to admit that she was never ideal mother material. She tried her best, she said, but she never much liked children and in any case she had her career to think of. It seems, unfortunately, that young Leo noticed this even when only a few weeks old, for she remembered that he snivelled unattractively for much of the time and, although the doctor said he was perfectly healthy, he didn't prosper.

There were other unhelpful early circumstances: in particular, strangers looming over his cot. Madam Sara's small Belsize Park flat, doubling at that time as her Séance Centre, was full of them and apparently their large mooing faces terrified him. The unattractive snivelling intensified and was accompanied at the other end by diarrhoea. His mother went about her Spiritualist business as best she could. He wasn't an easy child.

Eventually a nurse was engaged. Nurse no.1 didn't always see eye-to-eye with her employer and was quickly replaced. Nurses 2, 3 and 4 had similar problems with their vision. This was war-time so they probably took grateful refuge in munition factories or the WVS.

And then, as a final negative circumstance, there was Leo's lack, on the premises, of a father. As I've already briefly mentioned, Maurice Moon (*né* Bresson) was a professional conjuror and comedian, plus some nimble virtuoso pieces on the xylophone, and for a while in the thirties Sara had been his assistant as well as his wife. She'd grown out of him fairly quickly, however, and struck out on her own, as a psychic and voice medium in North London.

They stayed married, quite amicably, with Maurice mostly away on increasingly threadbare provincial engagements and now (mysteriously declared to be unfit for military service) playing mostly to raw army recruits in ENSA, until December 1939—at the beginning, coincidentally, of the Phony War—when, on learning that his wife was pregnant, he congratulated her warmly, went off on a Christmas panto engagement in far-off Wolverhampton, and never came back.

She didn't grieve for him. Not emotionally, and certainly not financially: her London connection was growing fast. They still met occasionally, and without rancour, when their professional engagements allowed. This left Leo effectively fatherless: maybe not a decisive factor for or against boldness in those early months, but it can't have helped.

In any case, shortly after his first birthday, Sara decided to donate him to her mother Clare, recently returned from India following the death there of her ex-Indian Army husband, Colonel Hesketh Barraclough. Sarah's father had been running a string of polo ponies in Gujerat for a minor rajah until cirrhosis and the DTs claimed him. Now, having braved the German submarine threat on the long voyage home, his widow Clare was living in Cheltenham, well-provided-for by the poor dear colonel but under-occupied, in a middling grand Victorian house on Tivoli Street, complete with cook and housekeeper. As Sarah pointed out to her mother, the house was obviously too big for her, so Leo's arrival in it would work very well. Also Cheltenham was undeniably very much safer for her grandson than London in terms of any future enemy action.

By the way, a belated manufacturer's warning: although in principle this is to be a true-life story, drawing heavily on newspaper archives and police reports, a good seventy-five percent of it still comes from Leo himself, who is well-intentioned but probably has a memory no less creative than the next man's. Also, sizeable self-serving chunks come from his mother's autobiography, and from her recollections shortly before she died.

Enough said. We do the best we can.

As for reported conversations, necessarily they'll be heavily fictionalised, but Leo claims to remember the gist. He'll keep an eye on the underlying truthfulness of what gets printed. Unreliable narrators may be permissible in books these days but not in this one.

Which brings us back now to the grown-up, forty year-old Leo, genetically not bold but on this occasion pushed into brave by the many tumultuous necessities of being in love with Rosie Krauss-Häber. He's in Cirencester, a few miles along the A147 from Cheltenham, in his male ex-lover's lamp-lit living room, in a sixties block of flats on the outskirts of the town, and he's looking out across the clutter of flowerpots on the narrow balcony to the corner where Declan leans silently on the metal handrail. Earlier, when Leo arrived, Declan had been watering his geraniums and dead-heading them. Now, his back turned, his head tilted, he's gazing down towards the bare concrete pathway five floors below.

He's just been exed as gently as Leo could manage, but apparently not gently enough. Not if his current posture, bristling, head averted, lengthily silent, is anything to go by. To be frank, in matters as abrasive as being exed, it's unlikely that *gently enough* exists. Leo is genuinely very sorry he had to do it, and he's eloquently said so, but who needs sorry?

So is Declan contemplating suicide? Crying *Willow, tit-willow, tit-willow*? By the look of the back of his neck, no. Muscles twitch there. Also his fingertips drum on the handrail. All this suggests that he's very angry.

Leo sees this and it scares him. He's no idea what Declan might do next. He came into this encounter hoping for the best, a gently regretful-on-both-sides parting, but realistically prepared for the worst, which he reckoned might involve Dekko being weepy, hurt, insulted, perhaps resentful, even waspish… but not just plain angry. Dekko was never angry. Angry was just so crude. Uncool. Like being drunk. The censors took a holiday. Anything might happen. Dekko was never angry.

He is now, though.

Eventually he raises his head. Sighs very audibly.

'Run it past me one more time, dear heart.'

He turns slowly, fixing Leo with an intent cold gaze. 'I need to get it straight. You say you're dumping me? Is that it? You're dumping me, and all for a poor little nothing called Rosie?'

Leo lets the insult slide. He doesn't have to defend his Rosie. 'I'm not "dumping" you, Dekko. I don't like "dumping". It's so theatrical. And it's not what I'm doing. Relationships change. I'm trying to be honest, that's all.'

'And you can spare me your word games, honey. If you're not dumping me I'd like to know just what the fuck you *are* doing.'

Leo comes forward a couple of paces, almost out onto the balcony. 'Truthfully, Dekko... what was there to dump? Tonight you're doing all this *honey* at me, all this *dear heart*, but that's all just a cheat. You're making this into a drama. We've never been like that.'

'Just good friends? Is that what you're saying?' Declan reaches for his cigarettes. 'A friendly feel-up and a wank behind the bike sheds, like at school? Sex, Leo? Just good sex? Is that what you're saying? Just good sex?'

Leo thinks about it. 'Yes. If that's how you want to put it, yes. What's wrong with that?'

'What's wrong with it, pet, is that it's bloody insulting. I'm not a schoolboy any more, Leo. Neither are you. I know quite well you've grown up a bit from that.'

It's a cool evening, but not unpleasantly so. Darkness is falling. Save for an occasional bright window, the houses and rooftops behind Declan are scarcely visible. He's an attractive man. This evening, possibly because he was expecting Leo's monthly visit, he's wearing one of his suaver outfits: silver-grey lycra polo-necked sweater, well-presented darker-grey slacks and red velvet house slippers. As already mentioned, his flat has white carpeting and he doesn't allow shoes on it. He cares about such matters, accessories and clothes and furnishings.

Leo, in his anorak and badly-darned socks, has always felt an oaf by comparison.

It would be good to be able to claim that his presence here on this particular evening was the result of a responsible, thoughtful decision—some sort of action was long overdue, for heaven's sake. He and Rosie have known they were in love for nearly a month now and he's blundered along ever since, avoiding Declan during all that time, spending every possible moment with Rosie, telling neither of them the truth, feeling bad about that and doing damn all about it, so he really should by now have found some decent manly reason for deciding to own up.

But no. Leo, thinking back and basically a truthful person, now remembers only that his job with his mother's SCT had required him to visit Declan that evening, and he could hardly turn up and chat with him happily, not admitting the change in their relationship. He had to tell Dekko. He'd dreaded this moment all day, getting through the rest of his round on auto pilot as he screwed himself up for it. And after his final call before Declan, he'd even parked his beloved Jaguar in a lay-by for a while and sat there, talking himself into going through with it.

No decent manly reason, therefore.

He does remember being relieved, though, to have had his hand forced by this unavoidable visit. He's always hated procrastination. It signals bad management somewhere, and it usually ends up with people getting unnecessarily upset. Life is better all round when things are conducted promptly and tidily. In this case, of course, Declan was going to be upset anyway, so at least delaying the actual moment hadn't done much harm.

' …I'm not a schoolboy any more, Leo, and neither are you. I know quite well you've grown up a bit from that.'

Leo ducks that one. 'Don't let's quarrel, Declan. All I'm saying is, we've had good times together. Why not leave it at that? Nothing lasts for ever.'

'*This too will pass*…. Spare me the eastern wisdom, *please*. You walk in here, tell me you're ever-so-sorry but you've fallen in love with some middle-aged Cheltenham tart—Christ, am I really fucking hearing this?—and you expect a friendly pat on the head, do you? Do me a favour.'

'I've said I'm sorry. What more do you want?'

'What more do I want? Now there's a question.'

As to Rosie, he's told her about being bi in general, but mostly in his youth and certainly not specifically about Declan. Now, now that Declan's safely out of the picture, perhaps he'll never have to. It's not that Leo's ashamed of him. Dekko's a bit of a ham, but most good mediums are, and Leo himself has done his share of performing, one way or another. From now on though, as far as telling Rosie is concerned, the man's an unnecessary detail. No woman expects a list of former lovers, queer or otherwise.

Not that his list that would have added up to much: seven or eight in thirty years perhaps, including schoolboy fumbles. As to later adult pick-ups, for a stammering chap like him for whom simply asking the way of a stranger in the street has always been a horrific ordeal, making sexual advances to someone, of whatever gender, was obviously out of the question. So he isn't exactly your average sex fiend. And in any case, on the subject of former 'lovers' there's a confusion in the terminology here: he's never been 'in love' with Declan or with any other man. Men offer him mechanics, basically the thrills: 'in love' happens to him only with women. Which brings the relevant number down to only two before Rosie, the first of whom he'd actually married.

As for the rest, for social sex—after parties, in hotels, that sort of thing—he's avoided it. Taking off one's trousers for the first time in front of a woman would have demanded courage and careful preparation. After all, as Nanny had years ago made briskly clear, one's winkle was hardly one's prettiest part. Then there'd be all that hopping about on one foot and getting his shoe caught in the other turn-up. He's pathetic at the best of times. He doesn't need that.

No, Rosie is only his third true love and now, at forty-plus, he thinks of her as probably his last and is grateful for this final chance. He doesn't consider himself much of a catch.

'What more do I want? Now there's a question.'

Declan takes his time. He lights his cigarette, leans suavely back against the balcony rail, hoists himself up and sits on it, one velvet-slippered foot hooked behind a metal upright, the other swinging just clear of the tiles. He tilts his head, raises his chin, and folds his arms high across his chest. It's a careful pose: surface calm, inner fury. He's looking at Leo down along his rather beautiful nose, and for all his elegance he has the potential of an IRA rusty nail bomb, primed and unpredictable.

'I want you to grow up, laddie. Face facts. You're a faggot. You talk a lot about being bi but you and I know better. There's no such fucking thing. Only the queer who's too chicken to own up. You're harking back to the fifth form, ogling tits and hoping it would make you just like all the other boys. It didn't then, and this time round it won't either.'

Leo knows this isn't true. Declan's got him completely wrong. It simply doesn't apply. It never has done. There are different aspects to sex. Different emotional vocabularies. Queers like Declan can be so defensive.

'I expect you're right, Dekko. But—'

'Too damn right I'm right.' He draws angrily on his fag. 'Dump me for another feller and the chances are I'd go quietly. For fuck's sake, Leo, these things happen. This Rosie, though… this fucking *Rosie…* where's your sense of humour?'

Standing there, at bay, just inside the living room window, Leo doesn't have one. What he wants more than anything is to be somewhere else. He doesn't know this man he's talking to. Cool? Dekko? What happened to cool? There'd always been an accepted framework between them. A structure. Limits. Declan's feelings are hurt, anyone's would be, but getting in a rage is so… destructive. So *immoderate*. Limits. They're what careful people like him, people like him and Declan, need if they're to function.

He glances nervously back over his shoulder, across the living room to the door out of the flat. Why hang around? He's said what he came to say, so there's really no reason. He knows about rows—they have shape, choreography, catharsis and nemesis, and some people love them. He doesn't. Quarrels suck him in and spit him out exhausted. He hates them. So why not leave?

He stays.

He believes it's the least he can do.

It's amazing, isn't it? People who say they hate rows—it's amazing how good they are at having them.

'Alright. Alright, Declan, so you tell me it won't work with her, and I expect you're right. Let's leave it at that then, shall we? Let's—'

'Married, isn't she? Safely unattainable?'

Cruel. Leo winces. That's a new twist. He's shocked to be reminded of just how cruel people can be when the censors aren't working. As if cruel's always there, just waiting to get out.

Of course Rosie Krauss-Häber is married. It had been her husband's interest in the paranormal that brought Leo and her together. Max Krauss-Häber is a writer, or was one until his current dire illness, a journalist specialising in ESP, exposés of spoon-benders and such, and a year or so ago he'd been working on plans for a serious study of Spiritualism. Leo was secretary of one of the larger Spiritualist groups in southern England, and happened to live just round the corner from the Krauss-Häbers, so it was natural that Max should contact him. Since her second stroke Madam Sara herself no longer conducted séances—guidance meetings, she called them—but the SCT was still very active, so when Max had telephoned early last year for an interview Leo had been happy to fix it. His mother's days were lonely and long. She loved visitors. She was also well accustomed to dealing with manipulative, semi-literate journalists.

Leo had expected very little of the meeting, mostly just some filling for one of her empty afternoons, but Max and his mother had got on. He was in his early fifties, Leo judged, neither manipulative nor semi-literate, and he had a sexy European way with him, helped by his slight German accent. He asked few questions, nothing in the least confrontational, and—presumably on account of her aphasia—he spared her the indignity of taping their talk. Instead he'd flirted with her, she'd flirted back, and he'd arranged to visit again the following week.

Leo was wary. Journalists who flirted with fat old aphasic female stroke victims were dangerous. They had hidden agendas. But the second visit had gone well too, devoted mostly to the books she'd written and the background of her church, so perhaps Max Krauss-Häber wasn't dangerous, simply kind.

Certainly, as Leo would soon discover, Max was a kind man. But he had also, by then, read Madam Sara's autobiography (a paperback bestseller back in the seventies) and had learned of her mind-reading act with her husband Maurice Moon, conjurer and xylophone virtuoso, just before the war. There was a book for him in that, he suspected: show business, audience participation, mass hypnosis, and the performers' prearranged codes that reportedly sometimes didn't seem to be needed. At the very least there'd be a substantial chapter for his Spiritualism study.

Leo hosted a light sit-down lunch next, a few days later, in the honey pine kitchen (they hadn't used the cavernous formal dining room in years), with Max bringing Rosie, and Leo serving a home-made quiche and green salad after a carton of Sainsbury's stilton-and-broccoli soup. Wine too, a decent white sauvignon. Rosie was younger than her husband, but not significantly, and they had made a good couple.

'...Married, isn't she? Safely unattainable?'

'Don't hack at me, Declan. I've not done this well. I know that. But—'

'Safely fucking unattainable, and you're dumping me for *that*?'

Cruel, cruel, cruel... Leo wonders how Dekko's got his information but he isn't going to ask. 'So I'm wrong. It won't work and I'm wrong. You've already said it. Do we have to go on like this?'

'Once more with feeling, love. *Oh, I'm so wrong, Declan. I'm so wrong...* You don't believe a fucking word of it.'

'Believe? What's that? I hope, Dekko. *I hope...* That's all.'

'And now the fucking word games again. You make me sick.'

'I'd better go, then.'

'That's right. Bugger off. Things get close to the bone so you bugger off.' Declan laughs unpleasantly, stubs out his half-finished cigarette on the rail, tosses it away. 'You can't win, can you? Stay, and bitch Declan hacks at you. Go, and bitch Declan says you're running away. You can't fucking win.'

At the lunch with his mother Rosie Krauss-Häber had said nice things about the wine. She wasn't obviously pretty. Not obviously anything. Quiet.

She and Max seldom talked about their marriage. They didn't have to. Leo put it together over the next few months and thought how lucky they were. They were completely happy together. They'd met in a dank Oxford basement, correlating flashcard results for an ESP experiment, back in 1963 when his first wife was still around. Megan was already on her way out, though, with a lover in advertising, and Max—after three weeks working with Rosie—had hurried her on her way. Rosie was at the LSE, the London School of Economics, reading sociology, which she'd expected to be all about people but was turning out to be all about statistics which she hated, so she'd been happy to quit and go off to live with him. And eventually, as a sop to her family's Christianity, to marry him.

No—frankly, as a sop to her own. Ideas of sin nagged at her. So she married him and helped him with his work. They had sixteen very good years.

In 1978 Max's unmarried aunt, a refugee from Hitler like the rest of the Krauss-Häber family, had died, leaving him her shabby ground floor flat in a scheduled Regency Cheltenham terrace. He and Rosie, then based in London, had moved in while they decided what to do with it. Cheltenham appealed to them. Its joke years as a retirement home for redundant alcoholic empire builders were passed. It had fine architecture, beautiful Cotswold surroundings, and a surprisingly daring musical life. The Krauss-Häbers were regular concert-goers—Max played a nimble, if over-breathy flute—so this aspect of the town turned out to be the decider. Max's most recent book, a study of out-of-body experiences, had done well enough for him to able to cut down on London-centred magazine jobs, so they sold up there and settled permanently into the flat on Cheltenham's Parabola Road.

'…You can't fucking win.'

'You think I want to win? Is that it? Winning and losing? Is that what we've come to?'

'I think you're a feeble, mean-spirited little shit. You've been dithering over this for weeks. Word gets round, darling. You and this Rosie-Posie, fucking up a storm—how long has it been now? *Oh, I'm so sorry, Dekko…* and all I'm supposed to do is lie down like some dog with his paws in the air? Well—'

'I'm here, Dekko. I needn't have come. '

'You're here, matey, because it's the last Tuesday in the month and your mother'd have your guts for garters if you didn't look in on me. But you're not getting away with it. She's the least of your worries This Rosie, this Rosie fucking Krauss-Häber… she's not going to be too pleased, I promise you, when I tell—'

'—when you tell her I'm queer? Don't bother, Declan. She knows.'

It seemed a necessary simplification. What a mess he was making of this. A better man than he would have 'fessed up properly to Rosie right at the start, but at least this break with Dekko was a step in the right direction. The two other women in his life had never needed to know. And the two different aspects of himself had never overlapped. One was sex. The other added… love?

'I wasn't thinking so much of your precious Rosie, dear heart. More of her better half. I hear the old man isn't in the greatest of health these days.' Declan pauses. 'But maybe he's broad-minded.'

Leo's heart had actually missed a beat. *Christ. Oh dear sweet Jesus…*

This invocation strikes him only rarely. Only in moments of extremis, and it's strictly conventional. No appeal to a deity is involved.

Maybe all this is showing Leo at less than his best, but it's also Declan at more than his worst. The fact is, Rosie's husband Max is complicatedly dying, close to dead, from painful afflictions that had started out a year ago as merely late-stage colon cancer, so it's seriously important that he shouldn't find out about Leo and his wife. Declan's threat is unconscionable. He isn't like that. Leo could tell you. Normally Declan's absolutely the best company. Cynical but never bitchy. Amusing. Cool. It's just his anger talking. No censors.

Max is Leo's friend. Probably, in the full sense of the word, his only friend. It has to be said, he's as bad at friendship as he is at love. Another man, older than he, his bridge partner Canon Beckerton, probably considers himself a friend—he's known him right back from when Leo was at Cheltenham College and he was teaching there—but Leo's sure that's mainly because he's sorry for him. It's the s-word again. Having learned very early on that his stammer made him boring, embarrassing and often, in his facial contortions, ugly, Leo knows how little he has to offer. Max is somehow different. By now, Max and he are long past all that.

So why is he bedding Max's wife? And he's a queer too, for God's sake. Well, half a one.

Bi-sexuals hadn't yet been invented. Yes, he knows it doesn't look good. It looks bloody awful. But there really are reasons, explanations, even excuses—at least, he thinks so. He may not be the best human being, but he isn't a total bastard either.

He and Max had started out sharing music, his limited piano skills meshing with Max's limited fluting. Early baroque to begin with, then recklessly on to Ibert and Poulenc. They played chess too. Max was much the stronger player, but occasionally Leo got lucky. And, Cheltenham being Cheltenham, they discovered, with Rosie, the unexpected delights of horse-racing at the famous course. Watchful leather-cheeked trainers, bookies in greasy black suits beneath their enormous umbrellas, the reckless tenner-each-way that never worked, the wild-eyed horses in the paddock on their skinny inadequate ankles, and of course the picnic hamper in the car park, perched uncomfortably around the open boot of Leo's precious dove-grey vintage Jaguar 340, drinking cheap Chianti before the final race.

There'd been quieter times of course: early morning walks in Cheltenham's Charlton Park, a winter visit, for no very clear reason, on a train up to London Zoo. Sometimes, quite often actually, Leo wondered what the older man saw in him. A son, would be the easy answer. Innocence? Leo had dredged up the word with some astonishment, only to find that it fitted. Certainly his gayness, or otherwise, wasn't an issue.

Max's cancer had been identified—after the usual oscopies and op-sies—last October. An inventive and determined version. Surgery, chemo-therapy, radio-therapy, no interventions seriously discouraged it. By May, Max had told one pushy health visitor on a bad day, the doctors had so mixed up his pipes that his bladder pissed out of his one good ear and his rectum suffered from halitosis. At least his hair had grown back, though, some of it, after the chemo. By July the cancer was busy in his liver too and specialists were talking weeks to Rosie, if not days. Hospice care was discussed. Then a quite inexplicable stasis. Now it was September. And through all of this wretched stuff Leo had been, totally and without question, the two Krauss-Häbers' closest friend.

At the beginning of the cancer Max had been a heavy man, too much for Rosie when home from hospital, needing to be turned and potted and blotted between his several pipe deductions and reconnections. A nurse had visited, but so had Leo, and more frequently.

And then there'd been the day, some time in June, Leo thinks, when his friend, now totally yellow and down to under nine stone, had returned after a longer-than-usual hospital stay with the bed sores on the sharp ends of his arse bones split open in soggy red runnels. The expensive private oncology department he went to in London might advertise its possession of a million-dollar state-of-the-art microencephaloplasticultraphonyectomy machine, but it clearly couldn't run to your basic antiseptic buttock glop.

The visiting nurse was off duty that day and Rosie, to her deep shame, threw up at the sight, so Leo rolled up his sleeves. He was good at potting and blotting and buttock glopping.

He was, in short, what his mother on a good day, when the comforts of familiar phrases were available through her aphasia, would have called a tower of strength. *A stringth of trowels* might well be another day's version. Either way, she was proud of him: she'd received similar medical services herself from him, if less intimate, after her own two stroke-caused stays in hospital.

And so it was, eventually, four or five weeks or so ago, that the time had arrived, quite naturally and quite outrageously, when a new element was added. Rosie and Leo had been nursing Max together for ten months by then, sharing just the edges of the shallows of his bitter journey. Counting his pills, cutting his toenails, catching his vomit. Telling him when his jokes weren't funny. Picking little hard white turds out of his anus. Planning menus from his impossible diet sheets. Welcoming visitors and knowing when to tell them to go. Dancing when his sun shone. Keeping his miseries proportionate when it didn't. For the two of them to fall in love was only too natural. But it was also, as admitted above, quite outrageous.

Understanding this, they fought it. Leo stayed away. Rosie, she told him later, wept in the kitchen. But Max repeatedly asked where Leo was, and excuses ran out, and Leo (who had wept also) resumed his visits.

The next stage, sex, was reached after a similar short period of token self denial—no physical contact, not the lightest brush of a hand. A few successful days, three, perhaps four. Then, sod's law and all that, events conspired to take Rosie plausibly over to Madam Sara's house on Tivoli Street one evening. A spanner, possessed by Leo, was needed to fix Rosie's car. By that time his mother, pill-aided, was as always, firmly asleep in bed, while back at Parabola Road Max would soon be sleeping also... which left unnumbered hours for diffidence, guilt, temerity, exploration, tenderness, acceptance, passion, striving, regrets, sorrow, love.

The decision, it has to be said, had clearly been Rosie's. Her car could perfectly well have waited. She never raised the issue with him, but Leo knew it would worry her in her relationship with God, and he was shamed. Decisions, though, were not his forte. Neither was God. In any case, Max was the person who mattered most and from then on, in every second when Leo and Rosie were together in his presence, they exercised the most subtle vigilance: he should never, never, never be allowed to see the truth. Never sense it. Never even breathe it in.

They loved him too much for that. What they felt for each other was need: a shared, scarcely bearable obsession. What they felt for Max was total caring. In their delirium it may well be that they loved him more than ever.

He picked up nuances. Or had simply thought for himself about the two of them and their closeness. There'd been the day a couple of weeks ago, after his morning medicine time, lying wrapped in blankets on the living room sofa, alone with Leo while Rosie banged about in the kitchen, when he'd reached for Leo's arm. 'Not long now, friend,' he murmured. 'We talk, you know. She's very fond of you...'

Leo had been appalled. 'For god's sake, Max—'

'No, no. We can say these things. You two might make a pair one day. I like to think of that. OK, Leo? No obligations—just I like to think of it.'

Not long now... a pair one day ... reading between those particular lines wasn't hard for Leo. 'Wait till I'm gone,' Max was saying. 'Wait till I'm gone.'

Should Leo have been honest? 'Too late, old man. We've already you-know-whatt-ed each other's socks off. Awfully sorry, old man ... Wasn't much fun, of course—guilt and all that—but we'll probably do it again.'

Leo (of course) chose silence and a comforting, mendacious hand squeeze. At which point Rosie had come back into the living room drying her hands on a dish towel and asking if either of them had caught the BBC's weather forecast.

'...I hear the old man isn't in the best of health these days.' Declan pauses. 'But maybe he's broad-minded.'

Christ. Oh dear sweet Jesus.

Leo doesn't believe it. This isn't simply anger. It's way beyond anger. It's disgusting. Monstrous. He simply can't believe it.

Then Declan sits up straight, grinning, his head on one side, doing his wicked pixie look, and Leo does believe it. Disgusting indeed. Monstrous too. But it still makes no sense. What on earth does Declan hope to gain, telling Max about him and Rosie?

A foolish question. He asks it all the same.

"What on earth do you hope to gain, Dekko, telling Max about me and Rosie?'

'*Me and Rosie...* oh, isn't it just too divine? What I'll gain, sweetie, is teaching you an important lesson. Kick people in the balls and they kick you back. It mayn't be very nice, not quite what they taught you at Cheltenham fucking College, but it's the way life is. Everything has its price tag. This one's really going to cost you.'

'Not me, Declan. Some dying, totally uninvolved German journalist. It makes no sense.'

'You should see your face, honey. You're hurting already. From where I'm sitting it makes every sense.'

Is he really so obvious? Of course he is.

'Don't do this. *Please*—just think about it. Be practical. We're going to have to work together for the SCT in the future, you and me, and—'

'Work together? Do you really think, dear heart, that they'll keep you on once word gets round that you're fucking the wife of your dying best friend in some sleazy Gloucester Road motel?

'Stop it, Declan. This isn't you. It's just vindictiveness.' The man must be made to see this. 'Come the morning, you'll think differently. Just now you're angry. That's understandable. But—'

'Don't give me *understandable*, you patronising little cunt.' Declan's suddenly quite motionless now, almost whispering. 'I'm not one of your buttoned-up public school chums. You've kicked me where it hurts. I need you to remember that, you and this fucking Rosie-Posie. Giving Herr Maxie von Krautheimer an enlightening tinkle sounds to me like just the very thing."

Buttoned-up public school chums? Oh dear lord. Poor Dekko. Leo suddenly understands. All this—it's really just about class, isn't it?

'Declan—Declan, that's crazy. You're making no sense. Max is a sick man. I won't let you do it.'

'You won't *what*?' A silvery trill of a laugh. 'I'd like to see that, pet. I'd really like to see that.'

So here we are. It's clear what's going to happen. Here Declan is, perched on the balcony rail, arms folded, velvet-slippered foot hooked round an upright. Here Leo is, in front of him, maybe six feet away, shocked and desperate. It's perfectly obvious what comes next. Declan doesn't see it because he has the not-bold image of Leo and because anyway he's on the high of his own destructive power. Leo doesn't see it because he's fixed on his need to get through to Declan, somehow bring him to his senses.

Well, that's what he now tells me his memory says, and he's no reason to lie—in a short while he'll admit to far worse than mere murderous intent—he's simply passing on the information. He swears that his two quick paces forwards to Declan are for emphasis, an unthought response, and his hands on Declan's shoulders are simply for contact, a literal reaching-out, an expression of his need to make Declan see reason. The different schools they went to are neither here nor there. Alright, so Dekko's been scorned, devalued, insulted. It's shameful... But what will he gain by destroying Max's marriage? What will he gain by ruining Leo's life? Everybody loses. Tomorrow, when he's calmed down, what will he think of himself?

None of that gets said, of course. Instead, Declan's velvet-slippered foot comes un-hooked all too easily from the baluster upright, his folded arms can't save his balance and he's gone. He's not there any more, his shoulders are no longer in Leo's grasp. He's given a shout, though, a single astonished *'What?'* very loud and positive, which is followed by a less immediately identifiable sound coming up from ground level.

Otherwise the night remains silent.

Leo backs away. He's confused. He backs away. How can Declan have gone? He hears voices and a sash window down across the road being raised. He's alone on the balcony. A moment ago Declan was there on the handrail. Now he isn't. The sash window's closed. Finally, at last, Leo, staring at the rail, horrified, joins the dots. It's five storeys down. He's murdered Declan.

Looked at objectively, that sequence is worrying. Only then, he claims, did he realise what he had done. At no time, he says, had even the smallest hint of violent intention, let alone of murder, been in his mind. It's how, he tells me, he remembers the order of events and that's fair enough. But it's still worrying. Assuming that his thinking up to then has really been so dis-associated, it seems curious that in that brief bewildered interval he didn't instinctively lean forward and look over the rail. Most people would have. First thing. If they'd really felt so confused and blameless they'd surely have looked. Simple curiosity. Incredulity. Had poor Declan really fallen? Had he hurt himself? How badly? Where was he now? Perhaps there was an awning or some such that had caught him. A tree perhaps. The sort of ornamental cherry architects love to plant. Most people would have looked.

On the other hand, for an angry man, a murderer now hoping not to get caught, a sensible man who knew very well that five storeys were a long way down and there wasn't any awning/cherry tree/ stupid fucking feather mattress... for such a man not to look over the rail would have been a very good move. With a plan already lurking in his mind to deny ever having been near the place (see below), the last thing he'd want would be for someone out there to hear Declan's shout and glance up and see his murderer.

It's a small point. And, as soon will be evident, it's a point that—as a contribution to Leo's eventual state of mind—quickly becomes quite secondary. But fair's fair. It needs to be made.

So now, one way or another, he's joined the dots. He realises what he's done. He's killed a man, killed Dekko, and it's decision time. He's killed Dekko. So what now? Regret? Sorrow? Dekko had always been so *alive*. They'd had Indian restaurants, and the Bach cello suites, and fun, and—but the voices across the road have stopped and he hears the window sash lowered. It's decision time. Not his forte, but you can't have everything. Quickly, lad. No dithering. No weighing of alternatives. Not a suitable moment for regrets, for sorrow. Action is required. Don't just stand there. He turns and hurries through the flat, making for the front door where he has to pause for his shoes. He reaches down to grab them and hop first on one foot and then the other as he puts them on.

Hang on a minute. His plan to deny he's been here this evening is idiotic. It doesn't matter that nobody saw him arrive or go. Today's the last Tuesday of the month. No excuse will work. On the last Tuesday of the month he always does his rounds of Madam Sara's truthsayers, and Declan's one of them. There's the SCT's newsletter to be delivered and Declan's report and expenses sheet to be collected. Not to mention the friendly chat that truthsayers like to have with someone from HQ. His mother knows that, so do all Declan's fellow truthsayers. For Christ's sake, he's mentioned his coming final call of the day to a couple of them, that afternoon.

Of course he's been here. He leans, considering, on the wall by the door and Declan's row of coat hooks, and at this point his bowels inconveniently spasm and require that he clear his system for immanent fight or flight. Social conditioning triumphs and he makes it to Declan's bathroom without mishap.

The recovery period, quietly seated, trousers round his ankles, gives him a chance to look properly at his options. Where's the rush? Of course he's been here this evening in Declan's flat. No harm in that. Surely the real question is, when did he leave? After Declan fell or before? Nobody saw him arrive. If he's careful, nobody will see him leave. He can choose a helpful time. His watch tells him it's now close to six fifteen. How about a quarter to six? What's wrong with having left thirty minutes ago? Plenty of time after that for Declan, on his own now, to have lingered on his balcony, smoked a cigarette, fussed with his stupid plants, lost his balance, fallen over the rail, and shouted something as he did so.

Leo hooks the bathroom door further open with his foot and listens. No sounds of neighbourly agitation. Just the one shout—a significant event once the body has been discovered but nothing just at this moment for people in the fancy houses out there to make a fuss about. They've better things to do. Six fifteen in this posh area is drinkies time. Reading stories to the kids time, before they're put to bed. Helping wives to keep stir-fries agitated. All Leo needs to do now is leave Declan's copy of the SCT newsletter, collect his monthly report and expenses sheet, and depart discreetly. The drive back out through Birdlip and down the hill to Cheltenham takes fifteen minutes—say twenty at the most—and he'll be home with his mother a bit before seven. With any luck moving his arrival back twenty minutes or so in her mind won't be a problem. Since her second stroke she's never been all that sure about the time. She relies on him mostly, him and the radio. Find an excuse to mention lightly that the time is half past six and she'll never notice.

He stands, wipes, flushes, arranges briefs, pulls up trousers, tucks in shirt, deals with buttons and zip.

Declan's desk is by the window in his living room. A smart affair, all minimalist satin chrome with a dark rosewood top. His expenses sheet lies neatly on it, invoices attached, ready for Leo's visit. How very Declan. No sign, though, of his monthly guidance meetings report. Leo isn't worried. He knows that Declan took his prose style seriously. Chances are the report is on the kitchen table where he would have been looking it over while he ate his lunch. He prided himself on his economy of phrase and thought.

On his way to the kitchen Leo collects his briefcase from the living room—he'd come close to forgetting it—and scoops out a copy of the SCT's newsletter, which he leaves as always on the kitchen table. And ready there, as expected, is Declan's monthly report, which goes into the brief-case, along with Declan's expenses sheet.

A quick glance round the flat. There must be his fingerprints all over the place, but that's to be expected. He's been *showing the flag* there on his monthly visit. Anyway, Declan and he are friends. They've been friends for years now.

Back at the front door, briefcase in hand, Leo staggers suddenly, gropes with his other hand for the doorknob, closes his eyes and leans there. He's heard himself and he's shocked. Declan's dead, lad. You're mixing your tenses. Declan's dead, lad. He was once alive, once your friend, and now he isn't any more. He's dead and you made it happen. And now you must get on with it.

The landing outside the flat is deserted. Leo runs along it. Not that there's any hurry—he's simply limiting his risk of being seen. At the stairs he hesitates, needing to make a choice, them or the lift. Behind him he thinks he hears a sound and turns. Nobody there. There are several doors to other flats on the landing and they're all closed. He chooses the stairs. They're safer. People never use them and the next four stairwell landings are deserted. At the glass door to the ground floor entrance lobby he checks again, peering out. Still nobody. He can leave the building through either front or back doors. Decisions, decisions...

When he'd arrived he hadn't been able to find a space in the flats' official parking area so he'd had to leave his car a fair distance away, out on the street. At the time, this had annoyed him. Now, as it's important that he isn't seen, that was probably very fortunate. Other residents of the flats, parking near him, might have recognized his car, and might now notice him driving away in it.

He chooses the lobby's rear entrance because it offers the shorter walk to the street. Significantly for him, though, its route includes the open concrete forecourt under the upper floor balconies and therefore—he should have thought of this—it now includes Declan Finsey's body which he comes upon as he rounds the first corner. Noone else. Nothing else. Just Declan Finsey's body.

A body is a body: he can deal with that. He walks on till he reaches it. Looking isn't morbid fascination. It's brave and honest. He's glad he thought of that. Now that he's here he needs to look and properly see. No denials. He needs to face what he has done.

There's a street lamp screwed to a wall nearby. Dim but bright enough. Declan's body is lying in an untidy sort of pile. An arm trails out from it. Leo doesn't immediately see Declan's head. Then he does. It seems to be in pretty good shape. Leo looks up at the building, counts the balcony levels. Number five's a long way up. The lamp in Declan's living room dimly lights the metal rail. Suddenly a thought occurs to Leo—what if Declan isn't dead? What if he's lying here, still breathing, conscious, paralysed perhaps, in terrible pain?

Leo puts his briefcase down on the concrete and when he leans closer he sees blood in a dark, heavy mass that he'd thought was shadow, a mass that spreads out from Declan's shoulder, under Declan's trailing arm, reaching Declan's wrist and hand and fingers, thinning there, thinning so that Leo can see how Declan's fingers have scraped at the concrete, back and forth, and Declan's fingernails as they scraped have gathered clots of blood and concrete dust, back and forth, back and forth, and now they are no longer scraping any more, just resting on the bloodied concrete, clotted and dusty, and his fingers are curled a little, resting, quite without movement now, resting, looking very white and dead.

Dead? Well, bugger it, lad, if they've stopped their scraping then they would look that way, wouldn't they?

Leo lifts Declan's head and finds the artery's place in Declan's neck, and that too is dead. For that he thanks the god he doesn't believe in. He lowers Declan's head. He's never before touched a dead person.

Later events in this story might well suggest that in all senses other than the strictly technical, Leo also, from that moment on, was dead. But maybe that's an over-blown notion.

Now, for Leo, another question remains. For how long, he's forced to wonder, for how long before Declan died did he lie here, scraping at the concrete, in unimaginable agony, scraping at the concrete, weeping perhaps, scraping and weeping? For how long?

It's too dark for Leo to see his watch but he knows how long. Eight or nine minutes. While he was getting himself sorted out. Ten, maybe. Not long. He tells himself, ten at the most. Only ten. He straightens his back and walks on by.

Walks on by.

Stops walking.

Clutches his briefcase to his chest.

Only ten minutes… Christ Almighty, how dismissive can a person get? How uncaring, how unconscionable? Only ten minutes for Declan, down here on the concrete, to lie in agony, weeping and scraping. Only ten minutes for Leo, upstairs in the flat, to sort himself out, have a shit and ponce around planning how he can fix things so he won't get caught.

Planning how he can cunningly lie and cheat and get away with it.

Somehow Leo walks on as far as his car. He glances round, there's still nobody, and he quietly opens the driver's door.

Only ten minutes. He gets into the car and rests his forehead on the steering wheel. Only ten minutes. Those very words. He'd really thought them. Those very words. Only ten minutes of agony, weeping and scraping. He raises his head. Quite by chance he'd parked the Jag on a downward slope. Simply releasing the handbrake is enough. He coasts down to the corner, fixing his seat-belt and jump-starting the engine on the way.

He drives off. Nobody sees him.

For the first mile or so, till he's out of the town and onto the lonely fifteen-mile stretch of Roman road between Cirencester and Birdlip village, he manages quite well.

It doesn't last.

He keeps on going all the same. Eventually, a mile or so before the sharp right in the village and the steep descent into Cheltenham, he turns into a lay-by and stops the car. He barely makes it. His eyes are salt-blurred and wide, his hands judder on the wheel, his feet seem to him tiny and useless, poking at the pedals. Vomit sours his throat as he swallows. He can't go on like this.

He switches off the Jaguar's lights and sits in total darkness, this time leaning the side of his head against the door pillar.

Only ten minutes.

To be honest, Leo has never been what you might describe as 'close to' Declan. They probably weren't even friends. He'd liked the fellow, though, and they had good sex together. They read the same books, they enjoyed Indian restaurants, they had good sex together. Both of them dreamt of owning an immaculate vintage Aston Martin. They had good sex together. No great emotional involvement, though.

That's not the point.

The point is obvious. It shouldn't have needed stating but it did: any ordinary, decent person would have gone straight down to see if Declan was still alive. If he needed help. Someone to hold his hand. To call for assistance. Their common humanity demanded it. The idea had never entered Leo's head. Just the one shamefully simplified concern—Declan is dead and how can I avoid being caught? Which meant that important things had needed to be done.

Up in the flat important bits of paper had to be found, important other bits of paper had to be delivered, important shoes had to be put on, important bowels had to be emptied, an important escape had to be made. And all that busy, busy, busy-ness had to be completed while Declan, the actual Declan, not dead yet but dying, while his actual ex-lover Declan lay in agony five storeys down on the concrete, scraping his fingernails back and forth and quietly weeping. Scraping and weeping.

Only ten minutes. For Declan, five storeys down on the concrete, not a measurable period. It might as easily have been ten hours.

Shuddering, Leo hunches his shoulders. He can't go on like this. There's his alibi to think of. It's high time he was on his way so he turns the key in the ignition. The engine is still running and starter cogs scream at him. For a while he hides his head in his hands. Then he sits up sensibly and smoothes his trouser legs over his knees. Life goes on. Well, his does. Checking that the road behind and in front is dark, he engages a gear, a wrong gear, and drives out jerkily, slipping the clutch. He turns on the car's lights. Soon a dashboard dial tells him he's travelling too fast. He peers at it, then back at the road ahead and drives on faster.

Entering Birdlip village, he has to press his elbow painfully into his right thigh to keep his foot from slipping off the brake pedal. Beyond the village the road winds so steeply that driving focuses his faltering attention. Somehow he makes it safely down Leckhampton Hill and into the lights at the top of Cheltenham town. Then it's only a short distance to Thirlstaine Road and left into Tivoli.

He stops the Jaguar outside number eighty-one, seeks to unclip his safety belt, finds he's never clipped it, gets out to open the garage door, then returns to the car and drives in. He switches off the engine, breathes deeply. With an enormous effort he gathers together the innumerable bright fragments of misery whirling in his brain. One thing is clear: the framework he's lived within has gone. Whatever senses he ever had, he's lost them.

First off, he'd taken Declan seriously, believed his threats. And then, letting him fall from the balcony, leaving him to suffer, picking up papers, shitting, taking his time down five flights of stairs, finding Declan's body, walking by, driving off, coming here... all of it one long shameful catalogue of inhumanity and folly. Tidiness? Order? Framework? Structure? You must be joking.

His miseries whirl. Rosie... Rosie... he did it all for Max and Rosie. All of it to protect them. He did it for love of Max and Rosie.

You're joking again. Who the hell does he think he's fooling? He did it for himself, because he couldn't bear to lose them. Declan is dead, after cruel suffering, and he's responsible. How long does it take to fall from a fifth-floor balcony? Long enough to know and be afraid? *Oh Declan, Declan...* He might have eased his pain. He might even have saved his life. He'd been given that chance. But he'd been too busy running, running away, and he's running still. Framework? Structure? He's junked them. Flushed them down the lav. And all for love of Max and Rosie. All because he couldn't bear to lose them.

Lose them? Pull the other one. It's got bells on it.

Dear Max... dear Rosie... Guess what—I've brutally murdered my faggot lover Declan Finsey because I couldn't bear to lose you...

They'll really go for that.

What, then?

Only ten minutes. The phrase recurs in his head. Three words, round and round.

Better to be dead like Declan. No more running. He's really blown it. Better to be dead too.

He looks out over the Jaguar's sleek grey bonnet. In front of him the garage's white-washed back wall, brightly lit in the headlights, is hung with sectional metal shelving and a coil of garden hose looped over hooks, two empty picture frames, a neat rack of tools. Better to be dead like Declan. Tidy again. Framed and orderly. He sits back in the Jaguar's softly sculptured leather seat and thinks about being dead.

The notion has a sad, bitter rightness to it. His being dead would spare the people around him so much trouble. And they'd never have to know his true shame. Even if they connected his death with Declan's, they'd never discover the whole, lonely, pain-wracked truth of it.

Being dead. Being nothing. He's no problem with that. Being something has been fine, up to half an hour ago, but being nothing is alright too. Leaving the party early. Taking his shame with him. Sparing people that. Choosing. Taking a decision. For the first time in his life, being in control.

He links his fingers behind his head and stretches, straightening his back and pushing his feet on the floor between the pedals. Lights flash behind his squeezed-shut eyes. He can choose to be dead.

Too easy a get-out? He thinks about that. Ah, sod it—when had he ever not done something because it was too easy?

Scared, then? Of course, but he can deal with that.

Besides, the car is there and the garage is there, and they're calling his bluff. Max has the Euthanasia Society's literature and Leo's read it. With a reliable internal combustion engine, a full-ish petrol tank and a well-built garage with well-fitting doors, death by carbon-monoxide poisoning is simple, fool-proof, painless, and only briefly unpleasant.

Unless, mind you, the car's a recent model, really up-to-date, and its exhaust system has a catalytic converter which cuts its poisonous CO_2 emissions to a relatively harmless level. It says so in the book, Max's book, put out by the Euthanasia Society. But Leo, with his sixties converterless Jag, will be fine. No CPR, no rushes to hospital, no pumpings-out. Just a cherry-red complexion from the CO_2 emissions, so the book says, and death…

He could use sleeping pills instead of course (his mother has Oblivons a-plenty), with the book's recommended plastic bag pulled over his head and tightened down round his neck just to be sure. His last, drug-dazed act when he's nodding off. Pills would be fine.

The garage is here, though, and the Jaguar. With these two excellent items, who needs pills and a plastic bag? He re-starts the car's engine and opens the driver's door beside him, preparing to get out and wind down the garage's up-and-over.

He doesn't get out. A new thought has stopped him.

Alright then, you at the back. So you're tempted to sneer. Once a man starts finding reasons to put off committing suicide, you can easily take that as proof that he's never really meant to do it. Or maybe he's just too chicken. He's simply been whipping up a drama, snugly, there in the solitude of his garage. Feeling sorry for himself. Scripting his funeral. Basking in the obits.

In this case, though, Leo's new thought is a good one. It's not about himself. For once, perhaps rarely, it's genuinely selfless. He's realised that while being dead would be fine for him, it wouldn't do much for anyone else.

Not for his mother.

Nor for Max. Nor for Rosie.

At the best, they'd simply miss him for a while. Probably quite badly. Suicides do that to people. It's not just the dying. Suicides claw at the survivors. A little more attention given, they say, a little more love, and it could have been prevented. At the worst, then, the survivors start to blame themselves. It's the sort of sad, self-destructive thing people like them do, nice people, decent people, good people, and he absolutely does not want to leave that sort of mess behind.

Certainly having him alive and nicked for murder wouldn't do much for them either. Nor for Leo himself, actually. But that's fair enough. There's still the alibi option.

He turns off the Jaguar's six potentially lethal cylinders. The dashboard clock tells him the time is a couple of minutes before seven. All that's needed, of course, when he goes into the house, is for him to suggest to his mother that it's actually rather earlier, say around six thirty, and then his visit to Declan will clearly have ended well before the poor man's tragic fall—the time of which will be established by the sash-window-opening neighbour.

It's certainly a possibility. A lot of pain would be avoided if it worked And as a final, admittedly saccharine thought, a few more years for him out in the world would give him a chance to make up for some of the worst of his iniquities.

All this depended, of course, on him now going in and not finding his mother glued her radio, the BBC's seven o'clock pips sounding just at that very moment clearly and unignorably.

CHAPTER 2

Back in 1941 Grandmother Clare had accepted without protest the proposed donation of her grandson. She hadn't yet got to know the child—Madam Sara hadn't encouraged her to visit the Belsize Park Séance Centre to any great extent and she hadn't insisted (the flat had bead-curtained doors, an unmistakeable waft of incense and a heavy mahogany table that looked suspiciously capable of rapping noises) but poor little Leo, she decided, could be her Good Work. A passable Jessie Matthews look-alike back in her youth and now a recent widow still capable of a smooth line in songs-from-the-shows at her big black Bösendorfer, Clare had no thought of re-marriage. Although still a child at the time of Victoria's death, she was a Victorian at heart and would, like the dear Queen, bless her, wear black for the rest of her life. She'd been back from India for several years now, however, and understandably had been finding Cheltenham on the uneventful side after Poonah society and their beautiful bungalow up in the Nilgris.

Not that she could have stayed on alone. India was changing beyond all recognition, even her several handsome Sikh household servants (a framed set of their portraits hung in her hall) were listening to the agitators. In any case her British friends out there were dying off at an alarming rate, and poor dear Hesketh had left her agreeably well provided-for, so here she was.

At least Cheltenham was Home, the bridge was decent, the house she'd found on Tivoli Street—although Edwardian rather than the high Georgian of Cheltenham's finest years—was a gem of its kind, and her younger sister Iolanthe's family were now nicely settled over near Bath which wasn't impossibly distant. Iolanthe, with a Channel Islander husband, Ian, and two sons, had been living in Guernsey at the beginning of the war. They'd got out virtually as Hitler's thugs were landing on the beach and the husband luckily had a small but respectable Somerset family property. No, all Clare had really found herself needing was a purpose, some sort of worthy activity—War Work was hardly her thing—and Leo's arrival would give her exactly that. With Sara now a mother and trying to make a living after being abandoned by that walking disaster area Maurice, she would actually be useful. In short, though she would never have voiced anything so trite, it would be nice to be needed.

(As to the present nature of the living her daughter was trying to make, the less said about that the better. Show business had been bad enough, but now this Spiritualist mumbo jumbo… She'd kept it from the Colonel while he was alive: she could only hope that the poor man had happier things to think about now that he'd joined the Great Majority.)

A delivery day was arranged. As I've already mentioned, Clare had of course visited her tiny grandson in London, but not frequently. London was bothersomely distant and in any case, like her daughter, Clare was not comfortable with infants. Or, to be honest, with children. An excellent Indian ayah, and teams of servants, had raised baby Sara until she was old enough to be sent to school back in England, from where Iolanthe, her aunt, married to her Channel Islander and living at that time in Guernsey with their two small sons, had coped with the holidays.

Even so, the skinny little baby boy, thrust into Clare's arms by his mother one hot late August afternoon on Paddington Station just in time for their departure from platform three on the Cheltenham Flyer, dazed her with such an extraordinary gush of emotion, quite unexpected and curiously physical—an astonishing sensation coming vividly and identifiably from around her heart—that small tears wetted her eyes and her hands trembled as she took the child and actually pressed him protectively to her breasts. All thoughts of Leo as her Good Work disappeared. He was amazing. He was her precious, precious grandson.

Fortunately for all three of them, Madam Sara noticed none of this. She'd already turned away and was hurrying down the platform to the station's Praed Street entrance. She'd left her taxi waiting there and the meter was ticking. She'd moved on.

Clare and Leo, too, moved on. She loved him, and would do so for the rest of her life—dote on him, one might say, but guardedly, in a very Victorian upper-middle-class manner Her passionate moment on Paddington's platform three had been so unexpected, so rare and dangerously intense, that Leo believes she spoke of it only once, years later, and then very Britishly, to her sister Iolanthe, his great-aunt, around the time of her final illness. Iolanthe, back in Guernsey now after the war, but over in England that summer for tennis at Wimbledon, was a frequent visitor. And Iolanthe, being British also, had chosen not to share her sister's intimate recollection with him until the funeral was safely behind them. In coming years, though, she would in fact usefully become his source for much of the early Cheltenham history appearing in this book

On their return from Paddington to the house on Tivoli Street the Norland-trained nanny, meticulously interviewed, checked and approved by Clare for a probationary period, was ready with supper, bath, and bed. In the first of many letters to her daughter—which Sara astonishingly kept—

Clare reported that Leo wept only briefly. If he had been chilled, in his time with his mother, by love's absence, then Clare's embrace had clearly warmed him. The nanny, an efficient if insecure person, deeply needing to love and be loved, took him to her heart. She survived her probationary period and stayed for the next eighteen years, promoted sideways to Clare's housekeeper as her nannying duties became no longer necessary. As might be expected, the two women's attentions clearly proved to be excellent for Leo's physical prosperity and for his peace of mind, but much less good in the matter of his lack of bold.

* * * *

"Ma? Ma—it's me.' Entering from the garage, through the garden door and the conservatory at the back of the house, along the turkey-carpeted passage beside the stairs and hanging up his anorak in the dimly-lit front hall. 'You alright?'

The house was silent. No radio was playing, no BBC pips, nothing.

Hallelujah.

Madam Sara's voice came faintly from her bedroom. 'Iss been a long day.'

Leo waited, counting silently. *One, two, three, four—*

She didn't fail him. 'And doan call me that *Ma*. I'm not some barmaid. It's so clower chass.'

He left the entrance hall, went across the hall and leaned round her half-open door.

'These Tuesdays always are long. Are you decent?' She was in her red brocade dressing gown, his Old Cheltenonian's black-and-magenta woollen school scarf wrapped round her neck, sitting on the edge of her bed. The room loomed round her, much too much mahogany. 'Hi there. So how was your day?'

'Sandra came. Man read the gash meter. The gas meter. Nice man. What I always say is. His wife's just had a... a... one of those—'

'A baby?'

'Doan prompt me. Sandra says you musn prompt me.'

Sandra was her speech therapist. An indomitable young woman, bright-eyed beyond the call of duty.

'Only trying to help. Anyway, it's nearly six now.' It was closer to seven actually but on his way along the back of the house after closing the garage door he'd rehearsed his new plan and it worked better with the extra half hour. This should be a safe adjustment—the alarm clock on her bedside table was behind her and in any case where the time was concerned she usually took his word for it. 'Nearly six now, so we'd better start thinking about some supper.'

'Warmed up that cuffleflower cheese you left me for lunch. Gash man helped me. Gas man. He was nice. But too much salt. I told him. I told him. You always put in too much salt, Leo.'

'I'll try to remember.' He went forward to the bed and held out his hands. How long she'd been sitting there was anybody's guess. He remembered the joke about the old man who's asked what he does with himself: '*Sometimes I sits and thinks,*' he answers, '*and sometimes I just sits.*' Christ.

She took his hands and pulled herself upright. He kissed her forehead. 'Shall we get you through to the kitchen, then? Keep me company while I see what's in the fridge?'

While they were eating supper—he didn't approve of fridge fodder but something simple was necessary once a month, on his *showing the flag* days—she told him more about the gas man. Her day's big event. Then she asked him how her truthsayers were doing. For a dangerous moment, his thoughts wandering, drawn constantly back to Declan's dying, he couldn't think why she wanted to know. Then he remembered. He'd been checking in with her bloody truthsayers all day.

'They're doing fine, dear. Busy as busy. The Patton woman won't be holding any more Coombe Hill meetings until after Christmas. Something about her brother's kids. She's fixed for Denny to go over from Stroud. His group is down to two and they can ride with him in the car if they want to.'

'Denny? Denny's no good with two. I seen him. What I always say is. Most people arn. The more, the merrier. Only two and there's not enough vort, not enough vart, not enough—'

'Voltage.'

'Doan prompt me.'

'That's why it's so good that he can join up with Mrs Patton's lot. That way he gets a decent-sized meeting.'

She nodded, looked at him sideways. 'What did you tell them?'

' The truthsayers? What about?' He knew what about.

'You know what about.'

'They're missing you. Missing you badly. I told them what I always tell them. You're fine. Getting better every day.'

'Thass what Sandra says.'

'Of course she does. She also says you must put the "t" in "that's." That's.' He reached across the table, patted his mother's hand. 'It's not easy, I know. I tell them they're never out there on their own. You're always with them.'

Madam Sara stared down at her plate. 'I *am* getting better. Look at me. I *am*.'

'That's what I tell them. You mustn't worry.'

His reassurances had kept the SCT's accredited mediums happy for a while, but not any more. On his round today he'd heard disloyal murmurs. People were wondering if Madam Sara would ever be back. That terrible Graham Courtland man over in Ledbury was in fact thinking of starting up on his own account. If the SCT was to survive, it needed—

His thoughts fragmented. He ran out of reassurances. *Only ten minutes. Scraping at the concrete.* In his head the tape loop played again. Dear god, had there really ever been a time, a blessed time when this wretched SCT stuff had actually mattered? A time when the biggest drama in his life could really have been bloody Sally Patton taking herself off to Tewkesbury till after Christmas?

He took a deep breath. The loop was hysterical nonsense. One dealt with it. Somehow one kept on. Kept on keeping on. 'Don't worry, dear. You're getting better. That's what I tell them. And you are.'

'Good.' His mother prepared her face for the effort of Sandra's 't.' 'Tha-t's good.'

After their supper and half an hour's TV in the chintzy small back sitting room (luckily nothing was on that she regularly watched on Tuesday nights so she wouldn't notice how late they were running), he got her into the shower and then on into bed. He gave her her pills, counted them out on her bedside table.

Two Oblivons for her sleeplessness, one Zestrol for her blood pressure and three Dolcelaxes for her constipation.

He stared at them. What the hell? Why not try a different approach?

Sixteen Dolcelaxes for her sleeplessness, three Oblivons for her blood pressure, and just one Zestrol for her constipation.

Or, better still: three jelly beans for her sleeplessness, one sugared almond for her blood pressure, and thirty peppermint humbugs for her constipation.

Declan dying on the concrete.

Christ.

Leaning over her, he smoothed the hair back from her forehead. 'Sleep tight, old lady.' He went out into the passage, pulled her door shut behind himself, and leaned against the wall, every muscle rigid. Photographs in fine gilt frames of younger versions of Madam Sara, often with the most unexpected celebrities, lined the passage, signed and inscribed with impressive testimonials. He closed his eyes, counted silently to ten, and then to fifty.

After washing up the supper things he returned to the small rear sitting room, where he found cat Rumple warming his chest at what was left of the fire. Mostly Rumple spent his nights indoors but if he chose the garden he had a flap in the door to the garage to get in by should the weather turn nasty. Leo stirred the fire, then made it up, settled in his usual chair, and turned on the TV again. He sat with the sound muted, staring blankly at its over-saturated colours, until his grandmother's long-case clock out in the hall, made in nineteenth century England but bought in Delhi, laboriously struck eleven thirty and it was time for bed.

How do people cope with personal catastrophe? Does it make a difference if the catastrophe is of their own making? Does self control help or is it better to be one of those people who shed theatrical tears, or raged up and down and broke things? No—forgive me. This isn't about people, this is about Leo. Only about Leo, sitting quietly there in front of the silent TV in his mother's rear living room in the house on Tivoli Street.

And how did he cope? Well, as one of those people who sought order in their lives, now that he had survived the initial trauma he coped with his catastrophe by making it tidy. Looking at it straight on and taking it in stages.

First, his sorrow. It wasn't simply conventional, a social response. Losing Declan would leave a gap in his life. Admittedly there was a fair chance that Declan, after being exed, would have taken himself off, severed the entire relationship. They might never by choice have seen each other again. They'd had their good times, though, and there'd surely be moments when Leo would miss him. And Declan would always be out there somewhere, a part—for good or bad—of who Leo now was.

But *sorrow*? To be honest, if it wasn't simply conventional it was something very similar. To be even honester, something he had already been working at. He'd decided to move on.

Second, the practicalities. Always assuming that Declan Finsey's death wasn't simply written off as accidental or a suicide (which seemed quite possible), Leo's arrest still wasn't inevitable. There was a sporting chance that he could get away with it. There'd been no scuffle, and therefore there'd be no signs of one. As to Declan's single shout, with any luck—and Leo would need plenty of that—his '*What?*' had been heard only unclearly by whoever had then opened the sash window. In any case, the time of his fall would be established as as somewhere around six thirty, which meant that if Leo admitted his visit but moved it back forty minutes or so (which period had in fact been filled by the time-out he'd taken in a lay-by while driving from his previous visit), then he'd have been long gone from Declan's flat by that time. So there'd be no need for the awkward question to be raised of why the poor man should have shouted something arguably suggestive of a second person's involvement. Solitary people falling by their own intent probably didn't shout anything at all, while solitary people falling by accident (Leo's preferred alternative) were likely to cry out more for help than for answers.

A blurred cry therefore, please: unsuggestive of another's presence but clear enough to establish the time of Declan's fall. Leo's arrival back in

Cheltenham, fifteen miles away, at just about the same time would then be established courtesy of Madam Sara, and Leo would be off the hook. The police would be left, in the absence of a suicide note or any conceivable suicide motive, with a tragic, if admittedly improbable, accidental death. They might have their suspicions about him, and his mother wouldn't be the ideal witness, but they'd need more than that, especially given the apparent total lack of motive, to secure a conviction.

To secure a conviction—Leo knew the jargon. He'd read his Ruth Rendells. Even had a go at writing one. Fitted it in around the SCT. A dud, of course. Even so, having read his Ruth Rendells made this whole wretched situation far less unthinkable. The mess he was in was a matter of contrivances. Mechanisms. Words on a page.

The practicalities, then, suggested a better than sporting chance. He must take it. Not only as a matter of crude self preservation: he had wider responsibilities. His mother depended on him, for her day-to-day living and for him as a son whom people—and she herself of course—thought of as a decent, respectable citizen. The SCT too, in its own small way, depended on him: a secretary revealed as a brutal murderer would do it no good at all. Also there were Max and Rosie—he owed them his best efforts to avoid the distress of his arrest and conviction. Nothing excused the manner of Declan's death, but now that it had occurred, surely any fall-out should be kept to a minimum? For everyone's sake?

Next, the moral side of things. His guilt in the matter. His shame. As to the former, Leo told himself guilt wasn't a useful thought. The phrase was Max's but Leo'd taken it to his heart. *Not a useful thought…* he'd found it an invaluable life simplifier. However you looked at it, guilt was pointless. Corrosive. The most destructive of human emotions. What was done, was done. One faced consequences, dealt with them, and moved on. One never wallowed. One accepted responsibility, ameliorated the human cost where possible, and moved on.

Declan was dead. No matter how—walk by that quickly. Declan was dead and dead was dead—neither good nor bad, no memories and no regrets, just *dead.* Nothing to be done about it. He had a family, though, a father and two sisters. The father had disowned him abusively years ago as a fucking bum-boy, no son of his, killed his poor dear mother, (not true— his mother, loving him dearly, had died of a degenerative lung disease), and hadn't spoken to him since, but the sisters were close. Carla and Mary ran a gift shop nearby, just down the road, in Bourton-on-the-Water. Leo felt bad about them. His responsibility there was real and he'd do what he could. It wouldn't, in the nature of things, be much but he'd do it. He remembered them as wary, cheerful, vulnerable girls. Neither had married, he thought.

Who else? Declan's little Cirencester congregation would miss him.

He was good with them, good at his job altogether, and the SCT had no truthsayer immediately available to replace him. Leo would make a real effort to find someone to help them. Denny could go over from Stroud, but only temporarily: he wasn't really very good with his people.

Any other human cost? Friends, presumably, but nobody close. Dekko'd never mentioned one. Not that Leo could remember.

So much for guilt, then. What did the man in the Strindberg play say? Cancel and move on.

Finally then, the legalities. Preserving the fabric of society. Punishment for his sins and the satisfaction this would give to the innocent. He didn't go for that. Certainly society needed to be protected, but not from him—he was no danger to it, none at all. And its innocent members weren't worth much if punishing him was how they got their jollies…

Hang on a minute—hasn't he left something out? A few moments ago wasn't he considering his guilt in Declan's death and his shame? And then, there in front of his silent TV, he'd dealt with, if you can call it that, the matter of his guilt. But now he's moved on to the legalities, quite skipping over his shame.

And shame, although possibly an even less useful thought than guilt, is seldom a condition that stays skipped over. Leo's shame did not go quietly. It beat at him relentlessly, refusing to be moved on from and cancelled.

He had no answer for it. Taken one by one, as they had happened, each of his acts seemed to possess a mitigating aura of accident, even of inevitability, but it was only an aura. One by one, each of his acts had been in fact callous, inhuman, immoral. One by one, each of his acts had also been short-sighted, stupid, seriously shameful. One by one, each of his…no, this individuation was in itself a delusion, a way of lessening his inhumanity. To separate each one of his acts into items was to devalue the truly monstrous overall brutality.

His acts were indivisible: a dying man, unimaginable pain surrounding every broken bone, blind perhaps, scraping, sorrowing hoarsely on the concrete… ah, all these dire imaginings. Perhaps, more mercifully, Declan had been unconscious, scraping and sorrowing only in his dreams. Perhaps he had been already dead, scraping and sorrowing the way the newly dead are reported, occasionally, to scrape and sorrow.

Nothing, though, for Leo's comfort. Nothing for a man who anyway would never know the truth because, shamefully, shamefully, shamefully, he'd been somewhere else, up in his victim's flat, working out a plan to stop him getting caught.

He did not have a good night.

It's not much, admittedly, but isn't Leo's shame perhaps a minutely cheering phenomenon? Isn't shame a proof of humanity? I feel shame, therefore I am?

* * * *

The following morning, Wednesday, 15th September, saw Leo up and dressed by seven fifteen, in time to get cat Rumple fed and stuffed out the window, and his mother's breakfast tray ready to go into her room punctually at seven thirty. Her nights were often uneasy, troubled by pains and weird dreams, and she woke very early, so that by seven thirty she was impatient for the day to begin. And she knew what seven thirty looked like on her bedside clock radio.

That morning Leo too, unusually, had long been awake and ready to leave his bed. He leaned on the cooker in the kitchen, breathing deeply, his eyes closed, as he waited the kettle to boil for her breakfast tea. The frying pan was warming on the gas. And Declan was with him there of course, weeping and scraping, dying on the concrete.

When he drew his mother's bedroom curtains the sun, which had been shining cheerfully through the kitchen window, shone equally cheerfully into her over-furnished, joyless bedroom. She eyed the tray suspiciously. There was a script available on Madam Sara's mental bookshelf for questioning the exact cookedness of her breakfast fried egg, and on bad mornings she used it. The yolk must be just right—not hard but not runny and cold to the touch either. There was also a script concerning the condition of her toast—she required it to be crisp and brown and hot enough to melt the butter. This morning, however—possibly on account of the sun—she left both scripts on the shelf along with her others. The egg, once carefully fingertip-touched, was judged to be acceptable. The toast too.

As he'd expected, the regional morning news on his mother's radio was unsensational stuff. There hadn't been time for Declan's body to be found and any Cirencester stringer to alert the local station. He reckoned noon was the earliest the media would get on to Declan Finsey. Declan must wait, meekly dead, at least another four hours before the world got to hear of him. Leo's press experience took over, writing the headline wishfully for them in his head: *Local Medium in Mysterious Death Fall.*

Meanwhile, in 81 Tivoli Street there was the morning to be got through. Today was Wednesday, and on Mondays, Wednesdays and Fridays a home help arrived at nine. Dear Hoppy, Mrs Hopkins to you, had been with Madam S for nearly twenty years. And for Leo today there were SCT clerical chores—entering Sally Patton's defection into his office diary, for example—and the health visitor Mrs Caudle at nine-thirty to check up on his mother (toenails, in particular, were a difficulty she didn't care to share with him). Then, at eleven, she'd do her speech therapy exercises. He sat with her for these and she always worked hard:

Arrround the rrrugged rrrock the rrragged rrrascal rrran.

Arrround the rrrugged rrrock the rrragged rrrascal rrran…

She rolled her 'r's like a side drum. She saw herself back in control of the church she had founded and Sandra said her exercises were the only way.

Before any of that, though, Leo had a phone call to make, from the desk in his office-bedsit.

'Max?'

'No—it's Rosie.'

He'd hoped it would be Max. He'd had a desperate urge to call them, a need for human contact, for adult communication, and Max would have been easier. Their relationship was simpler. Safer. Almost, he could imagine confiding those ten minutes to Max.

'Rosie. Rosie my dear… how is he?'

'A good night. This new cocktail from the hospital seems to be working.'

Leo stood his pen upright on his blotter and tried unsuccessfully to balance it. There was nothing he could say. Nothing about how much he loved her. Nothing. At any moment Max might pick up the extension by his bed and join in.

She waited, then went on. Silences weren't unusual. 'He's decided on a party, Leo. Saturday next—late morning coffee and nibbles.' Copying Max, she pronounced his name the European way—Leh-o. He'd been tempted to use that pronunciation himself, when introducing himself to strangers, but he never remembered. A lot of affected nonsense, anyway. 'No booze— we're keeping it simple. And we don't want people to linger. In and out— you know how quickly Max tires. This is your official invite, love. Sara's too, if she'd like to come.'

'Next Saturday?' He couldn't think about next Saturday. Would it happen? 'A party?'

'Quite a do. Lots of locals, all the people we've ever met—even that terrible headmaster man from Dean Close School.'

'The Closet.'

'That's right.'

'We used to call it the Closet.'

'I know.'

'For the lavatorial connection. We were awful snobs, we College boys.'

'You told me… Are you alright, Leo? Is something the matter?'

His pen skittered off onto the floor. Was it really that obvious? 'The matter? Of course not. I'm fine. Bit of a spat with Mother, but it's nothing important. I just thought I'd check in, see how you're doing.'

'Max is full of his party. He's tying it in with the autumn equinox—

some mystical German thing I think he's invented. But he's pushing the boat out. If he's well enough he wants you two to play something, *á la* Viennese *salon*. You two, and that organist woman from Christchurch.'

'Oh Lord.'

'Don't be mean, love. She's—'

'Not her—I was thinking of us. Max and me. You know how I go to pieces in front of people.'

'It'll have to be something simple. He doesn't have much puff.'

'Tell him, nor do I.' What he'd said wasn't funny, but he laughed at it loudly.

'Leo? Leo, are you sure you're alright?'

'Look, there's someone at the door. I've got to go. Perhaps I'll see you this afternoon. If I can get away. When stands the clock at ten to three. Honey for tea and all that. And I'm fine. Love to Max. 'Bye.'

He flung the receiver at its rest. If that was the best he could do he must never talk to Rosie again. The receiver bounced off and he caught it as it slithered away. A party? What the hell was Max thinking about? He never gave parties.

As he sat there staring at the phone, it rang again. He jumped. Rosie calling back? Had he really sounded so odd? He carefully let it ring several times before he answered.

'Good morning. Spiritualist Church of Truth. May I help you?'

A woman's voice, not Rosie's. Someone called Roxanne Fletcher, and on SCT business. Leo steadied his hand enough to wake up the SCT program on his Applemac. Roxanne Fletcher worked for a local Charlton Kings funeral provider and she wanted to book a qualified truthsayer for a post-interment guidance meeting on the coming Saturday. Leo cleared his throat and asked her about the wishes of the bereaved.

Much of his SCT work involved the telephone. Usually stammerers hate the telephone. Leo, however, was comfortable with people he knew, and for the rest his carefully announced identity as The Spiritualist Church of Truth gave him a safe, non-stammering persona. Back in his school days he'd been able to act on the stage in just the same way. Reading in chapel was fine too. The person who did those things wasn't Leo the stammerer. He was… someone else.

The choice of a truthsayer was a very personal matter, he told Roxanne Fletcher, and suggested that the bereaved might like to look at some SCT promotion material before making a decision.

The woman said she'd been given full authority. Leo didn't argue. They discussed fees, then he consulted the schedules and gave her Ledbury's T/S (truthsayer) Graham Courtland, not ideal but the only T/S available for a Saturday. Ledbury was without a guidance meeting for that week-end on account of repairs being made to the central heating in the village hall they used. Leo chose a man for the ceremony because funerals needed the weight, but he didn't mention that to Roxanne Fletcher. Women were only recently making their way in the funeral industry and they could be touchy.

At least she'd known better than to ask about a guaranteed spirit response. It was surprising how many people did ask. As if a truthsayer were some visiting TV serviceman.

They completed the arrangements and she rang off. He wished he'd found her someone else. T/S Courtland was a flamboyant, actorish man, his hats broad-brimmed and his gaze piercing. He'd arrived in the Spiritualist Church of Truth two years ago, after a time in the USA about which he was reticent in a manner that suggested a becoming modesty. In fact, as Leo's vetting process had eventually established, he'd been a sexually very successful barefoot painter/seer in Southern California whose departure for England had been the result of a difference of opinion with the tax authorities. He'd claimed he was a church, and therefore tax-exempt, and they'd thought otherwise. They were after him still, but with waning enthusiasm.

For Courtland the SCT was obviously no more than a place where he could develop a following of his own and then branch out. Meanwhile he'd got a day job teaching life classes in a local art school, and the rewarding quality of his truthsayer sessions, combined with his lingering handshake (and perhaps with thoughts of this risqué other job he did, drawing nude people), had made him, at least with the women, a popular figure.

Leo sighed. He was a snob. All that was really wrong with Courtland was his charm. He'd do a good, sensitive job for Ms Fletcher. Leo looked up his number, called him, got his answerphone, left him the Saturday booking on it. Then he sat on, telephone to his ear. His eye had been caught by a patch of wallpaper above the fireplace. It was clearly peeling. Back in the spring he'd put two coats of a silicone-based sealer on under it to control the damp but it was still peeling. The sealer hadn't worked.

His mother's health visitor arrived sharply at nine thirty. He listened while Hoppy let Mrs Caudle in, and stayed in his office-bedsit. He stared at his Apple's screen, seeing only darkness and Declan dying, weeping and scraping, dying on the concrete.

Between the health visitor and the speech exercises there was usually a break for coffee. He waved Mrs Caudle away down the front path, then closed the door on her and returned to the kitchen where his mother was already leaning her hip on the edge of the sink as she juggled the tap and the kettle in her one good hand. The other worked, but weakly.

He crossed the kitchen, tried to take the kettle from her, and she resisted. He stepped quickly away, wrong-footed. 'I'll get the instant out, shall I?'

She nodded. 'Fithy stuff. What I always say is.'

She positioned the kettle in the bottom of the sink, removed its lid and turned on the tap, edging the kettle sideways when the water missed it and glancing to see if Leo had noticed.

He was busy looking in the coffee-and-sugar-and-tea-and-biscuits cupboard. 'We're nearly out. You must remind me to get some tomorrow when I go to Sainsbury's.'

'Mind you get…' she braced herself, made a major effort '…freeze dried.'

He didn't applaud. Sandra would have, but Sandra believed in the everyone's-a-child-at-heart approach. His mother wasn't a child. Not at heart or anywhere else.

'Biscuits?' He rattled the tin.

'Narp. Fattening.' She turned off the tap, put the lid back on the kettle, carried it to the stove, put it centrally on a burner and turned on the gas, waiting there until the spark ignition had visibly lit it. She worked at her rehab.

Fattening? He sighed, put the tin back in the cupboard, and sat down at the table. She already was fat, there was no other word for it. And the eternal dressing gown didn't help. But circumstances conspired. It was hard to control your weight when you were almost immobile, and getting dressed was a battle. He helped her with buttons when he could but there was more to clothes than that. She'd given up bras on account of the fastenings. Even pulling up knickers with only one hand was a struggle.

A twice-daily nurse would have been the answer, and they could easily have afforded one, but she was obstinate—she hadn't yet come down to that. Twice weekly Mrs Caudle was bad enough.

She turned from the stove. 'What you been up to?'

'Nothing much. Undertaker called, those Charlton Kings people, wanting a truthsayer for the end of the week. I gave them Graham Courtland.'

'Thass Ledbury. Thass the town hall with the busted heat.'

'Right first time. Well done.' He let her thasses go. She'd a better memory than he had. He'd needed the Apple's.

She'd been working three of her four fingers into a mug handle. Now she lifted it to put it on the table. 'You confirm to him? Might be busy.'

'I left him a message.'

'Might be busy. What I always say is. Didn only work for us, you know.'

'Doesn't, Ma. He doesn't only work for us. *Didn't* means—'

'*Didn* means 'then.' I know.' She was suddenly furious. '*Didn* means then. *Doesn* means now. I know, boy.' Hammering the table with her mug. '*Doesn* means now. I know…'

He let her hammer. The mug was good thick china. 'Sorry, Ma.'

'And doan call me *Ma*. It's so clower chass.' Saliva trailed unfelt from the corner of her mouth. 'Makes me sound like a barmaid. I've always hated it.'

He'd been calling her *Ma* now for twenty-five years, since just after his school days, and she'd always hated it. 'Sorry.'

Ponderously, out in the hall, the clock struck eleven. It moved them on.

'What shall we have for this evening's supper?'

'You choose.' She sat down heavily. 'You always do. I'm the resident idgit.'

He hardly ever chose, but arguing wasn't worth it. He never won—not against the resident idgit. 'There's some best end of neck in the freezer. I could do a curry.'

She glared at him. 'Mean. Mean all through... You know I never sleep. Not after... after...' She'd lost the word. 'After that stuff with rice what you said.'

'That was only once. Months ago. And it was chicken. We've had lamb curry twice since then and you loved it.'

'Doan tell me what I love.'

He'd closed his eyes and moved his lips with hers.

He tried again. 'There's always pork chops. They're easy. I could rustle up some apple sauce.'

'Please yourself.'

He wanted to lean forward and wipe the drool from her chin but he didn't. He wasn't Sandra. She'd discover it for herself in a minute.

'Kettle's boiling.'

And Declan was scraping and weeping, dying on the concrete.

He got up from the table, eased her fingers out of the mug handle, spooned instant coffee into the mug and took it to the stove. There was just enough water in the kettle. She let him do all this without comment, didn't look at him, just sat. A synapse had missed a spark somewhere. He made a detour to the refrigerator, where he added fat-free milk.

The kitchen was honey pine from the Habitat shop up at the top of the Promenade, installed by his mother back in the sixties, when she'd moved in after Grandmother Clare's death, the only room in the house that wasn't still filled with Clare's Indian past—the past, faux-Victorian, that had shaped Leo's childhood. What-not shelves lined with mysteriously-echoing Benares-ware brass pots, an ornate ebony table on fiercely-tusked elephant's-head legs dangerous to schoolboy shins, sandalwood screens that creaked for no clear reason and breathed out fine grey powder, ominous coffin-sized chests in red-and-gold lacquer from Bareilly... Only the kitchen had been spared Indian Victoriana and he'd never liked it.

He still didn't like it. His mother was old now and it wasn't kind to her.

Its chaste spotlights and little bright knobs did her many inadequacies no favours. Everywhere else in the cluttered frowsty house she didn't look too bad. Here in the chic honey pine kitchen she looked like somebody else's dirty fat ugly bad-tempered retard.

It would be kinder on her, he suddenly thought as he put the mug of instant coffee in front of her and gently touched her arm, if he didn't keep the place so tidy.

She roused herself. 'I've been making plans,' she said with rare control and clarity. 'The radiant spirits agree with me. Nuna thinks we should take a cruise ship to the Greek islands in the spring.'

'Wouldn't that be marvellous.' He waited for her to go on but for the moment her resources of vocabulary and syntax were spent. He trimmed his enthusiasm. 'It's a long way, of course. And we never did much like travel.'

It was a carer-and-patient 'we.' He'd have loved to travel. For his mother, however, it had always required an undesirable broadening of her focus. She had her Gift. It was what she had. Travel, never undertaken willingly, was a distraction.

'Shunshine?' She gestured vaguely at the window. 'Shunshine before I pass onto a higher pla—' She broke off, eyed him sideways, didn't complete the phrase, and drank her coffee. 'Fithy stuff. Fithy stuff.'

He looked out. Saw drizzle. Apparently the morning's clear skies hadn't lasted. Cheltenham was notoriously damp.

'Greece sounds fine. I'll get some brochures.'

'Huh. *I'll get some brochures*... I know what that means. Humour the resident idgit.' She discovered her trail of saliva and wiped it away. 'My radiant spirits. And my Nuna. She's never wrong. I... trust my radiant spirits.'

'Of course you do.'

Of course she did. The fame, the Cheltenham house, the SCT—her radiant spirits had done her proud: Princess Nuna in particular, her personal spirit guide, a seventeenth century maharani. It was curious, though, that in these last few months she'd started challenging him. Challenging his position on... things. A lifetime of evasions, of silences, between mother and son, truly a whole lifetime of other, safer things to talk about, and yet now, again and again, these little challenges. Did she really want to know? Surely she didn't need his validation?

For heaven's sake, he'd never laughed at her beliefs. Her bag of tricks. Whatever they were. Such stuff wasn't funny. One man's side-splitter was another man's Immaculate Conception. He was here, wasn't he, working for the SCT? Wasn't that enough?

'It's after eleven,' he said. 'Time for your exercises.'

Power. He seldom used it, but he did have it, and sometimes it was all he had. Now, with Declan weeping, scraping, dying on the concrete, was one of those times.

He helped her up and they went into the small rear sitting room.

Arrround the rrrugged rrrock the rrragged rrrascal rrran.

Noon brought lunch in the kitchen, soup from a carton and a tuna-fish sandwich, and local news on the small TV set above the refrigerator. As he'd expected, the lead story was Declan Finsey's death: *Famous local medium in mysterious death fall.* He gave himself nine out of ten. 'Famous' was stretching it.

His mother often didn't listen, but Declan's name caught her attention. 'Thass one of our truthsayers.'

'You're right, Ma.'

'Wass he done?'

'Hush a minute—'

The reporter on the spot, an earnest young woman, wet and wind-blown, standing in front of yellow police crime-scene plastic ribbons by the entrance to Declan's parking lot, was describing the latest developments. There weren't any. Mr Finsey had apparently fallen from his Cirencester balcony and the police were considering his death suspicious. A neighbour had found the body and was helping them with their enquiries. Oh, and a police forensics team had arrived two hours before.

The reporter pulled up her collar against the rain. Mr Finsey, she went on breathlessly, had been a Spiritualist medium best known for his work with the Spiritualist Church of Truth, a religious organization that had its headquarters in nearby Cheltenham. Leo expected no snidery at this stage around the subject of spirit messages, and heard none. That would come later. Probably in the papers. *Spirits silent on identity of medium's murderer.* Columnists had more space and a greater willingness to take risks. Mr Finsey had been thirty-eight years old. Born in Cheltenham, he'd been educated at Dean Close School and before becoming a medium he'd worked in the retail trade. He was unmarried.

Leo chewed his tuna-fish sandwich. Poor Declan. It didn't add up to much.

Winding up, the reporter said the police were asking anyone who had seen Mr Finsey the previous afternoon or evening, or had been walking or driving in the Cirencester area after dark, to contact them at their Cheltenham headquarters. She gave the telephone number. Then she returned Leo and his mother to the studio.

'Thass you,' his mother told him.

'That's. Tha-t's. You really must try. And of course it's me. I saw him last night.' He stood up and turned off the TV set. 'Poor Declan. What a terrible thing. I'll give them a call right away.'

'Wass happened to him? I didn hear.'

'He's dead. Fell off his balcony somehow. Block of flats. He lives on the fifth floor.'

'Dead.' She thought about it. 'You were there.'

'Of course I was. Before he fell, though. He was fine when I left.' The reporter had mentioned a forensics team. He supposed that was inevitable. They'd be looking for signs of a struggle. That sort of stuff. 'I must call them.'

'You were there. You could have stop him.'

'He was fine. People do have accidents, you know. He was fine. When I left, I mean.'

'Troubled spirit.' She shook her head vehemently. 'Troubled spirit.'

He stared at her. Trying to make Declan into a suicide would never work. He pushed his chair back. 'I'll just go and tell the police I was there.'

She turned on the TV again and he went along the passage to the telephone in his office/bedsit.

When he told the man who answered why he was calling he was put through to a Detective Sergeant Wiler, a woman, who listened without comment, then thanked him for responding to their appeal so promptly. She suggested that he come to the Lansdowne Road station later that afternoon and make a statement. It would be very useful to us, she said. How about three fifteen?

He rang off, sat staring at the telephone. Very useful to them…. Christ, he hoped not. At least, on top of all his other troubles, he wouldn't have to worry about his stammer. Terror was a great clearer of word-jams. He'd found that the really bad moments in his life simply blew them away. Performance took over. He had his lines, and he'd say them.

* * * *

(click)

D.S. Wiler: This is Interview Room Four and the time is three thirty-eight on Wednesday, the twenty-sixth of September. Present are Chief Inspector Coade, Detective Sergeant Wiler, and the informant, Leo Anthony Bresson. The informant has been told that he may have a legal advisor with him should he so wish it, and he has declined the offer.

(This official police interview tape, and another later on, are of course both Leo's reconstructions but he vouches for their basic accuracy and the dialogue format speeds our story along without losing too much detail. He remembers Detective Sergeant Anthea Wiler as a cheerful young woman, ample and matronly for her years, while Chief Inspector Patrick Coade was tall, knobby-jointed, with a leisurely crumpled-suited professorial manner helped by a pipe and gold-rimmed half-spectacles straight from Central

Casting.)

C.I. Coade: Good of you to come forward like this, Mr Bresson.

Bresson: (laughs) I've a feeling you'd have scooped me in soon enough if I hadn't.

C.I. Coade: The social courtesies, Mr Bresson. Hm? They cost very little.

Bresson: Of course not. I'm sorry. It's just that—

C.I.Coade: If you hadn't come forward, Mr Bresson, how do you imagine we'd have known about you?

Bresson: You'd have talked to other SCT people and they'd have told you.

C.I.Coade: SCT?

Bresson: The Spiritualist Church of Truth. You've heard of it?

C.I. Coade: And what would these SCT people have told me?

Bresson: That I'd been on my way to see Mr Finsey. That it was part of my job.

C.I.Coade: I see. (pause) Mr Bresson has a high opinion of our investigative skills, Anthea.

D.S. Wiler: It's television, Boss.

C.I.Coade: I hope we don't disappoint him. (rustling) So on with the formalities, then. Your name is Leo Bresson, and—

Bresson: Leh-o. Leh-o Bresson. My father was French. Naturalised, of course.

C.I.Coade: I'll make a note. Hm? You must get tired of correcting people.

Bresson: Well… My father was in the theatre, you know. He—

C.I.Coade: And your profession?

Bresson: My profession? I'm the secretary and general administrator of the Spiritualist Church of Truth.

C.I.Coade: That is a paid position?

Bresson: Certainly. Pensionable too. We're a registered charity, and—

C.I.Coade: You were visiting Mr Finsey yesterday evening as part of your job?

Bresson: It's a monthly routine. Good for staff relations. I visit all the truthsayers.

C.I.Coade: Truthsayers?

Bresson: Mediums to you. Our church avoids the word because it has bad associations. Mediums haven't always had the best reputations.

C.I.Coade: And Mr Finsey was one? We have him down as a librarian.

Bresson: He was both. Librarian was his day job.

C.I.Coade: Do you like Edinburgh rock, Mr Bresson?

Bresson: I'm afraid I don't understand you.

C.I.Coade: It's a simple question. Edinburgh rock. I was about to offer you some. Here.

Bresson: I'm sorry. I thought you were getting out a handkerchief.

C.I.Coade: I like it for the ginger in it. Hm? Have you noticed how few sweets have ginger in them?

Bresson: I'm afraid I don't much like ginger.

C.I.Coade: I do. Luckily for her, so does Anthea.

Bresson: Look—I know most people think Spiritualists are a bunch of kooks. Fair enough. But—

C.I.Coade: Are you a Spiritualist, Mr Bresson?

Bresson: To be honest, Inspector, I don't see what that's got to do with it.

C.I.Coade: Nothing at all. I was simply curious. After all, a Spiritualist might be hoping for some sort of message from the dead man. Hm? A name, perhaps? An accusation?

Bresson: You're thinking of the famous Mr Rosma.

C.I.Coade: Rosma? Now there you have me.

Bresson: He's how Spiritualism got started. As an organised movement, I mean. Back in 1848.

C.I.Coade: It's an unusual name. Rosma… I like it. Enlighten me. And you're sure I can't tempt you to some Edinburgh Rock?

Bresson: Not just now. Thanks all the same…

C.I.Coade: You were telling me about Rosma.

Bresson: Well… well, it happened in an American small town called Hydesville—you really want to hear all this, Chief Inspector? Really?

C.I.Coade: If my sergeant will bear with me. She taps her watch if I over-run too badly.

Bresson: Ok. Fine… well, some Hydesville people heard rappings in a house there, telling them that a murdered man was trying to make contact, so a séance was organised, at which the dead man gave his name as Charles B Rosma and told them to dig up the cellar floor. And since there had indeed been someone with that unusual name living in the house some four years earlier they dug around and found human remains, and quicklime. You can imagine the sensation it caused. The boost it gave to Spiritualism.

C.I.Coade: And the murderer?

Bresson: Not so satisfactory. Too many years had gone by. The owner of the house at the time, a Mr Bell, was a perfectly respectable fellow. The police were never able to pin the crime on him. All they had to go on was a dead man's word, conveyed through spirit rapping. It wasn't enough.

C.I.Coade: You're well-informed, Mr Bresson.

Bresson: It's a famous story. Convincingly documented, too—interviews, depositions, that sort of thing. And it's really not all that unreasonable. Many people believe in some sort of life after death. Not just Spiritualists. They don't need proof—they just believe. So why jib at communication between the dead and us?

C.I.Coade: Why indeed, Mr Bresson. Hm? I'm partial to a bit of proof myself, but then of course I would be.

Bresson: Even policemen have their moments, Chief Inspector. Don't you people used psychics to find stolen property, kidnapped children, even corpses?

C.I.Coade: Not I, Mr Bresson. Not I... But in any case, I see that watch-tapping time has come.

D.S.Wiler: Mr Bresson is here to make a statement, Boss.

C.I.Coade: Thank you, Anthea. Busy, busy, busy... The point is, Mr Bresson, that our opinion of Spiritualists is neither here nor there. A signed statement is a signed statement. Hm? Now—you're here of your own free will, at your own suggestion, and we appreciate that. Especially since it seems that, as the book says, you may have been the last person to see Mr Finsey alive.

D.S.Wiler: Apart from the murderer. If there was one

.C.I.Coade: Also as the book says. So we need your input, Mr Bresson... You arrived at Mr Finsey's flat when?

Bresson: Around five. Can't be sure, though. You can check with my previous call. Mrs Denby and her daughter in France Lynch. I'll give you their address. I went straight on to Declan's place from them.

C.I.Coade: He was expecting you?

Bresson: Some time that afternoon. I told you. It's a regular thing.

C.I.Coade: But you didn't get there till five. Was he happy to have been kept waiting?

Bresson: Somebody has to be last. And no—to be honest, he wasn't pleased.

C.I.Coade: So how long were you there?

Bresson: I've thought about that. My mother says I was home around six and the trip takes maybe twenty minutes so it can't have been more than half an hour. Probably less. It was a fine night but I didn't drive fast.

C.I.Coade: Thirty minutes, then. What did you talk about?

Bresson: SCT business. Mostly we talked about Madam Sara. That's my mother. It's her church and she's supposed to be in charge, but she's been sick now for months and a lot of stuff isn't getting done. The truthsayers are getting restive.

C.I.Coade: Thirty minutes. Not long. Hm? Did Mr Finsey offer you tea? Coffee? Drinks?

Bresson: Not a thing. I told you. He wasn't too pleased.

C.I.Coade: He was fine when you left, of course?

Bresson: I'd made my peace by then. I think he'd forgiven me.

C.I.Coade: I meant—

Bresson: I know what you meant. You're wondering if I pushed him over.

C.I.Coade: My question referred to his mood, Mr Bresson. You say he'd forgiven you. So was he cheerful? Jolly, even? Or was he depressed?

Bresson: Suicidal, you mean? Not in the least. He was a very positive person. Suicide wouldn't occur to him.

C.I.Coade: You knew him well, of course?

Bresson: Fairly well. We worked together. If he had any problems with his group we talked about them.

C.I.Coade: Did people like Mr Finsey? Would you say he was a popular man?

Bresson: He was a very popular truthsayer. Yes…I think you could say people liked him.

C.I.Coade: Did you like him?

Bresson: I used to. We had a falling-out some time back. But I didn't push him over.

C.I.Coade: You seem very sure that he was pushed, Mr Bresson.

Bresson: I know that balcony. The rail's pretty high. It was council property once and I'm sure there are safety by-laws. It doesn't seem possible that he simply fell.

C.I. Coade: Anthea doesn't agree with you. Personally, I—'

D.S.Wiler: There are scenarios, Boss. If Mr Finsey owned a cat, for example, and the cat got into difficulties, and Mr Finsey had tried to rescue it, then he might have—'

C.I.Coade: Any cat, Mr Bresson?

Bresson: There was a Siamese once, but it peed on his carpet and chewed his indoor plants. He found it a happy home.

C.I.Coade: Personally, I see a plausible middle way. Not simply was he pushed or wasn't he… Hm? (pipe tamping noises) I'm willing to accept Mr Finsey and someone else being involved in a disagreement. Some sort of scuffle. Nothing intentional, you understand. A tragic accident.

Bresson: A scuffle? Not with me, there wasn't.

C.I.Coade: And when exactly did you leave his flat?

Bresson: We've been over this. I can't be certain. Twenty past five. Perhaps half past. I can't be certain… Sorry to be impatient, but may I go now? I've got work to do. This statement I'm supposed to be making, could we—?

C.I.Coade: (match striking) Your car, Mr Bresson. When you visited Mr Finsey last night, where did you leave it?

Bresson: There wasn't any parking. I left it out on the street.

C.I.Coade: Did anyone see you leave?

Bresson: How should I know? I didn't notice anyone. But I wasn't looking.

C.I.Coade: Anyway, it was getting dark by then.

Bresson: Dark? Not very. Sort of twi—

C.I.Coade: Tell me, Mr Bresson, did you leave the flats by the main front entrance?

Bresson: My car was round the back. I used the back door.

C.I.Coade: Don't you think that's a curious coincidence, Anthea? It means he walked across the very spot where Mr Finsey, only a few minutes later, would fall.

D.S.Wiler: Coincidences come in all sizes, Boss.

C.I.Coade: Very true… Mr Finsey didn't die quickly, Mr Bresson. Not, as we say, on impact. Hm? Did you know that?

Bresson: How would I?

C.I.Coade: The signs are that he moved his limbs. One arm, certainly. Or had it moved…

Bresson: Why should anybody—

C.I.Coade: Someone might have simply come on him. Looked for something to steal. Possibly while he was still conscious.

Bresson: That's horrible. Why are you telling me this?

C.I.Coade: Most people think, Mr Bresson, that when a man falls from a height his death is quick and painless. That isn't always so. The brain is displaced within the skull, certainly, and the lungs are often punctured, but many vital functions may persist. Consciousness too… and therefore pain. Victims sometimes cry out with it. Lie there and moan. It isn't nice.

(pause)

Bresson: Is that what Declan did?

C.I.Coade: I've no idea. I wasn't there.

Bresson: So why are you telling me this?

C.I.Coade: Perhaps there was someone else in the flat. Someone who stayed after you left. Hm? Someone you haven't mentioned.

Bresson: If there was, I never saw them.

C.I.Coade: Someone you're protecting?

Bresson: I told you. There was no-one there.

C.I.Coade: He sounds very positive, Anthea.

D.S.Wiler: He would be, Boss. I mean, either there was or there wasn't.

C.I.Coade: And you saw no-one outside? While you were leaving? Hm? On the stairs, perhaps?

Bresson: Not a soul. (long pause) May I go now?

C.I.Coade: Anything I've forgotten, Anthea?

D.S.Wiler: His mother. We may need to talk to her.

C.I.Coade: Your mother, Mr Bresson—you say she is sick. Will it be possible for us to talk to her?

Bresson: Perfectly. She's had a couple of mild strokes and she's aphasic, but she's mentally alert and perfectly understandable. Let me know when and I'll—

C.I.Coade: Detective Sergeant Wiler will be round in an hour or so. If that's convenient.

Bresson: I expect—

C.I.Coade: And as for your statement, Mr Bresson, the text of this interview will be written up in the necessary manner, which I hope you will approve and sign. Make an appointment with the desk sergeant. I suggest tomorrow afternoon. (chair scraping) Thank you for your co-operation, Mr Bresson.

D.S.Wiler: Chief Inspector Coade is leaving the interview room.

C.I.Coade: Oh, and don't leave town, please. Not without letting us know first. Nothing special, but we might need another word. Thank you so much. Good afternoon.

(door opens, closes)

D.S.Wiler: Chief Inspector Coade has left the interview room. The interview with the informant Leo Bresson is terminated.

Bresson: That's Leh-o, if you please, Sergeant. Leh—

(click)

* * * *

Leo had left his Jaguar only just round the corner from the Lansdowne Road police station. It felt like miles. He fell into the driver's seat, shuddering, and slammed the door. Cat and mouse. Coade and him, cat and mouse... He hunched down onto the worn grey leather. The moment was one of barely controlled hysteria. In consequence, so are Leo's recollections.

He hunched down into the worn grey leather. Cat and mouse, cat and mouse... The inspector hadn't believed him. *Don't leave town, please.* He hadn't believed a thing he'd said.

Victims cry out with the pain—why should Coade tell him that? *They lie there and moan...* Moan or weep—what's the difference? Declan might not have done either. Oh Christ. Dying, there on the concrete, he'd scraped but he might not have wept.

The inspector said he'd moved his limbs. Then fined it down to only one arm. How did he know? Leo hadn't seen the other. Hardly time for a robber? Those ten minutes? Before Leo got there, while Declan was lying there. In just those ten minutes, a robber? More agony?

Leo shook his head. All this, it was simply the inspector, picking at him. Suspecting him of murder, picking at him. Trying to break his story. Trying to break *him*.

Why? Leo wondered what he'd done wrong. What he'd said. How he'd looked. And he'd hardly stammered at all. Minor disruptions. Only one big hold-up, trying to get out his mother's name—anything connected with Madam S tended to do that to him—but it wouldn't have looked suspicious. He had a stammer, for God's sake. Anyone could see that.

Pick, pick, pick... why hadn't the inspector believed him?

Suddenly he sat up and reached for his seatbelt. He'd remembered his Rendells. The inspector hadn't believed him because it was necessary for him not to. A policeman needed his suspect to be guilty and therefore to be lying. It was how these things worked. A policeman's job wasn't to discover what had really happened. A policeman's job was to find a suspect and then put together a case against him.

Well, Coade had found his suspect—someone physically able to commit the crime, who'd been in the right place at more or less the right time—but unfortunately the suspect seemed to have an alibi. Admittedly it was early days. And Coade's answer to the alibi was simple: all he now had to do was prove that the suspect was lying.

Hence the inspector's prompt despatch of his sergeant to check with the suspect's mother. There'd been no mention of a time for the victim's death fall but clearly Coade had one. Which meant that he'd talked to whoever raised the sash. So now, with the time of the fall established at around six thirty, Coade's suspect either had to be innocent because he'd left the victim's flat nearly an hour before or he was lying. At the crime scene there was no proof either way. All the inspector had against the suspect was his apparent opportunity. Nothing else. No motive. No evidence. Nothing else. So if the suspect's alibi held and that opportunity no longer existed, all Coade had left was to pick at him. Pick at him, hope somehow to break his story.

So the picking was in fact a sign of how well Leo had done. The inspector's trick comment, *it was getting dark by then*—he'd spotted that little trap, its suggestion of a later time for his visit. He hadn't gone for the *disagreement, scuffle* and *accident* either. Nor for the suicide. Discounting all non-murder theories had been a good move. Coade was devious. They were just put in to tempt him. A guilty man would have helped them along.

As for his homosexual relationship with Declan, Leo had decided on his way to the police station how he'd handle that. If things went well he'd leave it out as a needless complication. If things went badly and Coade discovered it, Leo could say that he'd kept quiet about it on account of his job: there were SCT members who wouldn't approve. He hadn't lied, he'd simply left out a socially damaging detail. An irrelevance. After all, being lovers, even gay lovers, was hardly a motive for murder.

On the face of it, then, everything depended on his mother.

She needed to remember the time he'd established for his return and, when questioned, she needed to be able to report it convincingly… and suddenly, just as Leo realised that she could be depended on for neither, he realised also that he didn't bloody care.

He was too tired. He was just too beat-up, too alone, too inexcusable, to care. This was all so cobbled-together and false. In the real world, the world of his shame, the world of Declan weeping, scraping, dying on the concrete, his mother's inadequacies were of no importance whatsoever.

He covered his face with his hands. Coade. Where did people like Inspector Coade come from? Sitting quietly there. So much self. So much confidence. How did that ever happen?

Come to that, where did people like Coade go to? After their work-day, lacking official identity, how did they conduct their other lives? In just the same way, for certain. So much confidence. So much self. When had Inspector Coade, when had Sergeant Wiler, a pleasant woman, taking her own worth for granted just the way he did, when had either of them last felt afraid? Not of bullets, knives, bad people, just *afraid*?

He wiped his eyes on his sleeve. He'd sat there long enough. Somebody might notice. He started the car's engine and drove away, out onto Lansdowne Road and along to the Montpellier roundabout. Christ, how he hated self-pity. All his sort of person really needed was a shoulder—anybody's—to cry on.

CHAPTER 3

His sort of person. What sort would that be?

Since a very early age Leo has thought of himself as unusual. Different. His very first kindergarten taught him that. The other children didn't stammer. Also, as well as nannies, they had mothers who were often around, and hugged them. Fathers too. So that right from the beginning being different had clearly meant being in some way bad. Not liked. He would examine that thought later, and decide to perceive difference as a protection instead.

Not always successfully.

In any case, to begin with there were elements in his different-ness that he himself wasn't as a child aware of. His background, for one thing, not at all Tivoli Street: grandson on one side to a true Brit empire builder and his Poonah luminary wife, but on the other to a French upper deck steward on a Channel paddle steamer who'd got a Dover shop-girl pregnant in the usual over-sexed French way, and then surprisingly had done the right thing by her, even getting a job in a haberdashery shop and making his home with her and their child in her dank, Froggy-hating country.

Additionally, although the Bressons had raised their son Maurice devotedly if with little imagination, the wretched boy had rewarded them by moving in their terms decidedly down-market in his teens, going on the halls of all things, improbably combining conjuring with a talent for the xylophone, an instrument very common in nineteen-thirties Britain. Perhaps in disgust, Bresson senior had returned to France, taking his wife with him, and contact between them and their son had petered out.

Maurice meanwhile had chosen Moon as a stage name for the alliteration and for the magical notions it suggested. To begin with, however, his act was decidedly unmagical: a couple of raucous xylophone solos decked out with risqué jokes, palmed playing cards and disappearing goldfish bowls.

Enter, a few racketty years later, Leo's mother. The empire builder's daughter Sarah, reportedly a sensible girl, now nearly nineteen years old and in her final year at a fancy private school in Dorking, still theoretically supervised by her Channel Islands Aunt Iolanthe.

Sarah Barraclough had gone on a Thursday night in May to a theatre in nearby Guildford where Maurice happened to be playing and had been quite bowled over. Not by his prestidigitation, which was mediocre, nor by his music, which sounded to her like a birdcage being attacked by a toasting fork; rather she was beguiled by his louche personality, which she found knee-meltingly sexy. She'd gone again the following night, and yet again on the Saturday, volunteering to choose cards and check knots on all three occasions, and Maurice had noticed her, and one thing had led to another. (But not, surprisingly, in those pill-less days, to instant pregnancy.)

Officially she stayed at the Dorking boarding school (she told her parents Out East this was because she didn't like imposing on her aunt) through the rest of May, June and July, until the end of the academic year. In fact she spent her week-ends secretly with Maurice in whichever shabby Midlands theatre digs his tour took him to, and somewhere during that time she suggested to him that she might be useful in his act. She'd further suggested, apparently out of nowhere, that mind-reading might be her forte. He tried her out in Tunbridge Wells, after a half-hour rehearsal just before the Saturday evening show, and she did very well. She had good legs, an engaging way with the punters, and when he messed up the cunning arrangement of her blindfold she proved herself to be an extraordinarily good guesser.

It's only fair, at this point, to remember that her aunt Iolanthe, nominally responsible for her, lived in the Channel Islands and had children of her own and a busy life. This was before the war and their last minute escape from Nazi occupation. The eye she officially kept on her niece, such a sensible girl, was inclined to wander.

They got married the following week. She lied about her age and Maurice chose to believe her—he was a conventional person at heart—and a telegram from the two of them, reporting the event some days later, was the first that the Barraclough family heard of it. They weren't happy. Her parents blamed Iolanthe, of course, and wrote to her lengthily, telling her so. England was a long way away, however, and in any case the deed was done. At least this Maurice person had married their daughter.

Soon after the war began Maurice received his call-up papers. He failed his medical, for reasons he never quite explained (flat feet, Sara suspected), and from then on did his patriotic bit in ENSA, playing to long-suffering servicemen, still assisted by his intriguing young wife, who by 1940 had opened up their act, adding demonstrations of x-ray vision. With thick balls of clay over her eyes and a blindfold keeping them in place, Sarah could identify objects held up in the audience. The codes she and Maurice used for this were standard in the business but they worked well enough, when he remembered them. He was more reliable on the xylophone, but it was an instrument that had had its day. Wartime audiences were no longer impressed by its skinny clatter, however virtuosic.

The mind-reading, though, on good nights, was a winner. So much so that she started a profitable side-line in private psychic readings, one-on-

one. She'd long suspected that she saw things and heard things other people didn't. Maurice told her she was picking up on hints, body language and so on, but she thought differently. She hadn't yet recognised it for certain, but this was the beginning of her Gift. It was at about that time that she dropped the aitch at the end of her first name. Private readings benefited from a touch of the exotic.

All this Leo had gathered by the time he was in his teens, learned from Granny Clare and from his mother's then newly-published autobiography, *Spirit Truth*, where it was presented more romantically. As for the Bresson side of the family, Madam Sara would have been his only first-hand source of information. There'd been an Uncle Alphonse, on Leo's father's side, but he'd fallen under a bus outside a smart Brighton hotel while on a visit from Besançon soon after the war. Of Maurice's other relations no mention was made. He'd left Sara before Leo's birth anyway, early in the war, and although they never divorced, he saw his infant son—on sufferance—very infrequently.

After his departure, with Leo already nicely established in Cheltenham, she'd stayed on in London despite the bombing. Her *Gift,* she believed, was particularly needed there. Long distance telephone calls from Maurice came now and then—the Blackpool booking he'd landed that would put him back up where he belonged, as would the drink a few months later that he'd had the previous night with an important London Palladium producer who really understood his work…

VE Day, the end of the war, changed very little for him. Radio had taken over and television was coming. The music halls continued their downward slide. The new holiday camp trade was strictly seasonal. Then, in 1947, when Leo had just turned seven, his father had met his abrupt and messy end, at eighty miles per hour, on the North Circular near Wembley.

So far in Leo's life therefore, an undeniably different start. Damaging? Possibly. That remained to be seen.

Sara, meanwhile, had acquired an aristocratic female Indian spirit guide, the Princess Nuna, and a new Spiritualist profession. By now, also, she had thrown off the *Moon* connection and was using her husband's legal surname. *Sara Bresson* looked good on the business cards, with the *Madam* soon added. Obviously she didn't want any showbiz Maurice skeletons rattling in her cupboard as her reputation began to spread. The clubs and theatres were left behind, like him, and she was building a useful connection as a voice medium and clairvoyant in the Belsize Park area of North London.

By then Leo's life in Cheltenham with Granny Clare and Nanny had been supplemented by a tabby cat called Simpkin

The only vivid memory Leo has of his father dates from thenabouts, from a bench in a park somewhere, a year or so before his death. Maurice is sitting with the boy facing him on his knee, the sun is shining, large dead leaves are blowing around, and he is saying, 'Your mother's a re-markable lady, Leo lad. A re-markable lady.'

His mother remembered the occasion well: the park was Kensington Gardens and the leaves were from plane trees. She remembered it better than Leo did. But the plane tree leaves were a nice particularity. He's sure he remembers them.

Otherwise, Sara told Leo little about his father. He'd smoked the smell-iest cigars. He'd also had an irritating habit of balancing salt and pepper shakers on top of each other in restaurants. He'd been nearly bald, having lost most of his hair while still young, probably as a result of all the diving he did when a boy living near a town called Dover. Oh yes—and of course with Leo about to be born he hadn't cared enough about his son to stay.

Apart from that, nothing really. She took the trouble, though, in 1947, to travel down to Cheltenham and tell her son promptly of his father's death, the day after it had happened, and of its manner too, sturdily believing that the truth never hurt anybody.

Leo remembers weeping sensitively. That's snide of him. Perhaps he's being hard on himself. In any case, Granny Clare and Nanny rallied round, his father was rehabilitated with consoling words about the hard row creative artists had to hoe, his mother was spoken to severely (in the next room but very audibly) for her heartless announcement, and a new locomotive model, the streamlined 2-6-4 *Sir Nigel Gresley,* was ordered for the poor boy's electric train-set. Sensitivity, he had already learned, brought compensations.

* * * *

In an immediate sense, Sara was quickly forgiven, and when she returned to London the following day she probably carried with her her own model locomotive, in her case a comforting cheque.

In a non-immediate sense, though, Sara would never be forgiven. The details of her early years in India have never been told, but her going into show business was for her mother a transgression beyond redress. She'd been given every advantage. After her daughter's birth in the excellent Poonah hospital Clare had supervised the wretched ayahs every inch of the way and had sent the child Home at great personal sacrifice when she was only eight, so that she could attend a thoroughly progressive girls' boarding school near Dorking. One could laugh at Dorking, people did these days, but the school had an impressive record. Money no object, my dear. And for the school holidays, there were Aunt Iolanthe and her brood in Guernsey. She and her sister had never been close, but Iolanthe's husband was something in the Islands' legislature and—at least until Maurice Moon came along—the arrangement had been just about ideal. There were two little cousins also, David and Julian, so that Sara didn't have to be too much with grown-ups.

All that effort—and what happened? Show business happened. Pink tights happened. Maurice Moon happened, the Reigate Empire happened. Colonel Hesketh Barraclough, Sarah's father, when he heard, came *that* close to disowning her. No wonder Clare had kept their daughter's shift to Spiritualism from him.

These parts of the story come via Clare, of course, much of it passed on to me by Leo who, as he grows older in its events, adds increasing penn'orths of his own. He admits to have been a knowing child. Also an avid eavesdropper. At that time, however, not yet an active pursuer of different-ness.

Furthermore, watchful for any unfortunate inherited tendencies in that direction, Granny Clare and Nanny contributed vigorous opposition. *People are looking at us, dear,* was the worst criticism Nanny could make of his behaviour, and for a while he knew no better than to share her mortification.

From Clare too, her *You're making an exhibition of yourself* was the direst accusation. Respectability ruled. Take her daughter's shift out of show business, for example: a good thing, in principal, but for God's sake, my dear, into *what*? Spiritualism simply compounded the wretched girl's showy-off outrageousness. A little eccentricity was all very well, Clare often claimed it for herself on account of her years Out East, but table-rapping was so bourgeois. The *Madam* on her daughter's professional cards particularly stuck in Clare's throat. It reminded her of that Madam Something-or-other played by Margaret Rutherford in the Noel Coward comedy. She also wondered wittily to her friends what had happened to the aitch at the end of the silly girl's name. She knew that aitches could quite respectably be dropped at the beginnings of words these days, but surely not at the ends.

Still, one couldn't live one's children's lives for them. At least Sara was making a success of something, and Leo was a poppet.

Poppet. Leo liked the word. He was a poppet. He asked nobody, not even Nanny, what his grandmother meant by it. A poppet. It was enough simply to *be* it. It clearly signified approval. It was also a word he knew his mother would never use. His mother simply wasn't a poppet-type person. His mother was something quite other. He didn't have a word for it, but whatever it was, she brought great waves of it billowing round her on her occasional visits. He warmed his hands at it, knowing it would never be for him. He feared it also, for it was what made her so dangerous.

At a later time, a much later time, in a confidential pub reminiscence, he would tell a friendly chap called Peter—who would usefully turn out to work in the Condensed Books Department of the Reader's Digest in London—that the word he would have used for his mother's something-quite-other, had he known it then, was chutzpah. She was quintessentially shameless.

A more flattering word for which is *bold*.

So here we are, back at chapter one, page one. Sara was precisely what Leo was not. He wasn't bold. Sara hadn't helped. Neither had Maurice and her version to Leo of his departure. Even being donated to Granny Clare, although an improvement, held a bitter truth: his father hadn't cared enough to stay and then his mother hadn't either. Why not? What was wrong with him? His stammer was developing fast but he didn't yet have a name for it. All he knew was that it somehow put him... outside.

Granny Clare did her best. She loved him, maybe even still doted, but it wasn't enough. One could be only just so much hands-on. Granny Clare, now in her sixties, had a bright flirtatious eye and a busy social life of her own, and she doted distantly. Hugging was so working class.

But there was also Nanny.

Nanny, with a sister in Dulwich whom she never saw, doted hands-on, hugging right up close. For a three and four and five year-old this was very comfy. Somebody loved him and so he loved somebody. The situation was codified: as soon as he was old enough to count, Nanny would ask him, 'How much do you love Mummy?' with the answer of two or three table-spoonsful expected. 'How much do you love Granny Clare?' would give her an answer of five or six. And to the final question, 'How much do you love Nanny?' Leo knew enough to pitch his answer, in those early days quite honestly, at a reassuring ten or eleven tablespoonsful of love.

Sadly, as he now admits, his honesty didn't last. Since a very early age connections between cause and effect had been clear to him, and he well remembers the rosy glow that surrounded Nanny when she was awarded large numbers of tablespoonsful. So he gave her them and received favours in return, but the manipulations gave him no pleasure. Nanny shouldn't be like that. To keep him properly safe, Nanny needed to be clever. Not able to be tricked so easily.

She was also his first detected liar. He caught her at it often, usually to Granny Clare. If he and Nanny were going for a walk and his grandmother asked her to do some little errand, get her cigarettes perhaps, Nanny would forget all about it and then, on her return, tell Granny Clare (in front of him, bare-facedly) an elaborate tale about the many shops she'd visited in vain, looking for Mrs Barraclough's chosen brand. It was a confusing experience. Lying was bad—everyone told him that. So Nanny was bad. But she couldn't be. She was Nanny.

Which brings us finally back to Mother. Madam Sara, voice medium and clairvoyant. She was like no other mother he ever saw. By now very successful, and dressed to match, even on her visits, with strings of beads and self-designed robe-like garments, often thickly textured in brick red with black facings, and a heavy make-up style reminiscent of the pre-war theatre. He found her increasingly dangerous. She was large (Granny Clare's word for fat) and like many large people she had developed a gliding rather than walking motion, often with her hands held out as if to grab him and gobble him up. Her temper was large too, and she didn't like him. Playing cards with Madam Sara, Double Demon or Beggar-Your-Neighbour, was no fun: she played to win, quite ruthlessly, and always did. Also, unlike Granny Clare and Nanny, she was visibly irritated by his stammer.

'If I stammered as badly as you,' she once remarked, 'I wouldn't try to talk so much.'

Her visits were outsize events, exciting but also frightening. Fortunately they didn't happen very often, and never for more than a single overnight stay. She had her career to think of. Her profession—and that, when he discovered its exact nature, was frightening too. But that was after he got to school.

Prep school, that is. At five years old, an agreeably ordinary child apart from his slight speech difficulty, Granny Clare had sent him to an expensive nearby kindergarten where he'd managed well. He was bright, and big for his age, and the school was small. He received his first piano lessons there and especially recalls the deafening tambourine he played in the school orchestra.

Then, shortly after his father's death and now seven years old, he was approaching preparatory school age—to be followed by a suitable public school when he was eleven—so his mother was summoned from London and there were family discussions. His father, being recently departed, thank God, had not needed to be invited. His great-aunt Iolanthe, however, now back in Guernsey with Ian, was naturally included. Her own grandsons, David and Julian, had gone to Eton and were now making their way apparently quite successfully as somethings in the City. Their father had returned to Guernsey with Iolanthe and the boys after the war and Iolanthe had admitted to Sara that he was really rather vulgarly prosperous. Ian had a younger brother, Martin, who was biggish in UK insurance, and had never married. The Guernsey and Gloucestershire families, separated by more than simply geography, were not close.

Iolanthe, however, was often at the house on Tivoli Street. She regretted her neglect of Sara back in the days when Clare was out doing the Raj thing in India with the Colonel, leaving her theoretically *in loco parentis*. Her niece's subsequent life obviously left a lot to be desired but she wasn't a judgemental person. She was determined, however, to keep a great-auntly eye on basically parentless Leo.

Cheltenham conveniently had a public school of its own. Admittedly Cheltenham College was rated fourteenth on the list of Britain's public schools, but it had a preparatory school just across the road, and both were agreeably close to Clare's house on Tivoli Street—which meant that Leo would be able to go in turn to both of them as a Day Boy. He guesses now that his mother, if given the option, would have chosen to send him as a boarder (character building), but Granny Clare—who was paying—either didn't want to part with him or had noticed, and sympathised with, his solitary, not bold nature. His stammer was a worry, but it would be that wherever they sent him, and in any case, people told her he'd soon grow out of it. So the Cheltenham College decision was made, and the Day Boy decision was made, and the clothier Daniel Neal's in London was visited for the uniform, and in September of the following year, a month or so after his eighth birthday, Leo went off to the College prep school.

Given any luck at all, Leo's first year at proper shorts and blazer prep school would have been a doddle. He was big for his age (no peer-group bullying) and bright and biddable (no staff bullying), and although his mother's otherness would always have been a problem with the other boys, the only school event at which she might reasonably have been expected to make the effort to appear was Speech Day, in July, at the far end of the academic year, by which time Leo would have established himself. All he needed was for his mother to be regretfully unable to get away till then.

It didn't happen. The very first day of his very first term (an occasion for any sensible new bug to show a discreet level of ordinariness) unfortunately happened to coincide with a rare gap in Madam Sara's London schedule of séances so she decided to be present for the occasion, to accompany her son and personally to introduce him to his form master. And by then she was not only indiscreetly bold and large but also was a completely spectacular person: dress, hair, voice, glide, make-up, everything. Her profession demanded it.

Leo's career at prep school never recovered. Every boy in the school saw some stage of Madam Sara Bresson's visit and every boy in the school (save one) agreed that she was a hilarious freak and nearly wet his y-fronts trying theatrically not to snigger as she passed. The exception was a weedy fellow new-bug called Pimbury, who had a rather similar aunt, at that time safely out of the country in a Krishnamurti-type community near Palermo.

Pimbury was little help. His records turned out to be of songs generally considered to be totally feeble (*Open the door, Richard. Put another nickel in, in the nickelodeon),* and his mother sent him jars of Brylcreem. His friendship wasn't an asset. As for the rest of the lads, they had a freak's boy in their midst and they never let Leo forget it.

By now, unsurprisingly, his stammer, rather than getting grown out of, was firmly established. Not simply the hasty, cluttered speech that many young boys exhibit and do indeed soon put behind them: this was your genuine, head-jerking, mouth-distorting, life-changing stammer. It reads here so very much like an over-neat fictional device—the bitter poetic justice of his mother's lack of sympathy in his youth and her subsequent aphasia—that it nearly didn't make it into this story, but it's simply too much a part of him to be airbrushed away. It contributed to his isolation and shaped him crucially.

Main point: there's nothing basically wrong with the physical mechanisms of any stammerer's speech. His voice, his breathing, his tongue, his lips, everything works properly. He can converse with his dog, or an empty room, with perfect fluency. His problems are con-cerned rather with communication, the stresses of. He simultaneously needs and dreads human contact. The result is a battle fought within the otherwise excellent apparatus of his speech. In Leo's case his mother's bitter comment reveals a common situation: a stammerer, when too young to have become ashamed of his difficulties, does tend to talk too much. The harder it is for him to say things, the more he wants to.

Shame comes when he discovers that his way of speaking makes him ugly. He says a few words, stammers, and people look tactfully away. If he keeps silent they can bear to see him.

His struggles also make him tedious. He holds things up. Customers in shops have to wait while he grimaces. He appears to be stupid.

(By the way, the pronoun 'he' is used here for simplicity's sake and because, for no known reason, at least eighty percent of stammerers are male.)

Ugly, tedious, stupid... not a helpful start in life.

Leo still stammers. His difficulties are slight these days, and not always present, and he's much less troubled by them (people on the whole are very patient), but involuntary acts of any kind are undermining. No conducive to a rumbustious self image. And in any case, back in his childhood and teens, when he was learning who to be and what and how, his stammer was mostly a real humdinger.

Short lecture ends.

If you're looking for powerful writing on the subject of stammering, though, tough-thinking old Nietzsche is your man. In his mighty *Thus spake Zarathustra volume* Nietzsche gives his philosopher sage a hideous vision, the sight of a young shepherd choking and quivering, his face distorted, with a black snake hanging from his mouth. '*Never was such loathing and pale horror ever seen in one face,*' his narrator comments. And when the snake is finally banished, the shepherd is transfigured, bathed in light, a man who laughs…

Leo met the passage while in the sixth form. He knows it well. The trouble is, he also knows from bitter personal experience that the stammer snake is cunning and cruel, and up to now nobody has discovered a reliable way to banish it.

Curiously, his companions at prep school were far less entertained by Leo's stammer than by his mother. They imitated her glide and the swinging of her beads, causing wild laughter, rolling on the ground, tussling and punching each other. Having somehow discovered her profession, they then imagined the hooting cadences of her *Is there anybody there?*, and reproduced them to more tussling and punching. Leo watched them sideways, hiding his fear of such inexplicable behaviour. Tussling and punching. He did neither. Both, he finally decided, thus displacing his fear, were stupid.

Beneath him.

The cliché was soon established. His mother was a freak, making him fair game. Freak's Boy they called him, and after a while that was how he thought of himself. It made no sense, but little that they did made sense. And if he had to be a figure of fun, better pretend to enjoy it. He took to falling over funnily, and became quite good at it. *Hey, hey—Freak's Boy on his face again…* it cost him very little, a bruise or two, and it made them happy. Poor stupid things.

Some young people simply live their lives. Others try to conform, others try not to. Leo was in the last group. The combination of his stammer and his mother singled him out as a freak so why not go the whole hog? Falling down funnily was only a start. Later, at Cheltenham College proper a spectacular beige velour homburg would be worn around town. Grandfather Barraclough's silver-mounted army officer's cane would be swished theatrically between classroom buildings. He was the only Labour party member in his form. He scorned cricket but was required to play it.

Incidentally, Christmas day in 1949, when Leo was nine, was the occasion when Sara bought him his first Meccano set. This metal model-building system, with its nuts and bolts and cogs and plates and girders, introduced him to the wonderful world of three dimensionality, of miniature machines with strong sharp edges and hidden parts that could be made to whirr. They were a pleasure he'd turn to often, especially in the long school holidays when his solitary ways might otherwise have dragged him down a bit.

Madam Sara didn't always get things wrong.

Now that he was out in the world Leo had dropped the *Granny* from his grandmother's title. The change came at Clare's suggestion. She said it made her feel less old-fashioned—*less old* would perhaps have been more truthful, but that may be unfair. In spite of Clare's careful Raj-based respectability there'd already been that progressive Dorking school for Sara, and the early sixties were a great time for the rejection of conventional labels.

Sara herself had no such problem. Progressive she wasn't. Dorking had failed. The idea of being *mother* suited her perfectly. She had nothing to hide. To be forty and on the matronly side chimed both with her idea of motherhood and with her profession. Her Gift was strong. She was doing well, with a large following and a waiting list for one-on-one sessions. *Mother* suited her perfectly. It was what boys at public school called their maternal parent. It was proper.

Maurice Moon was far behind her.

As for Leo, without Sara his Freak's Boy school identity might soon have been forgotten. Boys' memories are short. Not as short as electorates', but short. At Leo's prep school, however, Madam Sara's occasional appearances needlessly revived them. He accepted that he needed to fall over funnily more often. But he'd also discovered the shocking pleasures of solitary sex (my phrase, at that time he had no word for it). These were so larger-than-life that he had to believe they made him in some way special. It was quite a while, being a Day Boy who went home every day straight after classes, before he worked out that most of the other boys did it too. Certainly Pimbury. Not that they admitted it. But the knowledge took away his specialness.

In any case, Nanny's opinions lingered. Bodily parts, on principle, were shameful. She was wrong about most things. Could she just possibly be right about that?

* * * *

And so life went. Simpkin died and was replaced by a Siamese called Ting.

And so life went.

By the time Leo was twelve—still a Day Boy—he had moved across the road from the prep school to Cheltenham College proper, liberally pinnacled in fake gothic Cotswold stone. His defences were expanding. There were other ways of—a new phrase—'going O.T.T.' By which point, ironically, they had become less needed. His fellows were older and more subtle now, aware of the burdensomeness of parents in general. And for many of them, Madam Sara was sufficiently far out to be awesome. She flaunted an almost pop-star quality of outrageousness. She was expansive. Unique. Entirely her own creation.

There were always jocks, of course, who found her appearances an affront, needing to avenged by mockery, but that was what jocks did. She was now, in Leo's social life, an asset. But he still feared her, and regularly failed her.

Beige homburg time arrived. Grandfather Barraclough's swagger stick time. And of course, hating Madam Sara time. To his disappointment, however, he quickly discovered that among his classmates hating one or other of your parents was acceptable, *de rigueur* even. He thought about that. At least his hatred was reasonable. For god's sake, looking back, didn't he have good cause? A classic case, he knew it now, straight out of the book: abandonment, rejection, belittlement, castration. He'd always hated her and now at last he was able to admit it. Madam Sara. Everything the name stood for was hateful.

Leo prospered at Coll. This was the 1950s and allowances were made. Eccentricities were accepted. There was even a Labour Government. He was good in class, he joined the chapel choir, alto then struggling bass. He persevered with his piano lessons and now composed sub-Chopin preludes on Clare's Bösendorfer. His height made him a useful second row forward on the rugby field. He also had a way with words, edited two issues of the Day Boy house magazine and wrote a couple of precocious one-act plays, and he showed acting skills. His appearances on the stage, or at the lectern to read lessons in chapel, were blessedly stammer-free. The words weren't his and neither was the identity: no longer being Leo, fluency radiated through his speech centres like a drug. He felt gloriously empowered. Tempted to follow in his father's footsteps, he considered putting on a conjuring show at a House Concert (he liked the idea of Maurice Moon and thought the poor man had had a rotten deal), but the notion didn't survive his first rehearsal. As a conjuror he was playing himself, the words were his, and his stammer wouldn't allow it. Still, he continued to get parts as other people in plays and at the end of his third year he would do a quite decent Stogumber in the *Saint Joan* put on for Coll's Speech Day play. His mother sat in the second row, outnumbering all the other parents by five to one. Or so a clever member of his fan club commented.

'Fan club' is Leo's unkind current phrase. Part of a warts-and-all approach to himself that has appeared only recently.

Life changed. He'd known for years now that he was unlike other people. Not worse, just different. And now he knew why. He had a genuine reason: this inferiority complex that his mother had created. The knowledge didn't cure his stammer—any more than had the several therapies Clare paid for—but it gave him both an excuse and someone to blame.

Please—he was sixteen. Later, at twenty-six and thirty-six, and now forty-three, if stuff like that were still part of his baggage, he'd be entitled to a healthy blast of your disgust. By now, though, we may hope he's become a more complex, slightly wiser person.

That was the year, his seventeenth, when Clare died of kidney failure.

For reasons never properly explained to him, dialysis sessions weren't possible and her body simply poisoned itself into a coma and death. She had claimed, from the bed in her museum of a house on Tivoli Street, that it was on account of something dreadful she'd caught Out East, but it wasn't. She was oldish, seventy-three, and her kidneys had simply failed. She wasn't, even in her dying, that exotic.

Leo's words at the time. She'd lavished her patience on him, her admiration, her sense of humour, much of her fortune and her considerable love, but she wasn't even in her dying, *that exotic*. A sad comment. But it's a measure of the anger, the fear, he felt at this latest abandonment.

In his entire life her occasional lavender-scented shoulder would turn out to have been his only gentle, kindly, uncomplicated refuge.

Clare's funeral brought Iolanthe and her husband and sons over from Guernsey, but only very briefly. Their embarrassment at Madam Sara's style of being showed.

That was also the year, in the school summer holidays before Clare's death, when she'd organised a visit for Leo to his mother in London, mainly to get him out of a house with so much sickness. One afternoon, alone in Madam Sara's new, much larger flat—arty Hampstead now, not shabby genteel Belsize Park—he'd trespassed into her forbidden Séance Room to see what she got up to. Crawling round underneath the massive table had revealed well-concealed devices. Unfortunately she'd caught him at it.

He told her he'd been fetching one of his ping-pong balls that had rolled off under the stupid table. She reminded him that her Séance Room was a special location—he shouldn't have been there in the first place. He wasn't allowed in it unaccompanied, nobody was. He said he was sorry. She said that was all very well—sorry was easy. He asked her what else he was expected to say. They rowed unpleasantly and an outing to the theatre that night, his summer treat, was cancelled.

He never asked his mother about the well-concealed devices and she never asked to see the ball he claimed he'd been looking for (it didn't exist). His discretion was born of embarrassment and shame. Hers was born of... he doesn't know. Certainly not embarrassment—she didn't do embarrassment, any more than she did children or babies. A challenge to him, then—*question me if you dare?* He doesn't think so. She was a rogue but she was also a fantasist. If a truth was uncomfortable and she stared it down for long enough, it went away. Both of them, if for different reasons, were silently agreeing that what was, was not. It was a moment that would significantly recur. They were conspiring, looking each other in the eye and laying up future troubles they couldn't begin to dream of.

Meanwhile, back in Cheltenham, as ever, Nanny lingered. Sara, still living in London, was grateful. The boy was long past the usual care of a nanny, but someone had to wash his College underwear and iron his College shirts and make sure that his College blazer went to the dry-cleaners. Cook could put his meals on the table but someone had to make sure he got his hair cut. Besides, Sara had a plan in mind. Her radiant spirits, especially her Princess Nuna, were telling her she had more to offer the world. Spiritualism needed her. She'd even had an episode with poltergeists, whose antics she'd routed with useful tabloid coverage. The potential for expansion was enormous, particularly outside London, and there were Leo and Nanny, in expensive-sounding Cheltenham, rattling round in the Tivoli Street house, now inherited, that was ridiculously big for just the two of them.

She moved in with them a few months later, as soon as her London affairs were in order. Clare's sombre dining room was perfect for séances. Her reputation had preceded her and the Cotswolds were ready. Even so, she now had the creation of a larger organization to work on and things weren't always easy. But her mother's money helped, once the Indian government had been persuaded to part with enough of Colonel Barraclough's shrewd investment capital, and in quite a short time the SCT was founded.

Leo, meanwhile, in his final two years at Cheltenham College, had a sort of friend, William, whose parents played bridge and taught the boys so that they could make up a four. They got together regularly. William played chess also and taught Leo the moves. William read chess books, however, learned openings, and always won. Leo started writing things instead, plays at first, with parts for himself in them, and a novel in mind, and school magazine articles, and had his fan club to entertain.

That spring one of his plays was put on in Coll's annual programme of one-acters. It concerned a tuxedo'd ghost in a casino who lured young men to their financial ruin and suicide. It went down well and confirmed his interest in writing. In plays and novels and all things literary. He discovered Ernest Hemingway and short sentences.

In his final year at Coll,, unsurprisingly, Leo was appointed editor of the Day Boys' House Magazine. Not the more prestigious College Magazine, you'll notice, any more than he'd played the male lead in *St Joan* or captained the rugger team. He undeniably prospered, therefore, but not extravagantly, and school reports spoke of the need to try harder. So did his very successful mother: 'I find it depressing, Leo dear, to see how often you seem willing to settle for the second rate.'

Lee saw things differently. Coming first or second or third was unimportant. Style was what counted. It even mitigated his stammer. The hat had been rejected as one O.T.T. extravagance too many, and the novel had died after thirty-odd pages, but he still had the silver-mounted cane and he wore bright cubist neckties. If people didn't like what he did, that was their problem. He was going to be a writer.

He was still falling over funnily, if by other means. No friends exactly, but an identifiable circle. His name *Freak's Boy* had stuck, becoming quaint and vaguely bohemian. He used it under reviews he wrote for the House Magazine. And at the end of that year, equipped with an adequate academic record in French and German and English classic literature but nothing that could seriously be called an education, he left.

A school career, eleven years, in a few brisk pages. The best years of his life. It was a phrase he never argued with. He'd coped with College. Nobody intruded and nobody asked for more than he could deliver. It was a small world and it played by rules he quickly learned. Leaving it was terrifying. Nearly twenty years would pass before he found another world he could manage so well.

Tivoli Street. The SCT. Aphasic Madam Sara.

CHAPTER 4

As Leo, eyes dried now, was driving back to Tivoli Street from the police station he glanced at his watch and remembered that Rosie was expecting him for tea. He'd been having a rough time this afternoon, and longing for a shoulder to cry on, but not hers. Never hers. Although he knew he wasn't the greatest catch, he could at least make sure he was never a burden. There were things he was good at, and among these asking very little of other people was a guiding principle. What he could give, he gladly gave—receiving was another matter. That was why he found excuses to look in on the Krauss-Häbers most days, not for the human contact that gave him, but in case anything needed doing. So he back-tracked now through side streets to Parabola Road. Madam S could manage without him. When D. S. Wiler arrived his mother would have dear Hoppy around to help her open the door and show the sergeant in. It might even be better if he wasn't there. The police wouldn't be able to suspect him of rushing home to coach her.

In any case, he didn't care what they suspected. Declan had died in agony while he was upstairs having a shit and making plans to not get arrested for murder by the police. He didn't care what they suspected.

The drizzle had lightened but Cheltenham was still grey. Cheltenham was often grey. The soft local grey-gold stone of its rot-pocked Georgian terraces soaked up the pervasive not-quite-rain that oozed in darkly beneath their crumbling sills and pediments. Street gutters clogged and flooded. Roof gutters too. Leckhampton Hill loomed dankly over the town.

Rosie'd given him a key to the door but he usually knocked. Since Max's illness you never knew. Sometimes the moment wasn't good. This afternoon she took her time. He waited, fidgeting until he noticed and practised being still instead. Their flat was on the ground floor of one of the town's less-grand crescents, just to the east of the Promenade. The exterior was bearing up and the rooms inside were very presentable—plaster cracking here and there, but nothing you couldn't paper over.

When she finally opened the door he bent to kiss her cheek but she turned her head away. He saw that she'd been crying. The moment wasn't good. He went past her into heavy antiseptic vapours.

Max was up and fully dressed, which was unusual, lying on the scuffed leather sofa in his study, his ragged post-chemo hair as wild as ever, ashtray on the floor beside him, smoking the usual thin cigar and staring at the

Guardian's crossword. His condition shocked Leo. It was the expensive Jermyn Street corduroy jacket and collar and tie that did it. Leo had grown used these days to Max looking old and yellow and little and sick, either half-naked while being washed or warmly bundled up in scarves and blankets, but today's attempt at smartness made his ribby neck stalks, now poking up inside an over-large shirt collar, look simply grotesque. Max's wrists were blue and ribby too, within their crisply-ironed cuffs.

'Happy Wednesday, Max.' Brisk and bright. Christ, how brisk and bright. 'I hear you're giving a party.'

'Party?' Max's eyes refocused slowly. He picked up the pace. 'Hey, why not? A few old friends. A little music. *Bonnes bouches*.... You're going to help me.'

'So Rosie tells me.'

'One of the Ibert *Histoires*, I thought. Just an early one. Not too many fiddly bits. Who needs the later acrobatics?'

'Just an early one, he says.'

'And for the encore, *Ave Maria*. Not a dry eye in the house.'

'You're joking.'

'I'm joking.'

He subsided. Smoked his cigar. In the short time he had left the condition of his lungs was no longer significant. Leo drifted over to the window, looked up at the grey, grey sky.

'Park your arse, friend.' Max gestured at a chair with his folded paper. 'Get rid of your coat. I need help with nine across.'

Rosie was at the door behind Max now, arms folded, visibly holding herself together. Leo caught her eye and she shook her head minutely.

He laughed. 'Thanks but no thanks, Max. I've got work to do. I just stopped by to see how you're getting on.'

'To see if the pathetic old sod was still *compos mentis*.'

'That too.'

'Well he is. Rosie—bring us some tea. Leo's staying.'

'I really mustn't.'

Rosie came forward. 'Give me your coat.'

He gave her his anorak and sat on a low buttoned-velvet chair beside Max. After she'd left the room Max unfolded his arms and patted his corduroy lapels.

'I've been trying on my party suit. Rosie says it's a disaster.'

'It doesn't fit, Max. Stick to sweaters.'

Max looked away. 'I was in a bad mood.'

'You're entitled.'

The room was cluttered, lined untidily with books, portraits and concert programmes in gilt frames on the plum-coloured walls where the books weren't. Files were stacked in corners, Japanesey pots with plants in them stood round the high sash window, small tables here and there, Max's computer incongruous on the leather-topped walnut desk now pushed back against the wall. A brass standard lamp with a sallow parchment shade leaned behind the sofa, casting a sallow light. Leo often nagged him to get the place brightened up but he liked it that way.

'Entitled? I don't think so.' Max thought about that. 'I don't think so,' he said again, and changed the subject. 'I've been looking at my notes, Leo. The research for my book. There's a couple of finished chapters. More or less finished. Sketched out... Rosie'll show you. She can do a lot herself but she'll need some help.'

'You know I'm not much of a writer, Max. Not any more. Never was, actually. Especially not non-fiction.'

'Moral support. An insider's view.'

They'd talked about Max's book before. Often. His study of show-business mind-reading had inevitably expanded to include professional séance material and their discussion usually concerned how he could take on that without taking on Spiritualism itself, which his publisher didn't want him to do.

'I'm not an insider either, Max. Most particularly not an insider. You know that.'

'What you're afraid of is that you may have to take a view.'

Leo frowned. 'In matters of faith I have a very clear view. You know it very well. Nothing in the universe is intrinsically holy. Men decide what they will consider so. It's a human notion. One man's sacred cow is another man's hot dinner. Me, I laugh at nothing.'

'That means you laugh at everything.'

'That's what you always say.'

'I also say that it devalues truth.'

'And I give you my toenail argument.'

Such well-trodden paths. Leo's toenail argument claimed that your truth was all the stuff that you needed to be true. It was yours—like your teeth or your belly or your toenails. And how could you possibly devalue your toenails? They had absolute value or they had none. Either way, they had their own nature. They were still toenails.

Today Max let the argument go. 'So you won't help Rosie sort out my—'

'I won't help Rosie make a mockery of Spiritualism. It does very little harm and comforts a whole lot of people.'

'No mockery, Leo. I promise you.' He scrunched out his cigar. 'In the book Spiritualism mostly seems to be coming off pretty well. I find it delivers good value for money.'

'There's a cynical thought.'

'Emotional value for emotional money, Leo. Value for what people put into it. And it's not based on this-or-that morality. It's not judgmental. Not a rule book.'

'That's a lot of what-it's-nots. What about some what-it-ises?'

'I told you. It gives comfort. It's not about blood and punishment and suffering and sin. Nobody would ever go to war for it.'

A clincher. Leo wondered why then he despised it so.

'Write your own book, Max. Hang on there and write it.'

'Now you insult me.' Max pointed at him fiercely. 'Would I be here now, begging you, if that were possible? If I had the days? You insult me.'

Leo didn't answer. He was ashamed. Max was right—he deserved better of their friendship than social pablum.

Clattering china announced Rosie's arrival with tea. If she'd heard Max's words she chose to ignore them.

'No honey, I'm afraid,' she said to Leo, remembering Rupert Brooke.

Max looked up at her. 'Thank you, my dear. Good timing. We were getting very earnest.'

Leo turned on more lights, fetched a low table, she put the tray on it and poured the tea. There was toast and Max's specially-imported Austrian black cherry jam. They segued into Saturday's party.

'The spring and autumn equinoxes,' Max told them. 'In my part of Bavaria they're the only nights that witches fear. The balance between light and dark, good and evil, is too narrow. This makes them very safe for us humans, and country people celebrate them. Especially the September equinox, with winter coming over the hill. Great parties are held in the villages—at least, they used to be.' He'd eaten half a finger of the toast. Leo'd been watching. Now he put the remaining half back on his plate. 'Today, of course, they no longer believe in witches. But they still believe in parties.'

Leo clapped softly. 'Good for them.'

'And they still wear those terrible leather knickers—' He broke off, curled up suddenly on the sofa, knees close under his chin, weeping with the pain. '*Scheiss*. Ah, *Scheisse*...'

Rosie quietly moved the tea table back out of the way and Leo squatted on the floor beside him. 'Those bloody doctors. They're putting you through it, the bastards.' He took one of Max's death-and-bone hands and held it tightly. If he hurt it, perhaps the other pain would somehow be less.

Rosie knelt beside him. They were close on either side of Max, containing him. Eventually the pain passed and he relaxed. His eye sockets were puddled with tears. He took his hand back and groped for his handkerchief.

'If this is dying, I don't think much of it.' He blew his nose. 'I wish that was original. Lytton Straichey said it first, I think. Very Bloomsbury of him.

Queer as a fourpenny bit, Lytton Straichey…'

Leo stood up. Rosie leaned over Max, smoothing his hair. The room looked no different. Terrible events took place in it, again and again, and nothing changed.

'Sorry about that.' Max sat up straighter. 'Where were we?'

'I was just going. You'd given us your home-made folk tale and I was just going.'

Max didn't argue. 'Call me later. We must fix rehearsal times for the Ibert.'

He closed his eyes and paid attention to other matters.

Rosie fetched Leo his anorak and went with him to the door. 'It's not the doctors. He doesn't take their stuff. One lot lays him out, the others make him crazy.'

'I know.' The *bastards* in Leo's comment hadn't really been the doctors. They'd been just *somebody*: somebody to blame. God. 'Nothing I can do, I suppose?'

She shook her head, touched his sleeve very lightly, went back into the study.

He watched her go, and loved her.

On the grey gravelled path down to the road, as he was shrugging himself into his coat, the desperation of his non-Parabola Road life returned in a crushing, suffocating wave.

* * * *

Way back in 1958 on the 24th July, then only a month off eighteen years old, Leo left Coll. His last day at Cheltenham College was a downer. After morning roll-call, a house meeting at which his housemaster said nice things about him. Then a circuit of his various lockers, checking that he'd emptied them. Then a word with his piano teacher, who gave him a book of Bach partitas. Then… well, nothing really. The boarders were catching their trains and going home, in his case a brief bicycle ride he was in no hurry to face. He played some ping-pong with William in the Day Boy Room. Then he went and sat in the library.

On the last day of term Chaplain Beckerton always organised an Evensong service in the chapel and for the first time in his life Leo attended it. He sat in his usual place in the choir stalls. Maybe a dozen other people were there, sitting carefully apart. Leo cried silently into his handkerchief. Then he collected his bits and pieces, and his bicycle, and went home to Nanny and cat Ting. Madam Sara was away, addressing a Spiritualist convention in Bristol.

A few weeks passed. His final A Level examination results wouldn't be known until September but were expected to be respectable and he honestly didn't care very much. At the beginning of the year the school had assumed he would go on to university, Magdalen College, Cambridge, his housemaster's college, but he'd resisted. He wanted, he suddenly announced, to be a writer. He wanted to write plays and therefore he wanted to learn about the theatre. He wanted to be an actor.

He probably meant it. He'd been happiest on Coll's various stage occasions. But it was true also that university was real and threatening, while the theatre was a romantic fantasy and also, in College terms, undeniably different.

His housemaster accepted the choice of career—Bresson had always been a wayward boy—but suggested he got his degree first. While he was up he could always join one of the dramatic societies. Leo said no, he needed to get on with life. It was slipping away from him.

His housemaster gave in. He knew he should have tried harder but the boy's family background was notoriously unhelpful. Nobody was there to make a stand. Certainly not his mother, mostly away in London, busy with her Spiritualist connections.

There were, of course, no men in Leo's family. Madam Sara had men around when she was younger and was by no means past it now, at fifty-three, but she kept them for her London trips. She had a small flat on Drayton Gardens, off the Fulham Road, which she used when SCT business took her to the big city. So Leo grew up basically man-less. Short of role models. The masters at prep school and College were manly in their way, but it was a very public, uncomplicated way. Not much help with the nuances. These he dealt with randomly, idiosyncratically, as they arose. Usually by ignoring them.

He was eighteen years old and he'd never had sex with a woman. Never even seriously yearned for it. Blame the fifties' one-sex public school system. Actually, in Leo's case do no such thing. Blame the falling-over-funnily system, into which the pleasures of a woman didn't fit. They would have required reaching out, conceptually and emotionally, an activity he didn't know about. The possibility couldn't ever have entered his head.

He was over-large, stammering, conceited, cowardly and clumsy: this his mother had taught him and this, as we've seen, he'd dealt with. Nanny's inculcation of bodily shame had been harder. The experience of school changing rooms and showers, however, had quickly showed him that his fellow males simply weren't bothered, and what he saw there didn't seem to him shameful either, rather the reverse. Coll had taught him, in special Dr.Griffiths lectures, the mechanics of human reproduction: messy, by the sound of it. Thoroughly embarrassing. Still, he'd discovered wanking by now and, thanks to Dr Griffiths, it had a disapproving official dictionary name for itself in his vocabulary, and therefore an acceptable place in his life, so that when, one afternoon behind the bicycle sheds, he further discovered the astonishing pleasures of letting some friendly hand other than his own touch his cock, terminal doubt was cast on Nanny's teachings. Private parts might conceivably be reasons for shame, but they could also be totally stupendous. Not much emotional reaching out, though. None at all, really.

That sort of thing wasn't Coll's business. Homosexuality, if mentioned, was conflated with mutual masturbation and was grounds for instant expulsion if discovered. It was also illegal. Subtler issues of sexual identity were not considered. Coll was a Christian establishment. Sexual pleasures of whatever kind, outside holy wedlock, were sinful. God said so.

Not, of course, that Leo went all that much for God. The theatrics in College Chapel were good fun, but anything more than that would have required concern, involvement, at least a little of the above-mentioned reaching out. In any case, very soon after discovering orgasms, he'd reasoned that only a real sod of a god would have made wanking wicked and then provided arms that were so exactly the right length for doing it.

Coll had been strong on God, of course. Patriotism too.

Which in this case is actually an unfair, anti-Establishment dig. In fact, Leo's most sympathetic mentor at school has already been mentioned here: the chaplain, Alan Beckerton,. A tough-minded young cleric of wit and acuity, Beckerton was aware of Leo's unusual background and they talked often. Not much about sex, and not about religion either. His most serious concern had been with the boy's isolation. He'd never broken through it, but he'd tried.

As for his now being a presence again in Leo's life, he had quit teaching back in the '60s and had entered the Anglican church heirarchy, quickly becoming Canon Beckerton, with an office in nearby Gloucester Cathedral's ivied close. He and Leo had met again in 1975, soon after Leo's return to work for his mother's SCT in Cheltenham after a fairly disastrous time in London (more about that later). Since then, having discovered a shared enthusiasm for the partnership card game, bridge, they've played together at least once a week at the St Stephen's Road bridge club. Despite their twenty-year age difference they're often successful. Leo, trained by William back in his Coll days, is the more aggressive bidder, Alan the more cunning when it comes to the actual playing of the cards.

Canon Beckerton also runs a local country dancing group, but Leo has never danced. Not even the Twist fever of the sixties tempted him. This goes with his mother telling him at an early age that he was over-large and clumsy. She told him also, at various times, that he had no sense of rhythm. All in all, therefore, her comments suggested that he lacked social graces— which he had quickly decided, *pace* chummy punching and tussling a few years earlier, were beneath him. The idiocy of this teen-age decision would become clear to him in his twenties, but by then the clumsiness (and consequent isolation) was an established fact.

He never danced and he still doesn't.

So back to 1958 and Leo leaving College at the end of July and going home to Tivoli Street. Madam Sara had regretted his ridiculous university decision. It didn't surprise her, though—so like his father—and she was a very busy lady. Shortly after his birthday she booked driving lessons for him—every young man should know how to drive—and when he passed his driving test she bought him a little red secondhand MG two-seater sports car.

She wasn't, however, a generous woman. She gave him presents quite frequently, big presents, but always in a way suggesting that she despised him for accepting them. He took them gladly, explaining to anyone sufficiently interested that he strongly disliked her and one soaked the people one disliked for all one could get. His more general scorn for humanity at large—poor stupid things—he tucked away. He'd discovered it was an unattractive trait.

Now, with university scorned, it was time for his stage career. The writer bit would come later. And the difficult part of becoming an actor, as everyone knew, was getting started. You attended auditions. But he lived in Cheltenham and Cheltenham didn't do auditions. Also you found an agent, but Cheltenham didn't do agents either. You needed London for that.

In fact, despite what he'd told his housemaster, Leo wasn't in a hurry. He'd only just left school. He deserved a break. He was working on a short story, a mother/son conflict, trying to pare down his sentences in the Hemingway manner. He'd also written a tune for a popular song that Nanny thought was very nice (the tablespoonsful of love went entirely one way these days) so he had a lyric for that to come up with. And it was already almost September. High time he did something constructive about his theatrical career: he'd learn the Hamlet soliloquies. Not because he expected to be offered the part—he wasn't that silly—but because he'd need audition pieces when the time came (September or October, after he'd found himself a London pad) and Hamlet was full of them.

In early December, with no pad found, let alone an agent or an audition, Madam Sara struck. She arranged an appointment for her son with the Public School Appointments Bureau in London, drove him to it, and went up with him in the lift to the Bureau's waiting room where she sat while he went in to see the man.

The man Leo saw was helpful. He had two vacancies on his books, he said, that were just about ideal: one with Moyses Stevens, the top-notch florist on Berkeley Square, and one with Beals' of Bond Street, purveyors of furniture and hand-made bedding to Her Majesty Queen Elizabeth the Second. Perhaps Mr Bresson would like to talk it over with his mother.

Leo's life was being hi-jacked. Acting had been put on hold. He accepted this. Not bold people do. He was a good accepter. But at least he'd choose for himself between the two professions on offer. And furniture had to be better than flowers so he plumped for Beals, was sent for an interview two days later, stammered only minimally, and was hired. (In some social circles, mind you, a stammer, if slight, is perceived as a chic affectation.) His prospects were excellent: the Palace connection was important to Beals, especially the hand-made bedding, and the right trainee bedding representative, with the right public school accent, could expect to be groomed for prestigious (and lucrative) Palace visits. Ahem—*consultations.*

He never made it to the Palace. That would have taken at least ten years of very up-market retail experience, and on principle he despised the aristocracy. He'd joined Beals' simply to keep his mother quiet till a theatrical agent could be organised, and a job on the stage. Meanwhile, however, he of necessity learned a lot about hand-made bedding. About top-off mattress construction, about unbleached long-staple sheep's-wool, about the curled manes and tails of white Argentinean horses. About best white down pillows and inferior 'old poultry' fillings that caused FP (feather penetration) in their ticking. Foam rubber was all the rage, but Beals' didn't encourage it. *Who wants to sleep on old rubber tyres, sir? You need something organic, madam, something that can breathe...*

He lasted at Beals' longer than he'd expected. For a while the stage remained his goal, but it faded. Hamlet's soliloquies stayed with him, but to little advantage. He wrote bits of a play but he had nobody to show them to. Life in London wasn't bad. He couldn't afford many West End shows but BBC radio drama gave him access to the giants: Beckett, Dylan Thomas, Brecht, Pirandello, Donald Wolfit hamming his way deliriously through Marlowe's *Tamburlaine the Great...* The sports car helped too. His mother set him up with a decent top floor flat in Palmer's Green. Otherwise, as she'd always done, she left him to himself. The SCT was flourishing.

In due course Ting died and so did Nanny. He visited her once in hospital, found her thinned to the bone, angry, full of resentments, and didn't go again.

Then, passing through Beals' china department one morning, he was spotted by a new member of the sales staff, Jessica. He was twenty, she a year or two older. She was big of breast, big of heart, vivid, enthusiastic. She scooped him up. God knows what she saw in him. His body wasn't bad and he'd calmed down since his schooldays, but he was still on the flashy side, camp even, and notorious among Beals' younger female staff members for being always affable but never likely either to make a pass or to notice when one was thrust under his nose. The word was, in those newly-enlightened days, that he might be homosexual. Possibly she saw him as a challenge.

Looking back now, Leo knows very well what he saw in her: sex. She had his trouser zip open in the car the second time they went out together, and the hard-on she found underneath it did not disgust her. She was beautiful, golden-haired, full of laughter, she didn't mind his stammer, and up in his flat she sang Handel arias like an angel to his uncertain piano accompaniments. And easier stuff, like *The Beggar's Opera*. He fell in love with her.

At first the actual sex bit wasn't a success. He climaxed instantly, with little sensation, and was the one of them to feel post-coital disgust. So much heat. So many juices. So much need. He got used to it. In her presence he became little more than an impatient six-foot-two erection.

He moved her into his Palmer's Green flat. Life was tremendous. They talked, insanely, about marriage and babies. She took him to see her mother, who was dazed by them, her doubts swept away by her daughter's vigour. As for Madam Sara, he took Jess nowhere near her. Jess was his secret. Like him, she didn't have a father. He'd make up for that. He'd look after her.

They had dreadful rows—he meant well, yet constantly missed the point—but life was still tremendous. Everything was for the first time, hyper-bright, hyper-real, hyper-momentous. They married in a Hammersmith registrar's office shortly after his twenty-first birthday, telling Madam Sara about it only afterwards. Jess's mother had been present, and friends from Beals. Jess's friends. He didn't seem to have any. His fan club from College hadn't stuck.

Madam Sara wasn't pleased, but she wasn't all that interested. After all, she'd done more or less the same herself. The SCT was growing, taking all of her time. She'd noticed the lack of girls in her son's life. Now she didn't have to worry. She let a month or two go by, then gave the couple a bigger refrigerator.

Jess left, got a part-time office job, and a baby arrived in June, a little boy they called Jake. Her mother helped out with child care. Leo was good with Jake's practicalities, unfastidious and patient, but the rows continued. Jess's first lover was a sturdy, decent fellow. He didn't last very long—he claimed that he didn't want to be a marriage-breaker—and after he severed the connection he wrote Leo a letter, telling him that he respected them both and that all their marriage needed was for Leo to open his heart and show his love for Jess more clearly. If Leo just did that, he wrote, it would make all the difference.

Leo accepted that this was true, it explained a lot, and tried his best. Her next lover did it better though, whatever 'it' was, and the two of them went off together, taking Jake with them. Leo didn't make an issue of it. He was depressed, he hated living alone, but he didn't blame her. He'd never had the faintest understanding of her needs or wishes. As for little Jake, broken homes were a bad thing: divided loyalties, tugs-of-love, all that. The sooner the child settled down with his new dad—who seemed kindly—the better. The three of them moved up north somewhere and he quickly lost touch. By then, in the sixties, divorce was straightforward and not expensive.

The Meccano set his mother had given him was up in the Tivoli Street attic somewhere. He'd looked forward to sharing it with Jake one day, but he knew he wouldn't have been a good father. He'd never had one and he didn't know what fathers did.

Well, he did know one thing—they left their sons money when they died. (Not Maurice Moon, of course, but that was just shrug-worthily typical of the man.) So it was that when, a few years later, in a fit of fiscal responsibility brought on by a TV documentary on the subject, he made a will, he quite naturally left his entire estate to his son Jake—which entire estate at that time amounted to £332 and 71 pence in the Bristol and West Building Society, and a small clapped-out MG sports car. After that single somewhat theoretical and less than generous gesture, it has to be admitted that his son disappeared entirely from Leo's consciousness for a very long time.

For a while he tried sharing his flat with another man, no sex involved, just a person about the place, but for some reason they didn't get on. He never found out why. What he really needed, now and then, was friendly manual orgasms with no strings, no threat of babies, no dramas… and eventually a lad called Kevin turned up in Beals' Delivery Services, bringing in mattresses for remaking, who was looking for the same.

The orgasms, by the way, had been at Kevin's suggestion. Never in his life has Leo knowingly laid himself open to the risk of rejection by making a sexual advance of whatever nature. He simply cannot imagine himself ever being so brave.

He concedes also that there may always have been a lack of the necessary hormonal motivation.

He visited Cheltenham infrequently. His mother was a big wheel now, with a staff of mediums she called *truthsayers* and a best-selling autobiography just out. She never discussed her work with him but while he was at Tivoli Street she expected him to attend her séances—*guidance meetings* she called them. What he saw at them confirmed his father's opinion—she was a re-markable lady. Still hateful, but re-markable with it.

A bolder man than Leo would have asked her about her insistence on his presence at her séance table. Was it again a challenge—just another *question me if you dare*? Or was it simply for the look of the thing. A further agreement between the two of them that what was, was not.

He never asked her.

As to her views about his private life, he never asked those either and she seldom offered them. She'd expressed concern about losing contact with her grandson Jake but only, Leo thought, because her concern was expected. She'd rarely visited the child when that was possible. She had a well-filled life and she wasn't, in any case, good with babies.

When Leo left Beals' in 1973, it was to join up with a young woman, Marie Anne, from the London School of Architecture. He'd been with Beals' quite long enough and Marie Anne, who had designed *MA Works,* a range of drawing office plan-chests and other equipment, wanted him to market it for her. Beals' and furniture and training in sales were supposed to translate into entrepreneurial genius. She fancied him too.

Leo was wary. He knew about women now: they were capable of love and happiness and the best sex he'd ever known, and he wasn't up to them. Since Jessica he'd kept his head down. Literally. Women were, in the words of some Frenchman, a certain pain, an uncertain pleasure. But then came Marie Anne, and he risked a peep. She was quiet, professional, self-sufficient, safe. He made her laugh. They fell in love.

The business relationship didn't work. Neither did the love. He was good at neither. But where Jess had discussed his failings with him in bitterness and sorrow, Marie Anne was fiery. Her quietness had been self-imposed and was fragile. Not safe at all. She beat at him, demanding more. More what? She didn't know. Just *more...*

The parting wasn't tidy. It left him bewildered, wretched, and jobless. No glowing references. No references at all. He did some writing. It was rubbishy. He signed on at a Job Centre, worked in warehouses. Then, with a few trick visuals that he'd picked up while at *MA Works*, he went into retail display on his own account, doing Kings Road-type boutique windows and interiors pretty well on a production line basis all over the south-west for shopkeepers who couldn't afford anything better. Some months he prospered, others he scarcely broke even. A couple of years of that and he was drinking more than was good for him, and knew it.

In a pub one night, while drunk, he let himself be picked up in the gents' toilet. The experience was squalid, fumbled, unprotected: he was lucky AIDS wasn't around yet, and he didn't do it again.

And so things went. He acquired a cat but it got itself run over.

Eventually, in 1975, nineteen years after leaving College, he arrived back at Tivoli Street jobless, with three big suitcases and a fulsome forged reference on headed notepaper from the customer relations department of The Reader's Digest Association (courtesy of Peter, Leo's pub friend and RD employee). Not quite coincidentally—his mother had phoned him on the subject the previous week—the Spiritualist Church of Truth had just that week started looking for its first full-time secretary-cum-PR man. All hiring decisions had to go before the Elders, she'd told him, but now—glancing through the reference he thrust at her—*Leo has been with us for nearly four years... excellent team member... many valuable original contributions... very sorry to lose him but we quite understand... broader opportunities, possibly in a smaller organisation*—she foresaw no problems.

(She must have thought it odd that he'd never told her he was working for the Reader's Digest, but she still accepted the reference without comment. Unless '*That's nice, dear*' could be called a comment. This was part of a pattern he'd learned he could rely on. What was, if inconvenient, was not.)

He interviewed well—he was good with older people, respectful but not unctuous—and the Elders were impressed both by the letterhead, and by his filial relationship with Madam Sara. They hired him. That was six years ago so we're just about up to date. He got on with them—he got on with everybody, up to a point—and he computerised their truthsayer booking system. He'd accepted that he wasn't writing. He was a good accepter. He played the piano nicely at ceremonies where hymns were required. Also he had been friendly back at Coll with a man called Gordon Stavely, now *The Cheltenham Echo*'s assistant editor, which led to good SCT media coverage. He was an asset.

Still not bold, but it seldom showed. The conversational side of his work got by on the new identity that working for the SCT gave him. As when on the stage or reading in chapel, to be able to pick up the telephone and say, '*Spiritualist Church of Truth, Leo Bresson speaking,*' was a separation from his stammering self.

Three years ago Madam Sara had her first stroke, not serious, leaving a slight paralysis that the proper exercises, undertaken rigorously, dealt with. She returned to work after a couple of months, and continued to preside over regular guidance meetings. The second stroke was worse. It left her, as we have seen, crippled and aphasic.

At this point one of her cousins, Iolanthe's older son David reappeared. Iolanthe herself, and his father, as parents tend to, had died some years earlier and, in his sixties now, like Sara, David had retired and he and his wife were devoting themselves to restoring a small but exquisite Queen Anne house in Berkshire. David had mellowed. Unlike his brother Julian, he had long ago accepted cousin Sara's life choices, was concerned for her now and relieved that Leo seemed to be coping so ably. He kept in touch.

So that's our Leo. His sort of person. *Explained?* Not really. *Excused?* Certainly not. *Contextualised*, then. It's a graceless term. *Understood* does the job but it's wishy-washy. Also the French have a saying—and I bless them for it—that to understand is to forgive, and that involves concepts of blame and guilt that need to be forgiven and that Leo doesn't accept. So we're back with *contextualised*, a wretched neologism to end these flashbacks with, but it also does the job and he's happy with it today. A psycho-social context and a way of coping. Mean well. Keep your head down. It's who he is. Circumspect. Moderate in all things. Go with the flow.

And now, look where it got him, returning to his car, shrugging himself into his anorak, walking down the path from Max and Rosie's front door, Declan dying on the concrete, weeping and scraping.

* * * *

Back home from Parabola Road, he was met in the hall by Mrs Hopkins, her eyebrows signalling agitatedly. 'Madam S,' she told him, pointing at the closed door to the big front drawing room, two little secret finger stabs with her hand held close against her chest, 'has a visitor.'

He gathered his depleted resources. 'I know, Hoppy. I made the arrangement. It's a policewoman, asking about one of our truthsayers. He—'

'No, dear, that was earlier. This is one of the papers. He's in with Madam.'

Another crisis? A newspaper man? He thought about it, hanging up his anorak very carefully on his grandmother's kudu antler coat-rack, gaining time. No, there was nothing new the press could have found out, not so quickly. He could cope. Already that day he'd coped with far worse. So he smiled encouragingly at Hoppy, shooed her away, opened the door to the big front drawing room, put on his SCT secretary's face, and went in.

One of the papers, represented by a sharp-faced, skinny man in a tired suit, was sitting on the sofa opposite Madam Sara, his trouser legs pulled up high, showing a nervous amount of sock. The sofa was immense and he was not. The whole room was immense, and over-furnished with immense furniture, Clare at her most Anglo-Indian baroque.

Leo crossed the room to where his mother was seated in her usual high-backed wing-chair on the far side of the empty fireplace, and put a reassuring hand on her shoulder. Luckily this was a Hoppy day, so she was properly dressed. She usually got dressed for Hoppy days. One of her brocaded tents. Manageable buttons.

The newspaper man was clearly glad to see him. Madam Sara, alone and pressured by a second visitor in the one afternoon, wouldn't have been at her most coherent. He got up nimbly and introduced himself. He was Charlie Pratt from *The Daily Mirror* up in London and Leo would be young Mr Brissard. How d'you do. He'd come about the tragic Cirencester death-fall and he'd been talking to the lovely lady here, Mrs Brissard, and she'd been very helpful. He understood that the dead man had been a medium working for *The Spiritual Church of Truth.* This was the headquarters of *The Spiritual Church of Truth,* wasn't it?

Leo shook his hand minimally. *The tragic Cirencester death-fall*—already the media phrase slipped easily from this man's tongue. He doubted very much that Charlie Pratt was 'from' *The Daily Mirror.* He was just some local stringer following his much-boasted-about-in-the-pub nose for news.

Yes, Leo told him while his mother sat brightly nodding, this was the head-quarters of *The Spiritualist Church of Truth.* Mrs *Bresson,* Madam Sara *Bresson,* had founded the church back in nineteen sixty-six. It now ministered to one thousand three hundred and fifty-two members.

The two men sat down. Charlie showed little interest in the size of the SCT's membership. He wanted to know how far the dead man would have fallen from his—

Wait a minute. *The two men sat down* ... Words, words. Clarification's needed. It's a lightly tossed-off little phrase, *the two men,* but it comes with a mass of unnoticed assumptions about shared characteristics. Similarities. Words lump people together and they often mislead. Leo's similarity with Charlie Pratt went as far as an obviously male body, but not much further: very little other generally-accepted man stuff.

Not that he was effeminate. Bi, but hardly a transsexual-manqué. And he was too able in too many fields to be written off as wimpish. But he shared almost nothing, good or bad, of what was the essential Charlie. Ambition, physical pride, ready anger, competetiveness, greed, arrogance, he had none of those. He was someone altogether other.

So? So nothing, really. Words, words... just authorial pickiness. He still got asked to parties. Perhaps it was his sense of humour.

Back then, with apologies, to Madam S and the two generically male persons in the Tivoli Street front drawing room.

Charlie was still showing little interest in the size of the SCT's membership. He still wanted to know how far the dead man must have fallen from his balcony. Had he, in Mr Brissard's opinion, been depressed in any way? How long had he worked for *The Spiritual Church of Truth*? He wasn't married, was he? Word was that the dead man had enjoyed an unconventional lifestyle. Would Mr Brissard care to comment on the dead man's unconventional lifestyle?

Leo commented instead on the sterling work Declan Finsey had done for *The Spiritualist Church of Truth.* He'd been a fine person and a much-loved truthsayer (Leo spelled the word out and waited while Charlie wrote it down), and he would be greatly missed. Leo spelled out S*piritualist* as well. His own name and his mother's he let go.

Charlie asked him what sort of scéance things the dead man did, did he move tables about and float, and what were the were the views of *The Spiritual Church*—sorry,—*-tualist Church of Truth* on unusual lifestyles?

Leo told him that, as well as Mr Finsey's fine work for the SCT, he had been employed in Cheltenham's public library, where he had by all accounts made a splendid contribution. Perhaps Mr Pratt would like to have a word with the head librarian. And if Mr Pratt would bear with him for just a moment, he'd fetch him some SCT promotional materials.

Leo's office/bedsit was just across the hall and down the passage. He quickly returned with an SCT flyer and a paperback copy of Madam Sara's most popular book, *Spirit Truth*, which she now shakily autographed.

Charlie stuffed it in his pocket. Did Mr Brissard happen to know, he wondered, just how far Mr Finsey must have fallen? His flat was on the fourth floor, wasn't it? Also, there were potted plants and trellis clearly visible on the walls around Mr Finsey's balcony—was the dead man an enthusiastic horticulturalist?

Leo answered that the group of people Mr Finsey specially ministered to was situated in the Stroud area. He was a much-loved truthsayer there, and perhaps Mr Pratt would like to go and talk to them. And yes, Mr Finsey had been a great plant lover. He was well known for the wide range of his interests. He would be greatly missed.

Changing tack, Charlie asked what arrangements the dead man's church would be making in connection with his funeral.

Leo said that Declan Finsey had been a very thoughtful and religious person. His funeral rites—once the police had released his body—would be entirely suitable.

Suddenly inspired, Charlie asked Mr Brissard when he had last seen the dead man.

Leo told him that he and Declan Finsey had worked together very closely. They would meet professionally several times a month. Mr Finsey had been a tower of strength within the SCT. Church members all over the region would feel his loss deeply.

And now, (Leo stood up firmly), much as he appreciated the *Mirror's* interest in his distinguished colleague, so suddenly and tragically taken from them, he had a busy time ahead, what with finding a replacement for Mr Finsey and other urgent SCT concerns, so if Mr Pratt didn't mind...

On the way to the front door Charlie asked again about the distance Mr Finsey must have fallen, and Leo explained that Madam Sara had recently suffered a minor cerebral haemorrhage but was now well on the way to recovery. He opened the door, told Charlie the name was *Bresson*, not *Brissard*, it was spelled out on Madam Sara's book jacket, and watched ostentatiously while Charlie walked down the path and across the road, got into his car and drove away. The house had nothing to hide, but the thought of Charlie poking around at the back and peering in through windows was repellent.

When the car was out of sight Leo closed the door, leaned his head briefly on its cold hard panel, then went back to join his mother. As he'd said to Charlie, he had a lot to do. It was Hoppy's going-home time and she liked her day's work to be appreciated so he must find her and appreciate it. He must contact Gordon Stavely at the *Echo* and organise some serious coverage of Declan's death, a tribute perhaps. There was also Declan's Stroud group to be talked to and comforted. Supper needed to be thought about. And there was the matter of his alibi.

First things first, though. Hoppy was hovering, ready to leave. And Coade's Detective Sergeant Wiler had already been and gone…

* * * *

'Wiler? Thass her name? I never did get it.'

They were in the small back drawing room. Leo smiled encouragingly. 'But you talked to her?'

'Of course I talked to her.' Hoppy was gone and Leo'd lit the fire, bringing up a scuttle of coal from the basement (man's work, not Hoppy's) and using the gas poker. His mother and Rumple were warming themselves. 'Of course I talked to her.'

'What about?'

She looked up at him sideways. 'Nothing much.' She was in her mean child mode. Charlie had rattled her. 'Nothing much.'

It reminded him of what he'd told Coade about her condition: she was 'mentally alert.' True. But in fact—although he usually he chose not to see this—her second stroke had seriously damaged her mind, her identity, and she was only gradually rebuilding them. Along with many familiar characteristics, however, she now often showed a cheap sort of cunning that would have been totally foreign to the old Madam Sara. Did it come naturally, a part of old age perhaps, or was she learning it? Sandra was the only outsider she spent any time with. Much of her speech was straight Sandra so why not, eventually, her identity?

He allowed a pause, then sensibly changed the subject. 'I dropped in on the Krauss-Häbers. Had a cup of tea.'

His mother fidgeted resentfully. She repeated her *'Nothing much'* as if he hadn't spoken. Then gave in. 'We talked about you.'

If he'd pressed her she'd have held out against him for hours. 'Nothing nasty, I hope.'

'She wanted to know all about. I tell her, told her about you and College. What I always say is. About the play.' She was cheering up. 'The magazine. The piano. You were good at rugger. They made you a prefect.'

After six years there his housemaster had really had no choice. Poor Detective Sergeant Wiler. 'Anything else?'

'How you look after me. How you look, looked after me last night.'

'Last night? She asked you that?'

'When you got home. How you looked after me. I told her, nice. Like always. Nice.'

'When *did* I get home?'

'Thass right. I told her, nice. Just like always.'

He tried again. 'Did she ask you what time I got home?'

'Thass right. Tuesday. I told her. Always a long day. You visit all the truthsayers, talk to them, hear what they say. Mrs Patton's going away till after Christmas. Denny's taking over. His meeting's small and—'

'So Tuesday's a long day. Did you remember when I got home?'

'Nearly six. Nearly six. I told her.'

'Nearly six? How do you know that?'

'Looked at the clock.'

He turned away and poked at the fire. He was taken aback—he'd expected a very different answer. The truth: *Because you told me.* She hadn't looked at the clock while he was there. He'd watched her. Perhaps she'd looked earlier, while he was still in the hall, hanging up his coat. Or perhaps she just wanted to impress him.

'Was that all Sergeant Wiler wanted to know?'

'You and Declan. Were you frens.'

If she'd really looked, the clock would have told her nearly seven, so why had she got it wrong? A lucky mistake? She did get clock faces muddled. But *such* a lucky mistake?

'Friends? What did you tell her?'

'Not close, I said. But never nothing bad. You arn like that.'

'Thanks, Ma. And it's *aren't.* Remember what Sandra says. You must work on your "t"s. '

'Sandra says you musn nag me.'

'She's right.' Too often he used his corrections as barricades to hide behind. 'I'm sorry.'

'Thass fine, dear. You're a good boy. What I always say is.' She reached down to stroke the cat's ears. 'All those questions. I know what they're doing. They think you pushed him. He fell and you pushed him.'

'They have to ask questions. It's their job. I was there so I might have pushed him. So they have to make sure I didn't.'

'Of course you didn. I told her. I'd of known. I'm your mother. You arn like that. I'd of known.'

'That's what mothers always say.'

'Iss true. You arn like that and I told her.'

'Bless you.' All those missing 't's and he let them go. Instead he leaned down and hugged her.

He didn't often hug his mother. There was always the risk that he might find himself hugging Madam S. Even when it worked, as today, neither of them was sure how to proceed. Briefly she hugged him back, patting his shoulders which were all she could reach. 'There, there,' she said vaguely, as if he needed comforting. Which he did.

A shoulder to cry on. Which he needed badly.

* * * *

Later, while peeling potatoes for dinner, Leo decided that his mother's recollection of looking at the clock was real but false, a memory grafted in perhaps from many other Tuesdays, created in order to preserve her self-respect. It proved that she wasn't the resident idgit: she didn't have to be told the time—she knew how to tell it for herself. A fortunate circumstance, anyway. Assuming that Coade had a source for the time of Declan's fall, presumably the person who'd raised the sash, his mother's evidence put her son Leo at that particular moment firmly thirty miles away.

Assuming this, presumably that, firmly something else… he leaned his knuckles on the chopping board and groaned. All this shit, while Declan… while Declan… while Declan lay dying on the concrete.

He put the potatoes on to boil and washed the broccoli. These vegetables, together with sausages and generous fried onions, would be their dinner. Wednesday evenings at seven were his regular bridge date with Alan Beckerton, so he always cut down on the washing-up by keeping the meal simple. Curiously, since her second stroke, sausage-and-mash had become his mother's favourite. He couldn't blame *that* on Sandra. She was never around for dinner.

He'd already called Gordon at the *Echo* and left a stammer-free message on his voice-mail. Sometimes he astonished himself. He'd also checked with the Cheltenham SCT group up in Pitville and then contacted one of the elders of Declan's people in Stroud, conveyed to them all his deepest condolences and, as they were now tragically without a truthsayer until he could propose one for their approval, suggested that they join Cheltenham's guidance meetings for the next few weeks. They'd be very welcome there, and a special memorial session was being planned for Sunday evening at seven-thirty. Not necessarily a meeting, that would depend on what people wanted, perhaps simply an occasion for sharing their loss.

He laid the kitchen table for supper. Two knives, two forks, two serving spoons, salt and pepper. The original dining room—now aka Madam S's séance room—was ridiculously large and menacing for just two people. The conservatory at the back of the house could double as a dining room on sunny evenings but the kitchen, honey pine and chaste spotlights and all, was mostly where they ate.

Leo got out the ketchup and put it on the table. The kitchen hi-fi was giving him Scarlatti harpsichord sonatas, very loud, Declan was dying, mercifully unheard, on the concrete, and he was on his third gin-and-tonic. His mother, who disapproved of gin, was in by the fire with Rumple, watching TV. His day had been one long act of desperation, one long nightmare, and he felt he was breaking up. He'd have called Alan and cancelled bridge if he hadn't been afraid it would get back to Coade and make him suspicious. The same fear was all that kept him from screaming and breaking things. Only the blessed quotidian, helped by gin, kept him going.

The gin bottle lived in one of the kitchen cupboards, beside the olive oil. There was a formal drinks cupboard in the big front drawing room, but that was a long way to go. In any case, it contained only left-overs. Neither Clare nor her daughter, perhaps on account of the dear colonel, had ever taken much interest in serious alcohol.

Madam Sara enjoyed her supper. Leo ate his with her and chatted brightly. They laughed companionably at Charlie Pratt. Reporters were all the same. Remember that one who couldn't spell poltergeist...? Leo went easy on his gin. It wouldn't have helped his bridge.

Wednesday's was the one evening in the week when Madam Sara was left alone and had to do without a shower (in case she fell in the stall) and get herself to bed. Before leaving for the bridge club on St Stephen's Road Leo laid out her night pills on her bedside table, stoked up the small drawing room fire to last till her nine o'clock bedtime, and drew her attention, as always, to the bridge club's telephone number written in large figures on the board beside the telephone. Then, sustained by these small tasks, he left the house.

Most people don't know about duplicate bridge and don't want to, so I'll simply explain that it's a partnership card game of some complexity, with tricks and trumps and bidding, four players to a table, lots of tables in a club-room, and it's taken very seriously. A minimum of social chat at each table. Partnership understandings should be sorted out elsewhere. Thus you can play against the same opponents on many nights and never become entirely certain even of their names. As to your partner, bridge conversation is best carried out during the mid-evening break.

Leo, who would have preferred on that Wednesday evening to avoid conversation with anyone, even with Alan, mis-timed his visit to the gents and found himself peeing beside his partner.

'Glad of this moment, Lee. I've been worried about you.'

'Worried? That two diamonds bid, you mean?'

'Lord, no. I'd have done the same.'

'What, then?' Leo'd known the bid was fine. In fact they'd been getting good scores all the evening up to now. Which said something about the different areas of mind involved in games and in naked, minute-to-minute not breaking up. 'What, then?'

'Frankly, Lee, you look terrible. I've never seen you quite like it.'

'Tired. A busy couple of days.' Christ. If only he knew. 'Ma's been poorly. I expect that's it.'

'Then there's that colleague of yours dying. I saw it in the paper. A wretched business. Did you know him well?'

'Declan? Quite well. He'd been with us three or four years.'

'Upsetting.' Alan finished peeing, zipped his fly. 'Reminder of one's own mortality. Wouldn't you say?'

'These days, Alan, who needs reminding? Isn't death the new hot topic?' Chatter, lad. For god's sake chatter. 'Used to be sex, but that's old-hat. Ever since Köbler-Ross, death is all the rage.'

Alan wasn't to be put off. Lingering to wash his hands and fuss with his thinning grey hair in the mirror, he probed deeper. 'So your associate's sudden violent death really doesn't bother you? It isn't something you need to talk about?'

'Of course it bothers me. Violence always bothers me.' He concentrated on peeing. Nothing was coming. A sphincter somewhere had clenched. He gave up, put his penis away, and crossed to the basin. 'It's just that I'm never quite sure what good talking about it does.'

'Aren't you really?' Alan moved to give him space at the mirror and tugged noisily on the roller towel. 'The Roman church is very sure. I envy them their confessional. It institutionalises a valuable human activity most of us have lost.'

'Come on, Alan. People confide in you Anglicans, don't they? It's the same thing.'

'Of course it's not. Confession has status, rules, responsibilities. It's an official part of the divine totting up. Confiding in your nearest Protestant god-botherer may well be simply telling him some old story to make yourself feel better.'

Leo stared at him. This was really just too apt. Too embarrassingly serendipitous. The Great Novelist in the Sky was making the connection between demand and supply too neatly. Leo's need for a confidant, Alan's need to be one. There had to be a snag.

'*Some old story…* what more do you expect? Catholics guarantee confidentiality. You people don't.'

A call for them to resume play came from the other room. Leo turned from the basin, flapping his still-wet hands, but Alan stood in front of him, blocking the door. 'Technically that's true—I know that. I can only tell you,

Lee, that I've received many confidences in my life as a minister, often very ugly, and I've never yet seen the need to betray one. So let's play bridge, shall we?'

They played bridge. Their second half wasn't as successful as their first, but they still ended up third overall, with 67%. A pretty good result.

Alan's last words to him as they separated outside the club to go to their cars, were: 'You have my telephone number.'

Leo found them threatening. He'd revealed too much. He hadn't said a thing, he hadn't twitched or sweated, he'd just played bridge. But he'd revealed too much.

Was it really only yesterday evening that Declan had fallen? Fallen and died? On the concrete? Scraping? Perhaps not weeping, but certainly scraping? Only yesterday evening? The shame of the event had been with him all his life.

Back on Tivoli Street Madam Sara had remembered to turn off the TV and was safely in bed, sleeping peacefully. Her pills saw to that. Leo stole one Oblivon, then had second thoughts and stole another. If she'd had enough sleeping pills to be reliably lethal he'd have stolen the lot. It was a moment when other people's distresses at his death counted for very little. He honestly felt that he couldn't go on.

He could, of course. He paced himself—one pill to get him to sleep and the other for later, in case his shame woke him at some black, evil, middle-of-the-night non-time, which it did. He always slept naked and as he sat shivering on the toilet in the downstairs bathroom at that bitter pre-dawn hour, his reflection in the mirror on the wall above the bath caught his eye. The face was unrecognisable. He leaned forward, looked closer. Hair and flesh, flesh and hair. Unrecognisable. A grimacing stranger. He stood up and flushed the cistern. The body in the mirror was a stranger's too. Ugly. Hair and flesh, flesh and hair. He took the second pill and quickly turned off the light. Sleep did not come easily but finally it came.

CHAPTER 5

Thursday mornings often began badly in the Tivoli Street house. Madam Sara resented Leo's Wednesday bridge evening—not getting her to bed, coming home at all hours—and she woke in an angry, complaining frame of mind. Today, leaving the fried egg script up on the shelf in reserve, she took down the boiled egg script. As usual Leo had done his best: he had the kitchen timer permanently set to ping at him when the specified four minutes and twenty seconds were up. He would then immediately take the immaculately-timed egg out of the water, put it in the egg-cup on the plate on her breakfast tray beside her just-popped-up toast, briskly carry the tray through to her, make sure the egg-spoon was conveniently to hand, and then return to his sugar-free meusli in the kitchen.

This morning, however, he'd hardly sat down at the kitchen table before she called him back, reporting that her egg-white was over-done. It was a no-fail claim, totally subjective and impossible to disprove. The timer was of course consistent but eggs came in slightly diferent sizes, and anyway any egg would continue to cook until its shell was cracked open, so the possibility of error undeniably existed during its transfer from the water to the egg-cup to the tray to the bedroom to the moment of its being actually cracked open. Any delay there (always possible on account of Madam Sara's uncertain left hand) and a nearly-hard egg-white became fatally nearer-to-hard. The difference, he strongly suspected, was undetectable. But a properly-cooked egg, she told him, wasn't much to ask, so he apologised, wrapped her toast in her napkin to keep it hot, took the egg away, and ate it himself while he boiled her another.

The second egg was fine, and her tea too, but the toast was now soggy. Sufficiently hot but, on account of the napkin, undeniably soggy. Enough was enough, he decided. The boiled egg script allowed this. He met her gaze and coldly held it, not moving till she looked away and conceded that the sogginess might be her own fault—if she had eaten the toast while she was waiting for her replacement egg it would probably still have been crisp.

Back in the kitchen he snatched up the bread-knife and stabbed it so hard into the butcher's block under the window that he was able to twang it. Rumple, on the windowsill, craned down to watch. Leo remembered how easily his friend Alan had spotted his desperation. If it was so obvious, how was it that his mother, arguably his closest companion, remained so unconcerned for him?

Not a useful thought, he told himself. Carefully he un-Excalibered the knife, put it back in the bread bin, returned to her and made his peace. On Thursdays there was a schedule to follow. Sandra arrived at nine, and Madam Sara had to be up and dressed and ready.

That done, he remembered that he'd promised to ring Max the night before to fix a time for a rehearsal. He did it now. Thursday was also Sainsbury's day, the weekly supermarket visit, which was Rosie's too, so he'd be meeting her there, but rehearsal arrangements were Max's business. The Parabola Road telephone rang for a long time, so long that the answerphone cut in, but then Max arrived and over-rode it. He sounded bad. Leo kept their talk short, tomorrow morning, Friday, why not tennish, and promised he'd look carefully at the Ibert. There were fingering problems. Then he rang off. How the hell he'd make time for piano practice between now and then he couldn't imagine.

At eight thirty he checked on Madam Sara, who was muttering her *Rrround the rrragged rrrock,* then left in the Jaguar for Sainsbury's. He and Rosie had been meeting there regularly for months now, doing their separate shopping, comparing special offers, and then taking twenty minutes off for a chat over coffee in the caféteria. It was a precious time, when they could talk away from Max's ears, mostly about him, his condition, the doctors, what could best be done. Recently a more troubling element, their lust, had been present and on one occasion its wild delirium had taken them down the road to a shabby motel. The desk clerk there, a haggard individual, clearly gay, who said his name was Henry, was impressively incurious. Their first love-making, back on Tivoli Street, had been frantic and finally sad, a mistake, and they'd vowed never to do it again. Their second love-making, in Henry's motel on the Gloucester Road, had been sadder, even more a mistake, and since then the vow had held.

On this particular Thursday, with freeze-dried instant coffee a priority (Madam Sara's *fithy stuff,* which she drank copiously), and a saddle of Danish boiling bacon as his choice for Sunday dinner, Leo quickly got his shopping done. Rosie was usually slower, fussier about the vegetables, and this morning she was also buying for Max's party. Arriving ahead of her in the supermarket caféteria, Leo parked his trolley, bought *cappuccinos* for them both and laid claim to the last empty table. He'd picked up copies of the *Echo* and the *Mirror* on the way in, which he'd disciplined himself not to open up anxiously and scan at once (it was just possible, he thought, that he was being watched), so he casually glanced through them now.

Right at the bottom of the Echo's front page, eight lines. A mere eight lines. Tragic death of local librarian… blah blah blah… fall from balcony… blah blah blah… as usual in cases of sudden death, police are pursuing their enquiries... blah blah blah... no sign of foul play... Leo turned the page lightly, stared at a headline about fox-hunting protesters. So far so good. Interesting decision, to describe Declan as a librarian—which he was of course, but his second profession would have been more of an eye-catcher. It looked like a poor reporting job, some cub simply copying the official police hand-out. No harm in that.

As to the *Mirror*, Charlie'd made it only to page four, and with even fewer lines, beside a shampoo advertisement. Declan's mediumship led, but any mention of the SCT or its secretary had been subbed out. Clearly his death wasn't considered a story that would be going anywhere. Relieved, Leo turned to the funnies. His hands were shaking but he didn't think it showed. He held the paper up and watched over it for Rosie to appear round the ground-glass screen by the check-out. As always, when she came into sight she was an astonishment to him.

A tender person, contained, calm. Softly shaped black-brown hair above a gently rounded face. Strong eyebrows, though. Bright eyes, very blue, her nose flatter than perfect, her mouth blunt at the outer edges, honest and passionate. No make-up. He looked at her and was astonished.

'Over here.' He folded the paper and waved. 'I've bought.'

She came to the table, stooped, held his skull carefully while she kissed his forehead, then sat down opposite. 'You're bothered, love. What is it?'

'Bothered?'

'You were yesterday. It's the same this morning.' She hooked her bag over the chair-back. 'You're... not quite here. What is it?'

Christ... Only just arrived, and already this. He'd prepared nothing. No story. He didn't know how to start, how to go on, how to end. There were decisions he still hadn't taken. But he couldn't just blatantly lie. She wasn't Alan.

'One of our T.S.'s, Rosie—he got himself killed yesterday. No, the night before. Fell off his balcony. A long way down. It was on the local news and the police talked to me, asked me questions, all the usual sorts of questions, suicide, that sort of thing, was he depressed, and I told them no, all the usual sorts of answers. Declan Finsey. His name is, was, Declan Finsey. No, that's silly. It still is. His name doesn't change because he's dead.'

'Of course it doesn't.' She reached for his hand across the table. 'He lived over in Cirencester, didn't he?'

'That's right. He had a group in Stroud, and I'd been with him on SCT business just before the accident. It's just that he wasn't depressed or anything, and I've had to talk to the police, and... and I'm not making much sense, Rosie. It's just that I was upset.'

'Of course you were. Of course you were.'

'I still am. They talked to me yesterday and I've got to go back this afternoon and sign a statement. I still am.'

' We never catch the local news. What do you think happened?'

'His flat's on the fifth floor. If he'd slipped somehow he wouldn't have had a chance.'

A narrative framework was forming. The police story. The police story minus any outright lies.

'Finsey... Isn't there a Finsey composer?' She thought about it and shrugged. She took her hand back. 'Of course you're upset. And the tea with us yesterday... you'd just come from the police. We should have noticed. Tried to help. Max and I get so self-absorbed. It's inevitable, I know, but... So were they alright with you? Not pushy?'

'They do their job. Everything has to be reduced to jargon.' He considered constructing an anecdote. Nothing came. 'This afternoon, the statement, the signature, and with any luck the whole thing'll be over.' He stirred the froth on his *cappuccino*. 'Tell me about this crazy party.'

She looked away, down at the table, not answering. It was as if there'd been a quick little *one-two-three* clap of hands, ordering a change of her pace, of her attention, of her intensity. Everything about her moved more precisely. Moved less, but more precisely. Her interest in his troubles had been a busy surface.

He waited. The caféteria murmured about them, knives clicking. Eventually he said, 'It's what I think it is? This party?'

'A farewell? It might be. I don't think so.'

He winced. First Declan's dying and now Max's—did he really need this? Does this author? Isn't it just too morbid, too much of a bad thing? Certainly there are happier processes in life to write about. But not, unfortunately, in Leo's particular life at that particular time. For him at that particular time Max's dying was what insurance companies nowadays like to call a pre-existing condition, something unpleasant that they can choose not to deal with. I'm afraid this author can't. So hang in there, please. Max and Rosie will soon get lucky and things will go along for a while quite tidily.

Meanwhile, back in Sainsbury's cafeteria Leo stirred his *cappuccino*. He asked her, 'What does the hospital say?'

'Nothing. The remission's over. Weeks. Days. They hand out pills.'

'So it's up to him.'

'We always knew it would be. He's saving them up. We've discussed the whole thing over and over. You know that.'

'He'll need your help.'

'He's supposed to be able to do it for himself. That's what the book says.'

Leo had read the book. It said that sleeping pills on their own weren't reliable. The subject could doze off, then vomit them up. Or lie in a coma for days and then die unpleasantly of liver failure. No, once the subject had swallowed them and they'd started to make him drowsy, in his last waking moments he needed to pull a large plastic bag down over his head and tighten it round his neck, so that he would dependably suffocate when he was too deeply asleep to notice. And that, the book said, was something he could do for himself. No third party involvement. Which was important, the book said, so that under current law when the police arrived they wouldn't be able to accuse anyone of the serious offence of assisting in his suicide. He'd done it all himself.

No third party involvement. Book talk. Lawyer talk. How Leo hated it.

'Come on, Rosie love—everyone knows that's just for the look of things.'

She turned her head away.

'He'll want me with him. What I do is my business. But he's not saying when. He says he'll just know. Then we'll get it quickly over with. No hanging around.'

Leo took a deep breath and held it, slowly shaking his head. Who was he to give advice about who died how or when? A cruel irony. It would have been pathetic if it hadn't been so shameful.

'Will you be able to?'

'I don't know.' She faced him. 'Yes. Yes, I will.'

He imagined her sitting beside Max, holding his hand, watching the plastic bag fill and empty with each breath, waiting for him to suffocate. Would some reflex make him struggle? Would she have to hold him down? For his sake, because she loved him, would she have to hold him down?

'If I were there too,' he said, 'perhaps we could—'

She held up a hand to stop him and he didn't insist. To be honest, he didn't know if he'd have been able to deal with those long, wretched moments. A cruel irony indeed.

Rosie lowered her voice till it was no more than a whisper. 'God knows what happens afterwards. To me, I mean. Afterwards. Living with that.'

For which he had no answer. What answer was there? From him, of all people?

She saw his pain, if not its true reason. 'I'll manage,' she told him. 'It's the only way, Leo. You've seen a lot of our horrors, I know, what he's been going through, but… well, it's worse. It really is. Not just the pain. Since hope went it's been hell. Any sane medical system would have helped him out of it months ago.'

'You've discussed it?'

'Recently, you mean? About the actual moment, not just the timetable?' She shook her head. 'I'm not supposed to let myself think that far ahead.'

Her voice broke. 'I wish I understood, Leo. God… Jesus… compassion… all that stuff I grew up with. I wish I understood.'

He wasn't the person to help her with that either. He looked for something he could give her. Something positive. There wasn't much. 'You know how Max is. He does things well. He won't let it be difficult. He'll support you.'

'I've heard that one. Love will find a way. And it probably will. But I worry, Leo. Christ Jesus, I worry… The fact is, my dearest dear, I haven't the faintest idea how I'll actually cope with it.' She leaned forward, placed three fingertips on the table, made the outside two of them walk like a little animal while the middle one tapped, feeling for the way ahead. 'I'll manage somehow, of course. People do. One thing at a time. No need to rush. One thing at a time. Of course I'll manage.' The fingers walked across the table, their middle one groping blindly. 'Pull down the bag and tie the string, of course I'll manage, and I'll wait and watch and cry a bit, and untie the string and take the bag away away so nobody'll ever know, and I'll manage the whole stupid fucking business but I don't know how. Not today. Not here. I don't know how I'll do it.' She made a sudden fist and beat silently at the formica table-top. 'I don't know how.'

'Nobody could.' Leo folded her hand into his. 'These have been terrible weeks for both of you, Rosie. But they will pass. And afterwards—'

She snatched her hand away. "Tell me more. Tell me about the merciful release.'

'Don't knock it, love. Just give it time. It'll be there and it'll be merciful. Trite but true.'

She massaged her walking fingers. 'Do you know how long we've been married?'

'Tell me.' He knew, but she wanted to say the words.

'Twenty-three years. Of course I must help him. It's not asking much. Twenty-three years.'

'More than half of your life so far. I can't imagine that.'

'Nor can I. But it's happened.' She paused, thinking back, then smiled. "I've warned him that you'll suspect the worst about the party.'

'And I know what he said. He said, "of course he'll suspect it, but he'll be brilliant at pretending that he hasn't."'

She smiled again, quite differently. 'I do love you, Leo.'

'*And I love you too.*' He made the words silently with his lips.

She gathered up her bag. 'I must go.'

'You haven't drunk your coffee.'

'The nurse's coming at noon. You drink it. Waste not, want not.'

'Nanny's Human Dustbin. See you tomorrow morning. Tennish. Max and I—we've got to rehearse.'

'He mentioned it. A little Palm Court with their coffee and cakes. God knows what they'll make of it.'

'Do 'em good. Take care, love.'

'And you.'

He watched her move away between the tables to where she'd left her trolley. A small, extraordinarily brave person. He was so much in love with her. What would she do, he wondered, after Max was dead? No lack of money, probably. She had a brother up in Liverpool. Phillip. Max and he had never got on. She'd hardly go to him but she'd never stay in Cheltenham either. Both parents dead. A gentle, beautiful widow, not poor, she'd quickly remarry. Dear god, he'd miss her.

Their two cups of *cappuccino,* now tepid, were still in front of him on the caféteria table. He cleared his throat. Ever the Human Dustbin, he carefully drank them both. Nanny, in heaven, nodded approvingly. Waste not, want not. He wiped his mouth on a paper napkin, eased back his chair, stood up, lifted the two cups on their saucers and carried them to the attendant's dirty cup counter where he found a place for them. He always liked to spare the attendant that small simple chore. From the dirty cup counter he returned to his shopping trolley and surveyed the available check-outs. Rosie was at the far end, nearly finished. He chose the nearest queue. Two customers were in front of him. One of them had her trolley piled high with large packets of disposable nappies called *Huggies.* When his turn came at the check-out he cashed in three cut-price coupons, paid for his stuff by credit card and trundled his trolley out to the Jaguar.

A memory came crowding in, unbidden, certainly unwanted, of the wretched afternoon Rosie and he had spent in that motel out on the Gloucester Road. How muddled their life had been together… He remembered the homo desk clerk there, impressively incurious and businesslike. Henry? Yes, his name was was on a pinned-on lapel badge. And on a printed nameplate propped on the reception desk in the motel office. Henry…. yes, that was it. And then, suddenly, with no apparent intervening mental process, Leo wondered if it was Henry who had been the source of Declan's information about him and Rosie. Photos of Max and Rosie had appeared quite recently in the *Cheltenham Echo,* in support of a hospital fundraiser—his writing had made him a small local celebrity over the years—and if Henry, no matter how incurious, had seen one of them he might have recognised her from it that day at the motel. Coming and going she'd stayed in the car, but he could easily have glimpsed her and then mentioned her assignation with some Carter fellow to Declan. Nothing malicious, just gossip one evening in some gay bar. Just a giggle. But more than that for Dekko.

Carter. Thank god he'd thought to use a *nom de plume.* But why *Carter*? He'd no idea. It was the first name to come into his head.

But this connection, once made, had the potential to bring Leo's most deeply regretted folly out into the public domain. Regretted, and now, furthermore, an indiscretion with possibly dire legal implications.

At present Chief Inspector Coade suspected him of involvement in Declan's death but lacked a motive. Henry, if found, gave him a marital mess and therefore the beginnings of something to fill that lack. Henry, if found, made Leo vulnerable. Henry, if found, could send Leo, false name and all, to jail for a very long time.

Henry if found... not an easy task for the chief inspector, with nothing whatever to suggest such a line of enquiry. Should Leo's picture and real name become known in the media as a possible murder suspect, however, then Henry himself might recognise him and do the sums.

At least the false name had necessitated no credit card, so this Mr Carter had paid in cash, which would have left no record to jog Henry's memory. Certainly cash customers would be unremarkable in Henry's experience. Leo remembered that he'd had only just enough in his wallet for the rental and a blessedly unmemorable tip.

No, for Henry to have recognised him that day in the motel office he needed to have chanced to see Leo before and then had a reason to find out what his name was and to recall, perhaps many weeks later and in a completely different context, that it wasn't Carter. All of which required too many special circumstances. Reassuringly too many.

He stooped in the supermarket carpark, opened the Jaguar's boot lid, leaned his forehead on its edge. No, it was much more likely that when Declan taunted him out on the balcony he had simply been making adroit inferences from stuff Leo had told him over the last many months about Max and Rosie and their situation. There was in fact no need at all for a gossipy Henry to be involved.

Mechanisms. Surprise identities. False names. Final chapter revelations... The butler who was really the victim's long-lost uncle. More of the Rendells. Dear lord. As if, in his tiny, shameful personal scheme of things, any of this mattered.

Declan, Rosie, Max, and now Henry... For God's sake, as far as Henry was concerned there was nothing Leo could do, no matter how discreet, that would make the slightest difference to anything.

He unloaded his supplies, returned the trolley, waved to Rosie who was still unloading hers, and drove away.

* * * *

In Tivoli Street Sandra was just leaving on her yellow motor scooter. She waved him down, tipped back her smart little helmet and leaned in at the Jaguar's window.

'I've left you a note,' she said. 'We must work on getting Madam Sara's speech forward. Front of the mouth, you know. Patients tend to gargle. It's easier. Get the action up and forward. *Tip of the tongue, the teeth and the lips.* I've left her an exercise. Help her say it.'

Before Leo could think of an answer the helmet descended and the scooter whizzed away. He reversed into the garage and filled all his fingers with plastic bag handles, carrying everything into the house in one trip. One trip Leo. He always made a point of that.

His mother was waiting for him in the kitchen, Rumple winding round her ankles, and she helped him put away the groceries, inspecting each item suspiciously. She knew he'd do her down if he could: buy foolishly, uneconomically, unhealthily, anything to get at her. Today the bacon he'd chosen was much too fat and the brown sugar was barbados when she'd asked for demerara.

Sandra's note was on the table. Leo opened it and read it: 'We must work on Madam Sara's articulation. Plosives. "The tip of the tongue, the teeth and the lips." A hundred times a day.'

Catching his mother's fiercely accusing stare, he passed the note to her.

She read it and snorted. 'Mrs Clever... I tell her, one thing I do know about is articlation. Clear to the back of the hall... How does she think I worked?'

Once the groceries were put away Leo dished up lunch. Nothing grand, soup from a carton, corned beef sandwiches and a shared large Jaffa orange. Rumple got the second half of his breakfast tin of *Seafood Platter*. On television the local lunchtime news reported a pile-up that morning in fog on the M5 near the Burford exit. Three people dead, seven people injured. Motorway madness was blamed.

No mention of Declan's death. Some man falling off his balcony—it wasn't much of a story. The TV people would have to be pretty desperate before they used it. The *Echo* would be another matter. They had more space to fill. Leo realised that Gordon hadn't yet called him back about Declan's obit, some sort of tribute. Perhaps Gordon could be guided tactfully to play down his, Leo's, involvement.

Lunch over, Leo went across to his mother's bedroom and turned on the electric blanket for her nap, then helped her to the bathroom, stood outside, and made sure she got herself safely into bed. Her bedroom was opposite his office/bedsit, on the eastern side of the staircase at the back of the house. It had been her office in the old days when she slept upstairs, and her faded ormolu desk still stood in front of the window, covered now with piles of letters and photographs and clippings, the SCT archive that she spent much of her time sorting for the history of her church that Leo was going to write one day. Since his mother's second stroke he'd moved her bedroom downstairs, into what had previously been the library, and they both lived entirely on the ground floor. The house was much too big for just the two of them, and expensive to heat, so they'd converted the butler's pantry into a downstairs bathroom and in the winter they shut off the basement and all the upstairs rooms. They were by no means poor—Clare's investments had taken a bad hit in the seventies but Madam S's SCT portfolio paid well, together with continuing sales of her books, and there was always Leo's salary—but she'd never been one to squander money. It didn't grow on trees, she'd tell him.

He reminded her now that later that afternoon he had to go to the police station to sign his statement and he also had SCT office work to get through. She liked to know these things.

Out in the passage again, her door closed behind him, he ran out of daily drivel. He stood quite still, fighting his demons. Henry was the least of them.

His office/bedsit, across the rear hallway past a door set with blue stained-glass lozenges that opened into the conservatory, had been the library back in his grandmother's day. Madam Sara had moved him into it at the start of his job with the SCT. She had interfered very little from then on, and the hugger-mugger was all his: evidences of short-lived enthusiasms, a quite expensive classical guitar, small panels of wooden inlays from a DIY kit, an unfinished oil painting on an easel with a broken leg, untidy stacks of computer print-outs, a vivarium that had once housed terrapins. His bed was single, out of consideration for his mother's sensibilities, but a wide single just in case. It had recently accommodated two quite needlessly well.

Curtains, carpets, furniture, rooms, pictures, books, ornaments, doors, passages, stairs. The house didn't change. It just went on and on and its continuity calmed him. Not ready yet to face his SCT work, let alone calling Gordon Stavely for a second time, he turned right from his mother's bedroom and walked slowly down the passage, past the doors first to the small and then to the big drawing room and across the entrance hall with its kudu hat-stand and its long-case clock to the formal dining room, once but now no longer Madam Sara's séance room. There he paused, brought up short in the open doorway. As usual, he didn't quite believe it. Entering it required courage. Shipped out to India in the late twenties by his grandmother at the time of her marriage and shipped back again by the grieving widow, regardless of cost, thirty-odd years later, enough mahogany had gone into the room to ruin a rain forest.

Huge table, ten huge chairs, two even larger carvers, thrones for emperors, two huge portico'd and pedimented sideboards, and six huge waist-high Doric pedestals for plants, two at each of the room's velvet-curtained floor-to-ceiling windows. There was also a huge slate-tiled fireplace with a baronial overmantel that had probably come with the house, and two substantial brass-and-glass candelabra. And on the plum-coloured flock-papered walls, sombre paintings of Barraclough ancestors, in heavy gilt frames.

The room struck awe. His grandmother had assembled it and his mother had preserved it. Madam S knew a good thing when she saw it. It had been ideal for her clientele.

Leo walked quietly round the table, one hand trailing along its finely polished surface (Hoppy cared about such things), and sat down at its head. He hadn't arrived there consciously but he now thought that this was perhaps the one place where the tumult in his head might be called to order. It battered in on him. Sooner or later it had to be dealt with.

What was it the man in the Strindberg play had said? Cancel and move on?

Declan, dying on the concrete. He, Leo, in Declan's flat five floors up, totally self-concerned. Ten minutes of panicky thises and thats. He, Leo, then fleeing in terror. Out of his mind. Not so much out of his mind, though, that he couldn't work out how to trick his mother into providing him with a fake alibi. Not so much out of his mind that he couldn't lie smoothly to the police the following day, and congratulate himself on his performance afterwards. Not so much out of his mind that he couldn't lie also to Rosie, if slightly less smoothly and only by omission. Rosie whom he couldn't bear to lose. Rosie whom he'd lost.

Lunacy. All framework gone. The limits he'd lived within, gone. And now this bloody Henry, this fellow with prison in his eyes, waiting at the motel to do his sums.

And finally there was Max, who had cherished his life, loving it for as long as he could bear it, and who would now soon be discreetly moving on. Max, the only man he'd ever loved. Max, whom he'd betrayed. Max, whose suffering he was now fitting into his thoughts only when he didn't have anything more important ... Grovel, grovel. Grue, grue. Ah, how self-pitying and foul he was. Ah, the wretchedness of Leo.

Cancel and move on? You must be joking.

Behind him, from the other side of Clare's baronial overmantel, he heard very faintly the ringing of the telephone on the desk beside the computer in his office/bedsit. No big deal. On the fourth ring, as with any other calls that had come in that day, the answerphone would take it.

Except that it might be Rosie calling about Max. Or Max calling about the rehearsal. Or Coade. Or bloody Henry. Or Declan, weeping, scraping, dying on the concrete.

Running, holding on to the dining room door jamb as he swung round it, he reached his desk in time to take the call before the machine cut in. It was from the firm in Wolverhampton that supplied him with SCT t-shirts and pens and other small fund-raising items. The salesman had a new line in genuine calf-bound organisers that would take the SCT logo very nicely. The price was right and they were going well. Would Mr Bresson care to place an order? Leo, his hand shaking so that he could hardly hold the receiver, told him yes, my goodness yes, provided that he could guarantee November delivery, in time for the Christmas trade. The salesman was sure that could be arranged.

Leo ordered three dozen, rang off and eased down into his chair. His shaking calmed. The little electric man who lived in the telephone told him that three other SCT calls were waiting for him. The first was from a potential new guidance meeting member, asking for a contact in the Coombe Hill area. Leo rang her back, gave her the Coombe Hill telephone number and told her he looked forward to seeing her soon at a meeting. The second message was from Paul in Declan's Cirencester group: he wanted to confirm that at least four of them would be taking advantage of the Pitville group's generous invitation for Sunday. Also, now that Leo was there on the phone, Paul told him the group had decided that someone ought to find out from the police when poor Declan's body would be available for interment, and he was just the man. He was good at these things. They could rely on him, couldn't they? Leo answered incorrectly that the matter was really for Declan's family, but he'd do what he could.

The third caller was Mrs Bunty Carstairs.

Leo knew Mrs Carstairs all too well—even on a good day she was the last caller he needed. A mathematics teacher retired from super-elite Cheltenham Ladies College, the widow of a prominent local lawyer and now Senior Elder on the SCT's Governing Board of Elders, Mrs Carstairs was trouble. Any call from her would be long and boring, about administrative minutiae of one kind or another. Perhaps his laggardly refunds of her postal expenses. Or a comma he'd omitted from her column in the latest *SCT Newsletter.*

Life was grotesque. It really was. He laughed wildly, and tapped in her number.

Her call proved to be long, as expected, but had nothing to do with postal expenses. First she complained at the time he'd just taken to get back to her. She wasn't impressed, Mr Bresson. Not impressed at all. She didn't have all day. Then she told him why she was calling, which was a bombshell. She and eight other Elders from around the region had held an extraordinary Governors' Board Meeting. They were concerned about the future of their Church. Madam Sara had been a wonder, an inspiration to them all, but now, tragically, it had to be admitted that she was a spent force, a spent force. The Spiritualist Church of Truth was to all intents and purposes leaderless. Something had to be done. Mrs Carstairs and the eight other Elders had unanimously agreed, unanimously agreed, that a new Director should be appointed. First of all it was essential that—

Leo tried to put in a word here but Mrs Carstairs quietly asked that she be allowed to finish.

First of all, Madam Sara had to be apprised of the Board's decision. For her own sake, and the SCT's, it was to be hoped that Madam Sara would then tender her resignation, presumably giving ill health as her reason.[1]

Leo would then organise the necessary postal ballot, Mrs Carstairs continued, with the replies to be returned to an election committee drawn from the Governing Board, led by herself, which would examine them and—after first consulting Madam Sara as the by-laws required—would make its decision. Again Leo tried to contribute but Mrs Carstairs talked through him.

Obviously telling Madam Sara that she was to be forcibly retired would not be easy, not at all easy. Even so, this was an official matter, a job the Elders had no intention, no intention at all, of delegating to Mr Bresson. Three of them, herself as Senior Elder, the Membership Secretary and the Treasurer, had agreed to visit Madam Sara as a group and explain the situation to her. She had been an inspiration to them all, an inspiration, but the time had come—as it must some day to all of us—for her to step down. All they required of Mr Bresson was that he arrange a time slot in Madam Sara's day when they could have a little talk with her. They realised that Madam Sara wasn't well, not well at all. Even so, a visit in the very near future was clearly desirable. And Mr Bresson should start distributing ballot forms immediately to all staff members and group Elders. As to the duration of the time slot for their little talk, Mrs Carstairs thought that half an hour would be sufficient. She was sure that Mr Bresson would agree.

Leo cleared his throat. 'Mrs Carstairs,' he said, 'I'm sorry to have to tell you this, Mrs Carstairs, but you're a fat pompous old bag, Mrs Carstairs, and I don't give a shit for you, for your ballot forms, or for any of your moronic Board Members. Flush my mother down the toilet if you like, Mrs

---

1   In her autobiography Madam Sara had described the founding of her Church, back in 1953, in the reading room of the Moreton Hampstead public library. She'd composed its constitution herself, over a long week-end, and in the unlikely event of the Directorship becoming vacant it required that all SCT group Elders, together with every full- or part-time staff member, should take part in a secret vote for their choice among the SCT's employees for the position. A prior list of candidates would not be necessary. Any staff member could be voted for—including, quite naturally, oneself. This, Madam Sara had decided, was true democracy. It also simplified administration. And the person chosen would of course accept the honour gratefully. This too Madam Sara had decided.

Carstairs—it's your privilege and she probably deserves it. But please don't ask me to care about little talks and bloody time slots. There's a real world out there, Mrs Carstairs, where real people suffer real pain. Real shame. Real desperation. There's a world where the dead aren't magicked away into a comforting haze of hellos from happy heaven. Where the dead are dead, Mrs Carstairs, rotting meat, Mrs Carstairs, and where their survivors have to fight real grief and real hopelessness to make new lives without them. Where the place in the bed beside you is definitively cold and empty, and—'

He said none of this, of course. The whole harangue, sadly, was entirely in his head. Instead, after he'd properly ascertained that Mrs Carstairs had for the moment finished speaking, he cleared his throat, politely told her he quite understood her problem, thanked her for the board's considerateness, and suggested the coming Saturday afternoon at four thirty as a suitable time for their appointment. A half-hour time slot should indeed be sufficient. Thank you so much, Mrs Carstairs. Yes. Yes, he'd refer to his bye-laws folder for a sample of the necessary ballot form. He was confident that he could format it and distribute it, together with a covering letter, within twenty-four hours. Next Wednesday, he suggested, should be set as the deadline for the ballots' return. And he hoped her daughter was in good health. Good bye now. Good bye. And thank you.

He rang off. A half-hour time slot indeed. Ha. Half an hour in which to write off an entire life's work. What a truly terrible woman. He gathered his thoughts. He should have seen this coming. He had, actually, and had ignored it. In any case, he couldn't have stopped it. It was a perfectly reasonable course of action.

As for his not telling his mother, though, and leaving it to the Elders, that was ridiculous. She'd want to know why they were coming—what could he tell her? Anyway, he'd rather be the messenger. He couldn't have them just go blundering in: the words needed to be chosen very carefully, and the moment. Only he could do it. She'd blast him, but that was what happened to messengers and it wouldn't be the first time. This evening, maybe. Some time this evening, perhaps over a cup of cocoa.

Poor old Ma. She'll be shattered. Everything she did was leading her towards the day when she'd be back in charge again. Without the SCT, who was she? Poor old Ma.

* * * *

Next for him that afternoon, once his mother was up and about again after her nap, came the trip to sign his statement at the Lansdowne Road police station. First though, as he was driving out of the garage, he had a most curious and troubling encounter.

Driving across the pavement and entering the roadway, he halted the car and, as one is supposed to, looked to left and right. Drizzle was falling. No vehicle was coming from either direction but, before he could drive on out, a man ran along the pavement towards him and knocked on the Jaguar's passenger window. Leo reached across and wound it down.

'Mr Bresson? Leo Bresson? I was just coming to see you.'

'Sorry. Can't stop. It'll have to wait, I'm afraid.'

'My name is Peterson. It *is* rather important. Couldn't I—?'

'I'm sorry, Mr Peterson. I have an urgent appointment. I really can't—'

'Just five minutes of your time. Not a moment more.'

Leo stared at him. He was a decent, Marks-and-Sparks-suited sort of man, forty-ish, anxious, sandy hair and not much of it, with a thin plastic raincoat pulled on hastily. Harmless. Probably some SCT enquiry. Getting rather wet.

'Five minutes then. And I mean it.' He wound the window up again and unlocked the door. 'Get in.'

Mr Peterson opened the door and scrambled in, bringing with him a waft of strong but not unpleasant aftershave. 'Very good of you. Super.'

Leo wound up his window and eased the Jaguar slowly off the pavement, out into the road. 'You have a car?' He'd have been wetter if he'd walked any distance.

'Parked back there. The Volvo. Just arrived. I nearly missed you.'

Leo drove on till he found a space and backed into it neatly. He left the engine running. 'So what now?'

'I'm one of Mr Finsey's neighbours. On his landing. You don't remember me. We met in the lift. Months ago. Um… he introduced me.'

'Sorry about that. I'm bad at faces.'

'No problem.' Mr Peterson dragged out a handkerchief and began blotting his skimpy hair. 'Thing is, I'm good at them. That's how I recognised you in the corridor the other night.'

There is a sensation, almost like what you imagine death will be, that comes when the blood suddenly drains from your face, when your anus clenches and your stomach heaves and your fingers and feet are stuck with sharp little pins. Leo closed his eyes.

He took a breath. 'What other night?' He knew what other night. He might be wrong, there were plenty of other nights. 'What other night?'

'Tuesday. Six twenty or so.' Peterson was drying inside the back of his raincoat collar. 'Bloody rain… Just after Finsey had fallen from his balcony.'

'You couldn't have.'

'You were wearing a blue anorak. Carrying a briefcase. You were in a great hurry.'

Leo remembered the moment. He'd turned at a sound half-heard. All the doors on the landing were shut. He'd seen them.

'That's... ridiculous.'

'I was intrigued. Went back and out onto my own balcony. Looked down. After short while, there you were. I saw you. Not Finsey's body, it was too dark. Just you.'

'Of course I was there. But not at six twenty. And certainly no body. You've got it wrong.'

'First Finsey's shout. Then you in your anorak. Carrying a briefcase.'

'Why are you telling me this?' Leo was coping. Moment by moment, a step at a time, no more, but he was coping. It was amazing how one did.

'So there you were. You stopped, bent over, then walked on. Till then I thought I'd been over-reacting. Anyone can shout. You'd had a row and you'd left. Simple as that. Super.'

'What do you want, Mr Peterson?'

'I turned on the telly. I live alone.' Mr Peterson smoothed his damp handkerchief on his knee and folded it. 'I turned on the telly and had my supper. I went to bed.'

'You're crazy, Mr Peterson.'

'But then, in the morning, all those policemen. Questions. Well, you can imagine.'

Leo remembered his interview with Coade. This made no sense. Coade would have mentioned it. 'So what did you tell them?'

'Me? Nothing. I needed to consider.'

'So you're here for money.'

'I knew you'd think that. People are so uncharitable.'

'How much?' He wouldn't pay. He'd no idea what he *would* do, but he wouldn't pay a penny. That sort of thing never ended. But he was curious to know. 'How much?'

'For me it's a matter of understanding.' Mr Peterson gave a small self-deprecating shrug. 'Nothing to do with vengeance, deterrence, justice, all that Neanderthal stuff. Understanding. You've seen the famous statue. That's all justice is: a woman in a blindfold.'

Crazy indeed. Leo didn't need this. 'If you don't want money, what *do* you want?'

'I need to consider. I told you. I need to consider. Make enquiries. Observe and consider.'

'And when you've considered?'

'Then I shall... Um, then I shall act. What would *you* do, Mr Bresson? In my place, what would you do?

Leo didn't answer. He was thinking that if this man really hadn't told the police anything, he could hardly go back to them later with this mad story. He glanced at his watch. 'What *did* you say to the police?'

'Kept it simple. I heard nothing. Saw nothing. Watched the telly. Ate my supper. Went to bed.'

'So why are you telling me this?'

'I thought you ought to know.'

'Know what?'

'When you see me around. It's only fair. I thought you ought to know why.'

See him around? What a terrible thought. Leo summoned a moment's bravado. 'Mr Peterson, your five minutes are up. Get out of my car, please.'

'If you say so.' He opened the door just a crack. 'People fall off balconies for all sorts of reasons. Often quite accidentally. I know that.'

'I'm late, Mr Peterson. Please go.'

Mr Peterson pushed the door further open and put one leg out. Drizzle gusted in as he twisted his body sideways. 'You have a stammer, I see. That's interesting…' He leaned away from Leo, getting his weight over his knees, then paused. 'I don't suppose you believe in hangings, electric chairs, that sort of thing.'

Leo revved the Jaguar's engine noisily. 'Please, Mr Peterson.'

'Nor do I.' Mr Peterson looked back over his shoulder, a concerned expression on his pale bland face. 'I'm on your side, Mr Bresson. People fall off balconies for all sorts of reasons. I lied to the police because I wanted to help you. They're a blunt instrument at best and the system they work for stinks. I'm on your side.'

'So what next, Mr Peterson?'

'Well, I admit I'll have a problem if I discover that you killed poor Finsey on purpose. Out of malice or for personal advantage. I might have to think again.'

'You mean you'll punish me?'

'I mean I'll think again.'

'Judge and jury? God?'

'There has to be room for passion. We're not machines. You must know that.'

'You're joking.'

'Not at all.'

'Then you're crazy. How the hell would you do it?'

'Another problem. I'm not a violent man, you see.' Peterson heaved himself upright, pulled his damp trousers away from his bum. 'Something would come to me. It depends what I discover.'

'Oh for heaven's sake… just go, can't you?' Hang on, though. The man was crazy enough to mean it. Leo leaned sideways across the empty passenger's seat. 'No. First tell me what you mean by 'discover.' What can you possibly discover?'

'I've no idea. The sort of man you are. That sort of thing.'

'And you'd punish me for being the sort of man I am?'

Mr Peterson stepped back from the car. 'What other good reason is there?'

Which made so much sense that it took Leo's breath away. He reached out, trying vainly to catch Mr Peterson's sleeve, 'Wait. *Please…* I had no malice. None. And no personal gain either. I just—'

'You'd be bound say that. Of course you would. And it might be true. Might very well be true. I'm sure it is. But I must first make enquiries. Observe and consider.'

He turned away, nudging the car door firmly shut behind him with his foot. Then he clearly had another thought, came back and spoke again through the closed window, but Leo couldn't hear what he said. Seeing this, Mr Peterson gave up, pulled the sides of his open plastic raincoat ineffectively across his chest and walked away down Tivoli Street towards his Volvo.

Leo let him go. His capacity for decisive action was small at the best of times. And anyway, what else could he do? He'd really no choice. It was a funny old world. All his other problems and now this nutter had turned up. This nutter who happened to live on Declan's landing and happened to have been at home on Tuesday night and happened to have looked round the edge of his door at just the wrong moment.

So what could this Peterson actually do to him? Punish him? Such a schoolboy word. Keep him in after class? Cane him? Pathetic. And in any case, *how*?

Leo had seen him. So mild. So earnest. So *crazy.* Leo could well believe he'd think of something.

How, then?

A very good question.

Wait a minute. Pull yourself together. This Peterson, was he real? Did he really exist? Wasn't he just a guilty fantasy? A crude hallucination? Some sick need to suffer? For God's sake, Peterson made no sense. I mean, *come on…* an avenging angel in a plastic mac? *Do me a favour…*

Leo wriggled across into the passenger's seat and peered along the pavement. No–one to be seen. He scrambled back behind the wheel, lowered his window, put his head out. A Volvo was moving away from the curb a few cars away down the street. He watched it drive off. A Volvo? What did that prove? There were plenty of Volvos.

He raised the window. That was it. There were plenty of Volvos. Obviously he'd imagined Peterson. The man was a delusion, the embodiment of all his worst fears. He'd have to be more careful. He hadn't realised how far gone he was. How near to the edge.

He thumped the wheel happily. Peterson didn't exist. He never had.

Except that the leather of the passenger seat was clearly still damp where Peterson had sat in it. And there was still the stink of his aftershave in the car. He couldn't be imagining that...

Christ. And now there was the police station to be faced.

* * * *

During his time at the Lansdowne Road police station two additional bad things happened. First, as he entered the building, Declan's sisters were leaving and they recognised him. Coade was with them and thoughtfully made a room available so that they could have a private talk.

He hardly knew them. It can't have been an easy meeting for them and itt wasn't for him, either. Carla, the taller, older sister, was full of plans and good sense: no elaborate funeral—no money, no money—just a simple cremation and a scattering of the ashes. In their Bourton-on-the-Water garden, she thought. Declan had loved their plants, their garden. They often gave him green stuff, cuttings, for the pots on his balcony.

Mary's concerns were subtler: she wondered what Spiritualists believed, really believed, what Declan had believed, really believed, and she regretted that they'd never really talked about it with him. What would their brother have wanted?

As for Leo, all he knew was the passionate shame he felt, and his sorrow for these people he had so deeply wronged. All he wanted was to embrace them, to shed tears, to tell them how sorry he was. All he wanted was to bring their brother back to life again. And all he could do, *jabberdee, jabberdee*, all he could do was reassure them that when he'd last seen Declan he'd been cheerful, in fine spirits, not a worry in the world. And he was so very sorry that this terrible thing had happened. *Jabberdee, jabberdee...*

Oh, and as far as interment arrangements were concerned, Spiritualists had no strong preferences. Declan himself had occasionally officiated at funerals, but as a kindness and a duty to the bereaved rather than from any personal convictions.

Jabberdee, jabberdee.

Two hands to shake. Two shoulders to pat consolingly. How Leo got out of the room he doesn't remember. But he does remember wondering if Mr Peterson would have approved.

And then, while he was out at the police station's reception desk, trying to read his statement, trying to make sense of the words it was putting in his mouth before he signed his name to them, Detective Sergeant Wiler appeared through noisily flapping doors and invited him in, just for a moment, just to clear up a couple of points, if he didn't mind of course. And when he told her he didn't mind at all, Chief Inspector Coade, on the other side of the flapping doors, was waiting for him.

* * * *

(click)

D.S.Wiler: This is interview room three and the time is two twenty-seven. Present are Chief Inspector Coade, Detective Sergeant Wiler, and the informant, Leo Bresson. The informant has been told that he may have a legal advisor with him should he so wish it, and he has declined the offer.

C.I.Coade: Mmmm... I see from my notes, Mr Bresson that you're the man who doesn't like Edinburgh rock.

Bresson: That's right.

C.I.Coade: Fine. Then I won't offer you any. Hm? My notes also tell me that you claimed to have liked Mr Declan Finsey once, but then you'd had a falling out—in your words, Mr Bresson 'some time back.' Do you happen to recall more precisely when that happened?

Bresson: Two or three months ago. It wasn't anything major.

C.I.Coade: Enough to stop you liking him...

Bresson: It was about my mother, actually. He was rather abusive.

C.I.Coade: Your mother... that would be his employer.

Bresson: Ultimately. But she leaves most things to me these days.

C.I.Coade: You've met Mrs Bresson, Anthea. Would you say she leaves most things to her son these days?

D.S.Wiler: Absolutely, Boss. And she...mmm...

C.I.Coade: And she what?

D.S.Wiler: Nothing really. She prefers to be called Madam Sara. That's all. She's quite insistent. She prefers to be called Madam Sara.

C.I.Coade: Thank you, Anthea. A revealing detail. Hm? So you chose to retain Mr Finsey's services, Mr Bresson, even though he'd insulted Madam Sara.

Bresson: He was a good truthsayer. I told you. And my mother isn't always an easy person to work for. And I really don't see what all this has to do with—

C.I.Coade: The broader picture, Mr Bresson. It sometimes helps... My one small problem is that we have an apparently reliable eye witness who claims that you and Mr Finsey ate dinner together at an Indian restaurant in Cirencester as recently as the twenty-second of August, yet you—

Bresson: Was it really only then? I suppose it was... That was the evening when—we both liked Indian food and we often went to that Cirencester place—that was the evening when it happened. I thought it had been much further back. We went on to the pub afterwards and... well, Declan got talking about... well, he got talking about my mother's... well, her mediumship style, which used to be a lot more florid than people are comfortable with today, and…

C.I.Coade: And you'd both had a glass or two, and one thing led to another… Hm? I quite understand, Mr Bresson. So this August date was the occasion of your falling out, and you'd simply lost count of the weeks. Would that be a fair description?

Bresson: It's been a busy time, Chief Inspector. I—

C.I.Coade: Was Mr Finsey on the balcony when you arrived, Mr Bresson?

Bresson: What? When are we talking about? I thought—

D.S.Wiler: The Chief Inspector's changed the subject, Mr Bresson. He's asking you about last Tuesday, when you arrived at Mr Finsey's flat.

Bresson: Was he on the balcony? No, he wasn't. He was in the living room. We talked in the living room.

C.I.Coade: You're sure of that?

Bresson: Of course I'm sure. It wasn't all that warm. I think the windows were closed. The French windows, you know—yes, they were. We sat in the living room.

C.I.Coade: And not for very long.

Bresson: The whole visit was a bit of SCT routine. Once a month I—but you know all that. I ask about their problems. Often they don't have any. Declan didn't. Didn't have any problems, I mean. So there wasn't much to say.

C.I.Coade: Just the recurrent problem of Mrs Bress—the problem of Madam Sara's leadership. Thank you, Anthea.

Bresson: That's right. And I'd nothing new to offer.

C.I.Coade: So off you went. Hm? Dry weather, would you say?

Bresson: The weather? It hadn't rained for days. Thursday was when it started.

C.I.Coade: What was Mr Finsey doing when you arrived?

Bresson: Doing? He had the CD player on. He was reading on the sofa.

C.I.Coade: And he turned the player off.

Bresson: That's right. I'd come to talk. We could hardly talk through Marian McPartland. Not that I've anything against piano jazz. But—

C.I.Coade: —But you can't talk through it. Quite so. Did you notice his hands, by any chance?

Bresson: His hands? What an extraordinary question. He had fine hands. Really quite delicate.

C.I.Coade: But you didn't notice anything unusual about them. They weren't dirty, for example.

Bresson: I don't think so. He was a very clean person. Fussy. But I might not have noticed. It's not the sort of thing I look for.

C.I.Coade: Most men don't…Well, Mr Bresson, you've been very helpful… Just one last thing—a matter of personal interest, really. Hm? Back on the subject of Spiritualism again, of communication from beyond the grave. If Spiritualists takes seriously the possibility that a murdered man might return in some way to confront, or even expose his murderer, why don't we hear of more cases when that is claimed to have happened?

Bresson: That's an interesting thought… Two reasons really, I suppose. First there's the problem Spiritualism has with the public. It doesn't get taken exactly seriously, shall we say. Spiritualists are touchy these days—they keep themselves to themselves. And secondly—

C.I.Coade: But what, Mr Bresson, if a spirit message came up with a clue that only the police knew about, something like that? We'd have to take that seriously.

Bresson: Come on, Chief Inspector—how would you ever get to hear of it? And in any case, the real point is that people forget one basic fact. Spiritualists believe that the dead take their natures with them. They don't suddenly become saints. They're as reliable or unreliable as anyone else. As truthful or untruthful. As wise or as silly. And of course, in your terms, they can't be put on oath.

C.I.Coade: *Touché*, Mr Bresson. …Put baldly, though, what would people at the SCT's next séance do if Mr Finsey's spirit appeared and accused you, for example, of his murder?'

Pause

Bresson: I've no idea. If they'd known him personally then they'd probably have trusted him, so they'd believe him. All very awkward. My word against his and all that… I expect I'd swear I was innocent and resign before they found some excuse to give me the boot. What else could they do? Some of them might try to involve the police, but I doubt it. You do ask the oddest questions, Chief Inspector.

C.I.Coade: Simply curious, Mr Bresson. Simply curious. (Sounds of movement.) But I appreciate your frankness… So now I'll simply thank you again for sparing us so much of your time, and—

D.S.Wiler: The statement, Boss.

C.I.Coade: Thank you, Anthea—I was coming to that. It's simply that the new information you've given us today, Mr Bresson, clearly needs to be incorporated into your statement, and you're a busy man so perhaps we could send a revised version of it round to Tivoli Street in the morning for your attention. Hm? If you would be so good?

Bresson: Anything you say, Chief Inspector. But I do have a ten o'clock appointment tomorrow and then a lot get through before the week-end, so it'll have to be pretty early.

C.I.Coade: I think we can promise that. Don't you, Anthea? Nine fifteen sharp sounds about right… Good day to you then, Mr Bresson. And thank you again.

D.S.Wiler: The informant, Mr Bresson, is leaving the interview room. (click)

* * * *

Dirty hands? What was that all about? Leo sat in his car and marvelled at the human constitution. He was still upright and breathing. Mrs Carstairs, crazy Mr Peterson, the Finsey girls, not to mention the threat Henry presented… all these, and he was still upright and breathing. He was still more or less making sense. He'd even survived another session with Chief Inspector Coade. Better than that, he'd actually done rather well. McPartland had been a brilliant touch. Maybe placing himself and Declan safely off the balcony, inside the flat, well away from what had actually happened, had been a fairly obvious move, but he'd nearly missed it. Especially after Coade had caught him out (bad stammer there, but hardly conclusive evidence) on yesterday's totally unnecessary lie about the date of his row with Declan. He'd been sloppy, thinking more about providing them with an outsider's view of his mother, but really, why bother? Let them see her for themselves. Make their own judgments.

And all that stuff, thrown in by Coade at the last minute, about spirit accusations—the point there presumably was obliquely to ridicule the whole séance rationale, and therefore to ridicule (and so unsettle) Leo himself. Well, the Chief Inspector had misjudged his man. Leo had courted ridicule for most of his life. There was safety in ridicule. He was a man who fell down funnily. It precluded anything worse.

Briefly he wondered if any of the SCT's truthsayers hated him enough to do to him what Coade had suggested. He thought not. They seemed to like him. Most people seemed to like him… which augured well, incidentally, for the results of the peculiar Mr Peterson's enquiries.

The matter of the dirty hands remained, however. It was a puzzle. In fact, Leo hadn't actually seen Dekko's hands. Coade had given him a fifty-fifty choice, clean or dirty, and he'd opted for the most likely. Dekko's hands were always clean. Dekko was like that.

And the merciless thought-question came down on him then, blasting his cheap complacency, tearing away the tidy frameworks, the Meccano he was so good at. The thought-question came down on him, what of Dekko's clean clean hands as he lay weeping, scraping, dying on the concrete? What of his clean hands then?

* * * *

There's a gap now in Leo's recollections. He mentions this not in order to suggest that otherwise he has charted his every single moment during those wretched days and nights, but rather because, when the gap occurred, he was immediately aware of it. First he had been in his car outside the police station, then he found himself in his office-bedsit at home on Tivoli Street and his computer was printing out Director Ballot Forms, plus a covering letter, for all the truthsayers. Nothing in between, and it worried him.

A black-out? He believed so then, and still does, but he has a tendency (understandable in the circumstances) to sensationalise. It may just as well be that the automatic nature of so much of his life, of everybody's lives, simply left nothing in particular to remember. The drive from Lansdowne Road to Tivoli Street he could have done in his sleep. The same with whatever passed between him and his mother before he sat down at his computer. The ballot form's program similarly would hardly have been memorable. The covering letter—it was a good one, he saw, tactfully describing the Governing Board's regret at Madam Sara's retirement decision (a face-saver he knew she'd eventually come to), and setting the form's Wednesday return deadline—was harder to discount, but it was really quite standard stuff.

Not that a black-out wouldn't have been natural response. The mind coming to its own rescue and all that. It's mentioned here in this account because from now on there's an increasingly emotional, over-wrought quality to Leo's recollections. Furthermore, although he's unlikely to lie straight out, he inevitably has an agenda. This needed to be said.

So here Leo is, and the thirty-three ballot forms (his number for the SCT's staff and group Elders, including himself) are waiting to be put in their envelopes, and Leo rejoins his remembered world in the middle of wondering how the hell he's going to tell his mother what the Elders have decided. They'll be round on Saturday afternoon, three of them, banging on the door. Today is Thursday so he has a full day-and-a-half in which to do it. No, not really—she'll need fair warning, time to prepare herself, so he must tell her tonight. He's no idea at all how she'll react. Do sudden shocks give people strokes, or is that only what happens in books? If it gave her one, that would be her third. Perhaps she'll keel over dead, which would solve a lot of things.

He considers the possibility. He'd miss her—an amazing thought—but it wasn't as if being dead would do her out of much. A release, really. She was never going to make it back as the SCT's boss, whatever Sandra might say. Being dead would spare her all those empty days. But she mightn't be so tidy. She might just keel over paralysed, which would be hell for all concerned. *Christ...*

Anyway—god bless the quotidian—it was nearly five o'clock, time to go and do something about dinner. People had to eat.

* * * *

Being Thursday, supermarket day, there was plenty of fresh food in the fridge. The two lamb chump chops would be perfect, he decided (he'd even brought mint to pound for the sauce), with glazed carrots, runner beans (they weren't too stringy yet) and new potatoes, which the label oddly told him came from Egypt. Banana custard to follow. A bit on the juvenile side, but he tried to keep his mother's weekday puddings low on stodge. She was supposed to be losing weight.

Anyway, a nice bottle of wine would cancel out any nursery tendency. He went out to the cupboard under the stairs, which passed for a wine cellar now that they'd closed off the basement except for coal, and picked out a Sauvignon de Touraine. *Unpretentious,* he told it reassuringly as he tucked it into the door of the fridge.

Since her nap that afternoon his mother had been at her desk, working on the SCT archive. She'd heard him go for the wine and called out to him, but he'd pretended not to hear her and returned to the kitchen without answering. He wasn't yet ready to face that side of his filial responsibilities.

The SCT archive took up most of Madam Sara's long days. Possessed early on in life with a sense of history—or at any rate of her place in history—she'd kept copies of just about every letter, newspaper cutting, bill, advertisement, testimonial, book review and bank or building society statement remotely connected with her or, later, with the SCT, the result being a considerable stack of neatly-filled and dated cardboard boxes that occupied one of the unused upstairs bedrooms, boxes that were brought down by Leo, when needed, one by one in strict chronological order for her to sort and annotate in preparation for the book he was to write. She'd started this work some two years earlier, while recovering from her second stroke, and she'd reached 1979. Thirteen years'-worth remained, some of her busiest. Having only a hand and a half didn't help but it wasn't really that she was slow, and certainly as far as the papers were concerned she wasn't stupid. She simply wanted to get it right.

They usually ate at six. She appeared in the kitchen at around five-thirty.

'Where were you in nineteen seventy? Your thirtieth birthday. Where were you?'

Leo had mint in the mortar and was pestling it. 'My thirtieth? God knows. On the dole, I expect. Honestly, Ma.'

'No. I remember. You were working in that shop. Records, wasnit? I juss published my book. The other one.'

Oh god. *A Little Slice of Heaven*: he did remember. And as a birthday treat she'd taken him to Selfridges for tea. Selfridges, for god's sake. Tea there been one of his grandmother's treats for him. Twenty-odd years later, Clare long gone, and it was still Selfridges for tea. Good old Ma.

'That's right. I do remember. We had tea at the Stores and you signed autographs. People had recognised you. In leather goods, I think.' The joke was unkind but his alone. She wouldn't catch it. Not any more. He resumed his pestling. 'So what about it? What's your question?'

'Why was I in London? That lawyer, about the copyright—was I see-ing him?'

She couldn't have been in bloody London simply because her son lived there and it was his bloody birthday, could she? Of course not. 'You're right. You were all steamed up about it. Some other group were calling themselves 'truthsayers.' You'd seen him in the morning.'

'Carn find... *can't* find his invoice. Sure it was then?'

'I told you. You'd seen him that morning. I can't remember his name. He was advising you to sue.'

She nodded. 'Barnaby. But no invoice. Mr Barnaby.'

'You'll find it. You always do.' Who bloody cared? Leo put down the pestle and reached for the vinegar. The mint needed to steep for at least half an hour. 'By the way, Ma—did I tell you Max and Rosie are giving a party? Saturday drinks and nibbles. We're both invited.'

'Party?' Her eyes refocused. 'I doan go to parties. And doan call me *Ma*. It's so clower chass.'

That was better. Anything rather than the birthday bit. 'You might go to Max's. They've come here often enough.'

'I might.'

'No need to make up your mind. It's not till Saturday.' Her speech de-serted her in crowds. He knew she wouldn't go. 'Park your bum. I'll open the bottle.'

The lamb chops, crumbed with rosemary to keep them moist, were in the oven, the dinner plates were in the grill compartment above them, getting hot, the potatoes and carrots were stacked in the steamer, with the beans ready to be added later, and the banana custard was cooling on the windowsill. He really was the most well-organised fellow.

She sat down at the table and he opened the wine. It wasn't chilled enough but she didn't complain. He'd been to the police station that af-ternoon and she remembered it so they talked about that. He told her the police said he'd been very helpful and someone would be over in the morn-ing with a new statement for him to sign. She asked about Declan Finsey's Cirencester group and he reported that some of them, three or four, would be joining the Sunday meeting here in Cheltenham. She said they must advertise for a replacement truthsayer in the... she tried for *The Spiritualist Gazette* but its name defeated her. He supplied it for her and suggested that finding a replacement wouldn't be easy—the group was small and Cirencester offered little scope for private clients. Declan had been so perfect because he had a flexible job schedule at the library. She frowned and her gaze wandered.

He leaned sideway, turning on the gas under the steamer. Something had to be said. No moment was good, but this one was better than many.

'I've been thinking,' he said. 'All this paperwork, all this admin—do you really want to be bothered with it? It's pretty boring.'

'Mr Barnaby. I sued and I won. Truthsayer was mine. The SCT was mine. I knew what was what.'

Dear lord... 'Of course you did. You still do. Nobody's questioning that. But—'

'They'd steal the shoes from your feet. A woman has to be watchful. What I always say is.'

He persevered. 'Nobody,' he said gently, 'goes on for ever.'

'Thass true.' She wiped a fleck of dribble from the corner of her mouth. 'Thass what I tell Sandra. Nonsense, she says. There's life in the old girl yet, she says. We laugh. There's life in the old girl yet.'

He stared at her. *Life in the old girl yet...* pure Sandra. His mother would be hanging up cuddly kitten calendars next.

But he'd started. It had to be got over with. 'The SCT's governors want to see you, my dear. Three of them. I've made an appointment for tomorrow afternoon. They—'

'See me? Whaffor? Whaffor they wan to see me?'

Instant outrage. The tone was fierce, the eyes were afraid. He reached for her hand. 'They've decided that—'

'Doan matter. I wan to see them too.' She took her hand carefully away. Her eyes sharpened. Sandra's influence went so far and no further. 'Plans. I've been thinking. Getting better every day. Plans. They woan know what hit them.'

'I'm afraid it's not going to be—'

'Woan know what hit them. I've got plans. Show them who's boss. Sit up and pay attention. What I always say is. Iss my church, Leo. I made it.'

'Of course you made it. But—'

'Cruising. Pottling along. Thass what they're doing. Pottling along. Look at the numbers... Iss my fault. Doan say it. But I'm back now. Plans. A membership campaign. I'm back now. Sit up and pay attention. You tell them, Leo.'

Poor Ma. What could he say to her? The water was boiling fiercely in the steamer under the potatoes and carrots. *Poor Ma?* Garbage. She was a mean old cow. She'd been a mean old cow for as long as he'd known her. What could he say? He scraped his chair back and turned down the gas.

'They're coming the day after tomorrow,' he said. 'It's you they want to see. You know that terrible Carstairs woman. You can tell them yourself. I know they'll listen.'

He'd given up. Today was only Thursday. There'd be other opportunities. Perhaps he'd feel tougher in the morning.

As he'd hoped, the mention of Bunty Carstairs distracted her. They were old enemies. Since her election as president five years earlier Mrs Carstairs had been pushing for decentralisation, greater autonomy to individual meetings. Madam Sara specified voice-only truthsayers. Direct communication. No hanky panky. Some meetings, Mrs Carstairs said, might prefer spirit writing; materialisations even. They ought to be allowed to choose. Madam Sara decried spirit writing as impersonal and over-laborious, and reserved her opinion of materialisations other than to say she didn't believe the radiant spirits had need of them and she'd never known a practitioner who wasn't a fraud. And up to now of course Madam Sara, although impaired, had prevailed.

She prevailed now. As Leo got on with dinner, melting the redcurrent jelly glaze for the carrots, Mrs Carstairs *in absentia* was routed and routed again. The Sauvignon de Touring helped. While Leo, who had no reason to suppose he'd feel tougher tomorrow, regretted having funked the truth. Cruel in order to be kind, that's what was needed.

He laid the table round his mother's vehement elbows and got the now-hot dinner plates out of the oven. God bless the quotidian.

* * * *

It kept him going through dinner and out across the hall to the small drawing room to settle his mother for her hour or so's TV, but it failed him as he returned to the kitchen to face the washing up. They had a machine but he seldom used it. Washing up was satisfactory: you started with a mess and half an hour later you had order. Would that the rest of life was so amenable.

This evening, though, he came close to flinging the whole lot, knives and forks and spoons and pans and plates and bowls and glasses, straight into the rubbish bin. Mashing them down. Crunching them. His day had been unrelievedly terrible. His world was in shreds. Death and destruction, death and destruction. He was like some SF monster, a functioning, human-looking exterior with a shapeless mass of seething secret ugliness inside. And now he was expected to mop at dirty dishes with detergent and a sponge.

For a while he rested his forehead on the brilliant white door of the refrigerator and sobbed. TV noises reached him. Soon his mother would be tired and wanting to go to bed. He straightened his back. Then he mopped at dirty dishes with detergent and a sponge.

Later, when his mother was pilled-up and safely in bed, he went to his grandmother's Bösendorfer in the cavernous front drawing room, and turned the light on beside it. The room was, as always, pompous and depressing, a musty assemblage of swags and ruffles and over-bearing furniture. The piano, though, calm and orderly and immaculate, was always a refuge. Always, but not tonight. Tonight the piano seemed closed to him: steely; frozen.

Death and destruction, death and destruction.

The piano's music stand held Jerome Kern. *Smoke gets in your eyes…* Grandmother Clare and her foxtrots. Leo never danced. He opened the lid of the piano stool. He needed the music for the Ibert Max was planning to play at his party. The first of the *Histoires*, the easy one. He'd been meaning to look it over: the accompaniment had difficult moments. To be honest, most music had difficult moments if you practised as rarely as Leo did these days.

He searched down the dog-eared pile in the music stool. Bach… Poulenc… Grieg from his schooldays… *Albumblätter*, Album Leaves, lord how he'd hated them… He found he was crying again. Where the hell was the bloody Ibert?

The front doorbell rang. The time was ten past nine on a Thursday evening.

His thought was that the police had come for him. He mopped his eyes and hurried to the door, like any good citizen, not wanting to make them wait.

His caller was Canon Beckerton.

'Leo. I saw your light. You don't mind, do you?'

'Saw my light?'

'I was driving past. You were at the piano. Obviously alone. I couldn't resist coming in.'

Driving past? At that time of night? Leo didn't believe a word of it. But he supposed he might be better for some company. His head was a mess. Death and destruc—

He turned on instant sparkle. 'Of course you couldn't. Come along in, Alan. You must share a snort with me. I need cheering up. I'm supposed to be playing for Max at his party on Saturday and you know how I hate practising.'

He led Alan back into the big front room. It wasn't a jolly place, but it was where Grandmother Clare's black-lacquered drinks cupboard lived. He opened the cupboard and peered in doubtfully—neither he nor his mother entertained much.

Alan crossed to a standard lamp with a ruched brocade shade and turned it on. The improvement was minimal. 'There's a chap in the next street over,' he said. 'We play Scrabble once or twice a week. He's losing his sight, poor man, but he can just about see the letters on the pieces. Can't read, though. Not even the large print editions. It's a terrible loss.'

Leo moved bottles. 'Port? Madeira? A dribble of Scotch? There's brandy but I suspect it's only fit for a rural dean.'

'I'll risk the brandy. Something to hold, really.' He sat in the chair that Charlie from the *Mirror* had found so disproportionate, and filled it more successfully. 'I've been concerned about you, Lee.'

Leo wasn't surprised. He groped for glasses on the bottom shelf. 'It's the window you look through, Alan. You're a clergyman. It's a concern-shaped window.' He stood up with the brandy decanter and two fairly suitable glasses, put them on the mahogany pedestal table by Alan's chair, and squatted on a nearby footstool. 'I'm fine,' he said. 'You needn't worry.'

'You didn't look fine yesterday. You don't look fine tonight. I'm poking my nose in, I know. But you're right—the window I look through *is* concern-shaped. And not just because I'm a clergyman. I've known you a long time, Lee. I—'

Suddenly, in a vivid flash of understanding, Leo remembered why, yesterday, he hadn't looked so fine. Why and what to do about it. Grandmother Clare's foxtrots. *Smoke gets in your eyes.* He'd never danced. Obvious, really. He'd never danced. It all went back to his mother. To Madam Sara.

'It's the dancing,' he said, and laughed extravagantly. 'That's what the trouble is. *Smoke gets in your eyes...* I'm not properly hearing the music.'

'The music?'

'That's what the trouble is.'

'What music?'

' You're being stupid, Alan. How can I dance if I can't properly hear the music?'

' Dance? You mean dance at the party? You're talking about the party? Max's party?'

'Dancing, Alan. It's what I never do.'

'At Max's party?'

'Max's party? You're crazy. Of course I'm not talking about Max's idiotic party. Why should I talk about Max's sodding party? I'm talking about—' He tailed off. What *was* he talking about? Dancing? He'd never danced. Over-large. Clumsy. No sense of rhythm. His mother said so. He was appalled.

Lurching forward, he jostled the table, caught the decanter as it teetered. 'Pardon my French, Alan. I was thinking of something else. Something quite different.' He removed the decanter's stopper, slopped brandy into both their glasses. What *had* he been thinking of? His mother's words?

How pathetic. All those years ago? How pathetic.

He gathered more recent, more useful memories. Built on them.

'I was remembering those Austrian peasants. Max's Austrian peasants. He says... Max says they dance at the time of the autumn solstice. Or they used to. Something to do with frightening away witches. But they didn't always hear the music.'

He brightly smiled at Alan and sat back, warming the brandy in his sweaty hands. It wasn't perfect, but he thought it sounded pretty good. It made a sort of sense. What the hell had he *really* been thinking of? *Christ...* He was breaking up worse than he'd feared.

'That must have been before those terrible Bavarian oom-pah euphonium people,' Alan said cheerfully. 'Nobody could fail to hear those.'

Alan was a professional. Jokes already. He'd done this before. His expression of friendly, unjudgemental interest hadn't sharpened by the smallest degree. Leo noticed and was grateful.

'I've a feeling Max made up the whole story,' he said, following Alan's lead. 'That's Max. You can never tell if he's being completely serious.'

'How is your friend these days?'

'Not good. Not good.'

'I'm sorry to hear that. You're very fond of him, aren't you?'

'He's been very good to me.' Leo tried the brandy. It was rather nasty. He drank some more. He'd never much liked brandy. 'He and his wife, they've been very good to me.'

'I don't imagine you've been exactly horrid to them. Relationships work both ways, you know.' Alan left a pause for Leo to fill. Leo stayed silent. 'Your friend in Cirencester who died a few days ago—you were very fond of him too.' A statement.

'Declan? Fond? I don't know about *fond*...'

'A weak word. You're right, Lee. How about, *you loved him*?'

Leo flushed. At last, a simple question with a simple answer. No more of the grubby evasions he so hated. For once, he could be totally truthful. 'Loved him? Certainly not. Not at all. No.'

'Oh, come on lad. This is me you're talking to. I could see how upset you were the other night. And of course I understand how hard it must be, even these days, not being able to admit your grief. Having to pretend. But not here, Lee. We know each other too well for that.'

Leo had a sour urge to laugh. The conceit of the man. Alan understood nothing at all. Declan weeping, scraping, dying on the concrete. Leo fucking his sick friend's wife. Lies to the police, lies to his mother. Lies to Rosie. Grubby evasions. Death and destruction. Alan understood nothing at all.

But he'd come to help. He was a kind man. He meant well.

The two of them hadn't exactly talked about it, lord no, but Alan knew he was queer. A long-distant wife and son were acknowledged, but they'd been left discreetly vague: early experimentation perhaps, attempts at the conventional. Alan was a solitary: he might well be homo himself, or as homo as his god would allow.

There was a puzzle, though, and it usefully shifted the conversation away from Leo himself.

'Who the hell told you Declan was queer, Alan? You never met him, did you? And in any case, he never advertised it.'

'I'm on Cheltenham's library board that hired him. I made enquiries. The police told me—confidentially, of course—that they knew him. Cruising and so on. Nothing they could prove. I pushed to get him taken on. He came with excellent references.'

'Nobody minded his connections with Spiritualism?'

'Some did. You know my answer. The C of E has always accepted an afterlife, visions, messages... Not in my line, obviously, but the doctrine's clear.' Alan put down his glass, its contents untasted. It *had* been simply to hold. 'There's nothing shameful in grieving for a lover.'

A lover? Leo started to protest. Dear lord, what catastrophes came from the dangerously different meanings of that word. Had he been Dekko's lover? Of course. Had he been Dekko's *lover*? Never. It was an important distinction... He started to protest but then he reconsidered. Should he really be so picky? At this moment? Better for Alan's peace of mind that he admitted to both than to the true causes of his distress.

'You're right, Alan. Of course you are.' He modestly lowered his gaze. 'Thank you for saying it.'

And Alan blundered on. 'Bereavement is a complex matter, Lee. A natural process, of course it is. But society these days is mostly in denial. You're not supposed to brood. You're supposed to brace up and get on with living. And added to all that, of course, being gay you have an acceptability problem.' He paused. 'If you thought you'd like some help I could put you on to a therapist I know in Gloucester. Transactional therapy. Which basically means she goes for the now rather than for the details of your potty training. She's very good.'

Therapy. Transactional therapy. Any sort of therapy. Ah, if only.

Leo forced down the last of his brandy. 'I'll see how things go.' What else was needed? Oh—'And I'm very grateful.'

'Don't leave it too long. Lee. I mean it.' Alan took out his wallet and a pen, found a piece of paper, wrote down a telephone number and held it out. 'Mary Figges. For my sake. She's very good.'

Leo took the paper. Stood up. 'I'll see how I do. And thanks again.'

Alan didn't take the hint. 'How's your mother these days? Haven't seen her for quite a while.'

"Ma?' Leo tried to remember. 'Oh, she's fine. She's sticking with her blood pills and physically she's fine. The aphasia's hit a bit of a plateau but she's working on it. She ought to get out more, take more exercise, but you can't have everything.'

'Excellent. Glad to hear it.' Leo got the impression that he hadn't heard a word. 'Ever think of taking a break?' he went on. 'Go off on your own? Change of scene? Hire a live-in nurse for a couple of weeks? You could do with a breather.'

That concerned-shaped hole again. Bless him. Alan didn't give up.

But he was such a bloody idiot. Somebody ought to tell him.

'I really do have to practise, Alan. We're rehearsing tomorrow morning, and—'

'Of course. It's nearly my bedtime anyway.' He joined Leo and together they walked out into the hall. 'I've been pushy, I know. But—'

'Nonsense.' Opening the door. Shoving him through. Well, almost. 'That's what friends are for.'

'Think about it, Lee. What I've been saying. Think about it.'

'I really will.' Closing the door. 'I really will.'

Leave Ma? Hire a nurse? One second longer there on the doorstep and Leo might have done his clerical friend an injury.

Back at the piano stool the Ibert was just two sheets down from the top of the pile. He didn't see how he could have missed it. But the notes on the staves remained elusive. He poked at piano keys with stumpy starfish fingers. Nothing came right. He tried again, counting the quavers.

Where had all that dancing stuff come from?

He never danced.

CHAPTER 6

Friday morning, after he'd fed Rumple, when he took in his mother's breakfast tray, Madam Sara ate her egg—poached on Fridays—almost without noticing it—she was full of her new plans for the SCT. Evidently her early sleepless hours had been fruitfully filled—which is more than could have been said for his. The Church, she told him, was in need of new blood and she had a membership drive in mind, something that would appeal to younger people.

He escaped back to the kitchen as soon as he could and poured out his usual bowl of sugar-free meusli. He'd known that it wasn't going to be easy, telling her what the Elders had decided, and this latest enthusiasm wasn't making it any easier. He still had a bit of time, though. The immediate priority was the mess inside his head. He'd purloined two more of his mother's Oblivons last night, but they hadn't helped much.

The trouble was, the problems he had were insoluble. They were all associated with people—Coade, Wiler, Henry, Peterson, Alan, Rosie, Max, Bunty Carstairs, his mother—so dealing with them depended on variables completely beyond his control. Usually that thought would have been a comfort. He wasn't an innovator. He waited for life to happen to him, then he did his best to cope. He didn't fret. If unwelcome events proved to be beyond his control he sighed and accepted them. He was, as has already been said, an excellent accepter. But not this time round. This time round life was happening to him with an ingenuity far beyond any acceptance. So what next? If the problems he had were unacceptable but could not be made to go away, what happened next? Leo had no idea.

The telephone on the wall by the refrigerator rang. Nothing he'd want to hear about, he guessed, getting up from his meusli and answering it.

'Leo? Gordon here. Sorry for the hour. Got your message. Meant to call yesterday. Chaos this end. Bloody flu—two able bodies missing. Look, what say you do us the obit? Photo too if you—'

Deckan's obit? Dear lord. 'Absolutely not, Gordon. No obit. No obit.'

'Far and away the right person. You knew the poor man. Eight hundred words. You know the sort of thing. Usual—'

'I said no, Gordon. It's simply not something I feel I could—'

'Eight hundred words. Need them this evening. Saturday's edition. You're just the fellow. Usual fee. We'll—'

'Fee?" If Leo had needed a final straw, that was it. 'You're not listening to me, Gordon. No fee and no obituary. That's final.'

'Don't be like that. You're going to need me one day, then you'll be sorry. Look, I simply don't have a spare man. And you can put in a puff for your old mum's church. What say I give you a by-line? Doesn't your dead Mister Whatsisname deserve a few moments of—'

'Finsey. Declan Finsey.'

'Say again?'

'His name, Gordon. Declan Finsey. You might at least have bothered to-'

'Eight hundred words. Six will do. Look, I'm right up against it. Won't there be a memorial service? You'll want to mention that. Next of kin. Photo too.'

'No photo.' Leo's determination was crumbling

'Maybe the *Echo* will have something on the file.'

'I doubt it. Declan wasn't the sort of man who—'

'You were friends. Who could do this better?'

'And what about the police? Shouldn't you wait until they've finished their—?'

'As a case it's a non-starter. Trust me. They have to ask questions. It's their job. It's what they do. That's all. Your friend was alone. He fell from his balcony. You'll see. Trust me.'

'All the same…'

'Do it for me, Leo. Please.'

'Six hundred words?'

'By six pm. I'll send round a lad. And I won't forget it.'

'You're a bully, Gordon.'

'Six pm. I'll send round a lad. Knew I could rely on you.'

'And no fee. I mean that. Give it to the cats' home. Declan liked cats.'

But the line was buzzing at him. He hung up the handset.

He'd been wrong about the phone call. In its last moments it had brought him the first bit of good news he'd had in days. In all his life. The police weren't all that bothered. Gordon was having one of his hunches and his hunches were usually right. They wouldn't be grubbing around, looking for a Henry. Their questions were just formality. And better even than that, Leo had just had the thought that perhaps he could write stuff in Dekko's obituary, good stuff, generous stuff, stuff that would make up for, in some tiny fashion would make up for what he'd done.

Make up for? It was a thought that lasted for only a moment. Not even that. A nano-moment but still shameful. Make up for? Words on a page? In some tiny fashion? Make up for what he'd done? Words on a page? Shitty words on a shitty page? *Dear God…*

He grabbed at the handset. Its white curled-up cable stretched as he tugged at it. Tugged at it, puffing and grunting. It stretched and stretched, refused to break, refused to dramatise his shame, refused to drag the rest of the telephone out from the wall or the house down around him in ruins. Refusing to care, the cable just stretched and stretched as he tugged at it, puffed and grunted.

So where then, ah dear sweet Jesus, did all honour go? All honour, dignity, shame, basic human decency? Words on a page. Words on a page.

Madam Sara was calling from her bedroom. Leo closed his eyes and rested, rested against the edge of the kitchen table. 'Coming. Coming…'

He hung up the handset. Its white curled-up cable, longer now, dangled almost to the floor. He jiggled it upwards, to no effect. 'Coming. Coming…'

He mopped his face on the dish towel that hung on the rail along the top of the oven door. It would have to do. There wasn't a mirror in the kitchen.

All that OTT stuff, it really did happen. Leo remembers it clearly, even now, all too clearly. It's not popped in here just for dramatic effect. It really did happen. Its immoderacy tied in with the previous night's lapse when he told Alan all about dancing and not being able to hear the band. That too, he swears, really did happen.

He replaced the dish towel on the rail and went out along the corridor, along to Madam Sara. 'Bloody cat,' he told her. 'Winding round my legs, tripped me up, had my hands full. Banged my head on the refrigerator. Bloody thing. Sorry about that.'

She sat up in bed, glared at him. He rescued her breakfast tray

'Scared me half to death.' One of her Sandra phrases, he thought, re-covered enough now to notice. 'All that banging.'

She didn't ask after his poor sore head, aching from the refrigerator. He wouldn't have expected her to. Madam Sara had never found other people's abrasions very interesting.

Apologising again to her, to Declan, to the world, he backed from the room, taking her emptied breakfast tray with him.

Today being Friday, which of course was another Hoppy day, it re-quired Madam Sara, who had her pride, to present herself properly dressed. Also, since Leo had warned her that the police would be coming again, this time with a statement for him to sign, there was always the chance that they might want to speak to her too, or that she might bump into them. Ac-cidentally, of course. And finally, since this was the first day of the newly invigorated Madam Sara, ready to take control of Her Church again, there was perhaps the further thought that her comfy old dressing gown days were best put behind her.

In any case, whatever the cumulative reasons—the speculation is mine, Leo having other matters on his mind—his mother quickly let his noisy behaviour in the kitchen rest, and rose ponderously from her bed to shower and consider the contents of her wardrobe.

Leo, keeping himself protectively busy, washed up their breakfast things. Thanks to Graham's unwitting reassurance his list of unsolvable unacceptables no longer included Coade's investigations, but plenty of others remained. He knew that if his day was to be even remotely manageable it needed to be rigorously apportioned. The hour was eight twenty-five, a police officer was coming at nine fifteen, therefore fifty spare minutes now needed to be filled. He dithered briefly by the sink, then settled for the nomination form envelopes waiting to be stuffed and stamped in his office bedsit. And after them—eight minutes?—would come first-draught Declan obit time. Thirty-odd minutes of that, to be followed by statement signing time. Perfect. Off he went. Hardly had he stamped the last envelope, however, before it bore in on him that a rehearsal with Max loomed at tennish and his piano practice the previous night had been a calamity.

He was at the Bösendorfer therefore, in Jacque Ibert's demanding company when, only ten minutes later, his mother required urgent help with an inside-out sleeve, and he was still with her at nine thirty, unjamming a side zip, when Hoppy—who had arrived as always shortly after nine—knocked on her bedroom door to announce the police, waiting in the front hall

* * * *

The police: the phrase sounded ominously plural, more than just a humble constable wanting his signature. And it turned out to be so.

'Ah, Mr Bresson...' Coade, jaw clenched on an empty pipe. 'A fine morning, wouldn't you say?'

'Would I, Chief Inspector?' He hadn't noticed. His day that far had been occupied with other matters than the weather. He turned to Coade's companion. 'Good morning, Sergeant Wiler. How can I help you both?'

'I have your statement, Mr Bresson.' She produced a neatly-folded print-out. 'If you would just—'

'And after I've signed it?'

Coade examined his pipe and tucked it, safely cold, into his breast pocket. 'Mr Bresson has put two-and-two together, Anthea. My presence here correctly suggests to him further issues. A few more questions, Mr Bresson? If you don't mind?'

Of course he minded. Christ. Of course he minded.

'Not at all, Chief Inspector. Always glad to be helpful.' He paused, trying to remember if he'd made his bed. Risked it. 'We'll use my office.'

He led them through. The bed was fine. 'I'm afraid I've only got the one spare chair.'

The weather ameliorated this. Coade had been right: unusually bright sunshine beamed in through the window.

'The corner of the desk will do for me.' Coade perched on it. 'So this is where you work.'

'More or less.' In fact it was where he lived. It was all he had that was unequivocally his.

He took the swivel chair in front of his computer and Detective Sergeant Wiler sat in the spare chair beside his empty terrarium. She had a computer print-out on her knee, presumably his statement, and her notebook open on top of it. Sounds of Happy hoovering filtered in. Coade pushed the door shut with one foot.

'I'm afraid you haven't been entirely open with us, Mr Bresson.'

His guts clenched. 'Haven't I? In what way?'

'Understandable, perhaps, but not useful. The matter of sexuality, Mr Bresson. Hm? Yours and Mr Finsey's. You questioned its relevance.'

His guts unclenched. He'd made plans for this days ago, right at the beginning. ' I didn't see how it applied. I still don't. It's not a crime to be homosexual.'

'It can become a hotbed for criminality, however. All the secrecy. Blackmail, for example. I'm sure you understand me.'

'Of course I understand you. But Declan and me were discreet. We never advertised being queer. And besides, as I told you, that was over with weeks ago. So where's the relevance?'

Coade nodded a little wearily. 'We've had members of the public coming into the station, Mr Bresson. They're demanding that we provide a list of all known homosexuals. Castration is talked about. There are some who would like to see them made to wear a wear a badge.'

'As bad as that? Like the Nazis and the Jews? I don't believe it.' He did, of course. He lived in the real world. But not here in Cheltenham. It saddened him. 'The poor souls. They must be crazy.'

'But you didn't think it relevant.'

'I know there's prejudice around.' Leo heard himself. The year's worst understatement. Ashamed, he changed the subject. 'These people. You're not going to tell me who any of them are I suppose?'

'I don't think that would be helpful.'

'I do. I think it would help me keep out of their way.'

'People who come forward to the police have the right to expect confidentiality.'

Coade's evasion was blatant. Leo thought a little outrage was justified. 'And you're bothering me now on the strength of local bigotry. I'm surprised at you, Chief Inspector.'

Coade shifted his uncomfortable position on the corner of the desk. 'At least we know now that our protesters are right about Mr Finsey's sexual orientation.'

Which was hardly an apology. Could any of this have anything to do with motel man Henry? Leo thought that unlikely. Henry had hardly seemed to be a rabid anti-homo protester. Not a rabid anything, actually.

'Mr Bresson?'

Leo started. 'I'm sorry. I was thinking…why are you telling me this, Chief Inspector?'

He knew why. Just more picking at him. Chipping away… For god's sake, the whole protest story could well be an invention. In any case, for once Graham's hunch had been wrong. Coade was still hoping to break him. 'These members of the publid, sir—are you allowed to say if any of them are associated with the SCT?'

'No comment.' Coade spoke abruptly, frowning. 'You're trying to push me, Mr Bresson. I will say, though, that nobody I've seen at the station has any connection whatsoever with your mother's Spiritualist Church of Truth.'

Which was thoughtful of him. So none of them were truthsayers. 'Thank you, Chief Inspector.' At least he wouldn't look sideways at the SCT's mediums in the weeks ahead, and wonder.

Coade went on. 'And as for my reasons for telling you, Mr Bresson, the relevance should be clear enough. Your personal position. The relevance…'

'More stuff for me to add to my statement?'

'I don't think so. My sergeant has her notes.' He pushed his spectacles fustily up his nose. 'One final observation, though. A few minutes ago, at the beginning of this conversation, when I told you about the protesters and what they were saying, your reply to me was…'

Tailing off, he made a small beckoning gesture with one bony finger. Detective Sergeant Wiler quickly picked up her cue and flipped back through her notebook. 'He called them poor souls, boss'. She found the place and quoted. 'He said, "They must. be crazy."'

'Thank you, Anthea. You weren't annoyed, Mr Bresson. Hm? You simply said they were poor souls and they were crazy.'

'So?'

'People were spouting vicious sexist slogans and yet you weren't noticeably angry.'

'I seldom am. I don't do anger. Anyway, they have to be crazy. Not responsible.' A comfortable thought. Very Max. 'Either that or what they're saying is true. Which it isn't.'

He wasn't certain, but fleetingly it seemed to him that Coade's eyes and his sergeant's had met. It suggested that a point had been made. He'd no idea what.

Coade glanced at his watch. 'Thank you for your time, Mr Bresson.' He eased himself down off the desk. 'The statement, please Anthea.'

Leo tried again, more boldly. There had to be something more. 'That's it, then? No new evidence? Just sexist rabble on police station property?'

'Mr Bresson's statement, please Anthea.'

D S Wiler had been unfolding the print-out. Now she smoothed it, put it on his desk, and tapped it firmly. 'Signature and date, please sir.'

He gave up, leaned forward, looking awkwardly for the print-out's final sheet. He'd completely lost interest in what might be in it. 'Where do I sign?'

'You must read it first, sir.'

'It's awfully long. I'm sure you've got it all right.'

Coade leaned forward and squared the disordered print-out. 'Even the police someimes make mistakes. Your signature is legally very important. Hm? It says you've read it and you approve. Otherwise, sir, you could always say we set you up.'

The detective sergeant's tone was light. Her meaning wasn't.

Leo gave in. He turned over the pages of the print-out one by one, head down, letting his gaze wander. He was totally exhausted. Bloody Coade.

After what he hoped was a plausibly lengthy scanning delay, during which the chief inspector dug his empty pipe out of his pocket and sucked on it noisily, Leo let himself reach the final page, took up his pen, wrote his name and the date on the dotted line. There really was one.

'Good of you, sir.' D S Wiler took the papers from him and refolded them. 'That's it, then.'

Coade was already at the door. He seemed unreasonably pleased with life. As if their visit had achieved some hoped-for result. He opened the door and went out into the hall, followed by the sergeant. Madam Sara, who must have been watching and waiting, just happened to emerge from the drawing room opposite.

'Good morning. I know you, Sergeant Miler.' She turned to the chief inspector. "We havn met. My name is Madam Sara Bresson. I'm the founder and director of the Spiritualist Church of Truth.'

It was a fine effort. And her hard-to-get-at side zip seemed to be in excellent order. Perhaps Hoppy had helped.

'Chief Inspector Coade, Ma'am.' Discreetly pocketing his pipe again.

'How do you do.' Her hands stayed lightly clasped at about waist level. His mother's left arm tended to dangle a bit if it wasn't held in place. 'Iss a fine morning. My son have been helping you, I think.'

Leo inserted himself. 'The chief inspector's just leaving, Mother. He's a very busy man.'

'Well, yes,' Coade admitted with a professionally charming smile. 'I do have rather a lot on my plate this morning. But I'm very pleased to have met you, Madam Bresson. My sergeant tells me she's had a really interesting talk with you.'

'We talked about my son. A member of the rugby first fiffleteen at Cheltenham College.'

'For heaven's sake, Mother, that was only because—' Leo stopped himself. Coade really didn't need to be told that every other possible second row forward had had chicken pox that week. 'Well Chief Inspector, if you need me again you know where to find me.' He chuckled cheerily. 'We're not planning any world tours, are we mother?'

'World whats? I've got plans too. No more pottling along. What I always say is. Woan know what hit them.'

'Of course you have plans, Mother.' He hated to see her slipping so quickly. It had to be on account of the sense of occasion that Coade brought with him. He was impressive, Leo conceded as he led him round his mother to the door. Empty pipe and rumpled suit or no empty pipe and crumpled suit.

'You're busy man too, Leo. Look at the time.' She nodded at Clare's long-case clock. 'Iss nearly ten.'

'I'm being reminded,' Leo explained to his visitors as he showed them out, 'that I need to get going. I'm supposed to be somewhere else.'

'Good of you to have spared us the time, Mr Bresson.' Coade looked back into the hall, where Madam Sara was still standing. 'Pleased to have met you, Ma'am. You have a fine house here. And good luck with your plans.'

He went away down the sunlit path, closely tailed by D S Wiler. At the gate, he paused. 'Mr Finsey's sisters will be making the funeral arrangements,' he told Leo. 'When the time comes. I understand your organisation has no strong views in the matter.'

It might have been intended as a question, but if it was the chief inspector gave Leo no easy opportunity to answer, striding briskly off down Tivoli Street, his sergeant still in tow, presumably in the direction of their car.

'Nice man.' Leo's mother had come up behind him and was looking over his shoulder. 'Nice man.'

Leo didn't disabuse her. She might even be right.

* * * *

At tennish that Friday morning Leo too, his old initialled school music case under his arm, was walking away from Madam Sara's house on Tivoli Street, pausing to post his bundle of nomination form envelopes in the red octagonal VR pillar-box on the corner. The radiance of the day had wooed him from the Jag. Also his need for a quiet fifteen minutes to himself before rehearsal stresses set in. Fifteen minutes of walking, just one foot in front of another, and thinking absolutely nothing. Not even Coade's unexpected visit. For Leo walking sometimes made that possible.

Let it today, please god.

And today, bless him, god obliged.

The Friday morning streets were quiet. The sun had dried out the worst of Cheltenham's damp. Tall golden terraces, proportionate and discreetly pillared, curved fittingly behind their iron railings. Cats soaked up the warmth on windowsills. Au pairs walked dogs and children. Butterflies wafted themselves fleetingly among dusty buddleia fronds.

Ahead of Leo, just as he reached Montepellier Street, a soft rushing sort of roar came from the north, more or less in front of him, and a small column of dust and possibly smoke rose above the rooftops, spreading gently sideways on the wind. Another of the city's Georgian houses out beyond Pitville had either succumbed naturally to the general mining subsidence there or had been demolished ahead of it. The maze of underground workings that had once brought prosperity to the town was now mined out and dangerous. Bits of Cheltenham, some of the classier bits, were falling in.

His grandmother's choice of area—and therefore his mother's and Leo's too—had been lucky. Even as recently as 1950 there'd been few warning signs. Back in the forties Clare could just as easily have bought property out in classy Regency Pitville as in Victorian Tivoli. The pit-head buildings long gone. Pitville at that time had been a very fancy location.

Leo crossed the Upper Promenade by the Wintergarden and arrived in Parabola Road. The Krauss-Häbers' terrace had shiny bitter-smelling laurels with yellow-edged leaves in its narrow front gardens. This was the middle of the town. Geologically very stable.

Rosie let him in. She looked terrible. Leo rejoined the world of sickness and pain.

'He's ready and waiting,' she said brightly. 'I see you've brought your music.'

Max was in the cluttered living room, sitting by the upright rosewood Steck, puffing into his flute to warm it for tuning. As usual these days he'd chosen his wooden instrument, of French manufacture: it spoke more readily and didn't have the silver concert flute's edge, which made it more suitable for ordinary room acoustics. From the window bright panels of sunlight slanted across the dusty carpet. Max hadn't shaved and he was still in his nightshirt and dressing gown. Music asserted its own priorities and a dome he was family.

Returning briefly to Cheltenham's subsidence problems, it's likely that some readers will be peevishly thinking that they've lived in Cheltenham all their lives and they've never seen a bloody coal-mine within a hundred miles of the place. Not a one. Not coal, nor copper nor lead either. No mines. That's understandable. But the explanation is very simple: they're thinking of another Cheltenham. Not Leo's. Theirs. Which is fair enough. Furthermore, their Cheltenham, with no coal mines, sounds much nicer than Leo's, but that's not the point. The point is, this story is about Leo, and his Cheltenham had clearly once had coal mines, since it now had subsidence above where they've been.

OK?

Back, then, to Max's cluttered living room.

'Welcome,' he said as Leo came in. 'We've got a lot to do.' The sections of his flute squeaked faintly as he pressed them together. 'And I don't last.'

Leo sat down at the piano, gave him an A. Max puckered and blew.

This was preposterous. Another world. He felt far, far away. He told Max, 'You're going to have to be patient with me.'

'When was I ever...' Max over-blew a shade, then settled. 'We'll start with the Handel slow movement. Something we know.'

Rosie leaned round the door behind them. 'I'm just off to the library. Anything you want?'

'*Leb' wohl...*' Max blew her a kiss and she went away, closing the door behind her.

Leo leafed through his Handel book of sonatas, found the page by its tattered upper corner and spread it on the rack. Max played the piece from memory. A tiny nod and they started.

To begin with Leo simply played the notes, mostly the right ones in this familiar composition, and the sounds were disciplined and pleasant in the sunlit room. By the first repeat he could feel the wildness in his head diminish, smoothed by the sounds and the surprising neatness of his fingers. Max leaned closer, eyes shut, listening, totally absorbed. They agreed to dare the scampering final movement and on the second time through Leo was listening too, hearing the music, and had forgotten about fingers and notes and daunting words like *presto*. Two people, but becoming larger than two. No, not larger. Not more truthful either. Leo's never found the word for it. He gets embarrassed. Romantic stuff and nonsense.

They moved on to some Johann Quantz. Earlier but more demanding: whole pages that could easily become just finger exercises. Max called a break. He was breathless and Leo saw that his hands were shaking as he lowered the flute. He went away, slowly, to the bathroom, was gone for quite a while. When he came back he seemed much recovered. They started the Ibert.

The *Histoires* were short pieces, very youthful, little melodic narratives, not obviously difficult, modern in feeling but seldom strident, and Max said the trick was to keep the story going. Then he shook his head, too much lit. crit., and said the trick was just to play them. The first two, he thought, one perky, one langorous, would be enough. Five minutes in all, if that. Rosie had warned their guests roughly what to expect, but some of them would quickly fidget.

The trick indeed was just to play them. The sunlight on the carpet moved significantly as Max and Leo laboured, fighting the temptation to slow down the perky one for the sake of Leo's sloppy fingers and to speed up the langorous one for the sake of Max's lack of puff. It needed to be fought. Part of the point of playing these two was for the contrast. And as encore Dvorak's crowd-pleasing *Humoresque,* in Max's own arrangement which they could play in their sleep, for the giggle. The rest of the floor-show would be the organist woman from Christchurch, giving *Jesu, Joy* in the Myra Hess arrangement, which was a no-fail winner. Her name was Myra Bunn and she was actually a very nice performer.

Noon came, with Rosie still out at the library. Or wherever. She'd have foreseen their difficult morning and she wouldn't have hurried. Finally Max called a halt. He was worn out, his face bloodless and damp with sweat (Leo, who hadn't said a word, would have stopped far earlier), but until the actual moment when he put down his flute, the demands of the music had sustained him. Then, suddenly, he was very old. Then, suddenly, like all of us but more immediately than most, he was dying.

'Lunch,' he said. 'And a good burgundy to wash down my pills.'

Rosie had laid it all out, ready in the kitchen for Leo to carry in. Food, wine, plates, cutlery, a corkscrew, glasses, four tiny plastic pill bottles. Leo opened the wine.

When he returned to the living room with the tray, Max was back on his sofa. He seemed asleep but he sat up briskly enough.

'You're a good fellow,' he said. 'A thoroughly good fellow.'

'You don't know me,' Leo told him, pouring a sturdy glass of wine, 'like I know me.'

'True.' Max accepted the glass. 'Two bars before the *accelerando,*' he said. 'That *tam*-tiddy. Not too heavy on the *tam*, don't you think?'

Leo left Max's some ten minutes later, first tucking a blanket round Max's shoulders. Rosie was still out, but Max said she wouldn't be much longer and he could perfectly well manage. Leo's pretext was the Declan obit he had to write: his true reason was Max's clear need to be alone with his pain.

Briefly, as he walked away down Parabola Road, Leo had a problem. Max must be perfectly aware that he himself was no more than ordinarily competent on his instrument, and Leo far less so on his, and that any perfor-mance they gave, no matter how carefully prepared, could never be other than really rather dreadful. Where the hell, therefore, did Max's literally life-threatening degree of intensity come from, his concern for the music, and how the hell—even more inexplicably—did it manage to spill over onto his accompanist?

It was an interesting question. Sadly, though, not interesting enough. Two minutes later, forty paces down the road, and Leo's wider life had battered in through to him, and this time the walking didn't help. Leo's wider life included concrete, scraping, Mr Peterson, and now Coade's informant.

He kept on walking. The moment he entered No. 81 on Tivoli Street, as if he hadn't enough on his plate, he knew there was something wrong. Hoppy and his mother should have been having lunch in the kitchen, a cheerful, chatty affair, but the house was silent.

He banged the door and called. 'I'm back. Yoo-hoo. Sorry it took so long. Where are you? Where's Hoppy?'

'Go away!' Madam Sara limped down the passage from her bedroom, her good arm raised, pointing. 'Go away! Get out of my house!'

'For heaven's sake, Mother. What's happened? What's the matter?'

'Snake. Get out, snake. Snake in the glass!'

He backed against the closed front door. 'Come on, Ma. Calm down. Tell me. Tell me what's happened.' But he already knew. He couldn't imagine *how* it had happened, but he knew there was only one event that could have caused such anger.

'Carn wait till I'm dead.' She stood by the foot of the stairs, her arm still raised. 'Narp. Dump me. Silly old idgit. Thass right. Dump me.'

'Not me, Mother.' Somebody'd told her about the Elders' decision. He'd known it. 'I wouldn't do that—you must know that. The bloody Elders. It was the—'

'Get out. Carn you hear? Get out of my house.'

Away down the passage in his office-bedsit the telephone started ringing. He ignored it.

'The Elders had a special meeting. They took a vote. It was a unanimous decision. I should have told you.' He walked towards her. 'Bunty Carstairs? You remember Bunty Carstairs?'

The name, as he'd intended, sparked a memory. They'd been talking about Mrs Carstairs only yesterday. Her arm wavered and she let him take it and lower it gently to her side. 'Doan touch me.'

'Bunty Carstairs. Over in Pitville. She's only their spokeswoman, but—'

'I remember Bunty Carstairs… Scout mistress. I call her girl scout mistress.'

'A good name. I know you did. She's the Senior Elder now.'

'And she banjax me?'

'Not just her. All the Elders. They banjaxed you.'

He held her hand in both of his and stroked it, watching the anxious thoughts behind her eyes as she looked up at him. He knew what would be coming next and got in first.

'I didn't tell you, dear, because I couldn't bear to. I told you they wanted to see you but I didn't tell you why. I kept on putting it off. I was looking for the right time and it never seemed to come. I'm sorry. Very sorry.'

'You should tell me.'

'I know.'

His office telephone stopped ringing as the answerphone clicked in.

'You should, Leo.'

'I know.' He put an arm round her shoulders.

She dwindled. Without the anger she wasn't very much. 'That man say an election. I doan remember no election.'

'It's in the by-laws. If there's a tie you get the casting vote.' He frowned. 'What man?'

'Telephone. Smarmy.' Her outrage sparked again. 'My telephone. In my room. My telephone, not office. Smarmy.'

'What did he want?'

'Ha. My job. Says he was sorry to hear. That Courtband. Sorry to hear the news. Wants me to know it. Ha. Smarmy. Wants me on his side. Wants my job is what.'

'You're talking about Graham Courtland over in Ledbury.' It had to be. Calling straight through on her private line. The personal touch. A cunning man. Ambitious, opportunist... smarmy. It had to be Graham. Madam S had seen through him right away.

'Courtband. Thass right. Came from America. I remember him. Not right for job but nobody asks me.'

Graham Courtland. He'd been right for the job then, a decided success. He could well be right for this new job now.

'Of course we asked you, Mother. That was before your last stroke. We needed someone urgently and you told the Elders he was fine. Afterwards you told me that it didn't matter how awful he was because he wouldn't stay.'

'Wrong. I was wrong. He still here.'

'People like him, Mother. He's done well.'

'Smarmy, Leo, clower chass.'

Blessèd are the smarmy, Leo thought, for they will inherit the earth. 'Anyway, Scout Mistress Carstairs is the Church's Senior Elder these days. And she's worse than ever. She and two others are coming to see you tomorrow afternoon. They're going to explain about what's been decided.'

'Good.' She shook his arm off her shoulders. 'I've decided too.'

'I'm afraid they won't like that. They've had a meeting. I told you. It's all being done according to the SCT's by-laws.'

'Doan tell me that. Didn I write them? Didn I?' She turned angrily away and started back along the passage. 'You'll see. Woan know what hit them. Woan know what hit them.'

'Mother…' He called after her. 'Mother—where's Hoppy? Did you send her away? What happened?'

Madam Sara paused. 'None of her business. *Do this, Madam Sara. Do that, Madam Sara…* What I always say is. None of her business. After Courtband I was very angry.'

Leo could imagine it. 'So you sent her away.'

His mother was on the move again. 'Very angry.' Having second thoughts. 'I was very angry. You must call and kiss it better.' She disappeared into the small rear sitting room.

Leo was struck by a sudden flash-back. His grandmother's voice: *Shall Granny kiss it better, dear?* The memory was untimely, sharp and extremely painful. Grandmother Clare had been good to him. Good and kind, good and kind… That stupid bloody woman who'd just lumbered off down the corridor, when had she ever bloody offered to kiss something better for him? *If I stammered as badly as you I wouldn't try to talk so much…* And now he was supposed to care that she might have hurt Hoppy's feelings. He was supposed to care that the SCT's Elders were finally giving her the old heave-ho. He was supposed to do up her buttons and buy her freeze-dried coffee and listen to her *rrragged rrrascal.* He was supposed to ring up Hoppy and kiss things better. He was supposed to care.

And all the while Declan. And all the while Declan.

The telephone rang again in his office. Being available and with no excuse, he went and answered it. He was losing his grip, he was pretty far gone, but not yet quite that far.

Gordon from the *Echo*, very brotherly and laddish, was asking after Declan Finsey's obituary. Leo told him it was going well. It would be ready for Gordon's boy at six.

After he'd rung off he looked in his Applemac. A document called *Declan Obit* was there but it looked to be completely blank. Leo was puzzled. He'd written a para or two, he was sure of it. Never mind. He must get to it at once.

First, though, the message waiting on his answerphone. It turned out to be Rosie, saying Max had really appreciated their morning together, and thank you. Leo was touched: as far as he was concerned, his times with Max were always special.

After that, Declan's obituary fairly rattled along. Nothing excessive, mostly stuff about his dedicated library work, with a carefully brief mention of his long-term SCT connection. Certainly not a word about the violent nature of his death, let alone any possibly suspicious circumstances. There would be a Spiritualist memorial meeting at seven thirty pm on Sunday in the Pitville home of Rear-Admiral, ret. Sir Barton Daubney at 4 Wellington Parade, all comers welcome, no flowers by request. Declan Finsey had been unmarried, and left two younger sisters. He would be greatly missed.

He will be greatly missed... Leo stared at the words on the screen and was mortified—not by the sentiment but by its trite expression. He thought, for no very clear reason, of Mr Peterson. The man was making his enquiries. The man was judging him. Not that obits like this got by-lines, but Mr Peterson's enquiries wouldn't be stopped by that. And '*He will be greatly missed*' was disgraceful. Leo high-lighted it, stabbed 'delete,' considered, and tried again. *His untimely death is a tragic loss to our whole community.* There. Not world-shaking, but also not something Mr Peterson could seriously hold against him.

The hour was two thirty. Gordon's boy would come at six. A time gap loomed. He spell-checked Declan's obituary, printed it out, put it in an SCT envelope ready for collection, then called up Hoppy on the telephone and kissed things better. His mother had been upset, he said. He knew she could be difficult, he said, but she was old and sick and he hoped dear Hoppy would make allowances. They couldn't possibly do without her, he said. She conceded this and was mollified.

Poor old Ma. She was what she was. She didn't always make the best out of it, but who did? The hour was two forty. He joined her in the small rear sitting room where he found her cultivating her anger, with Bunty Carstairs as its principal target. Bunty Carstairs and also smarmy Graham Courtland. Thanks to them, Leo's own transgression, not daring to tell her what had been decided, was passed over. He wondered what she would do if Courtland were chosen as her successor. Theoretically she could work some kind of veto, but would she dare?

This was the first time he'd considered the result of the SCT's election. It was a future event and the present was hard enough to deal with. If he survived that far, if Coade let him, if Peterson let him, if his own despair let him, then he didn't think he'd care very much either way. He wasn't exactly wedded to the SCT. To be honest, he detested it. If he no longer had loyalty to his mother as a force keeping him in his job, he'd quit it tomorrow. He had other skills. He'd scrub public toilets rather than what he was doing now.

Gordon's lad came promptly at six.

CHAPTER 7

On Saturday morning the sun shone again and Leo took his mother for a drive. When the second of her Oblivon pills had finally got him to sleep the previous night he'd had a dream about her—very odd, Madam Sara in a sort of white night-shirt, swimming, and an atom bomb attack, lots of little atom bombs, apparently not very serious, nobody seemed worried, the planes that delivered them diving in impossibly tight spirals, like the cord on the telephone by the refrigerator in the kitchen—but he hadn't suggested the drive on account of that. It was simply what they often did on Saturday mornings. Her life was dreary and she didn't get out enough.

The time from after dinner on Friday till ten on Saturday morning has been sensibly omitted. Readers will have a good general idea of Leo's life by now, of his routines and his present disintegrations, so Friday evening can be taken as read. Even the grimmest self-flailings bore with repetition. Outings in cars can be boring too—often for the participants, always for people reading about them—and this one mainly conformed to that norm.

First Leo drove his mother by a roundabout route to Chipping Norton, a Cotswold town with sentimental associations since it was where back in 1969 she'd established her first regional SCT group, (and also where there was a convenient public lavatory). Then he drove her by a roundabout route home again, stopping on the outskirts of town to buy little custard tarts (her favourites) and a fresh loaf of bread for the week-end. The round trip took just over two hours. During it, however, one tiny fragment of conversation between them proved in retrospect to be worth reporting here.

They were driving down the Golden Valley below France Lynch when Leo's mother asked him, 'You remember my guide? My Nuna? My radiant spirit?'

A question out of the blue. They'd been silent with their thoughts for a long while. Hers we'll never know (what she'd say to Bunty Carstairs at the coming meeting?), while the general tenor of his can be guessed at all too well. He dragged himself back from them, widening his eyes as he drove, theatrically registering incredulity at his mother's behaviour to the invisible sympathiser who often accompanied him when he was with her.

'The Indian princess? Of course I remember.'

'She still talks to me. Gives me messages.'

Oh lord. 'What sort of messages?'

'Private. Private messages. Advice…' She fidgeted her bad hand into a more comfortable position. 'You think thass silly?'

'Of course not.' Millions of people heard Jesus giving them private messages. Why shouldn't Ma have Princess Nuna? 'Of course not.'

It was very odd, though. Never before, ever, had his mother asked for his view of her profession, even obliquely.

The car hit a minor pot-hole and she lurched in her seat.

'Doan bump me up,' she told him angrily. 'Doan you ever look? Hole back there. Doan you ever look? Drive more slower.'

Presumably his answer had been satisfactory. The moment came and went. Advice? That sounded very practical. Usually Princess Nuna dealt in cautious generalisations. He shared a wry smile with his unseen sympathiser. And anyway, what would have happened if he'd told her the truth? Yes, he did think her messages were crazy, but as human crazinesses went, they were fairly harmless.

Nothing much else was said. Just that unexpected question and his nondescript reply. They registered, though, and would come back later.

Back on Tivoli Street he helped her into the house, then put the car away. The day was still fine and he'd walk to Max's party. There was no hurry. He was dreading it. All those idiot quacking people, and the music would be a disaster. He could scarcely hold himself together, let alone Ibert as well.

His mother, as he'd expected, had decided stay at home. He left her half a smoked mackerel for her lunch, to go with the crusty fresh loaf. And the custard tarts of course. Then he went to change his clothes. He usually wore polo-necks but Max's party rated a shirt and jacket and tie.

He looked himself over in the mirror on the back of his wardrobe door. Even in shirt and jacket and tie, well-chosen shirt and jacket and tie, he was breaking up. Anyone could see that. He fetched his music case.

Today the walk to the Krauss-Häbers didn't help. He'd started worrying about the nameless informant again, who led him back to Coade, and Coade led him back to Declan and concrete. Max's party was audible from fifty yards away. The door was on the latch and he let himself in. The flat was packed and hardly recognisable. Rosie must have worked all the previous afternoon and evening. She'd opened up the folding doors between the living room and the never-used dining room which she'd dusted and polished. Months of Max's untidily-read and muttered-over newspapers had disappeared, the big television set had been trundled back into its cupboard, house plants had been purged of their dead and dying rags, Max's CD collection was all in one place (not in an identifiable order though), the pictures on the walls were straight, and not the slightest trace of rotting old man lingered in the air. No trace, either, of the roistering medieval Austrian peasant theme that Max had threatened.

Coffee, in two gleaming antique silver pots, stood on a fine lace cloth on the table in the dining room, together with sugar and cream and plates piled with praline fingers, biscotti, tiny cream-filled profiteroles on sticks, and coloured marzipan thingummies. All very stickily indulgent and *Mitteleuropäische*.

Max, too, had been made over. His ratty post-chemo hair had been clippered, probably by Rosie, into a decentish crew-cut, and instead of his usual hit-or-miss shave she had scraped and polished up his face to a presentable yellowish glow. A knitted sweater with a tactful shawl collar masked his neck strings and bulky corduroy did wonders for his skimpy bone legs. Nothing could have helped his hands, but their knobbed joints gave reality to a presentation that otherwise might have seemed dishonest. Morticians' handiwork. Strictly for family viewing.

There were many guests. Leo shouldn't have been surprised, but the solitary, privately dying Max of the last six months had dulled his memories of the earlier, intensely social man. He watched now as Max talked politics with one guest, football with another, something very jocular in German with another. Looking at him, Leo wondered what additional medicinal make-over had contributed to his present relaxed and happy spirits. Or perhaps Max was simply relaxed and happy. He was smoking one of his cigarillos.

Rosie looked marvellous. She was dressed, as always, not to stand out, and, as always, it didn't work. That Leo observed all this, despite his condition, and remembers it now, is remarkable. But he reckons that most people have compartments. This was his Max and Rosie compartment. The thing is, he says, nobody can be scared and falling to pieces all the time. Nobody can be *anything* all the time.

Some people can. If they're mad enough.

And in any case, his compartments hadn't been working worth a damn for the last few days. Where had his Max and Rosie compartment been then? And soon, as things turned out, they wouldn't be working much at the party either.

None of the guests, at least none that Leo heard, asked Max how he was. They told him instead that they were glad to see him looking so well. He didn't pursue the subject. There were plenty of other things he wanted to talk about. The *Echo*'s music critic was there, full of the new *Cosi* production in drag at the Playhouse. Max wondered why, if the public wanted invert opera, nobody was writing it. The *Cosi* show was nothing to do with being queer, the critic told him. It was an examination of stereotypes.

The headmaster of Dean Close School was there too, recently back from a visit to China. Capitalism there was coming along very nicely, he reported—or very badly, depending on your point of view. Max's view was that capitalism wore its evils on its sleeve—its virtues it practised mostly in secret.

At one point Leo found himself beside Max's chair when Max was unengaged. He leaned on the chair back. 'Good to see such a turn-out of Cheltenham's finest.'

'Don't snipe, Leo.' Max smiled at him quite sharply. 'One might think you were jealous.'

Seeing a truth there, Leo dodged. 'You flatter yourself.'

'Not very often.' Max reached for his hand and squeezed it gently. 'These festivities don't suit us—do I look as bad as you do?' Then he waved to someone across the room. 'Jonathon—how good of you to come. How's your house? Has it fallen down yet?'

The subsidences, laughed at, were always a safe subject.

Leo drifted away. Look bad? Of course he looked bad. Suddenly the thought came to him that, like Max but in his own way, he was ready to be dying. If one couldn't cope deeply enough, and for long enough, one quit. The thought of an effortless end in sight cheered him. Except that nothing usually worked out that way. Instead, if one couldn't cope deeply enough, and for long enough, one either pulled the plug or went inconveniently mad.

So that settled that. Not much for his comfort.

He looked round the room. What next? He'd already tried in vain for a quiet word with Rosie. She moved among her guests with amusing comments and plates of thingummies, calmly and unstoppably. Instead, he found a woman whose name he didn't quite catch, who said she was interested in modern furniture. Stretching things, he told her he was too, and dragged in the Swedish chair designer Akerblom from his Beals' days. She was impressed.

Suddenly he saw, away in the dining room, Mr Peterson. He gaped. A disjunction. Mr Peterson of the clammy plastic mac, now in very classy pinstripe and what looked like a regimental tie, talking animatedly to an elderly man with a fierce moustache. A mixing of compartments. It wasn't possible. On the other hand, if Mr Peterson wanted to observe and make enquiries, this party was just the place. And surely, like the modern furniture woman, he'd be impressed. But even so, how the hell had he heard of it and got himself invited? Leo excused himself from his furniture woman and filtered over to find out.

"Mr Peterson. We meet again.'

'We do indeed.' His man with the moustache politely saw someone else he knew and melted away. 'Um…You're well, I hope?'

'I'm terrible. How did you get here?'

'Like you, I imagine. An invitation.'

'You know Max and Rosie?'

'I know Max. Have done for years.'

'How?'

'I don't think that's any of your business.'

'Everything about *me* is of *your* business.'

'Ah. Point taken. Fair's fair and all that. Super.'

'Well?'

'I knew Max in London. I'm a friend of his agent.'

'Simon? A friend of Simon Dell?'

'My dear fellow—you make it sound so improbable. Ask Max if you don't believe me.'

My dear fellow... were they really on *my dear fellow* terms? Wasn't Mr Peterson a sort of twentieth century fury, hounding Leo to his comeuppance?

'In any case, I'm afraid I have to go now. End-of-season cricket match out in Prestbury. You've played there, I believe. I'm meeting some archivist. Super party. See you tomorrow evening.'

'You will?'

'Pitville's Finsey memorial meeting. *All comers welcome.*' He made quotation marks in the air with his fingers: Declan's obit had appeared in that morning's *Echo*. 'You'll be there, I'm sure.' He turned away, then had a thought. 'Your mother,' he said. 'She and I need to have a talk.'

'Madam Sara? She's busy. She's got people coming today at four thirty.'

'This afternoon's no good anyway. I told you. Prestbury. I'll be in touch.'

He wandered off. He wasn't tall and was quickly lost in the crush. And Leo had just remembered the man with the moustache: he'd been the golf pro at Lilybrook back in 1968. Cricket and golf... it was odd of Mr Peterson to be going for his almost non-existent sporting background. Nothing there worth punishing, surely? Unless total mediocrity were culpable, which in Mr Peterson's eyes it might be. Everything depended on the hole one looked through.

As for Mr Peterson meeting his mother, Leo had no fears on that front. The version of her son that Madam Sara presented would be one hundred percent loyal.

Back in the living room somebody tapped a coffee cup. Rosie was helping Max to his feet. She'd been watching the clock and Max's limited resources, and it was time for some music. Perhaps that was why Mr Peterson had remembered another engagement.

Space was cleared round the piano, a chair and music stand arranged.

People sat and perched and leaned where they'd found themselves. Myra Bunn from Christchurch hovered discreetly, waiting her turn at the piano. Max's tuning ritual gone through, he announced the Ibert. Two *very* short pieces, he reassured them, laughing to suggest that they could laugh too. Leo stretched his fingers and prayed for it all to be over. Two taps of Max's foot and they started.

Ten or so bars later, tidily, with no warning, Max was unconscious. He didn't exactly slump but subsided rather, neatly enfolding his flute. Leo, who'd been keeping an eye on him as any good accompanist should, was beside him instantly. Max's head jerked slightly and he subsided further. For a moment everyone else in the room had been frozen in place: now they moved and murmured. Rosie knelt briefly beside Leo, then elbowed a way out through the crowd to the telephone in the kitchen. Leo eased Max's flute from his crumpled twitching fingers.

Max's doctor had been invited to the party but he hadn't made it. No other doctor was present. Myra Bunn, who'd done first aid with the WI, ascertained that the patient was still breathing and then recommended laying him face downwards on the floor, a cushion under his neck, his head on its left side. This was done. Rosie returned from the kitchen and reported that an ambulance was on its way, but it might take twenty minutes. The service was overstretched. Max remained apparently unconscious. Breathing steadily. Not dead.

Not dead, but it seemed likely that he soon would be. Mind you, 'soon' is an unreliable adverb when used in relation to the eternity of death. If you're Nietzsche and your mum gave birth astride a grave, then 'soon' might suggest an interval in the neighbourhood of three score years and ten. In Max's case, however, 'soon' had a less philosophical context: neither years nor months nor weeks, but at most only a day or two.

In the meantime, though, Max's next few hours would be orderly and predictable. A social construct. Systems took over. First the ambulance system delivered two sturdy paramedics plus well-worn survival machinery. Next the ER system provided a grubby office corridor for patient and companions to wait in and eventually a curtained cubicle with a mostly similar purpose. And finally the hospital system took over, supplying a proper bed with proper tubes, in a proper ward, with a proper waiting room close by (magazines, coffee machine, tasteful Cotswold landscapes on the walls) for the patient's equally proper companions. In Max's case, Rosie Krauss-Häber (wife) and, arriving slightly later, Leo Bresson (close friend).

The party had sidled tactfully away. Leo, lingering, had been excluded from the ambulance when it left for Cheltenham General Hospital with Max and Rosie, for reasons of space and too remote a relationship. He'd walked to the party so he didn't have his car, but Cheltenham General wasn't far away, overlooking College playing fields, so he went there on foot. His mother would still be having her nap, he reckoned, so he didn't call her. If she woke and he wasn't there she wouldn't worry—Max's party could easily have run on a bit. A deadline loomed at four thirty, however—the arrival of the three SCT Elders—and he needed to be home well before that to help her get ready.

Till then he sat with Rosie. *Sat with...* dear god, was that really all he did? A woman's beloved husband of twenty-three years is dying (they both assumed this) and all you do is sit with her? Simply *sit...*? Actually, that's just about what you do do. The wife beside you is somewhere else. Wait mode has set in for her. Suspended animation. Footsteps pass. Slightly adventurous Paul Klee prints hang on the walls here, the man who took a line for a walk. She doesn't see them. Doctors come, say things, and she listens and nods. They go. She's told you that she's glad you're there to help, but she probably wouldn't notice if you weren't. She's somewhere else.

One thought got spoken. After about an hour.

'It's what he's always dreaded, Leo. To be in a place he can't choose to quit.'

Leo, remembering, didn't have an answer.

'Choice. It's what made the last weeks possible.'

Leo silently squared a magazine on a glass-topped table.

'He's a brave man, Leo. But only so far.'

'We'll get him safely home, love.' Which Leo knew was a lie.

* * * *

At three-thirty Leo remembered the Elders and left the hospital for the twenty-minute walk home. Out on College Road he felt that he ought to be carrying something, his hands seemed empty, and then he remembered that he'd left his music case in the Krauss-Häbers' flat. The explanation was comforting: it told him his hands were paying proper attention.

Back on Tivoli Street his mother was up from her nap, had also remembered the Elders' visit. She'd done her face, and now was struggling anxiously into the clothes she'd picked out as suitable. He helped her get her left arm through its arm-hole, at the same time telling her about Max. She heard and was concerned—he'd had a good relationship with her, fond and respectful yet never quite serious—but just then her worries were elsewhere. Leo left her to them.

Finally she was satisfied and called him. Leaning unobtrusively on her dressy silver-and-ebony stick, she presented herself in her bedroom's open doorway, lit from the side by a golden ray of sunlight beaming in through the tall, west-facing window.

She looked really rather fine. The lighting was kind, no doubt of that, but she was still, left eyelid droop and all, a handsome old woman. And the outfit she'd chosen—black-on-black brocade jacket loosely open over low-waisted dark red roses (her favourite colour combination), with not a belt or brooch in sight, just a long three-stranded necklace of tigers'-eyes and pearls—was bold, timeless, and defiantly *her*. The Elders wouldn't know what had hit them.

He told her that. 'The Elders won't know what hit them.'

She frowned, twisting her head a little. 'Buttons, Leo. Buttons.'

He went to her. 'What buttons?'

'Here.' She lifted her chin. Close to, he saw that her lipstick was smudged. But the buttons in question were the top two of at least a dozen up the front of her dress and she'd managed the rest.

'Keep still now. Who on earth ever designed such a stupid arrangement.'

'Stupid arrangement.'

'Looks good, though.'

'Woan know what hit them. Ha.'

He smiled at her. It cost so little.

The time was four twenty. Things had worked out very well. He settled his mother in the big front drawing room with her glasses and the newspaper, and retired to his office-bedsit.

Once in his room all the surviving he'd been doing collapsed. He thought about Max and Rosie. Yesterday had been for lies and manoeuvers. Today was for sorrow. He sorrowed for Rosie, sitting in that quiet, calm, terrible waiting place. Max he couldn't picture, neither the transitory processes surrounding him nor the man himself. Max on the gurney being trundled out of the flat had been conscious but already diminished, already strange. Someone else staring at the ceiling. Staring at the ceiling.

He'd probably be doing that now. Not Max. A patient. A hospital adjunct.

The memory tore at Leo and he shuddered. Later, perhaps this evening when the hospital's processes had settled themselves, he would visit Max, perhaps with Rosie and perhaps on his own. He knew the scene from a hundred films. Hospital beds provided a good strong rectilinear element. White was good too. Pointedly impersonal. It kept the edges sharp. But the Max he now pictured would be shabbier than the patients in the films. Yellower and more ragged. Leo saw him clearly, propped on pillows. Homeless. Nowhere. Staring at the ceiling.

The front doorbell rang, announcing the arrival of Bunty Carstairs and her fellow Elders. Dragged violently back into the moment, Leo looked at his watch: the time was exactly four thirty. She'd have been waiting down the street with them till the critical moment. He imagined her, stopwatch in hand, marking time on the pavement.

He wiped his eyes, blew his nose, and went to let them in.

'Mrs Carstairs, Miss Minshull, Mr Doyle—good afternoon. Madam Sara is expecting you.'

The perfect butler. It was one of the very few perfections, and certainly the least desirable, to which he thought he might realistically aspire.

He stepped back, allowing them to enter. 'My mother is in the drawing room.' He tilted his head respectfully towards the closed door. 'May I take your coats?'

The afternoon was still quite warm and in fact only Mr Doyle had a coat. Mr Doyle was a professional man, the SCT's treasurer and a chartered accountant. Leo took his coat from him and hung it on Grandmother Clare's kudu coat rack.

'Mrs Carstairs—I'm afraid my mother knows the purpose of your visit. I couldn't keep it from her. You see, not all the truthsayers have respected the confidential nature of the election process.'

Mrs Carstairs snorted. That's not just a shoddy cliché—she really did. 'Only to be expected, I suppose. No standards, these days. Well, better get this over with.' She squared her shoulders. That too. 'I'm sorry, Leo, that it's had to come to this, but Madam Sara's really left us with no alternative. Douglas… Annette… come along now.'

Leo took them to the drawing room door and opened it. 'Mother? Mother, the Elders are here now.'

Seated inside the room, Madam Sara was waiting for them, erect and emblematic, like an ancestral portrait. Her visitors went in to her and Leo closed the door on them. He began the small journey back to his office/bed-sit, his sorrow gathering again, then remembered providentially that he'd bought a saddle of Danish boiling bacon at Sainsbury's for their Saturday dinner, which would require at least an hour-and-three-quarters' cooking, and his mother liked to eat early, around six, so he'd better get it started instanter. And once he was in the kitchen, of course, one thing led to another, and he was still there half an hour later when the Elders' meeting with his mother ended—a less-than-thrilling thirty minutes that gives me an opportunity to get something sorted out.

Just as there may well be readers having difficulty accepting Leo's Cheltenham versus theirs, so there'll be long-term residents worried that they remember reading some time ago about the tragic death of a medium which doesn't quite match this one. There'll be detail differences—the medium's name, the organisation he worked for, even the precise time of year—and they'll wonder how these can be explained. And the two Cheltenhams explanation sounds just plain silly.

To which there is only one simple answer: all this shows—and for good legal reasons—is that their Cheltenham absolutely isn't the same as Leo's. Theirs has no coal mines, no subsidence, no victim called Finsey, no SCT—clearly it's a different place. It's a bit of a coincidence for a medium to fall off a balcony in both these Cheltenhams, but it's no more than that. If they accept that mediums do fall off balconies sometimes, then a Cheltenham of some sort or another is as good a place as any.

The existence of two Cheltenhams may well strain some readers' ability to suspend disbelief, but don't let's be too literal-minded. There's no Statute of Limitations on prosecutions for the crime of murder, and Public Prosecutors read books, as do their assistants, so for a little healthy disbelief to be going around is surely quite a good thing.

OK?

Back then to Leo's half-hour in his kitchen. He consulted the clock there often and anxiously—a lot of talking could go on in thirty minutes. The kitchen, at the back of the house, was a good way from the closed door to the big front drawing room but on several occasions he was sure he heard raised voices. He let well alone. Bunty Carstairs was tough and had the by-laws on her side, but his mother in her present mood was tough also and had written them. Minshull and Doyle were cyphers. There was the strong possibility of a nil-nil draw. Whatever, in the present contest, that might represent.

He was melting the butter for the roux for the caper sauce when Mrs Carstairs loudly cleared her throat behind him. 'We're just leaving.'

'What's that?' She'd made him jump. He swung round and saw her, standing in the doorway. 'I'm sorry. I didn't hear you—'

'Not to worry. We can show ourselves out.'

But she made no move to go, just stood, arms folded, examining him.

He checked, as men do, even in life-threatening situations, on his zip. 'Mmm... how was your meeting?'

'Stormy. But we expected that. Douglas had the resignation letter ready. Your mother has a very forceful personality, young man. She signed it, however. Eventually... She's still very sharp. Frankly, I was surprised. Very surprised. It's a pity more of that sharpness hasn't been put at the disposal of her Church in recent months. A great pity. A very great pity.'

Leo offered a small, ambiguous gesture. 'There have been... considerations, Mrs Carstairs.' It was a bit late for him to start defending his mother. All the same: 'Her speech, in particular, is no longer reliable.'

'I don't think you need fear, Mr Bresson, that your mother had difficulty today in making herself understood.' Mrs Carstairs rearranged her breasts portentously above her folded arms. 'I assure you that what she meant was made abundantly clear to us. Abundantly clear.'

Which was more than she'd done for him. Apart from generalised warnings that they wouldn't know what had hit them, she'd told him nothing about what she planned to say to the Elders. Not that he gave a shit. Max was dying, Declan was dead, he himself deserved to be. *Christ...*

'So what can I do for you now, Mrs Carstairs?' He advanced on her, almost as if to herd her. 'Your two colleagues will be waiting for you.'

'I'm curious, Mr Bresson.' She didn't budge. 'I'm curious about your views on Madam Sara's expansion plans. The possibility of a campaign.'

'I'm the SCT's secretary, Mrs Carstairs. My views are neither here nor there.'

'You're too modest, young man. Much too modest.' She smiled at him alarmingly. 'You've been with us a long time. The governing board appreciates your efforts.'

Then you can tell them just where to stuff their precious bloody appreciation.

Well, not spoken out loud... but he did think it, as he modestly shuffled his feet and made grateful noises. A long time indeed, six years, and in all of them these were the first approving words he'd received from any board member. Incredible.

'Well, well, well...' She unfolded her arms. 'The election forms did go off, I hope?'

'Yesterday morning, Mrs Carstairs. I'm expecting the first responses early next week. Monday even. I did mention the board's wish for a quick decision.'

'Good. Very good.' She looked past him, at the kitchen table. 'You cook, I see. You're mother's very fortunate to have you. Continuity, Mr Bresson. Continuity. It's very important.' She did the smile again. 'It's time we were on our way... Please don't bother to see us out.'

He didn't, just stood and watched her stride away down the passage to where Henry and Annette were waiting for her in the hall. Then he turned back to his roux. The butter was burnt and ruined. He washed the pan out.

Continuity—so that was it. The Elders were worried that, with his mother ousted and someone else, probably Graham Courtland, as the SCT's director, he wouldn't stay on. Damn right, he wouldn't. Scrubbing public toilets would be bliss in comparison.

He waited till Mr Doyle had retrieved his coat and the Elders had left, then went to see how his mother was surviving in the big front drawing room. People, especially people like that, took a lot out of her.

She was belligerent but exhausted. In her mean child mode. Simply repeating mantras about making people sit up and pay attention, telling them what was what. Other than that, giving Leo nothing about their meeting. He wondered briefly what she could possibly have said that had so impressed the appalling Mrs Carstairs with her sharpness, but soon lost interest. Max was dying, Declan was dead, and he himself deserved to be. Now, there was a mantra for you.

He returned to the kitchen and got on with dinner. At week-ends he allowed his mother fattening puddings. There was just about time, he thought, to whip up a jam sponge with custard.

CHAPTER 8

This story could do with a Max-and-Leo deathbed scene. For all his faults, Leo might well have been good at it. Max surely would have been. In spite of their differences he and Leo were surprisingly alike. Both were intelligent, neither was brilliant. Both were articulate. They used the same conversational short cuts, enjoyed the same ironies, threw away their lines in very much the same fashion. They agreed about what was important. Both were wary of emotion, but their regard for one another created a rewarding closeness. Strictly speaking we have only Leo's word for this, but later events suggest that Max shared in it. Their extremis, too, would have been shared, with wit and affection. A rare circumstance. A special moment for both of them, had it happened. One worth recording.

Deathbed voyeurism? Tasteless sight-seeing? Surely not. Isn't the occasional special moment one of the experiences we hope for when we seek out stories? A glimpse of the extravagant, astonishing, hilarious, moving, magnificent things quite ordinary people may sometimes get up to?

In this particular story, though, the moment simply never happened.

A different, smaller scene, then. No deathbed scene, just Leo at the desk in his office/bedsit, calling Rosie, first at the Parabola Road answerphone, then at the hospital, and Rosie telling him that Max had not yet regained consciousness and his condition was serious but stable, a result of his liver failure and no connection with his loss of consciousness at the party which had been on account of either of a mild heart attack or of reckless top-up pills he'd apparently taken. The doctors were advising her to go home, get a good night's sleep, come back in the morning, and she was saying she'd rather stay. Leo didn't argue with her, just offered to drive over to the hospital for a while after dinner, which she vigorously resisted.

For Leo, therefore, after a less than triumphant Saturday dinner—the bacon was coarse and over-salted, the peas minus their caper sauce were bearable but the mashed potatoes accompanying them were lumpy, the sponge pudding was damp in the middle, and his mother was still belligerent—he spent a standard Saturday evening at home on Tivoli Street, watching TV with Madam Sara until, still saying she knew what was what, she went to bed at nine, then doing the crossword with Rumple's assistance, backed by Bach, a two-CD set of the unaccompanied violin partitas, until around eleven, when he thought he dared go to bed and try to sleep himself.

He tried and for a long time failed. For one thing, he was wary taking any more of his mother's Oblivons (He couldn't think why. Drug addiction? In the circumstances, who cared?), and for another thing, two deaths now loomed over him: Declan's that we already know far too much about, and Max's that was still to come but clearly not distant. Plus of course his shame.

Around two thirty in the morning he stopped trying and got up, dressed, and went into the kitchen. The spot-lights in there were bright, bright with accusatory two-thirty-in-the-morning brightness, and he lingered only long enough to slop down some cold custard left over from dinner which he regretted instantly. He went for a walk.

Cheltenham's streets in the still, dead hours of that night were holding their breath. Well, that's how Leo, after a lot of thought, puts it. They were watching him, watching him, waiting for him to prance and scream and burst into a thousand pieces. He denied them the pleasure. Walking briskly, clip, clip, clip, he set off in the direction of the Leckhampton Road, unconsciously following his boyhood's daily route to school. So unconsciously that when he saw where he'd arrived he was genuinely surprised. He wasn't given to nostalgic visits, and certainly not in the middle of the night.

Coll was lit by a full September moon and the charmless yellow oxide street-lights of the main road. The night air was cold on his face. An owl mewed high in the trees around the Tavistock hotel. When a boy he'd have gone straight on across the road, making for the Day Boy common rooms, temporary wooden buildings with rotting verandas beside the old parade ground, left over from the war. Now he turned right instead, perhaps because then was then and now was now, and walked towards the school's grand main entrance. Here a semicircular drive served the impressively studded doors in their solemn gothic archway, to the left of which stood the lodge where, in Leo's time, Mr Bassett had lived. Mr Bassett, an ex-serviceman with a curious (and by the boys much copied) bouncing walk presumably the result of a wound bravely incurred in patriotic conflict, had been the school's care-taker, handyman, and general minatory presence.

And by means of this vivid and unexpected recollection, the purpose of Leo's curious pilgrimage was gloriously revealed to him. Its purpose was to remind him that at some time, probably quite soon, the present's horrors would end, and something would come after them. If they ended badly, then speculations about what that something might be were a waste of time: badly was badly. Badly was jail, frankly unbearable. If they ended well, however, then a future existed. A future for which Leo so far had made no decisions whatsoever, save that it would absolutely not include the SCT. The scrubbing public toilets preference, he acknowledged, was strictly metaphorical. So what *would* he do? And now, standing outside

Mr Bassett's old lodge at three in the morning, he suddenly knew. He was handy, he was good at taking care of things, and with a little practice he was sure he could be minatory. He was a natural for Mr Bassett's job.

He wasn't proud. Coll might consider him over-qualified but he'd talk them out of that. Coll had given him the happiest days of his life. Now he could give Coll something back.

He trotted up the side of the main building, suddenly bursting with energy, past the archway to the chapel cloisters and then right, echoing clip, clip, clip, into the quad. The science labs and tuck shop were to the left, under their arcade, the art rooms were opposite. There were the lavs too. He paused. Part of Mr Bassett's job? He thought not. Cleaning staff did those—he'd seen Mr Bassett ordering them about. He trotted on, passing the entrance to Big Classical lecture hall, out to the open area in front of the new classroom block, and stopped, panting. He was in terrible shape these days.

Coll. The hideous old Victorian gym away to the left. Thirlstaine House ahead. Coll. The place was co-ed now, of course. Coll. And in a sense, a valuable sense, it would be his...

He leaned on a worn gothic buttress, still panting. Breathing 'his native air, on his own ground.' That was Alexander Pope. A good man, Alexander Pope.

There was the strong possibility that Mr Bassett's old job would not be available. In that case he'd wait until it was. But that was negative thinking. Everything in his life couldn't keep on going badly for him. There had to be a turn-around.

He walked on slowly, thoughtfully, out onto Thirlstaine Road and turned right again, back towards Tivoli Street. The running had made his skin prickle. He'd never liked to run. A tom-cat howled somewhere, followed by ugly sounds of cat battle, then silence again. This early morning outing had been a fine idea. Days and days of misery, there had to be a turn-around. He was filled with joy.

A police car cruised softly up behind him and stopped. He kept on walking. Obviously it had come for him but that was just paranoia. The car overtook him and stopped again. The window on his side, the driver's side, was lowered. A huge red hand lunged out through it and gripped his arm. 'Leo Anthony Bresson, I arrest you on the charge of fucking Max Krauss-Häber's wife. You have the right to remain silent, but anything you say may be used in—'

'Wait a minute.' Leo frowned. Something wasn't right here. To have fucked Rosie was bad but hardly an arrestable offence. 'Wait a minute...'

The hand went away.

'You alright, sir? Need any help?' A different voice.

'Help?'

'You seemed a bit unsteady, sir. We thought you might need some help.'

'Unsteady? I don't think so. Not paying attention, perhaps. Couldn't sleep, you know. Went for a walk.'

'You live in these parts?'

'Just round the corner. Tivoli Street.'

'What number would that be?'

'Eighty-one.'

A brief consultation took place inside the car.

'Would you like a lift home, sir?'

'That's very kind of you.' What a terrible thought. 'Not really, though. It's the insomnia—what helps it most is lots of walking. No harm in that, is there?'

'No harm at all. We just thought we might help.'

'You thought I was drunk, officer. I can assure you I'm not.'

'We have to be careful, sir. The hour is unusual. I'm sure you understand that. Good night, sir. Enjoy your walk.'

The window was raised and the car drove off slowly, returning to its proper side of the road. Leo watched it till it was out of sight. The wretched man had a point—the hour was indeed unusual. He was glad he hadn't overdone things. He'd considered casually mentioning that he was an Old Cheltonian, but that could easily have put the policemen's backs up. It would have been tacky, too.

He turned right at the traffic lights and walked on down past Coll's main entrance and Mr Bassett's lodge. There on the corner were the old Day Boy rooms, and they brought with them a second extraordinarily vivid memory. There'd been a wintry evening in '56 or '57 when he and Colin Something (he wasn't good at names) had stayed on late for some reason, ping-pong possibly, and had ended up, after everyone else had gone home, sitting in the dark on the bashed-up sofa squashed in behind the billiard table in the Common Room, street lights shining in through the windows, talking about the House Play coming up at the end of the term, and when would wretched Pimbury condescend to learn his lines, and eventually tossing each other off, taking their time, stopping at the brink, *en suspension* they called it, seeing how close they could get and bearing down to put off the moment, until suddenly there were bouncing footsteps on the veranda and Mr Bassett was leaning in through the doorway, looking round the shadowed room.

Panic-stricken, they froze. This was expulsion stuff. There hadn't been time for them even to put their cocks away, let alone see to their flies. If Mr Bassett turned on the lights, or simply saw them down behind the billiard table in the dim light from the road outside, their lives were in ruins.

He did neither. He looked round cursorily, closed the door, locked it, and bounced on down the verandah to deal with locking up the other three Day Boy rooms. Eventually his footsteps departed across the parade ground.

Only then did Leo and Colin Something move. Their cocks were frankfurter-sized by then. Getting out of the Common Room presented a serious problem, however, since the door was locked from the outside and only the uppermost line of window-panes opened, hinged horizontally from the top. But desperation drove them, and the long, high-up horizontal slot proved just sufficient, even for Leo's length and breadth. Standing on the narrow interior window-sill risked smashing the frame, slithering sideways down onto the veranda outside was noisy, and anyone walking along the street could easily have seen them, but they got away with it.

Leo made an important decision, however. That night, fetching his bicycle from the racks, he decided that shared sex wasn't worth the hassle. However you looked at it, shared sex was more trouble than it was worth. People got hurt. Distrust. Jealousy. Possessiveness. Not to mention sin. You saw it all the time. And for what? Foreplay was nice, orgasms were nice, but the risks they brought with them were immeasurable. Queer or straight wasn't the point. He didn't yet know about straight—except that it had to be wetter and messier, much was expected of you, babies were always on the cards, and women were unknowable—but either way, shared sex was an over-rated enterprise. Better, when the mood drove you, to stick to the solitary. No, not just better—essential.

Most people thought differently. He knew that. Fine for them. He wasn't most people. He was so afraid. So afraid. Recognise that, lad. Remember it. Stick to the solitary.

Now, some quarter-century later, as he did indeed remember that moment, Leo's early morning euphoria froze savagely round his heart, clutched at his lungs, spread lower, shrivelling his diaphragm, and he came the closest he ever would to the dark streets' hoped-for total disintegration. *Stick to the solitary.* Yes indeed. A decision he'd never lived by. Look at him now. Yes indeed. Look at him now. Look at where shared sex had brought him. *Oh Rosie... dear darling Rosie...*He fell to his knees in the gutter.

All these theatrics. Leo's asking a lot of us. Bathos threatens. Or maybe does its worst and wins. Still, that's his story and he's sticking to it, and in that case it just goes to prove that a man's paths to breaking up are many, not all of which are well-judged, sympathetic, even credible.

He pulled himself together, of course. Well, effected some useful improvements. He scrabbled himself up out of the gutter, registered his good fortune that no police car had passed again while he was apparently at prayer, got himself back to 81 Tivoli Street and into bed somehow, and slept. At least, he says he did.

If he's right about that also, then it's a wonder he was wide awake again promptly at seven ten, only three-ish hours later, ready to feed the cat and prepare Sunday breakfast which was special, proper freshly-ground coffee, scrambled egg instead of boiled or fried, bacon, fried bread, tomatoes, the two of them eating together, him sitting on his mother's bed, at seven thirty sharp. But the human spirit has remarkable capacities.

His mother's fried bread was soggy. Having established this failure, however, she said it didn't matter, squashed her scrambled egg down into it and ate it anyway. Her night's sleep had calmed her down. Also she'd decided, very surprisingly, to go to Pitville that evening for Declan Finsey's memorial meeting.

Before that there were Sunday matins in the big church across the end of Christchurch Road, for which a non-SCT friend, Janet Burke, was collecting her in her car at ten thirty. Miss Burke was older than she but in better shape, had led a sheltered life, and was admiring.

After breakfast, while his mother was having her shower, choosing church-worthy clothes and putting them on, Leo retreated to his office bed-sit, made his bed, and called the Krauss-Häbers' flat. Rosie wasn't there so he tried the hospital, mentioned Mr Krauss-Häber and was put through to a nurses' station. When he asked how Mr Krauss-Häber was doing and identified himself as a close friend of the family, the friend who'd been with Mrs Krauss-Häber the previous afternoon, the nurse transferred him to a doctor and the doctor told him Mr Krauss-Häber had never regained consciousness and had passed away approximately an hour ago.

Passed away?

Leo raged. He lost it. For once in his buttoned-up public school life he totally lost it. He pounded his office desk-top, scattering papers. *Passed away?* Christ fucking Almighty—what sort of an unctuous fucking phrase was that? From a fucking doctor? He'd be talking about higher fucking realms next. The fucker had meant that Max had fucking died, hadn't he? Kicked the bucket. Popped his clogs. Dropped off the perch. Given up the ghost. Cashed in his chips. Max was dead. The only fucking absolute. *Dead.*

He pounded his office desk-top and wept.

After a considerate pause, the doctor cleared his throat. 'Mr Krauss-Häber was a very sick man. I'm sure you knew that.'

Leo didn't argue the point.

The doctor then suggested that Leo might like to speak to Mrs Krauss-Häber, who had just at that moment come into his office, and Leo asked him to put her on.

'Rosie my dear. I'm so sorry.'

'They'd never have let him come home again. I'm not.'

He understood what she was saying.

'Sorry for you, I meant. For the suddenness.'

'Yes. Well. I'm organising an undertaker. Will you want to see the body?'

See the body? What an extraordinary idea. Either a mortician's made-up simulacrum that Rosie would never allow anyway, or poor beloved Max's corpse, cold and empty... He had far truer memories to cherish. Mafia bosses looked at corpses in coffins in order to make sure they were dead. He couldn't imagine any other good reason.

'No, Rosie. No.'

'I didn't think so. I must tell his agent. I expect Simon'll want to plan a big memorial service. London, probably. Max was quite famous.'

'How about you?'

'Me, Leo? I've no idea.'

'Of course not. Silly of me.'

'I must go now. People are flapping at me. 'Bye.'

'Wait Rosie—'

The line buzzed at him. Anyway, what would he have said? He rang off.

Max was dead. A memorial service. Oh Lord... Declan's this evening and then another for Max...

Max, dead? Max, dead. The only absolute.

Never again. Never again. So many never agains.

The void Max left was dizzying.

His dearest friend. Yes, he'd been expecting this, so why was he so shattered? He'd warmed his hands at Max's life. That was why. Max had welcomed him in. That was why. Max had needed him. Trusted him. That was why. His dearest friend. His dearest friend was dead.

Why really was he so shattered? Max had welcomed him in and Leo had betrayed him. That was why. He'd warmed his hands at Max's life and, on the side, he'd fucked Max's wife. That was why. Max had needed him, trusted his honour, and had received his deceit. His dearest friend. That was why he—

'Leo? Leo, I carn find my gloves.' Madam Sara, indignant out in the front hall. 'I carn find my gloves, Leo. I'm sure they were in the drawer.'

She'd stirred the drawer into a terrible mess but the gloves were in it. He found them for her and sat with her, saying things, till Janet Burke arrived. His mother hadn't heard the phone so he didn't have to tell her that Max was dead. He couldn't yet have said the words.

After he'd helped her (as always with some difficulty) into Miss Burke's tiny Peugeot 209, he returned to his office/bedsit and tried to contact Rosie again. She needed his support. Well, somebody needed somebody's support. The Parabola Road flat gave him its answerphone and the hospital thought she was still on the premises but couldn't find her. Leo decided to drive over to the flat. She was probably en route there. Where else would she go?

On Sunday mornings most Parabola Road residents were at home, so parking wasn't easy. Leo had quite a walk from his car. Letting himself in, no sign of Rosie yet, he was shocked to find Max's party, like some *Marie Celeste* mess-room, unpeopled but otherwise still in progress. Crumbs on plates, coffee cups half-empty, Max's flute and sheet-music waiting on his music stand. They would be, of course, he should have worked that out—and, mercifully, here he was, ready to fill the dishwasher, rearrange the furniture. Ready to unyesterday today, if he worked at it, before Rosie got there.

He had another time constraint, the two-hours-or-so before his mother would be back from church, needing her Sunday morning glass of sherry before her lunch. He made it back home—even including a quick vacuum cleaner whizz round the flat, and still no sign of Rosie—with a couple of minutes to spare. Miss Burke was just arriving from Christchurch as he closed the garage door on his Jaguar. The sermon, his mother reported, had been pathetic. She sometimes wondered why she went.

* * * *

The Pitville SCT group held their meetings in Admiral and Lady Daubney's fine old house on Wellington Parade, the north side of a square just down from Pitville Circus. Wellington Parade's compass-bearing gets a mention because its houses were significant as being on the only side of the square not affected by the widespread land subsidence occurring above the mine workings in that area. The three other sides of the square leaned, boarded up, occupied by one obstinate geriatric, plus squatters too poor to care. The ancient plane trees ringing the grass in the centre of the square, their leaves now a fine September gold, were leaning also, and three had fallen. Only the houses on the square's north side, built on a narrow oölite ledge, had kept their vertical, ninety degree angles and therefore their wealthy residents. The ledge there was stable, geologists told them. The road in front was more doubtful, but they could probably park their BMWs on it if they kept an eye out. Any movement would certainly be gradual.

Number four, the Daubneys' place, was one of a pair of large white stucco houses with pillared porticos and magnolia trees in their small front gardens. Its two front rooms, in a more impressive version of the Krauss-Häbers' flat, were joined by high white panelled folding doors, now opened back to accommodate the considerable group that was expected for Declan Finsey's memorial meeting. Assorted seating for this, gathered from around the house, stood in curved rows across the gleaming parquet floor, facing the huge bay window at one end where a gracious upright walnut armchair, a carver from the dining room, was positioned with its back to this window, ready for the group's regular truthsayer, Robert Gifford. The joined rooms were impossible to curtain into total darkness but T/S Gifford used no special psychic effects and was willing to channel in broad daylight if necessary. He was a voice channeller plain and simple. He preferred a general dimness, for its restful qualities and churchy feel, but he didn't insist on it.

Gifford was one of Madam Sara's most valued truthsayers. She claimed to distrust all hocus pocus and approved of his technique. Once contact was properly established, her theory was that spirits would be helped by the group's psychic energy to use the chaneller's mental and physical voice centres for the transmission of messages. No phoney mimicry need occur. It wasn't the spirit speaking, it was the channeller experiencing the spirit's intention and conveying it. That way, since intention transcended language, even those spirits who in their earth lives hadn't known any word of English were able to communicate.

This evening the curtains had been drawn against the darkness outside and tall wax candles lit the front of the meeting space, with a dimmed electric overhead chandelier lighting the area behind the seats, where the Daubneys' maid had laid out cheese and crackers and wine on tables for afterwards. There was a strong social element in all SCT meetings, which tended to be improvisatory—and more so than usual today since nobody was sure what the occasion might produce. No formal guidance or channelling was programmed. Members were gathering to remember and celebrate the life of Declan Finsey.

Leo and his mother arrived in good time, shortly after seven. Madam Sara's presence caused a stir. Cheltenham's Elders were unsure of the protocol where an about-to-be-replaced director was concerned, but Madam Sara solved their problem for them, pointing decisively at a comfortable upright chair tucked unobtrusively against the wall some rows back, and firmly making her way to it. Once seated there, very straight-backed, she gazed expectantly about her, making it clear that she would receive the faithful.

Leo kept out of the way, settling himself discreetly at the far end of her row. This was clearly to be her farewell appearance. He wouldn't intrude.

Earlier that day, after Sunday lunch, carrot and coriander soup, Marmite on hot buttered toast, he'd left his mother to rest on her bed—still fully dressed, since her church outfit would do very well for the evening's Pitville outing—and he'd driven back over to Parabola Road where he'd linked up at last with Rosie, now home from the hospital. 'Linked up with' is a suitably vague phrase: she'd been tired out, hollow, scarcely there. She walked disjointedly from room to room, rubbing her pale, cold arms. Max had never been a noisy man, but without him the flat's silence ached in Leo's ears.

She'd telephoned her brother Phil in Liverpool and he was coming down on Monday to help tide her over the next few days. She had no other relative, and no Cheltenham friends close enough to burden seriously with her grieving. Only Leo.

He didn't stay long. He'd no idea how she felt for him just then, and his anguished self-disgust kept him from finding out. He could think of no way—and he tried to, he really tried to—in which his love for her had harmed Max, yet the self-disgust persisted. The principle of the thing. The deception... He made sure that there was decent food (not just left-over marzipan thingummies) and drink available for her in the kitchen, the things he was good at, and then went back to Tivoli Street. where he knew the previous evening's raggy ham and caper sauce could be served again if given proper attention.

Balsamic vinegar to sharpen the sauce, he thought, and a thorough bashing for the lumpy potato. The pudding was beyond saving and he'd serve his mother ice cream instead.

And now, out in polite society, here she was, smiling graciously, saying little and paying careful attention to her 't's. Among the loyal SCT members who came and went he'd watched Mr Peterson, in his formal party suit again, talking to her as promised for quite a while. She'd clearly had a lot to say to him. Now T/S Gifford—who wasn't a man for mediumistic yoga and deep breathing exercises in a back room right up to curtain time—was with her, leaning solicitously. Gifford was a decent man, no longer young, a retired social worker with all the right motives, who lived in a traditional narrowboat, copiously decorated with hand-painted roses and castles, on the canal near Saul village. He knew his Pitville group well and suited them exactly. Nothing gaudy. Nothing too intrusive. Like most truthsayers, he had a minatory spirit guide in the Higher Realm, an intermediary able to pick out the most suitable petitioners from among the many dear departed clamouring to be put in touch. His guide, Mehetmotep, an ancient Egyptian priestess, brought in spirit contacts that offered the broadest consolations.

No offence intended. This, of course, is glib Leo talk. Leo, back then. He's let it slip out. Back then he recalls finding Gifford's guide excessive—although an ex-priestess made sense, the Egyptian bit overdid things—but the Pitville group was happy with her and in any case, one man's excessive is of course another man's perfectly justifiable. *Vide* the Bible: the discomforts of Job, oxen and asses stolen by Sabeans, camels stolen by Chaldeans, sheep burned up by fires from heaven, plus seven sons and three daughters mowed down by an earthquake. With boils still to come. And all for what?

But one can't unfailingly be *simpatico.*

The rooms filled up. SCT members plus several outsiders, library staff who had liked Declan, someone from the *Echo,* several obvious queers. Leo looked for Mr Peterson but this time did not see him. The man had once again sensibly remembered a prior engagement. By half past seven, though, some forty people had arrived for Declan Finsey's memorial meeting. His sisters were there. And also, in the back row—bringing Leo back to the immediate, to astonishment and distress—the instantly recognisable motel clerk Henry.

Why the hell should he have come? Leo hunched himself down in his seat and cursed. There was another world, ugly and dangerous, not just his self-disgust and sorrow. Perhaps, if he kept his head down, it would go away.

'*Good evening. My goodness, what a crowd. What a crowd.*' Mrs Carstairs, of course, as Pitville's Senior Elder, and indeed the SCT's Senior Elder, was at the front now, calling the meeting to order. That other world. '*Thank you all for coming. First of all, for those of you who are newcomers, I'd like to introduce...*'

She did the job economically and well, out of many years' chairing experience, and Leo grudgingly recognized it.

'*I ask you, dear Lord, for your strength and guidance...*'

T/S Gifford had taken over, eyes closed, offering the usual opening prayer.

'*...Please make me and keep me an instrument for truth, to be revealed from realms of higher being to people here on earth.*'

He stepped back, seated himself, opened his eyes.

'*We're here this evening, dear friends, to remember and celebrate the life of Declan Finsey, a man known and loved by all of us, a brilliant truthsayer and guide, recently moved on to a higher realm...*'

Leo's attention ceased. Since Tuesday he had accumulated many vivid memories of Declan, all of them different from Gifford's and most of them extremely painful.

In due course Gifford finished. Apparently Declan's Stroud group had eulogies planned but first Gifford proposed a time for silent thought. Madam Sara had always encouraged this. She called it listening. No circle or linking of hands, however—she emphasised to her followers that psychic energy wasn't huggy-feely, it was an awe-inspiring supernatural force that moved quite independently of physical contact.

The silence lengthened. A silence that forty people make in a room has a special quality. Quakers know it well. The smoky scent of the candles helped. By the time Gifford shifted in his seat and gave a faint sigh the room's SCT members were ready for anything.

'We have a contact, I believe.'

Sweat was beading Gifford's forehead and his hands were tightly clasped, fingernails digging into his palms.

'Do we welcome it?'

Leo thought not. Gifford/Mehetmotep was rushing things. A meeting like this, especially with visitors, needed better preparation. And in any case a contact, of whatever kind, would lengthen an already embarrassing event. But then of course, he was one of the very few of those present—his mother was probably the only other—who were not there at least in part for sensationalist reasons. By now the nature of Declan's death, and the uncertainty currently surrounding it, were both common knowledge. If ever words from the hereafter might prove to be truly revelatory, this then was the moment... Leo, on the other hand, was there simply because his job demanded it. He had no interest in the outcome, and certainly felt no fears. The radiant spirits, in his experience, were unfailingly non-committal.

As for his mother, if questioned about said spirits she would robustly claim that they were by no means infallible, that headline-grabbing pronouncements would be cheap and irresponsible, and that she agreed with Jesus: matters pertaining to Caesar were best left to Caesar.

Gifford raised his voice.

'A contact... Do we welcome it?'

In the presence of so many outsiders his regular group members had been diffident. They took courage.

'We welcome it.'

Gifford relaxed. He closed his eyes again, took several very deep breaths. Soon channelling would begin. He unclasped his hands. At one meeting held by him Leo had noticed blood on his finger-ends, which he had quickly and without comment wiped away. Madam Sara discouraged melodrama. Meetings were for spirit guidance not grand guignol performances.

Gifford tilted his head, shaking it as if he had ear-ache. Sounds came from his mouth, a sort of tuneless singing. Suddenly his body stiffened and he sat forward, elbows close by his sides, hands raised beneath his chin, fingers spread and curved as if enclosing an invisible sphere. The sounds changed and became words.

'Mehetmotep... Mehetmotep has a message. Message... message for a woman here... for a woman called... called Carey... Carey? Names are so difficult. I think we have no Carey.'

Gifford frowned. Shook his head again.

'No...no message for a woman... Two women. Sisters. Carey? No...two sisters... Mary... Two sisters, Carla and Mary... Carla and Mary. A mes-

sage for two sisters, Carla and Mary.'

There was a pause. In the audience Leo saw Declan's sisters leaning together. One of them was trying to stand, to get away, the other holding her down.

'Carla... Mary... The message is from Mumma. Mumma...is that right? Yes, the message is from Mumma.'

Gifford brought his hands decisively together, interlocking the fingers.

'Carla... Mary... Mumma has a message for her daughters. Deckle-po's tired. He's very tired but he's fine. He's thinking of you. He loves you very much.'

There was a disturbance. The sister who'd been trying to get away succeeded and ran awkwardly, Leo thought angrily, from the room. She slammed the door behind her. The other sister stayed, hunched over, weeping.

'Mumma loves you very much. This is a sad time. Mumma loves Deckle-po very much. This time will pass. Tell your sister... Deckle-po is safe and fine, safe and fine. He's thinking of you. Thinking of you both. He's with you.'

A neighbour in the audience had her arm round the weeping sister.

'Deckle-po is with you both. Important. Mumma loves him. Tell your sister. Deckle-po is with you both. This sad time will pass...'

The sister's neighbour was weeping also. Around them the whole room was in movement, SCT members gathering in the centre, visitors edging away, muttering to each other, a few clearly making for the door. Leo remembered his *All comers welcome* in Declan's obituary. It had been a mistake. The immediacy and emotionality of Spiritualism wasn't for everybody. He was concerned in particular for the Declan sister who had fled—which name went with which sister he couldn't recall—and was himself hurrying to the door to find her when, as the result of near-suicidal negligence, he crashed into motel clerk Henry, bound for the same destination.

Their meeting struck Leo dumb. Not so Henry.

'Mr Carter... what a surprise. I'd never of put you down as a Spiritualist.'

Thank god for the *Carter*. "Nor me you.'

Did motel clerks admit to recognising their short-stay customers? Apparently this one did.

Leo cleared his throat. He had more conversation available, but it shrivelled as he suddenly, truly for the first time, saw the thought association that had connected Carter and Bresson, and was appalled. How could he have given a false name that was so obvious? Coade would love that. All that was now needed was for wretched Henry to be a Cartier-Bresson 35-mm photography enthusiast, and to make the connection.

'Me a spitualist? Do me a favour. It was alright for Dek, he never pushed it, but I ask you...'

'So you're here because you knew him?'

'Knew him? He was around. A friendly feller... I can see you've been about the place a bit—' a sideways glance with that '—so you'll know what I mean.'

Leo felt a little better. Although he had never joined it, of course, he knew that queers made up a considerable community in Cheltenham. Back at the motel Henry clearly hadn't hadn't seen Rosie. Now, recognizing Leo as Mr Carter here at Declan's memorial service, Henry had assumed that he was a sympathetic homo and that his motel companion lurking in their car had been another bloke. Hence the ready confidences.

'A friendly feller.' Henry liked the phrase. 'And then some crazy bugger comes along and snuffs him.'

"You really think so?'

'That's what the word is. You'll see... But all this spook stuff here, it's a put-up job. I shouldn't never of come. Disgusting. Wouldn't you say? Stands out a mile.'

'I'm sure you're right.'

'Course I'm right. Who doesn't know Dek's mum always called him Deckle-po, for fuck's sake?'

Leo knew. Right up to the day, in the natural course of medical events, when her failing lungs had taken her, she had loved him. And that despite the claims from his cruelly homophobic father that his lifestyle had caused her transition. Declan had been known to mention this and T/S Gifford had now emphasised it. No accusations had come from her departed spirit

Henry needed a punctuation. He looked at his watch. ' We'll miss him, mind. You'd better believe it. Not all this stuff here. Bugger that. I'm off. See yer.'

'See you.'

Not in this lifetime, Leo thought. Not if he had anything to do with it. Cheltenham was a big town. A city, really. They moved in different worlds.

He waited a couple of minutes, for Henry to be safely gone, then followed him out of the house to look for the sister. The pavements were deserted under the street lamps save for Henry, walking briskly away beside the plane trees, but an interior light shone in a car parked close by, and Leo could see her inside, sitting very upright in the passenger's seat, smoking fiercely. He didn't go to her. She'd lost her brother. And now this circus. There was nothing useful he could say.

He went back into the house. Christ, he'd be glad when he was shot of the SCT and all it stood for.

T/S Gifford tried hard, he was a decent man, but. he never got Declan Finsey's memorial service back into shape again. Memories of Declan were shared, and a joke or two, but the culture clash has been too extreme. Wisely, he kept even the final prayer to a very few words.

Leo meanwhile had been joining Henry's dots. The only threat he now presented came if he'd been the source of Dekko's Rosie-Max information, but in any case, Dekko was dead now. So Henry basically didn't matter. Leo told himself he should keep his concerns for things that really mattered, of which there were plenty.

Getting his mother home and fed and into bed at a decent hour mattered. Emptying the dishwasher and putting all the stuff away mattered. Feeding Rumple mattered. Ringing up Gordon and thanking him for not subbing Declan's obit out of existence mattered. Checking with that Charlton Kings undertaker—Roxanne Fletcher, wasn't it?—that T/S Courtland's post-interment meeting had been satisfactory mattered. The choice of Madam Sara's replacement as director of the SCT mattered.

His mother was tired out. He got her into bed just after nine. He dealt with the dishwasher too, and fed Rumple. The rest would have to wait until the morning.

What else?

What about the mess inside his head? Mr Bassett's job? The dancing? Max?

Leo still couldn't hear the music. And Max, of course, was dead.

He lay down on his bed fully dressed: not just sorrowful, crushed by his sorrow, brutalised, dry and black and cinder-cold with his sorrow.

CHAPTER 9

So now, with Max dead, our story has arrived at Monday morning. Has it really been only five-and-a-bit days since Leo Anthony Bresson was up in Declan's white-carpeted living room, looking out through the French windows and fussing with the zip on his anorak? It feels like longer. It certainly felt longer to Leo.

He'd telephoned Rosie the night before, unable to sleep, some time around midnight. No answerphone, not even a ringing tone. *Number unobtainable.* She must have un-plugged the whole outfit from its socket. There was a woman really wanting to be left alone. He worried briefly, thinking that perhaps he should drive over and check. Another man might have. Leo didn't. Respecting her wishes was reasonable and got him off the hook.

He hung up, went back to bed, and eventually it was morning.

After an uneventful breakfast, keeping on keeping on because that was what one did, he tried her phone again. She was plugged in now and she answered briskly. As soon as she heard his voice her performance faltered and she wept. The empty flat clawed at her, she told him. She needed to talk. Why didn't the two of them meet in the park? The day looked fine enough from her window.

Leo peered out at the world beyond his office/bedsit and agreed with her. Furthermore, this was Monday and he'd just heard Hoppy letting herself in, so he could leave his mother in her care. Ma had bridges to mend with her. He'd laid the groundwork, but a quiet time together would do both of them good.

Putting Rosie on hold, he went and checked the SCT's post-box in case something needed urgent attention. A thick wad of letters, but five of them were ballot papers incorrectly returned to him rather than Bunty Carstairs. The rest were bills and advertisements. He rejoined Rosie and told her the park would be fine, by the gate on the Old Bath Road, give him twenty minutes, and rang off. He tapped the five unopened ballot papers into a neat bundle ready for sending on to the Board. Only a couple of days more, then his mother would know the worst. He had his money on Courtland. There was the capable motherly type whom he'd voted for himself, who was much more suitable, Mrs Patton in Longleach, away just now but only until Christmas, but he suspected that the Elders were looking for bezazz, which Courtland had in spades. He chose a cleaner crew-neck from the drawer, cheered up his hair, and told Hoppy and his mother that he was going out for a while.

They were in the kitchen together, drinking mugs of Madam Sara's *fithy stuff.* She eyed him resentfully. 'It's Sandra tomorrow. I need my es-sercises. She left a paper. I carn find it. Where you put it?'

His clenched his jaw until his teeth hurt. Was no moment ever his own? When he was able, he carefully told her, '*The tip of the tongue, the teeth and the lips,* Mother. Lots of times. A hundred if you can manage. Hoppy will help you.'

' Sandra said do it with you. It was on the paper, Leo. Sandra said you.'

He turned away. 'Do it lots of times, mother. Hoppy's better at them than I am. *The tip of the tongue, the teeth and the...*' He was out of the kitchen and into the conservatory before he'd finished. He'd been remiss. Of course he had. Four days had passed since Sandra's last visit and he hadn't given his mother's bloody tongue and lips a thought. She needed him to remind her of things. Whom else did she have?

She didn't call out after him. He went along to the garage, opened its roll-up door, and drove off down Tivoli Street, bodging a gear change in his needless haste.

Rosie was standing just inside the gate on the Old Bath Road, in front of the park notice board, visibly worn down and weary, carefully reading the opening times and the council by-laws. The bereaved wife. She looked utterly wretched: but more than that. Bereavement. He stopped abruptly, arrested by the realisation that there, at that moment, he was truly seeing not just the word, he was seeing the reality. And he was seeing it because he now understood it.

Bereavement. Experiencing it, he understood it. In its first sharp agony, what it was. Emptiness. The central void. The pervasive never-again. Rosie looked wretched, anybody could see that, but you could easily look like that if your tooth was hurting. Rosie's whole self was hurting. Assaulted. Nobody who hadn't experienced it could begin to understand. He approached her slowly, held out his hand, she took it, and they walked together on the path beside the river.

What they said, if they said anything, in those first few minutes Leo doesn't remember. He walked beside her, kicking at the leaves.

Charlton Park was full of autumn. Piled-up conkers, smoke from bonfires, all the usual stuff. Willows dangled dried-out lambs'-tails over the Chelt's narrow, bright, fast-flowing water. Ducks protested ungratefully in the shallows. The swans that cruised among them in aristocratic silence seemed wiser but were really just more suspicious and bad-tempered. Leo looked out across the busy stream and tried to plan some sort of useful opening remark.

Rosie's question came from nowhere. 'Leo?' She took her hand away. 'What the hell are you going to do with your life?'

So much for plans. 'Do with it?'

'You can't go on living with your mother.'

Oh lord. Another Alan. 'That's easy to say, love. But I do have responsibilities.'

'Do you? She's got money, hasn't she? If you took yourself off she'd get a proper nurse companion.' Rosie snapped her fingers. 'Just like that.'

'The SCT's dumping her. I didn't tell you.'

'So?'

He was hating this. 'So nothing, really…'

'So what are you going to do?'

'Rosie… Rosie, why are you attacking me?'

'I'm not attacking you. Yes, I am. I need to know. I mean, it's not as if you believe in Spiritualism, is it?'

'I don't… disbelieve in it.'

'Come on, Leo. This is me you're talking to. Those people, sitting round listening to dead Uncle Marmaduke tell them their doggie's barking Happy Birthday at them?'

'I think they're idiots.' He thought about it. 'That makes me pretty stuck-up.' He walked on a couple of slow paces. 'But I also think they must be pretty desperate, more desperate than I've ever been, so I'm sorry for them. And that makes me stuck-up too.'

'Stuck-up, Leo? Don't hide behind feeble prep-school language. For god's sake, having standards isn't being stuck-up.'

'Rosie… this is crazy. We don't really have to quarrel about whether or not I believe in Spiritualism, do we?'

It was a cheating question and they both knew it: people seldom quarrel about what they're really quarrelling about. He and Rosie walked on in silence, stopping wretchedly at a place where the path ran close by the water's edge and tiny children, done up in bright, inflated-looking anoraks, were feeding flabby bits of plastic bread to the ducks while their mothers—

Alright, so the self-appointed Cheltenham experts are protesting that they've lived in the borough for sixty years and they've never been in Charlton Park when the River Chelt wasn't a rusty bicycle-laden trickle at the bottom of a narrow sort of gully between collapsed chain-link fencing. No grassy banks, no willows, no swans, and precious few ducks… Well, just as before, that is their Cheltenham and this is ours. Which one, frankly, is preferable?

In any case, ours perfectly suits this scene between Rosie and Leo.

Which really did happen.

They found a bench, sat on it, watched the urban scene. The sun, although not hot, was bright and cheery. She took his hand again.

'I shall miss you, Leo.'

His gut cringed. She really was coming from nowhere this morning. 'Where will you go?'

'I've no idea. *Somewhere...*' She gestured broadly. 'There has to be somewhere better than Cheltenham.'

'Very true.'

Only two words, but she hardly let him finish them. 'So why don't you come with me?'

'What?'

'You heard me.' Sharper still. 'Don't make me repeat it.'

Of course he'd heard her. He was shocked. Disbelieving. Terrified. His mind was in spasm. *Why didn't he go with her?* He had no answer.

She shook her head, frowning, her first brave impetus exhausted, and explained instead. 'This isn't a marriage proposal, Leo. I'm Max's widow. I think I always will be.'

She broke then, shuddering, caught in a vertigo Leo could now recognise, and stared away down the path to a distant bandstand. The moment passed eventually and she turned back to him. 'No commitment, Leo. Getting away—that's all. We could see if it works. I need it and so do you. We can prop each other up. Just for a time, perhaps... Till something else comes along...'

She'd started out so directly and now she was conditionalising their future life with ifs and perhaps, all away to nothing. He couldn't bear to see it.

'Hush, now. Hush, my love...' He moved closer, felt safe to put his arm round her shoulders. 'It'll be wonderful. We can look after us. Start again. Oh, my little love...' He hugged her. 'It's the perfect chance. Get away. Just get away.'

She stiffened. 'But...?'

'But what? What do you mean?'

'You have buts, Leo. I can feel them.'

'No buts, my dear.' This was crazy. Max was hardly twenty-four hours dead. Of course he had buts. 'No buts, Rosie. Not a one.'

'Your responsibilities?'

'Proot on that. I don't have any.'

She eased away and looked up at him. 'Yes you do.'

'Not a one.'

'You do, Leo.'

'The SCT doesn't need me. I could leave tomorrow.'

'Not the SCT. Of course not.'

'What, then?' He knew quite well. They'd been through this on other days. 'These are the eighties, Rosie. Sons aren't responsible for their mothers. Especially their well-off mothers.'

'We aren't talking about sons. Not just *sons*.'

'Alright, alright… we're talking about me.'

She was insistent. 'And?'

Well now… not just *sons*. This was different. 'I really think I've done enough, Rosie. Three whole years—virtually day and night. That's pretty good, isn't it? And as you said, she could get a nurse companion just like that.' He tried snapping his fingers the way she just had but it was a trick he'd never learned. The finger joints slid against each other ineffectually. One could still fall down funnily, even at forty-one, if one was small-scale about it.

'She won't want to, Leo.'

'Of course she won't. And I won't want to make her. I shall hate it. Dread it. But it's got to be done.'

'No it hasn't. Not unless you really want it.'

'Of course I want it.' She'd offered and he'd accepted. He was a great accepter. 'Of course I want it.'

'So you'll tell her.'

It wasn't a question.

And what about money? He'd have to get a job. What sort of job? The whole thing was folly. Dangerous folly. Completely impossible. 'Where shall we go?'

'Where?' Rosie paused, as if to consider. Had he convinced her? 'Max always said I should live in the country. We often talked about what I'd do after he was dead.' She checked at the word, eyes very wide and empty, then carried on. 'He said I should have a garden. He said I'd be good at it.'

Out in the country somewhere… why not? Leo had lived in towns all his life and never used them. Not a man for art galleries, libraries, visits to the theatre. Not an area of life Coll had made him all that keen on. He could still have a bridge club, though. A village hall out in the country somewhere, with a weekly bridge club in it. And there was always writing. It was a long time since he'd had that thought.

There was never writing.

'How about Devon?'

'Max thought Wales. It's closer to London. And Devon's so expensive.'

Max thought Wales. Aha. Max had thought the country too, and the garden. Clearly Max came as part of the deal. Which was fine by him.

'I love Wales. We'll need to get jobs.'

'You will. I'll have my garden. Max won't have left me broke, you know.'

A tiny shock. She'd thought it through. Unless, like him, she was improvising, making it up as she went along. He hoped she was. Follies needed to be shared.

'A job for me, then. What sort of job?'

'I don't know… You play the piano. You could play it in a hotel. Songs from the shows. A restaurant somewhere.'

She had to be improvising. Leo was reassured. 'Come on, love— you've heard me. I'm nowhere near good enough.'

'A parish clerk, then.'

'I don't think they get paid.'

'But you'll come?' She looked at him sideways. Lord, how he loved her. 'You'll quit the SCT? You'll leave your mother? You'll really come?'

He faced her, his hands on her shoulders. 'I'll really come.'

Cut.

Cut and print.

A useful convention. Creaky but useful. It permits omitting the really boring bits. There was more of the same sad stuff, a whole lot more, on that Monday morning in Charlton Park between Leo and Rosie, but the point is clear. They weren't making sense: Rosie more than Leo, but not much. People in love often don't. Additionally they suffered from at least one unresolved guilt and they were also, if unequally, bereaved. All in all, a mess.

Mind you, Rosie'd had a full twenty-four hours on her own with the fragments of rational thought that her grief allowed her. She'd have worked out that day was going to follow day and that she was going to have to do something about each one of them. Something more than just this flayed, unconscionable existence. A trial life with Leo in a Welsh cottage, possibly with apple orchard attached, wouldn't have seemed totally out of the question.

As for Leo, it was a long time—only five-and-a-bit days, actually, but we've already talked about that—since even fragments of wholly rational thought had been granted him. Shame, the music he couldn't hear, compartments, love, death, dancing, jail, Madam Sara… too much got in the way. So that the possible continuities of a cottage in Wales with Rosie were a marvel. A treasure. A notion so wondrous that it lasted him until after they'd parted in the park, she for a telephone appointment with Simon Dell in London about Max's memorial service and unfinished book, plus her brother Philip arriving on a train from Liverpool shortly after lunch, and Leo for the short drive back to Tivoli Street.

At which point, as he sat waiting, full of wonder and joy in his Jaguar at the Leckhampton Road traffic lights—and absolutely not before that moment (so fragmented was he)—he once again saw Declan weeping, scraping, dying on the concrete.

The image tore him apart. There at the Leckhampton Road traffic lights he despaired so extravagantly, wept and raged, waiting in his Jaguar there, that he missed a green light or two.

Three, perhaps. Unusually, nobody was behind him to honk. He pounded the steering wheel and wept.

Rosie? Wales? A cottage in the country? Was he really so demented? Rosie was lost to him. And with her everything. Life itself. He'd known that right from this nightmare's start. Now it was even more acutely true. If he was to accept her trust, the possibility of a future together, he must first tell her about Declan, about Declan left dying on the concrete. And he never could. He never could confess to her something so insupportable. What the knowledge would do for her present perilous exigencies he couldn't imagine. It would certainly load her with an intolerable dilemma—help him or turn him in. So he couldn't do it. Not to her. Least of anyone in the world, to her.

His game of let's-pretend with her in Charlton park had been blind and cruel. *He meant well... he was a good accepter...* dear god, what cosy, smug, repellent phrases he thought up in order to be able to live with himself. Even his careful literary construction, *Rosie was lost to him,* was deceitfully cosier than the truth. She wasn't prosily and impersonally *lost to him*; he'd trodden her love for him thoughtlessly underfoot with every self-serving step he'd taken since that moment alone upstairs in Declan's flat.

Eventually, there at the Leckhampton Road traffic lights, he saw these grovelling, mawkish thoughts for what they were and drove on.

People drive on, he told himself. It's what people do.

* * * *

Back on Tivoli Street Hoppy was vacuuming the bottom few stairs with the long hose attachment, making so much noise that he scarcely heard the telephone ringing in his office/bedsit. As he passed her he gestured wearily for her to turn the cleaner off. He didn't give a damn what the telephone was wanting of him, but it might be SCT business. And he hadn't yet, not quite yet, quit.

Out in the hall: welcome silence.

Less welcome, on the telephone in his office/bedsit: 'Mr Bresson? Glad I caught you.' Not SCT business. Detective Sergeant Anthea bloody Wiler. 'The Chief Inspector would like to tidy up a few small points.'

'Points?' The sergeant's voice, though affable, he didn't need. He hadn't heard it since—when was it?—Friday morning. Now it was Monday. 'More points?'

'A reconstruction, he thought, if you don't mind, sir. This afternoon, sir. Sorry for the short notice.'

Christ... A reconstruction? What of? Coade was wanting to put him back in that terrible flat? He couldn't do it.

'A reconstruction, Sergeant? What of?'

'You were in Mr Finsey's home shortly before he died. It's possible that you saw something. Something significant. Something that perhaps you didn't recognise at the time.'

No. Standing up there with Chief Inspector Coade in Declan's living room, inventing stuff. Inventing a whole visit. No. He couldn't do it. 'I thought reconstructions were of crimes, Sergeant. I've committed no crime.'

'Then you won't mind helping us, sir. Around five, we thought. The time you got there last Wednesday.'

'I—' He couldn't do it. 'This afternoon isn't convenient. I've an appointment. I don't think I can change it.'

'Do your best, sir. Call us if you can't. Otherwise we'll expect you. Cirencester. Down by the ground floor entrance. Five. And you may bring a solicitor if you like, of course.'

'You're advising me to?'

'Not at all. Just reminding you of your rights. Goodbye for the moment, Mr Bresson.'

Leo dumped the phone and leaned against his desk. A solicitor? He didn't have one. The SCT did, but he could hardly ask her. Not in his position. She was a fussy bore anyway.

He'd have to be there. The sergeant knew that. And what the hell. He was a good little liar... Another of his smug self-deprecations? Yes. But they helped, brought a distancing lightness, and the way he felt just then, he didn't bloody care.

Five o'clock, at the lobby entrance. That left the whole rotten lousy afternoon to be got through.

Madam Sara, just now, would probably be reading her newspaper in the small back drawing room. As he went to her Hoppy restarted the vacuum cleaner in the hall, rattling its nozzle bossily between the banister rails. He closed the back drawing room door against her racket.

His mother looked at him over the top of the *Cheltenham Echo*. The previous night, after the Pitville meeting, she'd been weary but very pleased with life. Word of her retirement was out, of course: her final appearance had been a triumph. Certainly Gifford's Mehetmotep had made a serious misjudgement letting Deckle-po's poor silly mother through at that moment, with that particular group, but it hadn't stopped the faithful from showing their appreciation. Their gratitude for her lifetime of service. Their love. Tears had been shed.

This morning, during breakfast, her mood had been bleaker. Final appearances were fun, but they were final. Leo, in reality absent in his sorrow, had been inattentive. Not sympathetic.

'Leo?' His mother folded the paper. 'Good walk?'

'Walk? I was seeing Rosie. Max's wife. His widow. I was seeing Rosie.'

'You see her yesterday.'

'I shall probably see her again tomorrow.' Keeping score, you nosy cow?

She looked down at her paper, then up at him again and changed the subject. 'Your *Echo* friend... Gridin... Gardin... Glardon... tell him—'

'Gordon. His name's Gordon.'

She pointed at the paper. 'Tell him nineteen sixty-six. He get it wrong. Founded in nineteen sixty-six. And I was born in India.'

So Gordon's man up at the Pitville meeting had phoned in his copy in time for today's edition. If those were all the sloppy fact-checkings he could find in it she was bloody lucky. He leaned forward, tipped the top of the paper towards him and struggled with the upside down headline. Finally he mastered it: *Matriarch Medium Retires Amid Acclaim.*

'Got it wrong, Ma,' he told her. 'Past tense. He *got* it wrong.'

She glared at him. 'Doan call me Ma.'

He waited for the 'clower chass' bit but for once it didn't come so he turned away, en route for the kitchen to see about lunch.

She called after him: 'Telephone rang?'

'Wrong number.' He kept going. Was nothing his? 'Just a wrong number.'

'You talk long time—*talked* a long time—for a wrong number.'

He carefully opened the door, his back still towards her, and leaned in the doorway. She was keeping score. ''I talked for a long time, Mother, because the man on the other end was ringing his new girl friend's number from memory, and he'd remembered it wrong, and he was in a phone box so he didn't have a phone book, so I looked it up for him.'

He was, as he'd already reminded himself, a good little liar.

'Thass nice. Who was she?'

He continued on into the kitchen. 'I can't remember.'

He opened a store cupboard. Serve the old cow right if he gave her tuna fish for lunch, which she hated. He didn't. There wasn't any in the house. There was corned beef, though, which she loved.

The afternoon passed. SCT business helped. Shortly after he'd tucked his mother up for her afternoon rest the Stroud group called, reporting that on Saturday the tea urn they used had sprung a leak and this morning's news was that it couldn't be mended. The local vicar was willing to let them use his *Mother's Union* tea urn for as long as they liked, but they felt that really they didn't want to be beholden to him. Would they please be allowed, Mr Bresson, to bill SCT Headquarters for a new one? And possibly one that used bottled gas because Colonel FitzSimmons said gas ones boiled water more quickly than the cheaper electric sort?

Tea urns. Hooray for tea urns. And for Colonel FitzSimmons, whoever he was.

Leo told them there was an *Emergencies Fund* established for exactly that sort of purpose. And he was sure the SCT could run to the more expensive gas model. Send him an invoice in due course and he'd pass it on to the treasurer. And if they needed help getting the new equipment to the hall they should give him a call. He knew of a Charlton Kings member with a very useful small van.

He rang off. Not a single stammer. With his SCT hat on he was a whizz. Who the hell was Colonel FitzSimmons?

There was also supper to be considered. He decided on beef stew with dumplings. If he cooked the meat this afternoon he could leave it maturing in the oven while he went to Coade's reconstruction, and fling in the dumplings on his return.

Chopping board. Sharp knife. Stewing steak. Heavy-based frying pan. Oil. Plain flour, salt and pepper. Apparatus, too, was a fine thought-stopper. Casserole. Beef stock from a Sainsbury's carton. Garlic. Red wine. Oven. Then the dumplings for later—flour (self-raising this time) and shredded suet. Water.

Apparatus ran out of oomph, though. Max was dead. Rosie was lost to him, and Coade's reconstruction loomed. Its implications, too, should he get it wrong. His death (if sudden enough) he could cope with. But execution wasn't on the agenda these days, only (*only?*) lengthy imprisonment, and that was beyond all endurance. His worst dread. Not so much the fact of incarceration as the iron walls and their echoing paroxysms of group misery. And the fractured, terrifying company. He must not get Coade's reconstruction wrong…

What worried him most was how little he remembered of the two Lansdowne Road interviews. What he'd told them. What they'd be checking. Declan hadn't been out on the balcony. The French windows had been closed. It hadn't been dark. Clean hands. No tea or coffee or drinks. What else?

Three o'clock came. His mother woke. She had to be told sooner or later about Wiler's phone call and his five o'clock Cirencester appointment so he took the opportunity as she was settling herself at her desk with the SCT archive. By way of explanation he paraphrased the sergeant: he'd been at Mr Finsey's home just before the poor man died and he might have seen something significant, something he hadn't at the time recognised… Put like that, it seemed perfectly reasonable. She nodded absently and asked him to find the 1965 carton of files for her.

Four thirty came. Time to leave for Cirencester. The stew was thick and rich and bubbling cheerfully. He turned the gas right down and left it in the oven to stay warm

* * * *

His arrival that evening at Declan's block of flats being nearly an hour earlier than last week's, there were parking spaces. He took one of them, which turned out to be alongside Coade's unmarked Rover. The morning's clear blue sky had clouded over but it wasn't yet raining. He got out of the Jaguar and Coade and Wiler joined him by the entrance to Declan's staircase.

'You parked here last week, Mr Bresson?' Talking round his empty pipe.

'More or less.' The first lie. Necessary because the truth would suggest a crowded forecourt and therefore a later time. 'I didn't really notice.'

People don't. Well, he hoped they didn't. In any case, Coade seemed to accept it.

'And the forecourt was deserted? Like this? No one about?'

'I don't think so. I'm sorry, Inspector, but I wasn't really looking.'

'So you called Mr Finsey and waited while he unlatched the door?'

'No need. I know the combination.'

He pressed the right four buttons and released the door latch. Wiler stopped him as he was leaning against the door to open it.

'Last week, sir—was that difficult? Were you carrying anything? Bundles of SCT literature? A briefcase?'

'My briefcase, Sergeant.'

Coade read his thoughts. 'There *is* a point, Mr Bresson. We're wanting you to think small. Detail. Focus in. Things that perhaps you didn't consciously register.'

Leo humoured them. 'Nobody out on the forecourt.' He eased himself past Wiler and into the lobby. 'Nobody in here either. I'm sure of that. The lift was up at the top and I had to wait for it to come down.'

'Show us.'

Leo showed them. This was ridiculous. In any case, the lift was only one floor up now and arrived almost immediately. He got in and they joined him. Up they went.

'You stood here quietly,' Coade told him. 'What were you thinking about?'

About how he was dreading having to tell Declan about him and Rosie?

'…Probably about supper. Yes, I'm sure of it. What I was going to get my mother and me for supper.'

'Which was?'

'Something from the freezer. A slab of lasagna, I thought, zapped in the microwave. We usually eat from the freezer on the Tuesdays when I'm out all day visiting the truthsayers. That's probably why I remember. Not ideal, but it's only once a month.'

It was all coming back to him. And he really didn't need to apologise to Coade for how he fed his mother.

The lift arrived at the fifth floor and the three of them got out. One of the doors along the brown-tiled passage, Leo realised, must be Mr Peterson's. He walked ahead to Declan's door, the third, with two more beyond it, took his key from his pocket and-

'We have a constable waiting inside, Mr Bresson. I was expecting you to ring the bell.'

'Declan and I had been friends. I told you.'

'He hadn't asked for his key back?'

'We hadn't quarrelled, Inspector. Not *quarrelled*... It probably hadn't occurred to him.' Leo put the key in the door and opened it.

The constable waiting inside must have heard them coming. He was close to the door, expecting to have to open it, and it banged into him. He was in uniform, his cap tucked awkwardly under one arm.

'Mr Bresson, this is Constable Drew. The Cirencester force has kindly lent him to us.'

Leo ducked his head politely. Only a twit, he thought, would try to shake hands.

'So, Mr Bresson, you let yourself in. Where was Mr Finsey?'

'In the living room. Corner of the sofa by the fireplace. Reading. He had a CD playing. Jazz. Piano jazz.' In his head he invented a picture of Dekko exactly, one leg crossed over the other, looking up from his book. He'd mentioned McPartland last time so that would be over-doing it.

The black leather sofa was visible from the small hallway where they were standing.

'Drew...' Coade made a shooing gesture with the backs of his hands towards it. The constable backed away and sat down. 'Reading, Constable. *Reading*...' Drew obediently reached for a book from the shelf unit on the wall beside him and opened it. 'Excellent... We can do without the music. What next, Mr Bresson? How did he greet you?'

'Depends what you mean by 'greet.' He said something—*hi*... *hello*... I don't remember. Nothing very much. He didn't get up. I was late and he wasn't pleased.' Leo could see it all now. Dekko's open book laid face down on his knee, Dekko drumming his fingers on it. 'Anyway, I slipped off my shoes and—'

'Your shoes, Mr Bresson? Not your coat?'

'I didn't have a coat, just an anorak thing. I kept that on. The shoes were on account of Dekko's—Mr Finsey's carpet. I mean, look at it.'

They looked. Leo could imagine how upset Dekko would have been to see them now, tramping all over it. 'Mr Finsey had slippers for himself indoors,' he told them. 'Shoes go on that mat there,.'

Coade ignored the hint. 'Doors? Open or shut?' He pointed to right and left. The wide open right-hand door led into the kitchen. On the left, down a short corridor, the doors giving access to bedroom and bathroom were closed. Leo thought back, went to the bedroom door and opened it about nine inches. Not enough to give a view inside of anything but wall.

'That's how it was?' Leo nodded. 'You didn't use the bathroom?'

'I went straight on in to Mr Finsey. I was late. I told you. So I apologised and he said it didn't matter, he hadn't been doing anything anyway, just reading. But not... you know... not *nicely*. Not as if he meant it.'

'Did you sit down first? Before the apology? Hm? I'm assuming you *did* sit down at some point.'

Leo concentrated, saw himself standing in the doorway, then seated, still in his anorak, on the edge of the matching black armchair opposite Dekko. Before or after the apology?

'After... I'm guessing, Inspector. Can't honestly remember. Apologise first, sit down second—it seems reasonable.'

'Do it, please.'

This really was ridiculous. Leo wrung his hands. '*Sorry, sorry, sorry—*'

'And you can spare us the theatrics.'

Leo went forward meekly and sat. He couldn't win. Another man had said that to him. Someone quite recently. 'Mr Finsey put his book down. At some point he turned off the music. Probably now. We talked. I asked him if he needed any SCT supplies—stationary, that sort of thing. He said he didn't. I gave him his STC newsletter. It was all very ordinary.'

'In your interview you said you were here for about twenty minutes. Twenty minutes of ordinary?'

'Well, he said he'd heard on the grapevine that one of our truthsayers, a Mrs Patton, was leaving and he wanted to know what we were doing about replacing her. In fact she wasn't leaving, only taking a break till Christmas. That led on to one of his harangues about SCT inefficiency.' Leo now clearly remembered wondering why Dekko cared a shit about Mrs Patton or her replacement. 'That led us on to subject normal with most of the truthsayers I'd been seeing that day—how my mother was past it, and when were we going to–'

'The flat's got central heating, Mr Bresson. If the windows were closed, weren't you hot? In your anorak, I mean?'

'Were the windows closed? I suppose they were. Yes...' Looking. Remembering. 'Not the curtains, though. Anyway, I wasn't hot.'

'How dark was it in here?'

'Brighter than this. The day was sunnier. Dekko—Mr Finsey had the lamp on there by the end of the sofa, but it wasn't really necessary.'

Without being told, Constable Drew turned on the lamp. Detective Sergeant Wiler had her notebook out. Leo couldn't imagine what she was writing in it.

'Mr Finsey's book—did you see what he was reading?'

He saw Dekko move his book, still face down, onto the sofa beside him. Even so, he couldn't manage a memory of looking to see what it was. "I'm afraid not.'

'He was a tidy man, though? I mean, this flat hasn't been touched since he died, and not a thing's out of place.'

'A very tidy man. If you're asking me whether he'd have put his book back on the shelf after I'd gone, I think he very well might have. He couldn't bear clutter.'

The constable dithered, then replaced the book where he'd found it. Leo saw that it was one of Dekko's Jung tomes. Dekko'd been a great one for archetypes. It could very well be the very book he had been reading.

'Was tea offered, Mr Bresson? Coffee? Drinks of any kind?'

'Not a drop. Mr Finsey warmed up a bit towards the end, but—'

'And in all the time you were here did you hear anything, did you see any sign that might suggest there was someone else, a third person in the flat?'

Leo paused long enough to show he was taking the question seriously. 'Nothing. Not a thing. The place was empty. You can see how small it is, Inspector. I'm sure I'd have felt it if someone else had been around.'

Coade and his sergeant exchanged glances. Meaning what? Leo didn't bother to guess. The chief inspector was wandering round the room now, peering at things. A scan of Dekko's LP albums caused him to shudder slightly.

'So eventually this rather curious conversation ended, Mr Bresson. What then?'

'I got up first, I think.' He did so. 'I'd said what I could. About my mother's position in the SCT, I mean. It hasn't been easy, not for quite some time. She's just resigned, in fact. You may have read about—'

'My sergeant's shown me the local paper. So you got up, and presumably Mr Finsey did, and you went together to the door…'

'Not yet. I needed his expenses sheet. And his monthly report.'

'And where were they?'

Simplify. 'There on his desk. He fetched them and I put them in my briefcase. That's right. It was on the coffee table.'

'Then you put your shoes back on and went out along the corridor to the lift, and down in it, and back to your car, and drove straight home, getting there shortly before six.'

The constable wasn't properly on his feet yet, but Coade had clearly lost interest. Leo wondered absently why on earth Drew had been needed... and suddenly the reason, the obvious reason, came to him. Constable Drew was there as back-up in the event of his arrest. And he had of course pushed Dekko off his balcony, he remembered that now, and he had of course left Dekko to die, weeping and scraping, out there, down on the concrete.

'...Detective Sergeant Wiler and I greatly appreciate your help, Mr Bresson. I think I can promise you that we won't be bothering you any further.' Coade had perched on Dekko's bleached maple sideboard, and was actually filling his pipe. It looked as if he might even smoke it. 'Occam's razor, Mr Bresson. Clearly in this case the simplest and most obvious answer is also the best. Potting compost was found on Mr Finsey's hands and under his fingernails. Since from what you and other people have said of him, he was not a man to sit reading a book in his sitting room in that condition, it must obviously have been after you left when he went out onto his balcony and decided to work on his many plants, several of which are attached to trelliswork extending beyond the sides of the balcony.'

He put his tobacco pouch away and stretched out one arm to demonstrate. 'A half-filled watering can standing in a puddle out on the balcony, plus several well-wetted flower pots, all support this theory. An accidental fall, therefore, while reaching out to one side or the other, perhaps kneeling on the rail, is entirely plausible. Hm? And indeed, in the absence of any evidence whatsoever to the contrary, in particular of anyone else out on the balcony, that is my firm conclusion. And finally, if of less legal significance, it is also my opinion Mr Bresson—and my sergeant agrees with me—that you do not have the violent, impulsive temperament of a man who pushes another man off a fifth floor balcony. All possibilities had to be examined, of course, and your help in this was very welcome, but I can report now to my Superintendent with confidence that Mr Finsey's death was the result of a very unfortunate accident.'

He eased himself down off the sideboard, struck a match, and spent a few moments lighting his pipe. 'I also want to assure you that any specific accusers in this case will be contacted by us, and their minds set at rest. You had no motive and since you have an excellent alibi, you had no opportunity either. In the circumstances I believe we will have no further trouble from that source.'

Leo hopes we've got at least most of that speech right. It's long, and he admits to having glazed over slightly once he'd realised where the chief inspector was going, but he's done his best to get in, briefly but Coade-ishly, all the important points. Most dialogue, in any fact-based book like this, is at best an imaginative reconstruction. And Leo does positively remember the Occam's razor reference. He admits, though, that he also had positively remembered those totally imaginary details of his time with Declan, details which clearly must have helped to convince Coade of his truthfulness, and this worries him. Declan had been out on the balcony tidying the plants when he arrived and stayed there while they talked. Being a good little liar is one thing. This is something else.

Even so—and it's fair to say this, even if banal—at that very stressful time it's hardly surprising that his mind did odd things. Furthermore, it all happened some twenty-plus years ago. He'd be far less convincing if everything made perfect sense.

As we admitted right at the beginning, we do what we can.

Leaving the three police officers in Declan's flat, Leo went back down to his car. He drove away through the gathering twilight. His thoughts were a tumult. Jail no longer threatened. Obviously this was a major relief.

* * * *

More than that, though, the chief inspector's official exoneration of him from Declan's murder had managed somehow to lighten the wider burden of responsibility he felt. His involvement in the actual fall from the balcony, of course, had never bothered him much, being completely unintentional. Not so his outrageous subsequent neglect. We've seen how comprehensively that had obsessed and tortured him.

But now, although nothing in fact had lessened his overall culpability, he remembers that being declared officially innocent made him feel better about himself. Life was offering him the miraculous chance actually to cancel and actually to move on. The chance to put his shameful behaviour behind him. The chance for him now seriously to consider the possibility of something he longed for above all else: the possibility of somehow blundering through to a future shared with Rosie. The future she had suggested for them only that morning.

He's not talking logic here, of course. He's talking need. He's talking desperation. He's talking all his remaining years in a lonely lonely world.

And all he had to do now was persuade himself that he could somehow earn a life, a trial period at least, with Rosie.

Certainly it was likely that very few people entered a relationship waving a confessional list of every sin, great or small, they'd ever committed. Usually the matter didn't come up—in which case they probably tallied up a private list at some time or other, and inwardly determined to do better—but if it did come up, well, they'd try to be truthful but proportionate. Selection occurred, therefore, and any list that finally got submitted would probably be short. Efforts towards taking on board the standards of the beloved would have been made, but the nuances of other people's standards were always unknowable, and ultimately those confessing had only their own judgment to go by.

In his current situation, though, the beloved's standards aren't at all unknowable. If he tells Rosie that he pushed Declan from his balcony and then left him to die slowly, weeping and scraping on the concrete, she'll want nothing more to do with him. Simple as that. She might also—though he can't quite believe this—turn him in to the police.

Nothing new there. So what has changed? The way, thanks to Coade's exoneration, he feels about himself?

The way he feels about himself?

Oh, come on—don't be like that. What other criterion does he finally have?

So the question in Leo's head as he drove back from Cirencester, literally trembling with pent-up possibilities, along the Roman road to Birdlip and then down Leckhampton Hill to Cheltenham and 83 Tivoli Street, was very simple. Could he allow himself not to tell Rosie of his responsibility for Declan's death? Did he feel sufficiently better about himself to allow that? Could he accept her loving trust, and manage to live every day thereafter with that deception? His willingness to dare to ask himself this question strongly suggested that his answer might be yes.

Time, after all, is a great healer. And desperation is a great persuader.

* * * *

As he turned into Tivoli Street, Leo's immediate future was mercifully simple. As soon as he got home he'd be able to report to his mother the happy outcome of Chief Inspector Coade's reconstruction. She was the only person, other than bloody Peterson, who knew that the police had been seriously considering the possibility that he'd been involved in Declan's death, so she was the only person he could share the good news with.

And then he'd call Rosie.

Halfway down the street a man stepped out from between two parked cars and waved at him urgently. As he braked Leo recognised bloody Mr Peterson in the car's head-lights. He skidded to a halt. For god's sake, the man must spend half his life loitering with intent in the Tivoli neighbourhood.

He wound down the passenger side window and Mr Peterson leaned in. He was wearing his usual, not-quite-shiny suit again. The pinstripe was clearly kept for high days and holidays.

'Lucky I spotted the Jaguar. I was just on my way to see you. This is much better... Mind if I park my bum?'

Leo could hardly stay there, blocking half the road. He leaned across and unlocked the door. Mr Peterson got in. 'Super. I had a talk with your mother at the memorial service. I'm sure you saw us. An impressive woman. Seriously handicapped, though. Perhaps not quite as resilient as she would like to pretend. I wouldn't want her bothered unnecessarily.'

Leo drove on, parking in a space a couple of doors down from number 81. This was not the moment, he decided, for sharing good news. Mr Peterson, who knew the truth, was clearly here to make a point, and he'd get to it in his own good time. The impressive woman was waiting for her supper, but she'd just have to wait.

There was Rosie too. He needed to talk to her. Simply for the joy of it. That too would have to wait.

'Thing is, Leo, we've hit a bit of a snag.' Mr Peterson paused, hastily got out a large very clean white handkerchief and blew his nose. 'Sorry about that. Sneeze coming... Where was I? Oh, and by the way, I was in Gloucester this morning, chatting with a good friend of yours. Canon Beckerton. On the cathedral close. A very good friend. Cleared up a number of points. I'm glad he was able to see me. Fitted me into his busy day ... He's concerned about you, Leo.'

'I know.' Alan's concern was neither here nor there. 'You mentioned a snag. What sort of snag?'

'Ah yes. That... Well, the thing is, Leo, I've been calling in a couple of favours and I got a look at the police's autopsy report. Seems that Mr Finsey... well, not to put too fine a point on it, he didn't die on impact. There would have been... an interval. The possibility of movement. Noises. So I was wondering, Leo, what you would know about that.'

Calling in favours had an ominous sound to it. Why must life always be so bloody complicated? What was the man? An ex-crime reporter? An ex-policeman?

'What I would know about it? I don't understand you. You're the one who's seen the report.'

'It all depends on where you left your car that night. Out in front would be fine. If you left it round the back, though, on your way to it afterwards you'd probably have fallen over his body. Mr Finsey's, I mean.'

Bothersome, bothersome... more decisions needed. But Leo could see that the man was basically on his side. *The possibility of movement... noises*—Mr Peterson was giving him every opportunity to deny both. Leo was getting to like him. Perhaps he always had.

'I did leave my car round the back. But I didn't fall over him. I saw him.'

'And?'

'He was dead. But you're quite right. There had been movement. And possibly noises.'

'Oh dear.' Mr Peterson ran his anxious, bloodless grey fingers through his thin sandy hair. "Oh dear.'

'There had been a time lag. I'd say ten minutes. I checked and he was dead. Then I walked on quickly. I was very afraid.'

Confession, he'd been told, was good for the soul. Nobody ever said anything about what it did to a man's other parts.

'You hadn't gone down to him at once?'

'I didn't think. I did things up in the flat. I told you—I was afraid.'

'Did things? Oh dear. What sort of things?'

'Things to help me get away with it.'

'You assumed he was dead. It was a long fall. You assumed he was dead.'

'No. I didn't think like that. I was afraid. I've just told you—I thought about ways to get away with it. Can't you imagine that?'

'Of course I can. But…'

'But what?'

'We were doing so well. This puts a different complexion on things. Quite a different complexion.'

Leo wondered, now that they were into confession time, if he shouldn't also tell Mr Peterson about him fucking his dear friend Max Krauss-Häber's wife. He decided against it as vulgar and gratuitous. Leaving Dekko weeping, scraping, dying on the concrete was quite enough.

Mr Peterson poked at one of the Jaguar's dashboard dials. He seemed not to know what to do with his hands. 'I shall have to think about it. And we were doing so well. You do understand, don't you? I shall have to give it some thought.'

He moved to get out of the car.

Leo grabbed his arm. 'I didn't push him. You do believe me? I got clumsy and he sort of fell.'

'Intention.' Mr Peterson disengaged Leo's hand. 'Intention isn't everything but it does matter.'

'I don't do intention much. I didn't then.' He remembered telling Inspector Coade he didn't do anger. So what did he do? Not only then. What did he do? 'I went with the flow. What seemed possible. I didn't—'

'Please. I do believe you. Enough now. You're not helping yourself. I need to give it some thought.'

Firmly he opened the car door, ducked out, and hurried away back down the road.

Leo watched him out of sight. He wondered if he'd sounded pleased with himself for not doing intention. He hadn't meant to. One had to be so careful. He sighed, then drove on, put the car away in the garage, and made his way into the house through the conservatory and the door with the red and blue glass lozenges.

He paused there. Mr Peterson needed to give it some thought.

What next? After he'd given it some thought, what next? What could the man do? He could go to the police with the truth, of course, and some sort of explanation for why he lied the first time round. And even though the chief inspector would know what fun a good defence counsel could have with that, it would certainly set him wondering again, which was deeply undesirable.

On the other hand, Peterson had expressed no enthusiasm for the British legal system, so probably that wasn't on. What else could he do?

Leo had no idea. Peterson claimed not to be a man of violence. He certainly wasn't a blackmailer. Poison pen didn't seem to be his style either. Nor dog turds through the letterbox. So what else was there? All in all the fellow came over as so decent. Not at all your average avenging angel.

Decent. Not a threat. Just a harmless crank. Stranger things had happened.

And now there was Rosie. There was still dear Rosie.

His mother was waiting for him in the kitchen. As always she'd turned on all the spotlights. The room was horribly bright. He dimmed a couple of them.

'You were a long time. Meaty smells. I came out to see. No glove.'

The oven glove lived in the top drawer beside the dishwasher. He fetched it.

'Sorry, Mother. These police things always take ages.' He crouched down, opened the oven door, slid out the shelf and lifted the casserole out onto the stove top. The stew was hot but nothing excessive. He closed the door and raised the oven temperature, gettng ready for the dumplings. 'Good news, though. They've decided poor Declan simply fell. It was an accident. Nobody pushed him. He was watering his plants and he simply fell. Chief Inspector Coade says I've nothing at all to worry about.'

'Thass nice, dear.'

'It's more than nice, Ma. It's bloody marvellous.' The little pile of dumplings was ready in its bowl. He tipped them in on top of the meat, stirred them in, and returned the casserole to the oven. 'I was worried. I mean, men do get caught for things they didn't do.'

'Your gridi... your glardi... your *guardian* angel looks after you, Leo. Always has.'

'I wish I had your confidence...' He'd left runner beans cut up in water in a pan on the cooker. They wouldn't take long. End of the season, but they hadn't been too stringy. The dumplings would need at least twenty-five minutes. He started getting out cutlery. 'No pud today, Ma. But I did have to open that cheap Beaujolais to put some in the stew and it's not too bad. Care for a glass? A little celebration?'

'Good idea. A cereblation.' She sat down at the table, pushed cutlery around, watched him fetch glasses and the bottle. 'I telephloned that Rosie. Mrs Krauss-Häber. Ought to done it yesterday. Said how sorry I am about poor Max. Nice man. Nice man…'

'That was good of you.' His voice broke at the reminder. Max's death, his name even, coming unexpectedly like that, cut through all his devices. 'I'm sure she appreciated it.' He eased the cork out of the Beaujolais and poured two glasses. 'He was a very special man.'

'She wans you to call. There's a brother. They're leaving in the morning. She wans to say goodbye.'

'Leaving?' *Rosie*? First Max and now dear Rosie? Leo was suddenly short of breath, as if kicked in the ribs. 'Where to? Where are they going?'

His mother shrugged. 'She said but I doan remember.'

'London?'

'I expect.'

'When are they leaving?'

'In the morning. I told you.'

'I mean—' He gave up. The questions were only panic noises. Rosie wanted him to call. He could find out everything then. He had to see her. 'I'll ring her now, Mother. Won't take a moment.'

If his mother showed any reaction to his choosing not to use the kitchen telephone for the call, he didn't stay to see it. The stew could wait. So could the Beaujolais. He dialled from the phone on his desk.

'The Krauss-Häber residence. Who's calling, please?'

'You must be Philip. I'm Leo. May I speak to Rosie, please?'

'*Leo*…' His tone suggested that the word was unfamiliar, and possibly obscene. 'My sister and I are just sitting down to dinner, Leo. I wonder if you could possibly—'

'Look, it'll only take a moment. I promise I won't keep her.'

'Very well. Wait, please…'

Leo waited.

'Leo?'

'Rosie—hey. I'm not sure I like your new butler.'

'He's protecting me. Apparently Max was quite famous. Now that the news is out the phone can be quite a bother.'

'Poor you. Aren't the media bloody…' Protecting? Philip was clearly within earshot. 'Look, love, Ma tells me you're leaving tomorrow morning. What's the rush?'

'Simon's full of plans. A Fleet Street memorial service. St. Botolph's, isn't it? And then there's Max's book. I have to see him. And we're selling this place so I might as well go straight on up to Liverpool afterwards. And I'll need the car, of course. It's all so complicated.'

'Selling the flat?'

'Seems sensible.'

Sensible, yes. But so soon?

Cut to the chase. 'So what time are you leaving?'

'Early. Well, tennish. I still have to pack. Say ten thirty.'

'It all sounds a bit of a rush.'

'Philip's being very helpful. I don't know what I'd do without him. He has his job, though. This isn't a good time for him.'

'Don't let yourself be hijacked, Rosie.'

'Ten thirty. That's right.'

'I have to see you.'

'I know.'

'Around nine, then. I can help you carry out bags or something.'

'Fine.'

CHAPTER 10

The final chapter. Not many more pages left. A lot to get into them.

Tuesday has come round again—we're in October now, but still quite warm and sunny—and, as Leo's mother has just needlessly reminded him, Tuesdays are Sandra days. Sandra days often begin badly for mother and son, since the speech therapist is an early visitor and her patient has to be up and dressed and generally put together in time for her: this can be a stressful operation.

Additionally, this particular Sandra day is to feature a variation in the always risky breakfast egg routine. The previous evening Madam Sara—in good spirits following a winning cribbage streak—had suggested a coddled rather than a fried egg for her breakfast in the morning. Leo had been there before, of course, and wasn't pleased. But what could he say?

So the Tivoli Street breakfast coddled egg script will be dusted off and in due course set in motion.

As with many Tivoli Street breakfast egg scripts, the story line here features a female central character who is a quite extraordinarily discriminating connoisseuse, and the plot hinge is concerned with cooking times. However, since the egg in this case is to be coddled, success depends not so much upon stopwatch exactitude as upon the cook's judgment, experience, and quite a bit of luck. The egg remains out of sight in its porcelain coddler until the lid is removed, at which point it's totally visible, and its appearance is vital. A runny egg-white is disgusting. It reminds the client of… you know what it reminds her of. She understandably rejects it. The cook apologises, replaces the lid and returns the coddler for a very short time to hot water in the kitchen.

In scene two, when the egg is returned with its white solidified, its yolk is warily prodded with the egg-spoon. Any sign of solidification here and the whole dish is over-cooked. Ruined.

Scene three depicts the cook returning to the kitchen with the offending egg and eating it there himself (throwing it at the wall is strongly considered) before he restarts the process.

Breakfast (as scripted above) came and went. So did getting Madam Sara dressed and generally put together for Sandra. But this was for the very last time, Leo told himself as he settled his mother in the small rear drawing room to wait for Sandra. 'This is my last Tuesday morning,' he thinks as he and Hoppy pass in the kitchen, she arriving for work, he on his way out to the car and Parabola Road, and he reminds her to expect the speech therapist at any minute. His very last Tuesday morning. By this time next week he'll be house-hunting in Wales with Rosie.

Utter nonsense. He knows that. It's simply wishful thinking. He could never dump his mother so abruptly, nor the SCT. And then there's Rosie—she's still in shock, lost in the emptiness left by Max's death. Whatever she'd said to him in the park, he can never hold her to it. He must wait, be patient, help when he can, keep out of her hair when he can't. Her brother sounded a blight on the phone but perhaps he's simply seen what needs to be done and is doing it. Sparing her any important decisions. Taking command.

Weeks up in Liverpool. Months even. All this romantic Wales stuff could easily never happen. They aren't teen-agers. For god's sake, he's forty-plus years old. She's the widow of his best friend... Put like that, it has an Italian feel. The brothers of Italian dead men traditionally marry the widows. And he's been as good as Max's brother. Well, pretty nearly.

At one moment he's squeezing past Hoppy in the Tivoli Street kitchen. At the next moment, and only a few seconds later, he's getting out of his car a short distance down from the Krauss-Häber flat on Parabola Road. Another of those instant translocations.

The door to the flat's communal hall is open and out in the street a burly middle-aged man in corduroy and Harris tweed, with a black band round his jacket sleeve, presumably Philip, is heaving a suitcase into Max's Ford Granada. Max had never had much sense of car identity. *Comfortable seats, Leo. Plenty of room in the back. Reasonable mpg. I got a good deal....*

Rosie comes out of the building, sees Leo and waves. He joins her on the path and she introduces him to Philip. They shake hands. Philip's surname is Bostridge. He stands for a moment, eyeing his watch.

'I expect Rose has filled you in,' he says. 'Haven't been down here much. Max and I never got on. Nothing against him, though. Just very different sorts of people.'

Rosie touches his arm. 'Not now, Phil.'

'Needed to be said. That's all.'

'Max was special,' Leo the peace-maker suggests. 'Perhaps you never got to know him.'

Philip eases his jacket sleeve down over his watch. 'I'll fetch your other case, Rose.'

'Plenty of time, Phil—those wretched people won't be here for ages.' She turns to Leo. 'The cremation providers—they're insisting on bringing round Max's ashes.' She smiles at him brightly. 'Otherwise they say they'll have to send them up to Liverpool Special Delivery or something.'

Cremation? Already? Leo hadn't thought about it. A hateful image of devouring flames comes to him unbidden. He quickly replaces it with maggots, which are even more hateful. Choices, choices. And why Liverpool? Why not London and then back here while the flat sells?

Oh Rosie, Rosie my dear, what a struggle it is, simply to go on living...

'Mrs Krauss-Häber? Ah, there you are.' Behind them a lean young man, noticeably Adam's-appled, is standing in the flat's doorway. His suit too is lean: lean lapels, lean trouser legs. He's holding a clipboard and a spring-loaded tape measure. Clearly an estate agent. 'My name is Farnley. I was wondering about appliances...'

Rosie stares at him blankly. 'Appliances?'

Philip takes her arm. 'He's talking about the things in the kitchen, Rose. Cooker, refrigerator, dishwasher, that sort of thing. It all goes, doesn't it? It all goes, Mr Farnley.'

Farnley consults his board. 'There's a free-standing oil-filled towel heater in the bathroom, Mr Bostr–'

'That too. Fully equipped. The flat is fully equipped. I suggest you make a note of that.'

'That's a good little radiator, Phil. Why don't I keep it?'

'Presentation, my dear. Luxury detailing. *Feel good factor...* isn't that what you people call it, Mr Farnley?'

'If Mrs Krauss-Häber really wants the towel heater, sir, I don't honestly think—'

'Cross it off your list then, Mr Farnley. Simple as that. None of my business.' He angrily pushes past the young estate agent and disappears into the flat.

Farnley chews his ballpoint. 'I hope Mr Bostridge doesn't think I—'

'My brother had a bad night, Mr Farnley. A long drive, and then I don't think our spare bed suited him. Why don't you go and do some more measuring?'

The young man stares up at the front of the building, finds nothing there to keep him, and reluctantly follows Philip into the flat.

Leo catches Rosie's eye and looks away quickly. *Do some more measuring...* The shared joke doesn't last. Leo has so much to say to her. Everything. And now she's leaving. So little time in which to say it.

He casts around for a starting point. Just across the pavement at the bottom of the path the Granada looms. So little time. Nothing came.

'This is all a bit sudden, isn't it?'

'Phil's quite right. There's nothing here to keep me.'

'Of course not. We talked about that. But *Liverpool...*?'

'Eileen's not too bad. Phil's wife. And it won't be for long.'

'Then what?'

Philip bangs out through the door, hefting another suitcase. 'Too big for his boots, that one. Don't you think?'

He stumps past them, grunting.

'Then what, Rosie?'

She turns on him. 'A world cruise. A cottage in the country. A handful of Max's pills. How the hell do I know?'

'*Rose?* Rose, I think something's leaking in this case.' Philip is calling from inside the back of the Granada. 'There's a deafening stink of hair shampoo.'

'Then I expect it's the shampoo that's leaking, dear.'

'You're under a lot of stress, Rose. I know that. But please don't be clever with me.'

She flutters her fingers at him in a way that perhaps is intended to be sisterly, and escapes back into the house. Leo follows her. A cottage in the country? Monday's promise, his and hers. This is Tuesday. He must not remind her.

The shock he feels at the aching emptiness of the flat without Max in it is unexpected. Ridiculous. For god's sake, he'd been perfectly comfortable alone in the place after the party, cleaning up. But Max had been in hospital then. Now he's dead. It makes a difference.

He isn't sure why. An empty flat is an empty flat.

Rosie is in the kitchen, standing by the electric cooker her brother has told the estate agent she doesn't want. It's expensive, stainless steel, with a ceramic hob. She appears to be stroking it.

'I wish you weren't going so soon, Rosie. I'm going to miss you.'

'We'll work something out...'

Miss her? Looking at her now, at her tidy, gentle excellence, experiencing her entire, amazing presence, he knows he can't live without her.

She's been somewhere else. Now she pays attention. 'Don't look so bleak, love. Perhaps I'll come back. If this place doesn't sell quickly, I mean.'

'Come back? Your brother won't like that. I'm after your money. He's suspecting me already. I'm not wearing a black arm-band thing. I saw him notice it.'

'That's his problem. He's not my husba—' The word catches at her. She stares at him blankly, unable to speak, her eyes filling with tears.

Leo is aghast at her sorrow. And she's been managing the morning so well.

He reaches out to take her hand but she steps away. She wipes her eyes with both hands, smearing the tears outwards with her fingers, into her hair.

'Phil's the organising one,' she tells him, articulating very carefully. 'And if there's one thing I need just now, it's organising. He thinks of things…We're going to London first., to arrange with Simon for the memorial service. Yesterday afternoon he took me off to Max's solicitors, straight from the station. Those people up at the top of the Promenade. Zachary and Something. He'd actually phoned ahead for an appointment. The will and so on. He likes things done properly. Which reminds me—'

'Mrs Krauss-Häber?' Farnley is back. And there are noises behind him, suggesting that Philip is returning with the scented suitcase and going into the bedroom. 'Mrs Krauss-Häber, can you give me an idea of the rates and taxes here? We need to include them in the particulars.'

'Rates? Mr Krauss-Häber handled all that. We can look in his desk. Oh, and by the way—' she's remembered her manners—'I really should have introduced you two. Mr Farnley is from Cromwell's estate agents. Mr Farnley, this is an old family friend, Leo Bresson.'

'Good to meet you, Mr Bresson.' They shake hands. 'If you should be looking to purchase property anywhere at all in the Cheltenham area, sir, Cromwell's has a very wide range of excellent—'

'Me?' On another day Leo might have been flattered to be judged a member of the property-purchasing classes. 'I'm afraid not. No. Not at all.'

'That may well change, sir. The market is very fluid at the moment. Some really excellent opportunities out there… Let me give you my card.' He gives Leo his card, then returns quickly to his clipboard and Rosie. 'There's also the question of Inland Revenue tax liability, Mrs. Krauss-Häber. When exactly did you buy the property?'

'We inherited it, actually. But there was a valuation. Desk stuff again. Shall we—'

'Rose—' Philip, leaning in round the kitchen door: 'Rose my dear, there's detergent all over your jumpers.'

She'd been moving towards Max's study. She stares at him, waits a beat. 'That's a good line, Phil. I should keep it in…' She closes her eyes, breathes deeply, opens them again. 'Sorry, dear. Just shut the case up again, will you? I'll put them in Eileen's machine when we get there.'

'It's after ten, Rose. You do realise, don't you? When did those bloody funeral people say they were coming?'

'I can't honestly remember. They'll come when they come, Phil.'

'We need to get to Dell's in plenty of time. He's in Covent Garden, isn't he? Parking will be terrible.'

'I don't mind being late. He'll take us out to eat somewhere.'

Farnley clears his throat. 'Perhaps I should come back later.'

'Actually, Mr F., it's now or never.' She smoothes back her hair. 'We blast off for Outer Mongolia in exactly four and a half minutes.'

Leo jerks into action—something is needed—and grabs her brother's arm. 'Why don't I help you finish up loading the car, Philip? Leave these two to all the flat business.'

They go together into the bedroom, where the contents of the suitcase are spread across the bed. Leo starts repacking them while Rosie's brother tapes up a cardboard box full of shoes and takes it away, muttering. Once he's closed the suitcase, Leo follows Philip out to the car, finding him busy calculating which way round his cardboard box will best fit. They work together for the next ten minutes, basically not speaking as they load up the back of the Granada. Then, just as young Mr Farnley from Cromwell's is leaving, with much hand-shaking and labelling of front door keys, a large black car arrives, portentously shined up to cremation providers' standards. A large car, bringing a very small memento.

The ashes of Max's incinerated body—Rosie had abbreviated these to 'Max's ashes' but for Leo whoever Max had been isn't reducible to ground-up cinders—come parcelled in a neat dark red felt bag with a plaited bell-rope-type drawstring that, opened on the dining room table, is shown to contain a tasteful fake bronze Greek-style urn some nine inches tall with a snap-fit lid. Nobody checks on its contents. At some future time, presumably, they will be sprinkled somewhere. Leo, sticking to his principles, finds them totally unmoving. The man from the cremation providers, suitably non-existent, comes and goes non-existently.

Leo isn't sure, but at one point he thinks he hears the word *cremains* spoken.

The Granada is loaded. Leo carries the last two plastic bags filled with perishable food out of the Parabola Road refrigerator. Philip has been to the bathroom and so has Rosie. Earlier that morning she has paid for and cancelled milk and newspaper deliveries while he has dealt with post redirection. The flat is closed up now, to wait and gather dust. Nothing remains to keep them. Philip sits in the car drumming his fingers while Leo and Rosie stand out on the pavement. This is his last chance to bare his heart.

'I've got your Liverpool address.'

'Call me at the end of the week. I'll be making better sense by then.'

'I wish you didn't have to go.'

'So do I.'

'Then why—?'

She nods towards the car. 'He thinks it's for the best. Family. That sort of thing. I haven't the strength to fight him.'

'Oh, Rosie...'

'I know, love.' She stands up on her toes and kisses his cheek. 'Got to go now. And thank you. All these last months, Leo. Thank you.'

She evades his grasp, his need, and turns away to the car. When she's opened its door she looks back at him. 'We'll work something out. You'll see.' And, louder, 'Bye now.'

'Bye.' He ducks his head, looks past her and waves to Philip who, possibly not seeing him, doesn't wave back. He drives off masterfully down Parabola Road, making for Charlton Kings and London.

We'll work something out. That's the second time she's said it. *We'll work something out…* It can only mean that she's sticking by the offer she made on Monday morning, yesterday morning, in Charlton Park. The offer he accepted. And now that he's free of police suspicion, all that remains is for him to resign from the SCT—easily done—and then to break it to his mother that he's leaving and she'll have to hire a professional nurse/companion—not easily done but absolutely possible. Oh, and to find out what crazy Mr Peterson's plans are. After he's given them some thought. His plans. What he comes up with after he's thought.

This last proviso brings him up sharply. He realises that he's never really taken Mr Peterson all that seriously and perhaps he should. So what can the man do? Intention wasn't everything but it mattered. His words. For Christ's sake, Leo's never wanted Dekko dead. Peterson knows that. So what then—criminal neglect? Face it, lad, realistically there's not a thing harmless crank Peterson, nice decent Peterson can do.

Leo's free from police suspicion. Soon he'll be away from bloody Cheltenham and all that it stands for. *We'll work something out.* Rosie has asked him to go away with her. Not a proposal, she said, but the nearest thing. He's forty-three years old, not good with people, not good with women, not bold, he's accepted all that years ago, along with the solitary life, solitary bed, solitary death that it meant, and now Rosie, Rosie of all people, dear gentle beautiful Rosie, she's asked him to ring her at the end of the week.

Wales. A cottage in Wales. A cottage in a garden in Wales. A cottage any-bloody-where with Rosie…

Just for once life, for a moment or two, is being unreservedly good to him.

* * * *

When he gets back to the house on Tivoli Street Leo looks to left and right, half-expecting to find harmless crank Peterson lurking outside again, waiting to reveal what, after going away to think, he's finally decided. Empty pavements both ways. No Peterson.

Leo whizzes the Jaguar into the garage and tugs the door down with a happy thud. Humming a newly-composed going-to-Wales-with-Rosie tune, he bursts recklessly in through the front door, bangs it behind him and leaps from red diamond to red diamond on the passage's turkey carpet beneath Madam Sara's framed endorsements, making his way to the kitchen where, at this sort of elevenses time, his mother will probably be drinking freeze-dried instant coffee with Hoppy. And he's right, of course. There the two old dears are.

All this teen-age exuberance—is Leo over-doing it? Setting himself up? It's not a good sign, in a story like this, for a man to be so happy. Nor in life, actually, to which stories like this do bear a passing resemblance. Were there not considerations that he was overlooking? Were there not reasons within his very recent experience to make him just a little wary?

* * * *

But this is today and then was years ago, and when I ask today's Leo that question he claims that the Leo of years ago really was as extravagantly joyful as has just been described. So there he was, humming a newly-composed tune and leaping from red diamond to red diamond on the passage's turkey carpet.

It didn't last, of course.

* * * *

While Leo had been away on Parabola Road saying goodbye to Rosie, on Tivoli Street there'd been a development. During Madam Sara's exemplary *Tip of the tongue, the teeth and the lips* enunciations with Sandra in the kitchen, the telephone had rung in her bedroom, no answerphone there, and Hoppy had dealt with it. The message delivered eventually to Madam Sara was from Bunty Carstairs, reporting that the result of the SCT's directorship poll had been determined and the SCT's election team would be visiting Madam Sara that afternoon to discuss it with her. Unless Mrs Carstairs heard to the contrary, the team would arrive sharply at two o'clock.

Madam Sara had found no objection to this arrangement, so the two o'clock appointment stood.

Nothing there to sully Leo's joy. Rather it happily reminded him that one of his excuses for giving up his job with the SCT—the new director he really couldn't work with, whoever that might be—would very soon be known, and he'd better start putting together a suitable resignation letter. Also, once he'd supported his mother through the afternoon's inevitable post-election result trauma, he'd feel much happier about telling her they must at once start looking for a sympathetic nurse/companion, and why.

Because he'd be leaving. After a month. A month at the most. Then he'd be leaving. He'd be gone.

It was possible that she'd understand completely and give him her blessing. If she didn't, which she probably wouldn't, selfish old cow, then he might well leave sooner.

First, though, there was lunch. Lunches actually, maybe a month of them. Dinners too. Tuesday breakfasts. Meals. A month of Tivoli Street. For goodness' sake, it would take Rosie at least that long to work something out… He tried to remember what lunch he'd given his mother yesterday, so as not to repeat himself, but he couldn't.

She would, though, and he didn't blame her for that. Such things were important to housebound old people. Not many people really wanted the same lunch two days running.

To be safe, he decided on something unusual. He'd bought a slab of good strong cheddar last week and there was surely a left-over bottle of beer lurking at the back of the fridge. The poor old soul loved Welsh rabbit and never got it—far too greasy and fattening—so that was what he'd do. Melt some cheese with beer and mustard and serve it on buttered toast.

And that was what, in an hour or so, he did. She was very pleased. The failures of the breakfast egg were forgotten.

Rest time. Her Sandra outfit would do for Bunty Carstairs and Co, she decided, so she lay down fully dressed and he spread a blanket over her. Then he went to his computer and started on the resignation letter, for the moment leaving out the name of the new and unacceptable director who would be his main reason for leaving. One of the wonders of the computer—seamless later insertions. His mind wandered, though, returning to Rosie. She'd be expecting him to call her in Liverpool at the end of the week. She'd told him to.

Come ten to two he was rousing Madam Sara. Come five to two she was assembled and waiting. She'd see the Board of Elders in her bedroom, she told him. Her choice, and surprising, but he didn't argue. Come the hall clock's exactly two o'clock chime, as he'd expected, the doorbell rang. Bunty Carstairs was nothing if not predictable.

Today her election committee was down to one other member, librarian Annette Minshull, whose library fortunately could spare her. Mr Doyle sent his apologies, he had an important previous engagement. Leo showed the two of them into Madam Sara's bedroom where he found her seated at her desk, looking up from a busy sheaf of papers. He understood then her choice of room. For nearly thirty years she'd ruled the SCT from that desk. Its symbolism was just about all she now had left. He arranged two chairs in front of it for the visitors and went out, closing the door. He didn't stay outside to listen. He'd know the name of the successful candidate soon enough. His money was still on bloody Courtland.

Back in his office/bedsit he looked around, wondering what of all this stuff he'd take with him when he left. Not a thing. Wales. A cottage. Rosie. It would be a new beginning. He wouldn't take a single thing.

He finished his resignation letter. It was decent and respectful, grateful even. Not hard to do when one was decent and respectful and grateful, qualities which came with the life-long package, the meaning well, aiming to please package. Right from the start, whatever else might be said about him, Freak's Boy, Leo, Leh-o, dependable in this if nothing else, bless him, had always aimed to please.

Bad news, worse than usual, was just round the corner.

Politicians, when they see a policy not working, tend to respond by doing more of it. Doing it bigger, more expensively. It's the same with most of their electorate. Certainly Leo, down his entire post-infancy life, had pursued a policy of aiming to please. It had never worked, yet he had continued, with touching loyalty, to do more of it. He was at it now, and it was about to turn, at long last, and really bite him.

Miss Minshull was the first out of Madam Sara's bedroom. He heard the door open, rose quickly and met her in the passage. She held her right hand out, clearly expecting him to shake it.

'Congratulations, Mr Bresson. Congratulations… It's such good news. We really are so pleased.'

Leo, slow on the uptake, shook the hand doubtfully. 'I'm sorry?'

Mrs Carstairs joined them. 'Your mother's just confirmed the appointment. She must have discussed it with you. We really are delighted.'

She reached to shake his hand also. The three of them were rather squashed, half in and half out of his office/bedsit. 'I personally could not have hoped for a happier outcome. You'll do a marvellous job. An absolutely marvellous job.'

Leo gaped. Job? What job? The directorship? They had to be joking. He wasn't a truthsayer. Surely the SCT's constitution limited eligibility to truthsayers?

Joking, though? He couldn't see these two dull sticks joking. Not about the *directorship*.

'You're very kind. But there must be some mistake. My mother hasn't said a word. I'm not even eligible.'

'Of course you're eligible. You're a paid member of the staff. And it will be an excellent arrangement. Not being a truthsayer yourself gives you valuable objectivity.'

'I'm amazed. People voted for me? A majority?' It was a flattering thought. And he wasn't worried. Nobody could make him do it. He'd simply say no. They couldn't force him into it. He'd simply refuse. 'What were the votes?'

'Sufficient. You're a popular man. A popular man. And the constitution's absolutely clear. The vote is a recommendation, nothing more. Being picky over exact numbers misses the point. Final decisions rest with the committee, in consultation with the retiring director. Madam Sara. And she agrees with us.'

Sufficient… A nice word. Nicely meaningless. Like the election. They'd had it wrapped up right from the start. He remembered the raised voices at their meeting in this house last week. In other organisations and other times there'd been smoke-filled rooms, now there was Madam Sara's front parlour. His mother, bless her cotton socks, had beaten them down. Her SCT, her constitution, her decision… He could see it all now. No wonder she'd been so chirpy after their last visit. If they wanted her to go, and to go peaceably, these had been her terms. The dynastic succession, right for her and right for the Church she had founded. A Bresson at the helm, well on into the next century.

He collected his thoughts. There was one factor, only one, that she hadn't reckoned with. She hadn't reckoned with him. Aiming to please could be pushed only so far. Even for falling-down-funnily Freak's Boy, there were limits.

'Mrs Carstairs, Miss Minshull… obviously I'm grateful for your good wishes. And for your faith in me. But it's all so unexpected. Such a great responsibility. There are questions I must sort out with Madam Sara. I'm not even sure I'll be accepting… So please—both of you—please keep this to yourselves, just for a few more days?'

Mrs Carstairs leaned forward and patted his arm.'You need to think about it. Get used to the idea. Of course you do. And you must take your time.Take your time. So Friday, shall we say? I shall expect a call by noon.' She surveyed him frankly. 'We haven't always seen eye-to-eye, Leo dear, and we probably won't always in the future, but one thing's certain. You're Madam Sara's son. Her Church will be safe in your hands.'

Glory hallelujah! In a passage lined with testimonials this was one to hang with the best. And he was *'Leo dear'* now, he noticed.

Mrs Carstairs started for the front door. 'Got to run. I'm supposed to be at some wretched council meetin.' Don't come—we know the way.'

She went away, closely followed by Miss Minshull. Leo took her at her word. The front door closed behind them. He set off down the passage to his mother's bedroom. His moment of truth with her was coming sooner than he'd expected.

He found her still at her desk. She stood up clumsily as he came into the room.

'Don't be cross with me, Leo.'

The guilty child persona. *Cross?* What sort of word was that?

'Bloody hell, Mother—the least you could have done was warn me.'

'I wanted to surprise you. I thought you'd be pleased.'

'No you didn't.' Truth. Just for once, a little truth between them. 'You fixed it like this because then you thought I wouldn't be able to refuse.'

'You do it fine. They like you. My Church. Not that Courtland man. My Church. Not that Courtland man.'

First the guilty child, now the pathetic old woman. What would she come up with next? He was working on his anger. He needed to. Otherwise that was all she was: a guilty child, a pathetic old woman.

'I won't do it, Mother. I was quitting anyway. I won't do it.'

'Quitting?'

'I've already written the letter.'

'You carn quit. You carn quit.'

'I can. Watch me.'

'No...'

There was a lot more of this, mostly of the circular *I can, you can't* variety, which you really don't need. He never quite managed to fire up the anger but he never gave in either. He was going to quit. He'd given Rosie his promise.

Two moments stand out, however. Quite quickly their conflict had become episodic, itinerant, travelling around their small world in the house on Tivoli street. Leo would make what he considered one final refusal, leave the room, settle in some other, and wait glumly for her to follow him. Which she did. She was fighting, just as he was, for everything that mattered. Life itself.

On one of these occasions, when he'd centred his reasons for quitting round his disbelief in spiritualist phenomena and she'd goaded him till he'd actually accused her personally, for the first time ever, of fakery, with her radiant spirits and her idiotic Nuna, and had slammed out of the room, appalled at himself, she'd waited longer than before to pursue him. And when she sought him out, in the ceremonial dining room, standing by one of the tall side windows, looking blankly at the last of the roses on the garden fence, she seated herself at the head of the table, in her old place, and considered him for quite a while before she spoke.

There'd been times perhaps, since her second stroke, when she'd let herself go ga-ga. She wasn't ga-ga now.

'This is what I do, Leo.' Slowly and carefully, she was saying what she'd taken proper time to plan. 'People talk to me in their heads. What they want. Sometimes I hear them, Leo. Then I tell them what they say to me. They talk to me in their heads and I tell them what they say. I always do that ... It's all what I do. I tell them what they say.'

And that was all. So simple. Her tenses were spot on and the 't' in her 'it's' was perfect.

He didn't have an answer. The fact that he didn't believe a word of it didn't matter. Clearly she needed it so badly that she believed it. So what was he supposed to do now? Suddenly understand? Suddenly forgive? The change in register was more than he could cope with.

'Sometimes you hear them?' he asked her spitefully. 'What about the times when you don't, but the show goes on all the same?'

To which merciless question she too, in her turn, had no decent answer. Like him, only fear and resentment, spite and misery.

They battled on.

Until finally, when their dispute had shifted to the squalid ground of who'd failed whom and when, and he'd told her, in the small rear sitting room, that she'd never cared a damn for him, wafting down from London decked out like a circus clown, and she'd countered with the Christmas cards he'd never sent her, and then resorted despairingly, the non-paralysed side of her lower lip trembling, to tearful claims that she'd always been a good mother, a good mother, he'd never wanted, never wanted for anything, and he'd slammed out again, speechless with the cruelties he couldn't bring himself to remind her of—that was when she'd lumbered to her feet, close on his heels again, shouting after him.

Shouting after him, 'You said the time wrong on purpose, Leo. You made it up. It was a lie, Leo. A lie. You told me the time that you wanted.'

Shouting after him. 'And I lied too. When that Wiler woman came I told her the time you said. The lie. I told her the time you said. I told her the lie. I didn know why and it didn matter why. I told her what you wanted.'

Which was the moment when the two of them, crossing the rear hall, just beside the red-and-blue-lozenged glass door out into the leaky conservatory, the moment when the two of them halted in mid-flow, transfixed, not speaking, not breathing, and the afternoon halted with them.

Nothing moved. The exigencies of life had caught at the two of them, frozen them in that brutal moment. Leo remembers stillness and an amazing exactitude of surfaces. The possibility that something, anything at all, could happen next seemed to him unimaginable. Outrageous.

Her words weren't a warning of what it was in her power to do to him. He knew that. Nor were they a demand for gratitude. Nor even a plea for pity. Rather he recognised them as the bitter recognition, long avoided, wrung out of her only by extreme distress, brought home to him in a further deepening of his shame, the bitter recognition that no matter how inconvenient and dangerous life might be to them, finally and importantly, what was, was.

He and his mother, the two of them, they had lied. In their words and in their silences they had lied to each other, and through each other to the outside world. It was how they had protected themselves from each other down all the years of his life. He recognised that now. She, protecting herself from the intrusions and inadequacies of her son with denial, clothing herself in the strength of her own abundance. He, protecting himself with irony from his need for her love. Now, facing him here, driven and reckless, she'd stripped all that away and he saw for the very first time just who the two of them were.

She was Sarah, Sarah Ann Barraclough, Sarah Ann Bresson, Madam Sara Bresson, a woman who'd conceived and carried and borne a child, a brutal assault, an assault on all her being, on her body, her mind, her *Gift* and its potential; and he, a boy child, Leo Anthony, not easy from the start, who'd gone on that way, not bold, not industrious, not talented, content with the mediocre, a stammerer also, Leo Anthony, who'd grown up to be manipulative, a useless husband and father, professionally a nowhere man and a nothing, now an adulterer and a murderer. And she'd protected herself, Madam Sara Bresson, protected herself from him, from her son, for forty years. And now, knowingly, she had lied to the police.

He thought about that. She wasn't just a poor silly muddled old woman. Definitely not the resident idjit. She had lied to the police knowingly, not needing to understand the implications. Not caring. And now, pushed by him hard enough, she'd been driven to admit it.

Certainly this marked a rare level of truthfulness between them, but it was only partial. The real life-changer would be her fundamental reason for the lie. It was protective certainly but what or whom had it protected? Him? Herself? What happened next? Their future life together? And would it be useful for them to know this?

Suddenly weary, she sagged against the conservatory's door frame, and the frozen moment broke apart, releasing the two of them there, back in the house on Tivoli Street, naked and afraid but back in the relentlessly real world where things happened next, no matter what.

And what that would be, he supposed, was up to him.

She stirred herself, sparing him an immediate decision. Thought had gone on in her head too. Memories, apparently. Explanations he didn't need.

'That night, Leo. Before you came back from Cirencester, Leo, I was waiting. Sitting on my bed. Waiting.' She had a story to tell, the words almost whispered. 'Waiting, Leo. Sitting. Mother's Delhi clock out in the hall struck only one. Not six. Not lots. I looked. It was the half past six. You were late. And then you came. You said it was just after. Not half past. You said it was just after. I didn think about it then. You knew best. Just a muddle. Not important. Then the morning, and the TV news, and you go to the police station and that woman comes.' Speaking ever more faintly. 'That Miler woman. And I tell her the time you'd said.'

He nodded. It was a perfectly reasonable accounting. And the question remained, what should he cause to happen next?

After allowing himself a respectable pause in which to consider the possibilities, he decided that clothing their nakedness was their top priority. He smiled at her, he hoped as if fondly, and said to her, 'Of course you told the sergeant.' He said to her, 'Of course you did.' He said to her, 'Very sensible. I knew you would. Well done. Well done.' And finally, 'So what about I go and boil up the kettle for a pot of tea?'

He certainly knew a lot more now but that was still the best he could manage.

But he did reach out his hand and touch, just touch, his mother's arm, and she did let him.

And they were both, in their own ways, dressed and decent again.

Nothing had changed. Everything had changed. Nothing had changed. She'd told Sergeant Wiler the time he'd said. Their lives moved on.

Differently? He doesn't think so. Certainly she still hadn't been able to get him to agree to stay with her and take on the SCT directorship. But now, even though in his mind he was still totally determined to quit—either to make a new life with Rosie or simply because he couldn't face the adroit dishonesties that would be required of him if he stayed—to his mother he temporised, lied again, let her down lightly, patient and caring, promising to think about it, to let her know for certain in the morning.

Meanwhile the rest of the afternoon happened. Hours before, right after her rest, in preparation for her SCT visitors, she'd substantially cleared her desk, put most of the SCT archive back in its cardboard boxes and stacked them in her wardrobe. And she'd told Sergeant Wiler the time he'd said. Now, getting Leo to help her after their pot of tea, she set all the papers out again, cuttings in one pile, photos in another, accounts in another, miscellaneous correspondence in another, where she'd be able easily to find them. Cat Rumple helped too, as was his custom.

After which, of course, as their lives moved on, it was time for Leo to start thinking about dinner. The details of which Leo for once can't precisely remember.

They kept him busy, though, until his unexpected phone call from a Mrs Caroline Parks, of Zachary, Moorfield and Parks, which he took in the kitchen.

He unhooked the receiver. 'Leo Bresson here.'

'Mr Bresson? Mr Leo Bresson?'

'That's right.' He'd just said so. Why didn't people listen?

'My name is Parks. Mrs Caroline Parks of Zachary, Moorfield and Parks. And I'm speaking to Leo Anthony Bresson?'

'Right again. How can I help you?'

'Leo Anthony Bresson of eighty-one Tivoli Street, Cheltenham?'

'Is this some sort of game?'

'No game at all, Mr Bresson. Your mother is Mrs Sara Ann Bresson and you were born in London on the nineteenth of August, nineteen fifty?'

'You know a lot about me, Mrs Parks.' It was 'Parks,' wasn't it?

'I need to, Mr Bresson. I'm principal executor of the will of Maximilian Heinrich Krauss-Häber, and I need to establish your identity.'

'Well, I'm me alright.' Will? What the hell had poor old Max been up to? 'Mr Krauss-Häber was a very dear friend of mine.'

'In which case I hope you will be able to come to the office here. You have a legacy under Mr Krauss- Häber's will and there's inevitably paperwork. Documents for you to sign, legal proof of identity, a birth certificate, that sort of thing. Some time tomorrow, perhaps? Can we make an appointment?'

'A legacy?'

Dear god. 'Are you allowed to tell me how much?'

'Fifty thousand pounds, Mr Bresson. Not immediately, of course. After probate, which can take several months.'

'Fif*teen*? You did say fifteen thous—?'

'Fif*ty*, Mr Bresson. Forty-nine, fifty... Five-oh thousand. A considerable amount.'

'Yes indeed.'

Did it matter? Fifty thousand pounds'-worth of Max's love and trust? Fifty or only fifteen—did it really matter? Yes. To him, to the wrenching in his guts, to the tumult in his head, for some sad, excellent reason it did matter, finding out just how many thousands of pounds his lies to terminally ill Maximilian Heinrich Krauss-Häber had earned him.

And Rosie? As a reward for his not telling her he'd left Declan weeping, scraping, dying on the concrete, what was Rosie going to give him? A cottage in Wales? Deceive her enough, lie to her enough, and she'd give him a cottage in Wales?

'So is the morning convenient for you, Mr Bresson? Tomorrow morning? Shall we say nine thirty?'

'Very convenient. Nine thirty. Yes. Thank you.'

'We're on the Upper Promenade. A hundred and three. Opposite the Wintergarden. Zachary, Moorfield and Parks. You can't miss us. Good bye.'

'Yes. Till tomorrow, then. Nine thirty. Thank you.'

Sometimes the consequences of a man's actions, big or little, good or bad, creep up on him really quite slowly and may go almost unnoticed. At other times, when they finally get to him, they do their stuff within a matter of seconds and he notices them very much.

No prizes given for guessing which category Mrs Parks's telephone call belongs in.

* * * *

Leo hangs up the phone and goes back to preparing dinner. Things to peel, things to chop, things to stir, things to cut open to see how they're doing. Such a smart honey pine kitchen. Whatever the dinner is, he cooks it and he and his mother eat it. Next the dishes and cutlery they've used get racked for once in the dishwasher which is then set to *LIGHT LOAD* and switched on. When his mother asks him what the telephone call had been he tells her it was SCT business, something to do with the problems Stroud were having with a leaky tea urn.

At seven o'clock his mother watches the national news on TV in the small rear drawing room and he mostly watches it with her, when he isn't finishing up in the kitchen. After that they play some cribbage. He tries to let her win, but doesn't need to. The cards are kind to her and she wins anyway. She's knocked the afternoon's violations into manageable shape and is munching jelly babies in good spirits. He's going to agree to stay. She tells him so. Her lie to the police and her admission of it to him, his lie to her and her understanding that he needed her to pass the lie on, not even the bellowing rhinoceros in the room, Declan's murder, none of these gets the smallest mention. Perhaps she's managed to unremember it all. He's going to accept the SCT directorship. She *knows* it.

He doesn't argue. There isn't much he knows for certain, but on that one point he's unshakable. Accepting the SCT directorship would involve waking up again tomorrow morning in order to do so, and clearly waking up again tomorrow morning is no longer an option.

He helps his mother into bed. Gives her a glass of water and her pills. Tucks in her quilt around her stiff stout body. Kisses her forehead. Shoo's Rumple out of her room. Closes the door.

Waking tomorrow is no longer an option.

In the usual course of events people's minds are filled with gew-gaws a bit like the spingles and spangles in children's kaleidoscopes. Shake them up and they quickly settle down again into usually agreeable patterns. And the fact that this orderly pattern-making is simply an illusion, all done with mirrors, doesn't matter a damn. In minds, just as in kaleidoscopes, it's the appearance that counts.

A neat analogy. It breaks down though, should the mirrors happen to get broken. If that occurs when we're talking about kaleidoscopes, and the patterns fragment, what we find ourselves left with are very small sad scraps of plastic fakery, which dispirit but to be honest are no great disaster.

If we're talking about minds, however, and about patterns made up of human hopes and fears, and the mirrors should still happen to get broken, the results can be rather worse. And for Leo, on this day, at this moment, the patterns in his mind are already so fragile and desperate that when the thin, thin mirrors that have created them for him get shattered, what he finds himself left with is... but we don't need a list. By now we must know by heart the many items on it.

Boiled down to their elements, lies, terror and a pervading self-disgust.

After he's shut his mother's bedroom door he returns to the kitchen where the dish-washer is ticking quietly on *DRY*. He's been thinking about what would be best for her breakfast on her first morning without him. He sets out a tray on the kitchen table with a glass of orange juice, a jug of milk, a mug for either coffee or tea, and (in the absence of anything cooked) a bowl of his unsweetened *muesli*. When he doesn't appear she can either carry it back to bed with her or eat from it at the kitchen table. She may make phone calls. She won't think to go out into the garage.

As he stands by the table, uncertain as to what comes next, along in the front hall the Delhi long-case clock strikes nine. It reminds him that his clock-winding duties come round on Sunday evenings and that last Sunday he'd forgotten all about them. He'd had other, more demanding concerns. Today being Tuesday, he's surprised that the clock is still going. He goes down the passage, slides its key from the little ledge behind its upper pediment, opens its front and winds it.

He smiles. It's as if he has ensured that, even without him around, next week will now happen.

Next he looks in on the baronial front dining room with its enormous mahogany table and he remembers how on really long rainy Cheltenham days Grandmother Clare would let him lay out his electric train-set on it. Madam Sara, later, when she was using the table for her profession, had been more concerned about scratches. Leo's saying good bye and he spends only a token moment in the room, picturing his streamlined pale blue 2-6-4 *Sir Nigel Gresley,* rattling round the track and falling off at all the points. It's not a particularly happy recollection. He'd never been able to connect the points properly with the other rails, so that the *Sir Nigel Gresley* wouldn't fall off at them.

He's never checked, he realises, to see if the massive supporting framework of this table has acquired down the years the full gadgetry of Madam Sara's original London table. He's never been that interested. He isn't that interested now.

His relationship with the big front drawing room, with armchairs his feet had once actually dangled from, is more recent and acute. Charlie from the *Mirror*. The election Committee's first visit. The piano. He sits down at it and opens the lid. There was a similar-sized instrument on-stage at Coll and his most magnificent private moments have been spent seated at one or other of these. Seated. Not playing. Just seated. As soon as he played, even at his best, the magnificence disappeared. He had a discriminating ear for the ordinary.

He always did play, though.

As he sits at the piano, hands ready above the keys, and Granny Clare's *Smoke gets in your eyes,* heavy with left hand Charlie Kuntz tenths, whispers dustily among the room's sandalwood saddhus and elephants and tarnished brassware and monkeys hearing and speaking and doing no evil, it all sets him thinking how extraordinarily long and wearisome life is. And how easily, with one simple decision, he can free himself of it. The Jaguar beckons. Carbon monoxide. Not waking tomorrow.

At that moment, on cue, the front door-bell rings. He hurries to the door and opens it.

'There you are,' he says. 'I've been expecting you.'

Mr Peterson steps back off the door-step, surprised. 'Expecting me?'

'You had things you needed to give thought to. You said you'd be back.'

'You're right, of course. And I should have called sooner. It... wasn't easy. Thought. They took quite a bit of thought.'

Leo ushers him in. The night air is cold and Mr Peterson is wearing a puffed-up sort of waistcoat over his tired suit. He takes it off and hands it to Leo, who hangs it on Clare's kudu antlers. Then Leo leads him on across the hallway, not into the big front drawing room (too formal), not into his office/bedsit (too personal), but into the chintzy rear drawing room (just right). Bulgy old three-piece suite, Sandra-type table-lamp supported by a miniature wagon wheel, flourishing house-plants, his mother's 23-inch TV set. Before her second stroke she had hardly bothered with TV. Now it's a welcome day-filler.

As he sits Mr Peterson down and wonders what to do with him next, it occurs to Leo that getting himself slightly drunk might, in the present circumstances, be a sensible move. He toys with the idea of opening a very fancy *Chateauneuf du Pape* he'd bought for last Christmas and never got round to, but decides it would be, in the present circumstances, a waste.

'I'm getting myself a nightcap,' he tells Mr Peterson, making for the front room's drinks cabinet. He'd done this before, only a few days ago, with Alan Beckerton. 'What would you like?'

'Don't you want to know what I've decided?'

'Not particularly...' Pausing in the doorway. 'We've got Scotch, port, Madeira... Some pretty revolting brandy.'

'Thank you, no. I don't drink much.'

'Neither do I. But tonight is special. Won't be a minute.' He gestures towards a side table bearing copies of Madam Sara's *Spiritualist Gazette*. 'Read something. Improve your mind.'

He finds that there's more of the brandy than anything else but he'd chosen that last time and it was genuinely foul so he opts for the Scotch instead. No soda in sight. Typical. He returns to Mr Peterson with the bottle and two glasses, just in case. He's been flip with the man and it wasn't kind.

Mr Peterson hasn't moved from the low armchair where he'd been put. It has a rather collapsed seat. Leo waves the bottle in his direction—'I've found a spot of this'—and Peterson shakes his head.

Leo puts bottle and glasses on the glass-topped side table and sits down opposite him. 'Sorry about that. You were saying?'

'Last time we met, Leo, you presented me with a problem.'

'I know. I'm sorry. I've sorted it out now.'

'So have I. And I've come to the conclusion that—'

'I meant I've sorted it out for us both. I've taken over your job.'

'That can't be done. Who d'you think I am? You can't just—'

'You told me you didn't approve of the death penalty.' Leo opens the Scotch and pours himself a couple of inches. 'I've decided I do.'

Mr Peterson ruffles his skimpy hair. 'That was always a possibility. I don't recommend it.'

'I can't imagine why.' At least crazy Peterson, bless him, doesn't need any 'i's' dotted. 'You're a rationalist, aren't you?' He lifts his glass. 'Cheers.'

'Which is why I don't approve. We rationalists are a Puritanical lot. 'Suicide is a self-indulgence.'

'I agree. So is breathing. It's a question of how you do the sum. Like everything else in life. Indulging self, versus hurting others.'

'Hurting your mother?'

'In practical terms, quite a bit. Emotionally, not at all—she'll be able to blame me.'

'Your friends?'

'I don't have any. I had Max but he's dead now.' Rosie? The hurt from this will hardly be worse than from dumping her, and far better than from bashing on with Wales *et al* regardless. 'Sounds pukey, I know, but it's true.'

'You could be wrong. I've asked around. People speak of you very highly.'

'And I'm supposed to keep on keeping on for the sake of that?'

'Not keeping on devalues life. Everybody's. Theirs.'

'Not if they don't let it. Whose drummer are they marching to? *Mine*?'

'You're not as tough as you'd like to believe.'

'I'm not tough at all. I'm tired out. That's why I'm quitting.' Leo empties his glass, shuddering at its nastiness. 'Are you sure you won't have any?'

'Quite sure.' Mr Peterson watches without comment as Leo refills his own glass. 'And the dancing?'

'The dancing?' Leo reaches for the bottle again and glugs down more Scotch. 'I'd forgotten that. That was just me breaking up.'

'No it wasn't. It was you angling for Canon Beckerton's pity.'

Glug. 'If you say so.' *Glug.*

'I do say so. You've never danced. You've never heard the music. You're lacking the capacity. The awareness. Always have done. The intensity. No joy, Leo. Its absense is hardly a new discovery.'

'Did I say it was?'

'Then it's not a reason.' Mr Peterson is relentless. 'Not even an excuse.'

'And that's supposed to make me feel better? Christ, and you say *I'm* heartless... A lifetime, you're telling me? All those years of living blind and deaf? No joy? That's supposed to make me feel better?'

'Not what I do, Leo. Never has been.'

'This is a wretched conversation.' Leo finishes his drink again and stands. 'What the hell *are* we here for? You're crazy. I don't have to give you reasons. I don't have to give reasons to anyone.' He thinks about that. 'Only to me.'

'Which is what we're here for.'

'Very sharp, matey. One day you'll cut yourself.'

' Oh, *please...*'

Leo starts for the door, he's better things to do than this. Once there, though, he hesitates, then returns to the table by the his chair and pours himself the last of the Scotch. Sits. Mr Peterson's a decent fellow. He deserves to be heard. 'What *was* your decision?'

'I found mitigating circumstances. Also, the police report suggested that your friend had died very quickly. Three or four minutes after impact at the most. So I decided that—'

'Which is the most weaselly load of shit I've heard in years. I'm disappointed in you, Peterson. I really am.'

'Furthermore, proximate post mortem movement often occurs.'

'I'm so glad you told me that.' Leo puts his glass down. 'You're missing the point.'

'You didn't go down to find out.'

'Hey. Good answer. You're not just a pretty face.'

Mr Peterson struggles forward in his chair. 'I think I should go.'

'Please yourself.' But he doesn't want him to. 'Look—I shouldn't have said all that. I'm sorry. It's just that I hate to hear you making excuses.'

'So you want to be guilty.'

'I don't have to want. I am. And I've accepted it.'

'And you've chosen your punishment.'

'Punishment? This? Not at all. What a thought. The punishment would be to keep on keeping on. Every day after every day. I'm just so tired. I've chosen to quit. It's no big issue.'

'To you it is. It has to be.'

'You're trying to make it one.'

'Every day after every day isn't so bad.'

Leo stares at Mr Peterson, smiling patiently, till the wretched man looks away. The two of them, they've run the subject into the ground. Leo reaches forward, puts his hand out and pats Mr Peterson's knee. 'There's something I need to do. I'd appreciate your advice.'

Dumping the empty glass, he goes out through the hall to his office/bedsit and sits down at his desk. Advice? Not really. Simply his presence. Someone's. This is an unexpectedly lonely time. Mr Peterson follows him and finds the other chair, for once luckily not draped with crumpled clothes.

His mother: Leo has already organised her breakfast; now he has to write her letter. He tilts his chair back, finds a pad of notepaper in a desk drawer and props it on his knee. Basildon Bond. He'll leave her something old-fashioned, pen-on-paper. It seems more suitable than a smart word-processed print-out. He thinks for a moment, then knows what to write and writes it fluently, with no corrections.

> *Dear Mother,*
> *Sorry about this. You may have noticed that I've not been very happy recently. As for the directorship, why not push for that nice Mrs Patton over in Longleach? I'm sure she'll do a fine job. As for the rest, I suggest you contact Cousin Julian. He'll know just what to do. I also suggest you don't go out into the garage. I've been told that carbon monoxide makes the skin of corpses unpleasantly red. Just ring for an ambulance. They'll do whatever's necessary.*
> *I promise you, none of this has ever been your fault. I wasn't much. You did the best you could. I promise you.*
> *Love, Leo*

Perhaps the Scotch has helped him but he doubts that. Certainly he doesn't feel to the slightest degree drunk. He wishes he hadn't bothered.

He fans the letter, the ink's already dry, and gives it to Mr Peterson, who reads it quickly.

'This exoneration at the end—it's fake. You don't believe a word of it.'

'Not true. I do, Peterson. I really do.'

Mr Peterson looks down at the letter, re-reads it, nods and hands it back. Leo folds it, puts it in a non-SCT envelope which he doesn't seal, writes *Mother* on the envelope, takes it through into the kitchen and stands it on his mother's breakfast tray, leaning against the milk jug. Then, with one last small office job in mind, he returns to his desk. Mr Peterson hasn't moved.

Leo digs out his personal cheque book and, leaving the space for a recipient's name blank, fills in the day's date and an amount of five hundred pounds, which seems a reasonable figure, not vulgar but well worth having.

Mr Peterson watches, making no comment.

Another non-SCT envelope is found, the cheque is put in it, the envelope is sealed, and on it Leo writes, in large clear script: *For the poor sod who has to find my corpse—by way of compensation.*

He signs it. That'll cheer up someone's day, he thinks.

And Rosie's day? Can't be helped. He's been through this before. People die. It's only a matter of sooner or later. Things would never have worked out. She and her brother visited efficient Mrs Parks yesterday afternoon, so she already knows about Max's bequest. Perhaps, in the fleeting gaps between brother Philip and Farnley from Cromwell's and then the cremation provider's cinders, she'd been trying to break it to him. She may even find the bequest a sufficient explanation. And she certainly knows about Jake, so she won't worry that the money'll go to waste. People do funny things. She's wise and dear. She won't brood.

Mr Peterson stirs. 'You asked for my advice.'

'I did.'

Mr Peterson points at the compensation envelope. 'I think that's flashy.'

'Doesn't often happen. Indulge me.' He puts the envelope in his pocket and stands up. 'That's it, then. Are you coming?'

Mr Peterson stands up also. 'I still don't like it,' he says. 'It's crude. You hate yourself so you're killing yourself.'

'Not so. I don't do hate. In any case, there isn't enough there. Enough to hate, I mean.'

'It's a big decision. You're trying to make it small.'

'Read the Stoics. It's whatever size I want it to be.'

'You see what I mean? All these games? You're dressing this up. All this "quitting". All this "not keeping on". You've never said the s-word.'

'Suicide?'

'That's right.'

'So now I've said it. And again. Suicide. Is that better?'

'Listen to yourself. You need the euphemisms. You're naked without them. Frightened.'

'Frightened? No harm in that, is there? Seems reasonable. And I can be brave, you know.'

A silence.

'Then I give you my permission.'

Which astonishing notion, Leo thinks, Permission is the last thing he's been asking for. Still, if giving it makes old Peterson happy…

'Come along, then. You know where the car is.'

He leads Mr Peterson down the passage to the rear hall, looks briefly across at his mother's closed bedroom door—at this early stage in her night's Oblivons it would take an atom bomb to wake her—and goes through into the conservatory. It's dark out there: he'd disconnected the electrics back when the roof started leaking, so he has to feel his way round bits of garden furniture to reach the outer door. Peterson follows him. The path along the back of the house to the garage is easier.

Once inside, Leo switches on the bright neon tube. It's a small garage, room for the Jag, a few garden tools and not much else. He walks forward to the recently-installed up-and-over door, looks at the crack along the bottom between it and the concrete, and asks Mr Peterson, "What d'you think?'

'A rolled-up blanket?'

'That's what I thought. There's Ma's travelling rug on the back seat. It won't be long enough, but every little helps.'

Mr Peterson coughs apologetically. " As the actress said to the bishop.'

Leo is on his way to the Jag's rear door. 'I shall ignore that.'

Unfortunately the travelling rug is occupied by Rumple who leaps wildly out of the car and disappears behind the lawnmower. His outrage is justified: there's a cat-flap in the garage's back door and Leo always leaves a car window lowered, so the cat knows he's allowed to be comfortable in here when he can't get into the house and isn't about his outdoor business.

Leo bundles out the travelling rug, shakes it, and he and Mr Peterson arrange it in a fairly tight roll along the bottom of the garage door. It fills about two-thirds of the total width, which will have to do. Now they have to deal with Rumple.

Farce threatens. A reasonable cat, if poked with a rake handle, would flee through its cat-flap, safely out into the garden. Rumple prefers to cower more deeply behind stacks of flowerpots.

Farce is contingent upon haste, however, and Leo is in no hurry. It's around nine thirty and he has all night if necessary. So he sends Mr Peterson back to the garage's furthest, most unthreatening corner and lowers himself quietly onto the concrete in front of the flowerpots. He sits there making encouraging cat noises and in due course Rumple responds. He comes out, his outrage forgotten, and when Leo picks him up he purrs.

Leo carries the cat carefully round to Mr Peterson and transfers him into the other man's arms. Rumple goes peacefully. He's very amenable when not suddenly set upon.

'Take him a good way down the garden, will you? I'll block the flap from inside but I wouldn't want him trying to get back in. OK?'

You too, Peterson. Don't come back. The message seems to Leo clear enough and apparently Peterson hears it. Without further comment he takes the cat away into the night and doesn't come back. Not a man for lingering farewells, our Mr Peterson.

Leo closes the door, wedges a piece of two-by-four across the inside of the cat flap and gets into the Jaguar's driving seat. He adjusts the choke, starts the engine, listens. The purr might be Rumple's. He pushes in the choke and relaxes into the comfortably worn grey leather seat. Then he remembers the envelope in his pocket with the cheque in it. He digs it out and puts it above the walnut-veneered dashboard, propped against the windscreen inside the car, written-on side clearly visible. The Jaguar purrs at him.

He stares out through the windscreen at the garage's white-painted back wall. We've been here before in this story. Forgive the sense of *déjà vu*: it's only apparent. The garage-type bric-a-brac he sees hanging on the back wall may be the same, but elsewhere there have been important changes. He himself is very different. So is the world he plans to be leaving: last week it threatened public exposure, ignominy and jail, this week it promised professional advancement, power and wealth. Each alternative came with costs, of course. Those of the first week had been bearable, those of the second were not. So the choice between them had been easy.

So what else was there? *Fear*? Well of course. But not much. Most ways of dying, and certainly carbon monoxide poisoning, involve an initial loss of consciousness that he imagines must be pretty similar to falling asleep and he's done that almost every night for the last forty-three years. The trick is not to intellectualise it, not to hang it about with what happens next, the not waking up, the relatives weeping and calling him a selfish sod, all those Oxford and Cambridge rugger matches at Twickenham he'll never see. Of all the decisions anyone makes in their lives, suicide is the only one that no successful suicider ever regrets. Unless those trumpets-sounding-on-the-other-side people are right, which he's pretty sure they aren't. And if they are, he's even surer that they're wrong about their grotesquely punitive deity. Eternal damnation—eternal anything—has always seemed ridiculously excessive.

He coughs discreetly. He's sitting behind a 3.4-litre, six-cylinder, twin overhead-camshaft high performance engine and it puts out, even on tick-over, a hell of a lot of exhaust gases. He can smell them already, and a blue-grey haze is rising round the car.

So what does come next? *Peace*? That's surely not the right word for it. Peace is positive. Peace is things happening peacefully. And don't people tell you it has to be fought for? Really there ought to be something called negative peace, something that is simply the absence of everything non-peaceful. And that means the absence of just about everything and therefore is exactly what he's expecting.

He coughs again, less discreetly. He's been told that carbon monoxide is odourless, that the stink in car exhausts comes from all the other relatively harmless stuff that's getting burned. He knew it was going to be foul, and so it is. Typical, the way life's rigged. No gain without pain. Makes you want to puke… Which happens to be, just then, an unfortunate turn of phrase. Perhaps it's all that Scotch.

If not peace, how about *cessation*? *Ceasing* is better. Fewer misleading connotations. Stop, halt, whoa. Now you see me, now you don't. Shades of Maurice Moon. *Cease upon the midnight…* who wrote that? Christ, that bloody man Keats, with his nightingale and his *half in love with easeful death*. Won't do at all. All the wrong baggage.

Leo's eyes smart and his head's aching. Another second and he really will vomit. He vomits. It's very little though, which he spits into his handkerchief. The exhaust fumes are thick enough now to be dimming the overhead light. Breathing them in is surprisingly difficult. Sucked in through his nose, down his windpipe, into his lungs, they feel so poisonous. Which is the whole bloody point, you idiot.

Returning to the river. How about that? A drop of water. Just a drop of water, rejoining one billion billion other drops of water. It's not something, but it's not nothing either. It's everything. …Oops. He's come dangerously close to an uplifting thought. Let your guard down for a moment and you're back aspiring to the immortal bloody Bird, Bard, Bawd. Returning to the river isn't nothing, it isn't something, and it isn't everything either—it's simply returning to the river. It's—

Christ Almighty, he'd got one aspect of this dying business seriously wrong: there's no similarity whatsoever between this particular version of losing consciousness and simply falling asleep. This is unimaginably awful. His fingers feel bloated. His tear glands stream. The Jaguar ticks on contentedly enough, sod it. Fumes press against his face as if they're drowning him. Every breath, and he's keeping them as short as he can, every breath is barbed with hot sharp acid. He doesn't, oddly enough, consider escaping from the garage. It's doubtful that he could by now in fact get any further than flat out on the floor by the side of the car, but the idea doesn't occur to him. Noble determination? Probably not. A lack of get-up-and-go, more likely. He sits in the car, panting and sweating, his eye-ducts weeping, and waits now, really quite patiently, for it all to end.

Very soon, it does.

* * * *

Well, his consciousness of it did. But anyone who has read as far as this will know that his death didn't follow—he has to have survived for him now to be helping me to tell the tale. And, as once before in this book when Leo's suicide was unsurprisingly averted, it's easy to sneer: *How typical—the idiot couldn't even succeed at that.* But in this case, just for once, the failure truly wasn't his fault. He couldn't possibly have known in advance that Canon Beckerton would be passing at just the wrong moment, on his way home from that week's Scrabble game, or that the canon's attention would be caught by the lights on in both the two front rooms of No. 81 Tivoli Street and in the garage, or that he would drive straight on by, then stop, think about it, remember his last visit, and decide to back up and investigate, or that when he rang the doorbell and nobody answered he would decide to investigate further, or that… etc. etc.

Admittedly, with twenty-twenty hindsight it's clear that every one of these possibilities had always existed, and if Leo had turned off the lights in the two front rooms that would have dealt with them, but who has twenty-twenty hindsight? No, the only failing he might seriously be blamed for is his apparent refusal to listen to a life that had continually told him to expect the worst, and therefore to take steps accordingly.

Exactly what happened after Alan Beckerton decided on a further investigation Leo has no idea. He knows about Alan's driving by and then stopping and reversing back only because the canon mentioned it later, remarking in his tedious way on the tiny decisions a person takes that turn out to be so far-reaching… All Leo knows first hand, beginning very blurrily on the ground outside the open garage door behind the now-silent Jaguar, is limited to a splitting headache, the shivers, kind murmurs from his friend and a lot of vomiting.

It doesn't matter. This isn't the first car exhaust suicide Alan has interrupted—in pre-1980 catalytic converter days it was quite a common final exit—and he knows what to do. Get the patient breathing if he's stopped, and then provide oxygen if one has it or, *faute de mieux*, plenty of good fresh air. And hope that there hadn't been damage to the heart, which usually occurs only when the patient's exposure to carbon monoxide inhalation has been prolonged. In Leo's case, of course, Alan can only guess at that figure. Which leaves him doing what he can, and hoping. And possibly, in view of his profession, praying.

And Leo's still around now, all these years later, and in good shape, so clearly his exposure to poisonous inhalation was brief enough to be non-lethal.

Alan's next job is to find No. 81's front door key on the Jaguar's key-ring, enter the house, and go round turning off the lights. He calls neither the police nor an ambulance. At this time attempted suicide is no longer a crime or made much of an issue, but much still depends on the discretion of the officials involved and he doesn't care to take the risk. Leo is clearly recovering fast. The canon does attempt to wake Madam Sara but he knows about her pills and how difficult rousing her will be so he doesn't try too hard and is relieved when he fails. In his experience little is gained from immediately telling a mother that her son has tried to kill himself. One tidies up as best one can and then waits and sees.

The things on Madam Sara's breakfast tray in the kitchen he carefully puts away, and the envelope with Leo's letter in it he destroys. Also the envelope propped up behind the Jaguar's windscreen. He doesn't make use of its contents. He considers donating the cheque to a worthy cause, the Good Samaritans suicide counselling service came to mind as suitable, but finally tears it up. If Leo and his mother have a joint bank account she might learn of it and raise needless questions.

By now Leo is lying on his bed, fully conscious, his head still splitting. Alan brews him a large mug of tea and makes him drink it. He sits on the edge of the bed.

'D'you think you can manage tomorrow morning?'

Leo was putting events together. 'Do you see what you've done?'

'I think so.'

'I knew what was needed but you knew better?'

'I did, Leo. I cared. I took a decision.'

'And I'm expected to be grateful?'

'Beside the point. Not all at once, certainly. Perhaps not ever.'

'And you can live with that?'

'I can live with it.'

'You make me sick.'

'So I see. You didn't answer my question.'

'Question?'

'Tomorrow morning. Your mother's breakfast. Will you be able to manage?'

'I'll bloody have to. Shut the door behind you, will you?'

As Alan is going out Leo calls after him. 'One last favour. I put a bar across inside the cat flap in the back door of the garage. Take it off, will you? It might rain. The poor stupid animal might want to get in.'

* * * *

The rest of Leo's story is quickly told. He scrambled two eggs for his mother's breakfast, which went down very well. And when he took them in he told her he'd be calling Bunty Carstairs later that morning to assure her that he'd be honoured to accept the directorship. Family was important, he said.

He knew his mother would be pleased. She and Bunty Carstairs both.

* * * *

He's still the SCT's director. He does a good job and provides a reliable service. Many successful pub landlords don't drink. A capable girl from the Charlton Kings group comes in as part-time secretary and he handles the SCT's public relations and training programmes himself. Soon after taking over the director's job he launched the membership drive his mother had been planning just before her retirement, and it boosted the SCT's numbers to over two thousand. They've fallen off since then but they're still quite decent. Doggies still bark Happy birthday from heaven. He also now has a proper ground floor office: he's opened up the Tivoli Street house's upstairs, using a tiny part of Max's legacy, and sleeps in the big front bedroom, which he's totally refurnished.

The rest of that money he's leaving to Jake. They've met a few times but to no lasting effect. The SCT pays him well. He really doesn't need it.

By today, in the course of over seventy years, Leo fairly may be said to have wished ill on none and done ill to only a few. I exaggerate. The number of people Leo has known well enough to be able to harm noticeably, even if inadvertently, is far too small for them to rank as even a meagre handful.

Madam Sara died about a year ago. By then nudging ninety, she'd been frail and almost blind for quite a while, with a saint-like live-in nurse. Drugs and a careful diet staved off further strokes and she was still compos mentis when she finally dropped off the perch. Her speech, though, had sadly plateau'd long before that and she never took back control of the SCT. Leo continued to keep house and do all the cooking. He still does. He misses her badly.

He grieves for her. She was, as his father had told him, a re-markable lady. She may have made that up, but it sounds right, a very Maurice Moon description. He really grieves for her.

He never telephoned Liverpool. He didn't write either. After a longish interval Rosie wrote to him just once. She'd married a Welsh sheep farmer, she told him. He was small and strong and very kind to her. She was happy. She'd never put together Max's notes for his book, but otherwise things had worked out well for her. She hoped they'd worked out well for Leo too. He answered her briefly, telling her they had.

Years later, shortly before Madam Sara finally took to her bed, he hired a large RV and the two of them spent a pleasant couple of weeks driving round Wales. He had a cell-phone by then so he was never far from the SCT. He kept an eye out for Rosie as he drove but he never saw her. Even if he had, he wouldn't have stopped for a chat.

As for Max's book, he was unsurprised that nobody had approached him about finishing it. His mother's project though, the SCT history, came together nicely. Following what quickly became known in Leo's mind as 'the garage episode,' the two of them worked on it for nearly three years, while her memory for anecdote was still good, and it was published in hardback to coincide with the SCT's fortieth anniversary. A niche market, their publisher warned them, but it sold nearly twenty thousand. The paperback tripled that. Leo was a writer after all.

He hasn't married. There have been opportunities, two at least, but he's never quite taken them. He hasn't had lovers either. Male or female. There are cans of worms—forgive the Americanism—that he doesn't care to open.

He's also never tried again to kill himself. Not up to now. There will always be moments in a life when change seems possible and other moments, many more of them, when it doesn't.

When he does die he's accepted that he won't be leaving the world a better place, but at least he'll never have derived any pleasure from making it a worse one. In any case, keeping on keeping on isn't mostly all that bad.

Well, it sometimes can be, but the carbon-monoxideless alternatives these days all seem to him so untidy. Soporifics aided by plastic bags, jumping off cliffs... Even the reliably lethal small tanks of helium that used to be commercially available for inflating party balloons have been ruled out recently. He's saving Sara's many remaining Oblivons for when he gets his cancer. Dealing with something like that would justify a small untidyness here or there.

Forgive me. The claim a few lines back that keeping on keeping on 'mostly isn't all that bad' is a typically Leo understatement. Mostly keeping on is bloody awful. He might even, this being the enlightened twenty-first century, have put in a '*fucking*' somewhere, just to labour the point. But we mustn't appear to be sorry for ourselves, must we?

He did have several sessions, though, with Canon Beckerton's pet transactional therapist. Mary Figges was the price Alan exacted for saving his life and keeping quiet about it. Leo had predictably bitter fun with the canon's choice of words 'saving' was hardly the verb he'd have chosen. How about 'needlessly extending'? But Mary Figges turned out to be a treasure: thoughtful, non-confrontational, sympathetic, flatteringly interested, and she laughed at his jokes. She was also expensive, however, not at all NHS material, and he never quite felt that he deserved her. He discontinued his visits at about the same time that Alan was promoted from Gloucester and departed to higher ecclesiastical realms in Canterbury.

They quickly lost touch. Leo never precisely 'blamed' Alan for his part in 'the garage episode'—along with anger and intentions, he didn't do blame and in any case people came with their imperatives, you bought the package—but he was no longer comfortable in his company. Alan knew too much about him. He'd dragged Leo's lolling, vomit-streaked body out onto the drive and pounded and kissed it back to life. He knew too much about him.

By the time the canon was elevated to Canterbury, Leo had already replaced him with another bridge partner, a gay maths teacher who knew nothing of Leo's sexual interests and probably still doesn't. They play more often than Leo did with Alan and last year they were the St Stephens Road club champions.

Rumple's gone too, now, and so has Hoppy. Rumple he replaced with a fine sleek-furred tortoiseshell called Daisy. Hoppy's departure left him with a harder problem. The home help he now has is cheery and reliable, but she's young and might leave at any minute to get married.

The Jaguar has been well looked after. It's become a valuable collector's item and still gets an occasional holiday outing. The house on Tivoli Street, extensively refurbished in the proper Edwardian manner, now has a double garage, providing ample space beside the Jag for Leo's everyday transport, a yellow Mini Cooper with chic white stripes on its bonnet.

Leo may never precisely have blamed Alan but he's never precisely forgiven him either. There are many mornings, waking to another leaden day of keeping on keeping on, when we pause by the bathroom wash-basin, still pyjama'd, and raise a grey glass of tooth-pastey water to the tactful extirpation of interfering clerics, wherever they may be.

So here's our Leo.